Prophecy of Gods and Crows

Clan of Shadows #1

C.D. Britt

PHOENYX PUBLISHING

Phoenyx Publishing

www.authorcdbritt.com

Cover Artwork by GermanCreative

Editing by EFC Services, LLC.

Published by Phoenyx Publishing

ISBN (eBook): 978-1-7372652-8-3

ISBN (Print): 979-8-9872432-2-0

Content Warning

Dear Reader,

Thank you for taking a chance on my book! This entire book shifted and changed during the writing process until the end product was nothing even close to what I had planned.

Yet, it has been a labor of love, one that holds more of my soul than anything I've written so far, but I must ask that you take your time and read through the content warnings.

I am a huge advocate of mental health, and if anything on this page could potentially trigger you, I ask that you do not continue reading.

Trigger Warnings:

- sexual content
- religious trauma
- religious cults
- witch prosecution
- domestic violence
- child abuse (past and present by family member)
- emotional abuse
- scenes of war
- and death

Again, please take care of yourself and only continue reading if you feel comfortable in doing so.

C.D. Britt

Contents

To all the women before me, their voices unheard, this book is for you.

Chapter 1

B ryndis Kenneally had just slipped between the cool sheets of her bed as night relinquished its hold on the small desert town. The sun was just beginning its trek across the sky as it broke over the horizon, but the familiarity of another day ended when the warning horns rang instead of the typical church bells that announced the beginning of morning service.

The only reason for the city guards to sound the horns was one that made her heart pound as her skin grew clammy. Running to her window, she tripped over her bed sheet, catching herself on the sill and earning a splinter in her palm for it. Her concern was not about the small pain, but about what was happening on a much larger scale down on the street below. Something that rarely happened in their small town, and the last time it had, she'd lost her entire world.

The stifling heat radiating from her window did nothing to stop the chills moving along her skin as she took in what the horns meant.

The gate was opening.

Looking through the dirty window, sand having accumulated along the panes, she watched as the last true member of her family, her cousin Jace, stepped out of the church doors.

Just as her father had done ten years ago.

Her mind moving back and forth between two very different times in her life, she watched Jace, the town doctor, donning the same gear her father had to make the same trek.

The exact same type of mask her father had worn ten years ago on his final journey past the gate slipped over a different face. In a tribute to their god, the leather bull mask was adorned with brass horns that glinted in the sun and one glass eye blacked out in tribute.

That same mask now covered the face of the man who was the last of her family.

Her throat tightened as the same brown hood went up over his blond hair, taking all that identified Jace from the rest away as he became a symbol of the end of Bryn's world.

Identical to what her father had once worn and died in.

The town scrios, the leader of the Church of Baleros, stepped up next to her cousin and nodded as he affixed his own mask, before pulling the hood of his brown cloak up to cover his salt-and-pepper hair.

The two vastly different-looking men were now indistinguishable from each other after having donned the religious regalia.

Uniformity was the town's unofficial motto.

The town religion forbade anyone or anything to stand out, which was why their entire world was painted in the dullness of brown and gray. To be different in their community could very well get someone killed should the town decide a person was acting or standing out at the behest of a demon or witch.

Bryn pressed her fingertips against the glass, tracing the path her cousin walked as she prayed. Not to the god that the town would have her worship, but to some unknown higher power. There had to be something, some deity, who was more than what this town indoctrinated their youth to worship.

Someone who welcomed everyone, not just their chosen few.

She watched as the two men, her cousin and the scrios, turned as one and began to walk down the main road of the town. Saints' Road.

A road she'd walked herself only hours ago.

A road that had a duality to it just as the town itself.

During the day, it was the road the pious walked upon.

A place where families walked the streets for twice-daily church services as their children danced around their parents' legs. The livestock were moved by ranchers from one side of their town to the other all while shopkeepers pushed their wares.

People like Bryn were forgotten about during these times since there was no place for her and her ilk in the town of religious perfection.

At night was when the sinful, as named by the righteous, roamed Saints' Road, and Bryn was one of them through no fault of her own.

It was her "fits" as her father referred to them that earned her the title of witch and made her life in Ifreann dangerous, the possibility of them choosing to burn her at the stake always there. Her safety precarious in such a mercurial town.

The day her father made a promise that she would take over his role as doctor when she hit maturity was the day her fate was cemented.

With the first sickness came the fact that it was all too obvious she wasn't a born healer.

Not when she touched a patient and went into a seizure. At least that was what the town saw and what her father had led them to believe.

No, when she touched a sick patient, she saw and *felt* their death if their demise was imminent.

People began to grow curious as to why when she touched a person and went into a "fit," the person soon died.

The whispers grew. Narrowed eyes started to follow her.

The town proclaimed her a witch and that word alone was enough to have her burned at the stake. Her fear grew with every move the town made toward her in the following years.

People would leave bones out in front of the clinic. Smaller versions of the stakes the witches of old had been burned on would be erected near where a patient had died after one of her fits.

It wasn't safe any longer to try to heal the people of the town, not that she was great at it otherwise, and all too soon it wasn't even safe enough to walk among them.

So, Bryn took to walking Saints' Road at night with the other sinners.

Looking to the gate as Jace neared it, memories of the sickness that had caused the gate to be permanently closed to the outside world flooded her thoughts.

Now, only traders were allowed to leave once they had been issued a royal permit by the governor of Ifreann. While they did still trade with the other towns under King Bres, lands known as the Drystan Territories, they were never allowed to venture outside of those areas to other countries not under the king's rule.

Since they paid their tithe and worshipped the sanctioned religion, they were allowed to be mostly self-governing. Especially since King Bres was too focused on the countries that rebelled against his rule, sending out his bloody assassins, aptly known as wraiths because of how they became shadow and death while in combat.

The rebellious countries, as the church described them, were the reason for the sickness in the first place. Their sinful behavior created the need for unbelievers to be punished, and so their god created the disease. The wicked fell to it, and any devout who died must have been secretly wicked.

The god of Ifreann apparently did not take kindly to those who refused to follow Ifreann's religion and king.

Though Ifreann had a dark history all its own.

Ifreann had been a red-light district long ago, back when it was called Hell's Gate, and some of that darkness still clung to the buildings like shadows. The town having been around since before the collapse of the world as their ancestors knew it.

Bryn found her own irony in the name since the church taking over had made most days in Ifreann a literal hell for her.

Back when it had been Hell's Gate, people had freely roamed the streets day and night, finding pleasures of the mind and flesh.

The survivors of the Collapse rebuilt the town known for sin in the world left over from the destruction. They changed the names of the city and buildings, putting the church in the center of town next to where one of the most infamous brothels once stood, in an attempt to disabuse the citizens of its hellish past. The church worked hard to erase the sins of their ancestors.

Outside the gate of Ifreann wasn't much better.

It had once been a place where trees and water had been at one time plentiful, before the desert took hold, choking out the natural life that had once thrived. Nestled between two large rock formations, Ifreann was a desert with only brown and oranges as far as the eye could see. Cacti being the only color to break up the monotony.

Mother Nature reclaimed the world the humans had used and abused. Just as the scientists of days long ago had warned she would.

That mixed with the lack of color made the town seem even more hellish than saintly with the stone walls surrounding them day and night, and gates that rarely opened.

The same rusted, worn gates made of brass and wood that stood tall and proud day after day in the hot desert sun at the front of Ifreann.

Once a welcome, and now a warning.

At some point after the Collapse, Ifreann had once been a shining beacon in the desert for those in need. A walled fortress for wanderers who were lost in endless sand, desperate for a place to rest where heat and predators would not ensure their deaths. Where desert sickness would not bring their minds close enough to the edge of madness, resulting in death all the same.

Those same walls that encased the small town had been built to keep the worst of the desert out, but now that included outsiders, travelers not born to the people of the town or brought in before they closed the gates for good. Bryn was lucky enough to have made it past the gates before the town's paranoia had shut them off from the rest of the world.

Today they would open for something other than a small outfit of men leaving to trade since the horns never went off for such an event.

No, the horns were a warning for everyone to stay inside.

The sound meant that at some point overnight, the city guards had found people not of the town standing at the front of the gates.

Which meant her cousin was walking the same path to possible death that her father had taken years ago, and Bryn was trying to contain herself. Grabbing and folding her hands in her musty curtains, she bit her lip, a tear slipping from her eye as the last of her family who cared for her passed by her window.

The scrios and the doctor. Two men to both represent and govern the wellness of the town, spiritually and physically.

Jace, as the doctor, was needed to verify the people were not sick or, if they died, were not contagious past death. To make sure the horrible disease that had killed so many not that long ago would not make its way through their small population yet again.

Arioch, as the scrios of the Church of Baleros, was there to make sure the disease of sin was unable to make it past the gate.

Jace had stepped in as healer when she failed, and now she watched the consequences of her ineptitude. Her chest tightened with fear and guilt at what he took on for her sake.

I should be the one walking to my potential end, she thought.

Jace and Arioch made their way to the very gate no one was allowed to pass through without permission. The city guards took up formation behind the two figures, their faces covered only by cloth, with a uniform of jeans, flannel, and a wide-brimmed hat. They held their rifles at the ready as the gate slowly began to open. The wind and sand that had been beating against them all day and night found its way along Saints' Road in a sigh of relief from nature itself.

Each of the men steadied themselves against the relentless wind, bending at the waist to find their center of gravity as the desert pushed its way past the now open gate.

Watching as the scrios covered his eye and bowed low to the ground to make the horned sign of Balor in the sand, Bryn rolled her tear-filled eyes.

Why did they need to be sandblasted to do the prayer for a safe return to their fortress unharmed? When she had dared to ask once before, the answer had been that doing what was difficult showed one's obedience.

Bryn figured it just made them idiots not to do it beforehand when the wind was far calmer and the poor city guards were not struggling to keep themselves steady.

The guards widened their stances, their heads down not in prayer but to protect their faces as the scrios stood. His prayer ended while the wind howled in anger around him.

It seemed Mother Nature did not care for his god and was making her displeasure known.

As they began walking as one, in uniform and posture, she watched her cousin walk through the gate with the city guards at his heels just as her father had.

A mirror image of the memory of her youth.

The gate, just as it had that same day, slowly closed behind them, cutting her off from her beloved cousin who was as close to her as a sibling. The only other family member was her aunt, who despised her on a good day. There was no love lost between the two of them.

Closing her eyes, Bryn let her tears break free and roll down her cheek as she promised herself her cousin would be fine.

Logically she understood that, but emotionally she did not. A war between the mind and heart.

A sensation rolled over her skin like silk, her eyes popping open and her hands moving to see what could have caused such a reaction. Nothing physically was there, but a relentless tug in the back of her head pulled at her.

Something deep inside her said that although he would come back unscathed, something huge would follow him home.

Bryn suddenly wished her visions could see more than death in a person's immediate future.

Chapter 2

The desert heat did nothing to help with the smell of the dead.

Securing the bandanna over her mouth, Bryn tried not to gag at the stench of rotting and decomposing flesh, made all the worse by the sun.

While she was all too happy her cousin had made it back home in one piece several hours after he left through the gate, she wasn't pleased when he told her it was time for her to get to work on her day off.

Death waited for no one, he'd said, exhaustion evident on his face as he turned to his own apartment to clean up and rest.

Only to show up minutes after she'd arrived at the pyres to help.

Some clean cuts on the bodies that had been outside the gate showed a fight—with knives, not bullets—which usually indicated that rovers, people who pirated in the desert looking to steal supplies from travelers, had done the damage. Sadly, with the state of decomposition, she couldn't be a hundred percent sure. From the linen clothes and lack of jewels, they were most likely traders. One of the most dangerous jobs in the world now, as her uncle found out himself long before she came to Ifreann.

Used to handling one body by herself when they lost an elder or someone to a sickness, Bryn was overwhelmed by the ten bodies the city guards had moved in from outside of the gate. She supposed she should be happy that the guards carried them in at all and left them next to the pyres for her, but no one wanted predators hanging out on their doorstep, which a pile of bodies would certainly cause.

She dreaded transporting the bodies of the deceased . . . especially in such a decayed state. That would have been a long, smelly trek for her.

Bryn had done it before when a body hadn't been found for a week. Unpleasant was beyond an understatement in describing that aspect of her vocation.

"How long was this one left in the sun?" she wondered aloud as she secured the dead to a board with rope.

"Not long," Jace said from behind her, startling her from her musings.

Turning, she took in the bags under his eyes and pale skin from lack of sleep and nourishment. He'd been staying with an ill child night after night, and yet they had made him go out to check the bodies anyway.

It angered her he was in such a state, but she had only herself to blame for not being the healer Ifreann needed.

How her cousin was able to tell a sickness had killed them or something else, she had no idea. They had not been killed on the steps of the gate, but far earlier if their horrid state of decomposition could attest to anything. It always made it far too difficult to determine their death, yet Jace always managed to be right.

Bryn didn't mind Jace's help since she wouldn't find herself in a "fit" in front of him like she had when working as a healer. A person who had already passed on didn't trigger her episodes.

Her first fit came at the young age of four, when she saw her uncle's death. Jace's father was a trader, and when she told her father that her uncle would die at the hands of rovers, he'd laughed it off as the musings of a young, creative mind.

When they had brought her uncle's bullet-riddled body home, her father's eyes had met her own, his full of fear and panic. Grabbing everything they owned, he moved them south, telling her that she was not to speak about what she saw. That her seizure had done some sort of damage to her developing brain and that he would find a way to fix it.

She was the sole reason her father had taken her from her birth home. Bryn figured that deep down he knew medicine wouldn't fix his defective daughter. Perhaps religion could, and where was there a more religious place than Ifreann? A perfect place to exorcise demons.

Yet nothing had been fixed or cured by moving to Ifreann.

Now she was a failed healer with no aptitude for healing and a history full of unknowns, finding her calling working with the dead instead of the living.

It was, unfortunately, something that made her even more of a pariah since death was a taboo subject in the town. To speak of it, to even think of it, was to bring it upon your household. That was why they burned the dead since to have a cemetery was to invite death.

Bryn found peace in death because the dead never called her a witch, said a word against her, or whispered loud enough that it was obvious she was meant to hear. She felt comfortable among them as she prepared them to cross over into wherever one went when they died.

Something that in a town full of religious zealots made her little better than the imaginary demons that they prayed for protection from.

Witches.

Women born with magic and mayhem in their blood. Able to bring wrath and death down on the small town with their innate abilities.

While she held no true power, she knew where she fell on the town's spectrum of good and evil.

Had her father's closest friend not been Mr. Rafferty, the governor of their small town, she was sure she'd be dead by now. Keeping to the streets at night, letting people forget about her, was all that kept his job safe since too much interaction with her could doom him as well.

If only she could leave these walls, but she knew she wouldn't. She couldn't leave her cousin or her close friends since they were the only allies she had in life.

They were as much her family as Jace, but still, they didn't know her secrets. No, all her secrets died with her father.

"Why are you here? This is my part of the job," Bryn asked as she moved again to remain downwind of the smell as the wind changed directions. Even though the walls surrounding the town kept out most of the high winds and sand, it wasn't foolproof. "He is past your expertise unless you are able to raise the dead. You did your job in making sure they weren't diseased, now go get some rest."

"I have not been summoned to any bedsides, so why not help?" Jace asked as he moved to assist in lifting one of the heavier male bodies from the ground and onto a board, grunting at the weight.

Snorting, Bryn turned to her cousin, his cheeks pink more from the lie he just told than the elements and exertion.

"Your mother is on a tear throughout the clinic, isn't she?"

Sighing, he put his hands on his hips as he hung his head.

"It's horrible. As if sin is some airborne disease, and she needs to rid the town of it. I was just stopping in to put away my bag; the moment she saw me, she lit sage and started praying . . . loudly. Obviously, the sin is all over my clothes and bag." Lifting his head, he rolled his eyes as he reached for the cloth on the cart and used it to wipe his hands, blood and dirt staining it.

She tried to swallow the bile, making sure her own gloves were secured.

The sight of blood made her sick to her stomach, which was yet another mark against her as a potential healer. If a body came in from the desert having been feasted upon by scavengers, it was all she could do not to pass out working the pyres.

Her fear of blood was ammunition for her aunt to taunt her with, as if her aunt truly needed anything to assist in her cruelty.

After her father had died, leaving her at her aunt's mercy, Aunt Mallory's disinterest in Bryn had turned to loathing. Bryn learned quickly to make herself scarce as a form of self-preservation.

It was yet another of Bryn's secrets that even Jace knew nothing about.

His mother was abusive emotionally and physically, and yet the woman was seen as one of the most pious in the community for her undying faith and loyalty when she was pure evil behind closed doors.

The worst part was there was never anywhere truly safe for Bryn to turn to. Maybe she had friends with some power around town, but her aunt was engaged to a man who was the second most powerful in their community through the church. His own position was right behind that of the scrios, and the only one higher was King Bres himself.

Everyone would believe her before they would Bryn, and if her aunt ever used that against her, proclaimed her a witch, her life was forfeit.

The sound of hoofbeats in the sand broke her thoughts, and she turned to see the town sheriff heading their way on his horse. His loyal hound, Finian, running alongside the equine, bouncing around dangerously close to the horse's hooves.

Finian, the beast of a dog, was covered in black and gray brindle fur and almost as big as the horse itself, coming up to its shoulders.

Every human might have given a wide berth to Bryn, but Finian caught sight of her and barreled down, aiming his huge body in her direction.

"Brace yourself." Jace laughed as the hound knocked her to the sand, the air leaving her lungs on impact as Finian covered the parts of her exposed face with slobber.

"He used to strike fear in the hearts of most men until you, Bryn," she heard the sheriff grumble as he stayed his horse next to them, its hooves kicking up dust as it stomped in agitation at having to stop. She imagined the white horse running through pastures, free as the wind, not caged in this dull, sandy tan town with barely any leg room.

The horse shook its head, eyes rolling toward the fire, and aggressively chomped at its bit as Justin, the sheriff and their friend growing up, patted its neck. His touch calmed the horse enough to where it settled its hooves on the ground, no longer kicking up dirt, but its eyes kept rolling.

"Your beast has been tamed, Justin," Jace joked as Bryn rolled out from under Finian when he did his happy dog dance over her, barely missing a paw to the face. A sizable enough paw that should it manage to land on her nose could easily break it into pieces due to the one hundred and sixty pounds of dog behind it.

"It's Sheriff when I am on duty, Jace, you know this." Justin looked down at Bryn, his lips tilting into a slight smile at the sight of Bryn's attempt to escape Finian's adoration.

Justin was one of the few who didn't act like she had the plague when he was near her, and while there were not a lot of people who looked fondly upon her, he did. It was a breath of fresh air to catch sight of him in a crowd or when he was patrolling at night alongside the city guards.

It also didn't hurt the man had a smile that shone almost as bright as the sun, something Bryn would never admit out loud. That and she'd had the biggest crush on him growing up. Following her cousin and his friends around, she'd mooned over him for years until one of the other friends in their group decided she was his and not Justin's.

Her crush over the young soon-to-be sheriff went down in flames when the governor of their little town's rebellious son caught her in his sights. Declan Rafferty was not one to let his prey get away, and it didn't hurt that Bryn was more than happy to be hunted and caught by the man.

Justin became a close friend instead of a love interest. A choice some days she wished she could go back in time and remedy.

"Founder's Day dance is tonight, and I am making it an official mandate that you both attend," Justin warned, cutting into her thoughts as he steadied his horse again.

Turning back to face him, Bryn narrowed her eyes at the sheriff as he gave her a smile that was all mock innocence. Since she and Declan had broken up months ago, Justin seemed to have made it his life's goal to get them back together.

Not knowing the why of the breakup gave the man hope his friends would remedy the relationship, but she wouldn't tell anyone. It made both her and Declan look like fools. After four years together, he had kissed another woman. A girl who'd been one of Bryn's biggest tormentors when she was young.

Ava Stevens, the baker's daughter and pride of the town.

Bryn's nemesis.

Embarrassment and heartbreak renewed in her soul as she tried to push the thought away again.

"Pretty sure you cannot mandate that, *Sheriff,*" Jace replied, grabbing the cart by its handles, and moving it parallel with one of the bodies. Only three more left and they could call it a day.

She had been so focused on Justin that she hadn't noticed Jace had already finished with the body he'd been working on. Wrapping the body in cloth and securing it to the wooden board with the ropes, he moved it to the edge of the stucco pyre.

Bryn wondered if they'd soon have to find a new way to make the pyre boards since trees were not exactly a commodity around them in the desert heat, and there was only so much wood in their little town.

Finian sniffed one of the hands of the deceased men, sneezing immediately, his large head shaking as if trying to rid his nose of the stench. Poor hound. She could empathize.

Lying down with a whimper, he rubbed his paws over his long nose, giving Bryn a pitiful look.

"Good thing he is pretty because he's not too smart," Justin joked, his arms crossing as he leaned forward on his horse.

"Not pretty either." Jace grunted as he lifted a body from under the elbows and dragged it to the cart.

Bryn gasped, falling to her knees in front of Finian and taking his large head in her hands.

"Do not listen to them, Finny. They are just jealous because you get all the ladies." She smacked a kiss on Finian's head that earned her plenty of slobbery kisses in return.

"Come to the dance and you can make out with *Finny* all night," Justin teased, whistling to Finian to follow. Just as quick as Finian was a playful puppy, he was snapping to attention like a soldier and taking up his place at his leader's side. "But if I don't see you, remember, I can enter your home and drag you out. Permission from the governor himself to do so."

Justin nodded to them both, snapping the reins before she could reply, and took off at a quickened pace back to Saints' Road, Finian hot on his heels.

"I guess that's decided, then." Jace laughed as Bryn grabbed the ankles of another man Jace was trying to lift. Placing the lost soul onto another wooden board, they secured him with rope before moving the cart to the pyre.

"If I go, no one will have a good time. There is a reason I keep to my apartment and the night as much as possible." What she meant was it was better for her friends if the town forgot she existed. They only allowed her father in because they were promised healers in doing so.

They got that in Jace, but not her.

"Bryn"—Jace turned, stopping to lean against the cart— "these people are nothing but scared little sheep. They think only what Scrios Arioch tells them to think. Just stay with us and enjoy yourself for once."

Shaking her head, she pushed past her cousin to grab the board needed to slide the body into the fiery pit. Wiping the sweat from her brow, the sun beating down in all its midday glory, she was thankful when they were down to the last body.

Her heart hurt that these people were not given funeral rites just because they came from another place. Bryn felt like maybe, if there were a heaven of some kind, they would go there regardless of the actions taken here and now. That in not honoring them, they would not walk this earth in anger and loss.

The scrios wouldn't help with funeral rites for the strangers, always claiming he owed desert rovers and traders nothing. Blessings were for believers. Bryn guessed his god was pretty choosy about who he allowed to die with dignity.

Taking a moment, she prayed to her own imaginary deity. A deity who was just and looked upon humanity as a mother might her child, fierce in her protection.

One that, in her own mind, was strong and capable and nothing like the Church of Baleros's god.

Jace waited, not saying a word as she bent over next to the pyre in prayer. She wasn't sure what Jace believed since he, too, found excuses not to attend services, but they never said anything about it. Especially not around his devout mother where they were guaranteed the punishment of nonbelievers.

Bryn opened her eyes, the prayer lost to the wind as she took in the slackened face of the last man lost to death lying on the wooden board.

Readjusting the cloth to cover his face, she moved into position, and she and Jace placed the board along the rails to the pit where the fire burned. The stucco walls continued to contain the fire as they pushed the body into the flames. The man's hair and linen wardrobe caught well before his skin. The linens he had worn reminded her of some of her friend Sage's clothing that she still had from her mother.

Perhaps they were from Tanwen, the closest city to their own in the Drystan Territories.

Bryn watched as the flames took the soul to the other side of death, leaving only the burning remains of its worldly vessel.

Lost in thought, Bryn only noticed that Jace had pushed the cart back to the chapel when he yelled back over his shoulder to be ready in a few hours and then disappeared around the corner of the chapel.

Looking back into the fire, tingles ran along her skin so abruptly that she feared a predator was nearby. The sensation felt so much like ants crawling on her that her fingers curled and twitched to claw at her skin.

Trying to ignore it, Bryn walked to the end of the row of pyres and reached down to grab the torch from the rusted metal ceremonial stand.

The sense of someone watching her had her swinging around, her heart pumping blood faster as her extremities went cold, her body readying to make a run for it if needed, but only the pyres and dead trees were around her. Nothing and no one to account for the feeling of being watched.

Walking back toward the chapel, she extinguished the flame of the torch in the blessed water near the church before placing the doused torch in the box outside the building for someone to cleanse with prayers.

All while keeping her eyes and body on alert.

Another chill moved over her skin. This one was odd enough to raise the hairs along her arms and the back of her neck in a way that felt out of place in the stifling heat of the desert sun.

A sudden sense of doom made the sweat on her skin turn cold.

Shaking her head, she chastised her imagination as a headache started in her temples that had her groaning. It felt like the beginning of a migraine, yet something deep in her bones yelled at her to pay closer attention. To what end, she had no idea, but the sense of foreboding was intense.

A sense that the fear she had felt earlier that morning when Jace had left the gate to attend to the bodies was not to be ignored.

Bryn had learned the long and painful way to trust her instincts, so she knew better than to ignore them now.

Chapter 3

"For someone who normally looks like they were run over by a herd of buffalo, you look nice," Bryn greeted Jace as he finished tucking his button-down shirt into his jeans, his hair wet and combed from his face as he moved out from his apartment into their shared hallway. Each of them—Jace, Aunt Mallory, and Bryn—had their own apartments above the town clinic where her father, and now Jace, worked.

The apartments were nothing more than rooms of an old house refurbished into individual living quarters. They all shared a bathroom and a kitchen much like the places called "dorms" that she'd read about in some of the Pre-Collapse books.

A glitter in his blue eyes warned her before the words left his mouth, but she enjoyed the brotherly ribbing and teasing with the closest person she had to a sibling.

"You look decent enough to show your face in town, but only *Finny* will be brave enough to give you a smooch." Jace smirked at Bryn, his verbal retaliation earning him a punch to the shoulder. While Jace was clean lines and ironed to perfection, Bryn had never quite fallen into the same type of style.

Instead, she wore a white linen dress (slightly wrinkled) instead of the drab-brown skirt and tan shirt that matched the boring browns of the world around her. The town all wore their depressing browns, as if part of their culture was to blend into the drab desert around them. If they had always dressed this way, she'd think they just didn't have the means to trade for fine, colorful fabrics.

The uniform of their uniformity.

Shaking her head at the needless thought, because what could she even do, she chose to wear her decorative brown boots with their intricate beige details that looked like angel wings along the side of each boot. They were one of the few expensive items she owned since she'd invested a month's wages to procure them from the cobbler. It was worth it since it was her only other choice outside of her work boots that were also brown but not nearly as pretty.

Bryn was also able to tame her curly dark-auburn hair enough to where she could walk without it getting into her eyes and mouth. Not an easy feat on any given day, which was why she never wore it down except on special occasions. Ponytails and braids were a standard part of her daily uniform.

It was rare for her to dress up since she usually spent Founder's Day hiding in her room with one of her many books she'd pilfered from her friend Niamh. She'd never seen the extent of Niamh's library, but thanks to the woman, she'd found true joy and escape from her dreary and anxiety-ridden life in the pages of those very books, forbidden as they were.

Niamh seemed to know that as well. Every time Bryn went to have tea with her, there was always a new book on the coffee table.

One of those few friends Bryn had that she found herself thankful for every day.

Bryn watched as Jace tugged nervously at his sleeves, his anxiety overcoming him, and she couldn't help but smile. She knew exactly who he was thinking about before he even said it.

Sage, the town midwife and one of Bryn's closest female friends aside from Niamh, would be there tonight. The longest crush she could ever remember her cousin having was on Sage.

Though both of them found each other attractive, neither one acted on their feelings and were completely oblivious to the other person's affections. No matter how many hints Bryn dropped without betraying their confidences.

The longing in his eyes as he watched Sage walk down Saints' Road with her medicine bag, the late-night talks with Bryn on how to approach her, yet he always backed away. Watching from afar as she lived her life, including courtships here and there with the men in town. All the while Jace longed for her, and Bryn grew in frustration at the two of them.

As doctor and midwife, they had a rivalry born of mutual attraction and miscommunication.

It was a lesson in frustration. For two incredibly intelligent people, they were both incredibly stupid.

Bryn would watch as Jace worked up the nerve to speak to their friend in a nonprofessional capacity instead of mooning over her from the side of the road. She'd heard stories from Declan and Justin about how the man pined at every celebration, and no amount of good-natured ribbing changed it. Jace just wouldn't take action.

"Tonight. Tonight is the night I am going to ask her to dance," he promised, saying it more to himself than her, but she would give him that and not say anything about all the other times he'd chickened out.

She would be nice this evening and not give her cousin anything but a nod of confidence. If she made a chicken noise, well, that was by accident, of course.

Jace narrowed his eyes on her as he put his elbow out, and Bryn took it with a sardonic smile as she stepped out of her own apartment. Both of them knew to use the back stairwell if they wanted to avoid his mother. While he may not know the extent of what happened to Bryn behind closed doors, her aunt Mallory always had to speak up about her expectations for them in public.

Her aunt was to be a wife of the church as much as a wife to her husband, so her family had to fit into that overall picture of domestic perfection. Even her witchy niece.

Neither of them wanted to deal with her and the lecture on what was befitting a follower of Balor, the god the Church of Baleros worshipped. The lecture was always the same growing up. Enough so that Bryn could repeat it verbatim in her head. How to act in public and conduct oneself in the manner befitting a young lady and gentleman.

No drinking. No smoking. No dancing with anyone you do not have intentions toward. Anything fun was for the grown and *married* adults. Never make a scene. Be seen and not heard. Children were to be a point of pride for their families.

Like a living, breathing trophy of their accomplishments as a parent.

Look at what my genetics made and how well behaved it is!

Stepping out onto Saints' Road, what was once pavement and brick now broken, sand filling the crevices, Bryn stopped abruptly. Her nerves coming to life and her need to disappear overwhelming her as she watched townspeople walking along, laughing and dancing. Children ran through their parents' legs as family pets chased them.

Fires burned in tiny pits put in the middle of the road as musicians prepared their instruments. The torches along the buildings were full of enough oil to burn long into the night.

It was sensory overload for Bryn. The people, the sights and sounds, the fear of what they may do when they saw her.

Suddenly Jace was cupping her elbow, avoiding her skin, and helping her to sit on the stairs they'd just walked down.

Why can't I breathe? she thought as Jace pushed her head between her legs, careful still not to touch any skin.

"It's all right, Bryn. I promise," Jace whispered. "*Damn it, Justin.*"

She knew she wasn't meant to hear the last comment as Jace rubbed his hand along her back, careful to stay on the clothing.

Jace knew she didn't like to be touched, he just didn't know the why of it. Oh, he'd asked, but she played it off as just something that made her uncomfortable.

Finally, he stopped asking and respected her boundaries ever since. To say she was cursed would cause more issues than was worth it.

"I can't . . ." Her words stuck in her throat as tears came to her eyes and embarrassment overwhelmed her.

"Let's just go back upstairs. It's not a big deal if we don't show up. We can play that new board game that—"

His words were cut off as something licked the side of Bryn's face before nuzzling up against her. She found herself embracing the huge savior in fur.

"Finny," she whispered into his fur, and took deep breaths. He smelled like he'd been romping in the horse troughs, the sun from earlier doing nothing to make him smell any better, but it was soothing her all the same.

Looking up at Jace, she clutched Finian's fur. She wouldn't ruin her cousin's night. He might actually ask Sage to dance, and she would not be the reason her friends were denied that.

"I am good, Jace, but thank you," she whispered as she stood, faltering a bit, but both man and hound were there to help.

Chin up and shoulders back, Bryn walked out onto the sandy road, looking for her few allies among the population. Sadly, Ava Stevens was hovering near Declan. Bryn knew she shouldn't care, but it hurt to see them in the same place for the first time since that night she'd walked in on Declan and Ava kissing in his office at the Cauldron, his trading post.

Turning away, she looked for anyone else as Jace squeezed her elbow to keep her moving.

"Go find Sage," she whispered to him as her eyes found the woman in question walking along the road, saying hello to the women she'd cared for during labor.

"Not until I have you settled somewhere."

His tone allowed no argument.

Niamh wasn't out yet, the inn she ran was dark, and Bryn sent out a plea to her imaginary deity that Niamh would be here tonight. She was the only person the town shunned as much as they did Bryn.

It never bothered Niamh, though, as most people feared her abundance of confidence and backhanded compliments enough that the torment by the townspeople lessened when in proximity to her, making Niamh a safe place. Bryn would naturally still be friends with the woman, but it was a definite perk of the friendship. Plus, the inn had been a reprieve from her home life on many occasions.

Everyone in town knew there was no need for an inn when they never had anyone visit. It was a brothel, plain and simple, and as sinful as it was considered to be, no one had ever managed to shut it down.

In fact, Niamh called the place the Sanctuary to spite the church when speaking of her business.

How they hadn't kicked in her door and burned down the building already, Bryn did not know.

In fact, when Bryn had asked why they didn't find a way to close the inn's door for good, knowing what it was and it being such a religious town, she had earned one of Niamh's sardonic smiles.

"Because there are people at the top who gasp at the sight of my business yet utilize it themselves from their shadowy corners of the night."

So, while the old redbrick-and-wood building stood with the name "Saints' Inn," everyone knew it was a saloon and brothel and called it by the name Niamh had picked. That was aside from her aunt and the most devout of Ifreann.

The glasses etched with the name "The Sanctuary" were a solitary reminder that even though the church tried to conform the business, they were not as powerful as they pretended to be when it came to Niamh.

If they were meeting with Niamh, they would be meeting at the Sanctuary, not Saints' Inn.

Caden, one of Jace's school friends and the bartender at the Sanctuary, was moving through the crowd with nonalcoholic drinks.

The man would have been a rogue back in the day. His dark hair, soulful eyes, blinding white smile, and good nature made him popular with the ladies in town.

Bryn watched as he served outside the bar he normally tended, bantering with the people milling about and letting his infectious laugh catch through the crowd he spoke with. The people of the town were drawn to him like a moth to a flame.

She adored the barkeep, him being one of the few she could say hello to and not earn a scathing look, but she wasn't a close enough friend to stick to him for the evening like she would Niamh.

"You made it." Justin walked up to them, shaking Jace's hand and giving a nod to Bryn. Much like Jace, he was aware of her aversion to touch, just not the why of it.

There were few people she would risk a vision for, to know their death, as horrible as she thought that was to think. She couldn't lose Jace, so he was one of the few allowed to touch her arms or face on rare occasions when she was worried about him being called out for something risky.

If a vision came, she wanted to have a chance to prevent anything from happening to him. Still, he was careful around her since she normally shied away from touch, and she usually had to force him to shake her hand to get a sense of his fate.

Declan used to be the other . . . Nope. Not going there.

The tower guard, Travis, stepped up to them, his pistol on his hip as he nodded in greeting before turning to Justin.

With dark-blond hair and gray eyes, Travis held a serious nature that balanced with Caden's, his best friend. Even with his serious demeanor, she'd heard girls talk about how attractive he was, and it didn't hurt he was the quickest draw in town, but sadly his pistol and rifle were most likely his only bed partners. She wondered some days what the haunted look in his eyes was from but wouldn't force him to speak about something painful. Bryn understood having secrets.

She was all too aware of how difficult it was to hide the hurt from the ones you love. To never want to look weak even as your knees buckled, the pain as fresh as the day the emotional wound had been made.

"Bryn. Jace." Travis nodded as he finished speaking to Justin while she was lost in her thoughts.

"Hey, Trav." She smiled at him. With a tip of his hat, he turned to walk to his post at the guard station where he'd keep vigil until well into the morning.

"I'll be doing the rounds since I am on duty tonight." Justin tapped the sheriff's badge pinned to his blue button-down shirt. "Need anything, you come get me."

Looking at Bryn, he raised his eyebrows.

"Anyone or anything messes with you . . ." He let the words trail off, but she nodded, her fingers finding Finian's fur again.

Jace grabbed her elbow and pulled her toward where Sage was speaking with a young couple due to have their first child any day.

Several instruments were being tuned nearby, the sounds out of sync, but that hardly bothered the people dancing without music, already well into the ambiance of the evening. With their drinks poured and the lanterns lit, the people of the town showed their human side for a small window of time once a year.

These people were not so different as their counterparts that roamed the night. They just thought they were.

"Go, Jace. I will stick to the shadows."

She watched him hesitate, his loyalty to her at odds with his need to speak to Sage before another man asked her to dance.

"Go." She smiled and pushed him toward her friend. He looked back once, before putting his hands in his pockets and walking painfully slow toward where Sage stood.

Careful to maneuver her way through the crowd without touching anyone, not wanting to take the chance someone was near death and she went into a fit on the street, Bryn turned to take in the whole of the celebration before her. A pinch to her arm through her shirt had her hissing, but it was hard to tell which of the people she'd passed had done it, and honestly, it wasn't worth the hassle of trying to do anything about it.

Several people looked her up and down before speaking to their friends behind their hands, eyes on Bryn.

"Witch" carried on the breeze to her ears, and she tried to hold her head up high as she blinked away the tears. Why did she still cry when she heard the word?

Shouldn't it lose its meaning after hearing it for so very long?

Bryn just hoped she could make it through the night without finding herself burning for her perceived sins.

Chapter 4

Bryn tried to move away from the hateful stares and condemning voices. Her heart pounded as she felt like the whole of the town was coming down around her. The voices of the girls whispering about her loud enough for the whole of the town to hear, the chant of "witch" stuck like a bad tune in her mind, all told her very clearly she was nearing an emotional breakdown.

She needed to get somewhere safe before the town saw her tears and knew their cruel words had done the very damage they'd hoped for.

It was a horrible idea to come to the celebration.

A growl stopped Bryn in her tracks. The girls who had been talking and whispering about Bryn loud enough for her to hear quickly dispersed as Finian watched them with the eyes of a predator.

They scampered off, looking over their shoulders at Finian until they found the safety of their parents.

"Honestly, if you were human, I'd marry you." She laughed as Finian started walking, looking back as he waited for her. Smiling as much as she could, she followed as she blinked away her tears.

A man walking past her used his elbow to knock her to the side, laughing with his friends when she almost fell into the horse trough. Heat flooded her cheeks, and Finian went on the defensive again.

"Damn dog." The man kicked at Finian, but the hound bit into the top of the man's boot, lips pulled back as he held on. The man, unable to hold steady, fell backward, his friends catching him as Finian released his bite and backed up to Bryn.

Turning away, Bryn wiped her eyes.

Weak. She felt so damn weak and wished she could leave the town. As always, the questions rose in her mind: Where would she go, and could she leave Jace and her friends behind?

The answer was always the same. She couldn't leave them. If she asked, perhaps they would leave, but why should they uproot everything for her?

"Dalton!" Justin came up and stood in front of Bryn as he addressed the man who had shoved her.

No. Please, don't make it worse, Justin!

"Yeah, Sheriff?" The man turned, his two friends looking between her and Justin.

"Watch your step. You knocked a lady over."

Damn it, Justin.

Caden stopped in the street from where he was walking back into the bar, turned, and put his tray under his arm as he watched.

"Don't," she whispered, only earning a look from over his shoulder before Justin turned fully back to the men.

"Ain't no lady, Sheriff, and you know it. A damn witch, casting spells and killing people. If she wasn't spreading her legs for the governor's son, we'd be rid of her by now." The man spit on the ground near her feet, and Bryn moved away, hugging her middle and curling in on herself. Something she always did to make herself small enough to appear unassuming.

Finian growled a warning as Justin grabbed Dalton by the collar, bringing them both face-to-face.

"I don't give a rat's ass what you believe or the thoughts you have while sharing that one deranged brain cell between the three of you. That's none of my business, but I won't have you physically harming her again, do you hear me?"

Worse and worse. She knew Justin only wanted to help, but he was putting a bigger target on her back. Her eyes caught on the graying blond hair of her aunt, and the seething look she shot Bryn told her she was in for it later. As if her existence, and Justin's choice to step in, was all her fault.

Great. There would be hell to pay later.

"Gentlemen!" Caden walked up, shoving his tray into one of the men's chests. Their only option was to put their hands out to hold it. "Let's have a drink and be on our way." Throwing his arms around the shoulders of the two men not currently in Justin's proximity, he turned them away to focus on something else while Justin finished up with Dalton.

Such loyal friends, Bryn thought, regarding the men who left Dalton to Justin's wrath, but she wouldn't begrudge the small mercy of there being only one bully now instead of three.

Justin released Dalton, and she knew the glower the man was receiving from the officer of the law. Bryn could see it clearly in her mind's eye even if she were unable to see his face right then. Justin could bring a man to his knees and make them confess everything with that look.

"This is a warning and a promise. Don't mess with Bryn anymore. I won't have that kind of behavior happening under my watch, and not in my town."

Dalton gave Bryn a look promising retribution, and she knew he would make good on it. She'd need to watch her back.

"Yes, Sheriff. For however long you are in charge." His voice held a snide tone, almost a warning, and she feared Justin would find himself on the wrong side of the church because of her.

Dalton stood and dusted himself off before turning and following his friends.

"I thank you for standing up for me, but you know he will take a shot at me when you're not looking now, right?" she whispered as Justin watched Dalton wander off before turning to her.

"I wouldn't have to if you'd stand up for yourself a little. Why do you allow this, Bryn? You weren't always so ready to take people's crap when we were all younger." Justin turned to her as he folded his arms across his chest.

She'd had her father to protect her then. Mallory wasn't able to get through him so she could take her rage out on Bryn.

No, that'd come after when she was grieving his death and vulnerable. Mallory got her hits in and kept Bryn down so she knew it wasn't worth trying to stand back up.

It was physical attacks when she was younger, before Bryn became an adult herself, and then it turned into emotional manipulation that left Bryn living a life of fear. Her aunt always reminded Bryn that her future was in her aunt's hands, not her own.

"One word from me and they burn you to the bones, witch," she would say, leaving that as her last words to Bryn after an argument.

Just survive. Don't make waves. Disappear into the shadows.

He placed his hand on her shoulder, careful not to touch her skin, and she looked up into his clear blue eyes.

"One day, you'll tell me?"

Giving a small nod was all she had as an answer, but he squeezed her shoulder and let it go.

"Sheriff! Speech is about to start!" someone yelled out, and Justin gave her a wink before turning to help with the gathering crowd.

Slipping under the covered porches, she made her way toward Niamh's place, letting the shadows of the evening keep her from the eyes of those who would do worse than Dalton if given the chance.

"Sheriff won't always be around," one man growled as she walked past, but Bryn kept her face turned away so they couldn't see her reaction to their words. She wouldn't give them that.

"*Spreading her legs for him, too, I bet. Busy girl. No wonder she hangs out at a brothel . . .*"

"*. . . should've burned her at the stake a long time ago . . .*"

The last statement had Bryn running to the safety of her friend's establishment, brothel or not.

Slowing her pace as the crowd moved their focus to where the governor was readying to make his speech, she looked over toward her ex, allowing herself a little peek.

Declan tuned his guitar, the one he made himself long ago while she watched, talking and spending time with him. A memory that tore at her already battered heart. His eyes caught hers, and she watched a million emotions flicker through them before he turned away to look where the governor was calling for everyone's attention.

His father stood up on a wooden platform in front of the city hall as Bryn swallowed her own emotions to focus on his father as well.

Feeling eyes on her, she turned, but there was no one behind her. Bryn was good about not letting people sneak up on her usually, but if they had been there, whoever it was, they were gone now. Stepping closer to the shadows, she let Finian settle at her feet.

"Good evening! Welcome to our Bicentennial Founder's Day celebration!"

The crowd cheered at Mr. Rafferty's words, his dark eyes sparkling in the light of the lanterns and fires lit throughout the street for the night of celebration.

The large brass sculpture of their founding father stood strong and proud behind Mr. Rafferty. The grim face of a lost ancestor watching over the town from his spot near the governor's mansion. The long-dead man had his hands on his hips, looking out over the town he built, finding the descendants he left to rule in his stead long after he was gone lacking, Bryn was sure. Or so she hoped.

"Two hundred years since our world was lost to us, and we had to survive or die, and our great founder, Cadogan Rafferty, found a way to thrive!" Cheers erupted along with whistles. "He found this place, what was once a long stretch of hell, and turned it into the good city we thrive in today.

"So, on this day, let us remember our forefather and all those that came after, who worked to bring about an oasis in the desert. A place of sanctuary for the weary souls of those who would have been lost to Mother Nature's wrath."

Bryn wondered if Mr. Rafferty bought what he sold. She sure didn't. His too-large smile and false promises were catnip to the crowd, though. A politician through and through.

Just as fast as the cheers grew to a deafening level, they evened out as Mr. Rafferty moved from the platform, the instruments now tuned and in harmony as the music flowed along the road. People lost themselves to the rhythm as the celebration kicked off.

Turning back to look at Declan, his long, curly auburn hair falling around his face, his whiskey-brown eyes watching her as he plucked the strings of his guitar, the sound a siren call to her soul. As always with his music, Bryn was pulled in. Her worries and fears held at bay for another day. His music was almost magical in its ability to sweep the listener away.

Two familiar figures caught her eye, and Bryn looked to where Jace was dancing with a woman. A smile lit Bryn's face as she took in the couple. The dark skin of her friend with her natural curls free and not pulled back and away from her face like when she was working made her look like a goddess in the waning light of the evening.

Sage.

He did it, he had finally spoken to her, and they were dancing! She was so happy for him.

Both he and Sage laughed as he spun her out, bringing her back into his arms. Bryn sent a mental slap on the back to her cousin, hoping her friend gave him a chance for more than this night. The fact that they were laughing together, and not throwing sharp words, was promising in and of itself.

Leaving Jace and Sage to their joyous dance, Bryn heard the doors of the Sanctuary opening before Niamh stepped out onto the porch with a full glass of wine, the citizens keeping their distance from the place. Niamh nodded to her as she sat on the steps near where Bryn was standing, Finian not making an effort to stand and greet her.

Niamh's eyes moved over the celebration before landing on Declan with an intensity that gave Bryn goose bumps.

What was that about?

Bryn was sure demons themselves were less intimidating than Niamh as she skewered Declan with a look. It was far more than Bryn figured he deserved . . . unless she knew the truth of what had ended things between them.

Declan's father came up beside her, leaning against a post on the opposite side of Niamh.

"Enjoying yourself, Bryn?" Mr. Rafferty asked before she could inquire of her friend about her animosity.

Aaron Rafferty, the governor of their small town, descendant of the founder, and probably one of the few people who kept the entire town from coming down on her and Niamh. She never asked why, not wanting to look a gift horse in the mouth and ruin a good thing such as his protection.

Plus, he'd probably say something perfectly political.

It's my job to protect my citizens was her guess.

His salt-and-pepper gray hair and dark, almost black eyes were nothing like his son's, and Bryn wondered what Declan's mother had looked like. There were not any photos of the woman in his home when she'd visited the governor's home growing up.

One of Mr. Rafferty's three hound dogs moved closer, sniffing at Bryn's boot before trotting off to join the other two of his hounds. Unlike Finian, these dogs never bothered to make friends with anyone. While they never attacked, nor acted aggressively, people gave them a wide berth. It seemed the dogs were fine with that since all their loyalty was solely to Mr. Rafferty anyway.

Finian just watched them, not bothering to lift his large head to greet the other canines.

"I was told I had to be here. Governor's mandate and all that." She tried to smile, but it felt forced. She had no idea how to act around the man whose son she had broken up with.

Mr. Rafferty gave his winning-politician smile to her.

"Justin informed me you prefer to stay in your apartment, but is that any way to live, Bryn? Always hiding?" he asked, and something in his words pushed at something in her mind that she didn't understand. Something that felt familiar, but yet she couldn't access it.

Perhaps something from her childhood since he'd been good friends with her father before he had died. While she was not particularly close to him, her father had been, and she wondered what kind of friendship there could have been between a straitlaced by-the-books doctor and a politician.

He knew enough about what the town thought of her that it irritated her to no end that he'd all but forced her to come to the celebration, knowing how the town's people treated her.

As if some part of her traumatized psyche had called out to the enemy she'd learned to avoid at all costs, Aunt Mallory walked past, only acknowledging Mr. Rafferty with a greeting, her eyes staring past Bryn. Her aunt's betrothed, Daran Balcom, walked next to her and as always ignored Bryn's existence as well.

The man set her teeth on edge just as much as his brother, Scrios Arioch. Both men were the most verbal in their opinion of Bryn's perceived witchy ways and would see her dead without pause.

"You can guess why, Mr. Rafferty," she whispered.

"Say the word and I'll put a stop to it," he replied, his voice as soft as hers, surprising her. He knew she wouldn't let him and figured he knew it was safe to offer help to someone he knew wouldn't take it.

In the end, she could admit she needed him to stay in his position as governor since he was her only source of protection from being exiled to the desert should the scrios and his brother take it further than words and gossip.

Whispers were better than that fate, and if he took up her side, she could guarantee they'd turn on him as well. No, it was best to protect her few allies in the government that could truly protect her.

Even better would be to keep them safe by not associating with them at all and keeping her distance.

Giving him a small smile, she knew he had been speaking with her for too long already, and the sadness in his eyes surprised her. For a split second, she wondered if he could read her mind or if he cared more than she thought.

Turning, she faced Niamh, who was watching three women who were close enough to see they were talking about Bryn, but too far for her to hear their words over the music.

Unfortunately, she could see the words on their lips without having to hear them.

Witch. Witch. Witch.

"Buzz, buzz, buzz said the busy insignificant little bees," Niamh growled with a sickly-sweet smile to the woman nearest her. How they heard Niamh over the music, she was unsure, but the quick pace they made at getting away certainly said they understood they had crossed a line with Niamh.

A small laugh without any mirth left Bryn's lips as Niamh settled herself next to Bryn without a drop of wine spilling. Crossing her legs at the ankles like a true lady, she took a sip as a queen might, watching people she considered peasants, dancing in her court.

"I see Jace found his testicles," Niamh whispered conspiratorially as Bryn looked to see Sage laughing at something her cousin had said.

"Bottom right drawer. He forgets where he puts things sometimes," Bryn replied, smiling at her cousin and friend.

Two men stood just behind the dancing couple.

Justin was speaking with Kessler, the town blacksmith and one of the few who allowed Bryn to be around him without having to run to the church to douse himself in blessed water. Justin smiled when he caught her eyes, and Kessler nodded, arms still folded across his chest. She smiled back at the two men, happy to see a small lift to Kessler's usually frowning lips.

A sudden chill ran over her skin much like the day before. The hairs on her arms rose again, and she felt like something large was just over the horizon.

Shaking her head, she listened to Declan's tune, trying to shove the ominous feeling to the back of her mind, but her eyes kept moving back to the gate that was supposed to keep them all safe.

Chapter 5

T he sun had set, the darkness bringing shadows to life from the fires lit along the road, and Bryn smiled again, more than she had in years, as she watched the shadows dance beneath the last of the evening's revelers.

As the night wore on, more and more people made their way to their homes, but Bryn and Niamh stayed out here as their day was only beginning.

Bryn, able to walk the street without judgment, Niamh watching over the girls who stayed under her roof as they catered to the pious men, who were happily married during the day but came in under the cover of darkness to enjoy the hands of a woman not their wife.

She didn't judge her friend, nor her lifestyle. Niamh was her closest ally aside from Sage and Jace. She was the one who had taken her under her wing when Bryn was the most lost and scared she'd ever been right after her father had died and she was left to her aunt's care.

Teaching her how to be a woman when Mallory couldn't be bothered to speak of such things. Guiding her through her first love, Declan, and first heartbreak, also Declan.

It was a loyalty born from another's neglect.

The few women who worked for Niamh kept to themselves, even now they stayed inside, keeping to the shadows of the night as much as Bryn did these days. She never saw them unless she visited Niamh, but even then, they kept their distance. Yet when she did stumble upon one of the ladies, they were far more welcoming than any other in Ifreann, even in their reclusiveness.

Funny. One would think those of the church would have been opening their doors for all the "poor sinners."

"Glass houses all around and so many stones . . ." Niamh would say as she swept the church's behavior like lint from her shoulder.

No matter how much Scrios Arioch had tried to run Niamh out of town, to bring the townspeople together with the mindset she was running a house of ill repute, he failed every time. He finally gave up years ago, but his eye was on the house for anything he could throw at it in the hopes of knocking it down like the villain to their story that he was.

A glass of Caden's brew was suddenly blocking her vision, her hand moving to take it without thought as Caden moved to sit on the other side of Niamh.

"Thank you," she whispered before putting the glass to her lips, thankful that no one could tell she had an alcoholic beverage due to the dark glass. A sorely needed alcoholic beverage.

"Figured you could use a pint or so after dealing with the town idiots." He smiled at her.

He worked as the barkeep at the Sanctuary, but Niamh told her long ago that he never messed with any of the girls. A huge reason he had lasted there so long.

Even when the very serious Travis came to visit and have a brew, he also kept to himself, simply being polite company.

"Thanks for stepping in without making it obvious," she replied. Caden was good at that and had saved her more than a few times when someone was messing with her in front of the Sanctuary.

"He shouldn't have to. You should be safe in your own town," Niamh groused as she took a sip of her wine.

Caden settled back, leaning his elbows on the topmost step of the porch. How he managed to look comfortable lying across wooden steps, she didn't know. Her butt was going numb from the discomfort.

"Travis says the same thing. We wish it. We grew up with you, Bryn, and the town doesn't see you the way we do. If they could, they would know you are amazing," Caden said, referring to their small group of friends: Justin, Declan, Kessler, Sage, and Jace.

Still, even among them, she felt like an outsider. Hiding and keeping her secrets from them, like the fear she lived out in her own home or the fits she fell into when she touched someone who would die soon.

"Kessler is still pissed as a wasp bothered during mating season that you won't let him make you a weapon," Caden said with a nod to the forge where Kessler was ignoring the joyous revelers dancing outside on the street.

As if he could hear everything, Kessler looked toward them before hammering some metal hot from the fire. He'd made his appearance to appease his friends and got back to work. Smart man.

"I'll speak to him soon. Perhaps I should let him," she whispered, Niamh and Caden turning to her with raised eyebrows.

"You'd make his year if you did, Brynnie." Caden smiled. "He isn't law like Justin, not a trader like Declan with his own gang of thugs, so he wants to have something he can do to protect you."

Bryn gave him a small smile, wishing she felt like she deserved it.

"That's all for tomorrow. Tonight, we listen and wait for the peons to go to bed so we can rule the town once more." Niamh raised her glass, Bryn and Caden clinking their own against hers as they fell into the music of the evening. Bryn was able to listen to Declan's playing, ignoring the stares and whispers, which was a relief. His music was a balm to the weary soul.

Soon enough, only the light of the torches was left aside from the fires that burned only once a year along the street. The shadows took over the celebration as they danced along the buildings.

Settling back, she swayed her body to the last of the music, the night ending slowly as people stumbled and laughed after having allowed themselves the pleasure of being human one night of the year.

The feeling in her gut, the warning, grew at a rapid rate, and she found herself standing and looking around.

"What's wrong?" Niamh asked, standing as well, looking for a threat.

"I'm not sure. I've had this bad feeling," Bryn whispered as her system flooded with adrenaline.

The warning horns split open the joyous atmosphere of the night like a knife. The screams of the people matching the horns as they ran from the streets to take cover from the unknown danger.

Bryn and Niamh both turned as one toward the gate as small dust devils made their way along the street, trailing the panicked townspeople as they ran, shoving at each other like wild, mindless animals.

"Sandstorm," Niamh whispered, her eyes focused on something past the gate. Words in another language Bryn had never heard soon left Niamh's lips.

In her own panicked state, Bryn tried to calm her nerves, debating whether she could make it back to her apartment or if she needed to take cover with Niamh. The fact that Niamh was in a trance, staring intensely at the gate, made her hand twitch with the urge to slap Niamh out of it.

"It's going to be a bad one. I feel it in my bones," Niamh spoke, but Bryn wasn't sure who she was talking to since Niamh's eyes were glazed over.

"Sandstorm!" Justin yelled as he ran down the road toward them. "Get inside and take cover!"

The walls usually took the brunt of the weather for them, but the wind picked up as a dark cloud moved over the gate, the horns' mournful sound chilling as the storm grew in its intensity.

They'd never had a sandstorm this intense before.

"Now!" Justin was suddenly in her face, shoving at her shoulder and pushing her and Niamh into the Sanctuary. A horrifying cloud of red dust enveloped the building right as Justin slammed the door shut behind them. The entire road engulfed in tornadic sand was the last visual she had of Saints' Road.

"Away from the windows!" He herded them to an inner room in the Sanctuary, yelling for the others to do the same. Bryn didn't look to see what men from town were there. She didn't want that on her conscience, and since she was a horrible poker player, she didn't want to pretend in public when she watched them walking with their families to church service before she turned in for the day.

Settling down in one of the supply rooms, Bryn put her head to her knees, wrapping her arms around her legs. Focusing on her breathing and not the glass breaking, Bryn worked to calm her heart rate, trying to ignore the sobs of the other women in the dark room as the glass broke and the wind howled.

Finian whined, having moved back to Justin's side.

The only light came from the cracked door Justin looked through. He flinched every once in a while as he watched the storm bear down on their little town.

"Calm yourselves. Your yelling isn't going to change the course of this storm," Niamh chided, her voice barely audible over the furniture breaking outside their little room. Bryn was surprised by the calmness in Niamh's voice as her business was being torn apart. Her whole life was in the Sanctuary.

A tingling started in Bryn's fingers and toes, as well as the all too familiar feeling of ants under her skin. Bryn rubbed along her arms at the same time as Justin, their movements mirroring each other.

Looking to Niamh, her eyes focused on the wall as if she could see through it, as if her focus could stop the destruction, Bryn patted the woman on the shoulder before she pulled back. Her skin was growing more sensitive, and the anxiety building up inside her was becoming a raging inferno.

"*I am here, come to me, my child,*" Bryn heard the whispered words, and looked for who was speaking. No one else looked around for the voice; it was as if they hadn't heard it.

Bryn was sure her heart stopped. Was this a vision? It didn't feel like one.

When Justin looked at her, his eyes confused, she realized it wasn't just her who had heard the whispered plea.

The distraction of Justin kept her from noticing one of the men in the room sitting too close to her, his fingers brushing hers, and she knew before it happened she was going into a fit.

Feeling it come upon her, she scooted away from him, farther into the corner of the room right as the black stole over her vision.

Chapter 6

Her world was blindingly bright as she opened her eyes, knowing inherently that she had been pulled into a vision. The man who had sat next to her in the Sanctuary where they were hunkered down was the town baker. Ava's father.

The fact that he was in the brothel at all, his second wife just having had their first child together, Ava's mother dying from the sickness, made her wish she could pull herself from the vision and slap him for being here when his wife was recovering from childbirth. She knew no one had followed her, Justin, and Niamh in. He'd been here before the storm hit.

Perhaps her "fit" had her smacking him with her seizing body. One could hope.

Bryn watched as the baker grabbed a rifle from his bakery office before running to the front of the store and looking through the window.

"You said nothing would happen with Arioch taking over!" his wife yelled from where she held a mewling newborn behind the counter. "That was the reason I didn't fight you on it!"

Arioch taking over what? What would the scrios be taking over?

"Ted! Do something!" she turned to yell at Bryn, or Ted, the man who Bryn was looking through the eyes of. The man who was going to die. If she remembered correctly, he worked on the town's small farm and was most likely doing a delivery to the bakery during the vision.

"Shut up, woman!" the baker yelled at his wife, not looking at her as his eyes danced across Saints' Road, and Bryn wished she could reach out to throttle him. "You knew the demons would rebel as sure as I did. Now hush up and shut that damn baby up!"

Leaving the window, he checked the rifle before running to push the bakery door open, aiming at whatever was outside. The moment the door fully opened, blood splattered the walls of the bakery.

His wife was screaming, but Bryn was unable to focus on her or the baby. A cloaked figure walked in, and somewhere deep down, Bryn knew she was looking at a wraith.

Something rolled across the floor and stopped near the toe of Ted's boots. Bryn looked down to see the glassy eyes of the baker looking up at her from his severed head.

A sharp pain cut through her side, and she came out of the fit, gasping for air, and her lungs seizing as much as her body, while Niamh held a damp cloth to her head.

Bryn needed air that her lungs were unable to pull in. Pushing away Niamh's arms, Bryn stumbled like a newborn colt as she ran from the room someone had moved her to. How long had this fit lasted?

Stumbling down the stairs, she held on to the railing as her knees buckled a few times, but she finally made it to the front of the Sanctuary to see the door and windows gone, glass and wood strewn everywhere.

Focused on the world outside of the Sanctuary, she made it to the porch, the steps destroyed. Ignoring the debris, she fell onto Saints' Road before dry heaving.

Her mind reeled at the image of the death she had just seen in her mind's eye. Something she never could grow used to no matter how often it happened.

Rolling onto her back, she took in huge gulps of air.

The sky was growing brighter as the sun made its way higher in the sky, the storm having hit in the early hours of morning. The rays penetrated through the hazy sand still floating through Ifreann in the aftermath.

"Brynnie!" a man yelled, heavy footsteps making their way toward her, but she didn't have the energy to respond or move. One moment she was staring at the sky as the clouds of sand dissipated around them, the next she was pulled into Declan's arms, a spark of electricity moving between them as his face pushed into her neck. Tensing, she braced for a vision, relief flooding her when none came.

"You're okay. Thank fuck," he rasped against her skin. Pulling her into his lap, he took her face in his large hands, looking her over with those whiskey eyes she missed so much that it physically hurt.

"I'm fine," she rasped, her voice gritty from inhaling so much of the sand still floating along the air currents.

Placing his forehead against hers, they shared breath. She missed little moments of touch, the relief he was going to live another day, followed by the intimacy of it.

The intimacy she coveted, and yet he shared with another.

"Please, Brynnie—" he started, but she pushed out of his arms. She was too weak right now and would capitulate to his pleas if she were to listen further. Maybe, one day, she would be strong enough to listen to his why of what had happened between him and Ava, but this day was not it.

"Maybe later," she stated, the same standard response she had given him for weeks now.

Declan stood as well, his hands holding her elbows to steady her.

He was one of the few she'd allowed close to her since shutting people out had come far easier for her, and she hated he couldn't understand how deep his betrayal cut at her when she looked into those familiar eyes.

Shaking away those thoughts, she gave Declan a small smile.

"Thank you, but I need to check on my apartment." As she withdrew from his hold, he narrowed his eyes.

"Now is not the time, I understand that, but we need to talk. Soon."

Turning and walking away, he had the last word, but she agreed. It was going to have to be soon.

Bryn walked down Saints' Road, taking in the destruction, and feeling a sense of sadness. The town may not have ever welcomed her with open arms, but this place had been her home for as long as she could remember.

This sandstorm was on par with the stories she'd heard of the disasters brought on during the Collapse. When the oceans rose, earthquakes decimated, and the seasons changed dramatically.

Long ago, she'd read the world had four seasons. Now, there were two. Burning and freezing. One extreme to another, and they came on quickly. One day it might be burning, and the next it was freezing without warning.

Never, in all the time the town had been standing since the Collapse, had they found themselves in the center of such natural chaos like this, though.

No, natural was wrong. Bryn could feel an undercurrent of something that had nothing to do with the world around her, but as much as she dug deep down inside, she couldn't put what the feeling meant into words.

The sensation of being watched was back, and this time it had her inner-prey drive going crazy. Spinning, she noticed nothing out of the ordinary. A shadow moved, and she held still, wondering if it were some trick of the light.

Watching where the shadow had been, nothing more happened.

"You're being paranoid," Bryn growled out loud to herself.

Bringing her arm up, she noticed that the hairs along her skin had yet to go down. Everything in the air was still charged as if lightning were about to strike, and that worried her. The storm was over, so why was she still in a state of panic? Why was her adrenaline not lowering? Her extremities were cold, pumping blood to her internal organs in preparation for fight or flight.

"Bryn!" Sage yelled from the front door of the forge, and Bryn jumped, her heart pounding faster at the interruption to her internal panic.

Bryn moved to meet her friend in the road. "Are you all right? I heard you, Justin, and Niamh were out when Travis blew the horns."

Gold flickering in Sage's eyes stayed Bryn's lips.

A trick of the light . . . again, she thought to herself, but she was having trouble dismissing such things as her nervous system went haywire. The moment she made eye contact with Justin in that little room, when someone whispered to them both . . . the voice . . . She'd never heard the woman's voice before, but a sense of calm familiarity had clung to the words. A familiarity similar to hearing the soothing voice of a loved one.

"Bryndis!" Sage yelled again, and Bryn came back to herself, the gold gone from Sage's eyes.

"I'm sorry . . . I am just rattled, I guess?"

"Is that a question? Of course, you are! Come to my home, I'll make you some tea, and you can rest for the day." Not waiting for an answer, Sage took her arm, a small shock jolting Bryn at the skin-to-skin contact as she pulled her arm from her friend's hand.

Bryn did not have a vision, which if Sage wasn't near death, she wouldn't . . . but the shock she'd felt was a new revelation. The same shock she'd felt with Declan moments earlier. Could the sandstorm have caused some sort of electrically charged atmosphere around Ifreann?

Ignoring the weirdness of what had just transpired, mostly since Sage had no idea Bryn could see people's deaths when she touched them and obviously did not feel the jolt, Sage pulled Bryn to her small little cottage behind the buildings of Saints' Road.

"Jace is okay?" Bryn asked as she followed her friend.

"Left well before the storm to get some sleep before he was called out to a bedside," Sage replied, not missing a beat as she focused on getting them to her cottage.

A shadow moved in between the buildings as they made their way through, and again Bryn looked for who or what would have cast it, perhaps one of the guards doing a sweep, but there was nothing there.

Her eyes kept to where she saw the shadow, the flicker of darkness that called to something deep inside her. A memory rose to the surface, one lost to years of trauma. Bryn, a small girl, playing in her room talking to the shadows as they moved about almost as if sentient themselves. *Playing with her.* Bryn wanted to chalk it up to a small girl dealing with loneliness.

An agitated flapping of wings surprised her, and she ground to a halt, Sage being yanked back by the sudden cessation of movement.

"What is it?" Sage asked, looking around for what had caused Bryn to stop so suddenly.

"Have you ever seen a black bird before, Sage?" Bryn asked, her eyes focused, scared that if she were to look away, she'd lose it.

"Please tell me I am not hallucinating." Bryn's voice came out in a rasp and a plea as she licked her dry lips.

Looking up to the top of the forge, Sage gasped, her hand going to her mouth while the one clutching Bryn's arm dug in. Her nails were sharper than they looked, and Bryn was afraid to tug away lest she bleed to death.

A large black bird looked down on them. Were the birds in the stories she'd read normally this large? She'd thought them small, barely larger than a rat, but this one looked as large as some of the small dogs she'd seen. Its eyes held a steady, almost humanlike intelligence as it focused intently on Bryn.

"Please . . .," Bryn whispered again, but Sage was quick to tug Bryn and all but throw her through the door of her cottage.

Both women tucked safely inside, Sage paced as Bryn leaned against the door, her body stiff with fear as she waited for her friend to speak. Though Bryn was unsure what she really wanted her friend to say.

"That was a crow." Sage was breathing heavily as she whirled around and ran to a bookshelf in her small living quarters. "I cannot remember the old saying . . ."

A crow. Bryn tried to look out the dusty window, letting out a small scream as the crow landed on the windowsill, staring at Bryn with an intensity she was sure had to be abnormal, yet she had nothing to gauge it against.

There hadn't been a crow, or much of any species of bird, in Ifreann for far too long. The desert hardly seemed a place they'd thrive in. Sage might have seen them before she was brought into Ifreann herself.

Bryn remembered then that Sage, like herself, was not born in the town but brought here. Odd how so much of her past was so focused on surviving that she missed little memories and details about her and her friends from before her father's death.

Sage was from the town closest to Ifreann; the traders of her town were permitted to exchange needed goods with them. Though the town was relatively self-sufficient with underground water reserves, windmills to help provide the town with energy, and livestock that helped with the small farm and its meager crops, there were still crops one could not grow in the desert.

That was where trade came in, and they traded the most with Tanwen.

Tanwen was under the control of the king as well now, which was why Sage's family had left when he imposed the Church of Baleros as the state religion, only to find themselves in the same situation in Ifreann.

The Church of Baleros condemned those who followed the ways of any of the old religions from before the Collapse. Before the invasion of Tanwen, women had power there. They could choose their own clothing (Bryn would have loved to wear something other than skirts and with color!) or control over their own bodies (the brothel wasn't sinful so much for the sex as it was that women were allowed to choose who they gave their bodies to and earn a living while doing it).

However, the other rules of the church were for everyone. It was sinful for anyone to have an affinity with animals or nature in a worshipful way, no mind-altering substances could be consumed, and they must all worship Balor twice a day.

They stopped the sacrifice of a farm animal once a month on a religious pyre (not the ones used for the deceased) to the god who supposedly saved the world shortly after the Collapse. Killing the livestock turned out to not be conducive to feeding a town, and Bryn could only roll her eyes at the ridiculousness of wasting limited resources in such a way in the first place.

Somehow everything the Tanwenian people believed, their whole religion itself and what it stood for, was against Balor. The more Bryn learned about the fall of Tanwen, it was as if the Church of Baleros was actually only made to go against the old ways.

All the rules of the church were in direct opposition to the way it had been for hundreds of years before the Collapse.

Tanwen hadn't fallen under the king's thumb until her teen years. Bryn had planned many escapes to Tanwen in her youth before the invasion. Asking Sage questions of her birthplace was from which their friendship grew. Finally, Sage trusted Bryn enough to show her the books that would have been burned should anyone in town find them.

Much like Niamh's books, they were treasured secrets for Bryn. A library of forbidden information.

Sage's parents had secretly worshipped nature instead of worshipping at the king's orders. They believed in a mother goddess who created all, and it was their job as her children to preserve any and all they could of the natural world.

"We had no choice. Our people ran for their lives. The wraiths came overnight, and we didn't have the supplies to make it far. Ifreann was the closest, and once we were in, there was no leaving."

That was the extent of Sage's explanation. That the governor opened the gate for her family, and that there was almost a riot of the townsfolk from the entrance of an unknown, wicked family into their pristine town. That was her most prominent memory of the event.

Mr. Rafferty had made them a home here, and while they may have been uncomfortable, they stayed. They tried to teach people who would listen about nature and the old ways.

Bryn was sure that was what had caused their early deaths. She had no proof, but the visceral anger of the community and that Mallory called them witches as she did Bryn was a pretty large clue.

Every day since they had died, Mallory reminded her what happened to witches in their town, and that was proof enough for Bryn to keep her head down and not ask questions.

Rubbing at her cheek, Bryn remembered the words that came with the slap when Mallory had found her after she'd shunned the touch of a member of the church after service, consequently embarrassing Mallory.

Bryn had been young and naïve enough to think she could make a choice for herself and her comfort.

With the memory of the slap came the words that slithered through her head whenever she spoke of Sage's parents:

I should help you pack and send you off myself to that witch-and-demon-blighted city so you can join all the other witches there. Take your already damned soul and good riddance.

The night before Sage came into town, Bryn had packed a bag with the intention to leave and try her hand at making it to Tanwen, not knowing it was being torn apart at the seams by the king's army.

If Kessler hadn't found her with her bag walking toward the gate, she might have left. Instead, he made her sit with him as he prepared the fires for the blacksmith he was an apprentice under until her anger wore off. He never asked after that what had made her try to leave, but she was sure he knew something was up. Especially when she made sure he never saw her cheek, keeping her face away from him.

"Yes!" Sage threw a fist up as she did a little dance, her other hand holding a book not in the language of Ifreann. "A crow means change! Something will change soon."

"I'll say," Bryn muttered as she made a wave to the door they had just come through.

"Oh . . . but there was only one . . . right?" Sage asked, looking up at Bryn with a furrowed brow.

"That I saw." Bryn drawled out the word at the look in Sage's honey eyes.

"One crow . . . means death." Sage bit her lip as she turned the yellow pages of the book.

"For whom?" Bryn snapped, calming herself when her friend took a step back. Bryn was not lost to anger often, so even she herself was shocked by the outburst, the vision she'd just had coloring Sage's words in her mind. Were they somehow related? The storm and the crow?

Bryn was not one to believe in coincidences.

"I don't know, Bryn, but there is a prophecy among my people—"

A knock at the door had both of them scrambling to hide the book. Anything from Tanwenian history was outlawed after the king took Tanwen, and if someone saw Sage with it, exile would be the least of their worries.

Skirting around the small dining room table, Bryn put her finger to her lips as Sage calmed herself, having hid the book under her couch cushion. Wiping her sweaty palms on her dress, she nodded to Bryn that she was ready.

Opening the door slightly, Bryn felt a sigh of relief roll out of her mouth before she could contain it. She did not have the energy to deal with Declan after their moment outside the Sanctuary, and Justin would pick up on their behavior and investigate. She did not want to know how Justin would handle illegal contraband, friend or not. Justin was the law first and foremost, and she did not want to test how far she could push their friendship.

"Come on in, Kess," Sage greeted with her own sigh of relief while Bryn opened it the rest of the way so Kessler could manipulate his large body through the small entryway. The muscles were beneficial for smithing, but a small man it did not make.

"I didn't see you ladies outside with Niamh and Justin." His low, rumbling voice soothed Bryn's nerves, her skin less sensitive than it had been when she had been trapped in the room with all the others. One of his eyebrows went up as he gave a questioning look to both women. "Everyone and everything okay in here?"

Sage nodded, clasping her shaking hands in front of her.

Smooth.

Kessler returned a slow nod that declared he in no way believed them. At all. Looking between Sage and Bryn, his eyes held curiosity, but Kessler was not the type to overstep.

"Well, if you need anything, I'll be cleaning up the forge. Thankfully, most everything in that place weighs a good ton, so not too much damage to the forge itself, but the windows are broken."

Giving them one last long look, he turned away, and Bryn's brain finally clicked into gear. Her conversation before the storm with Caden and Niamh pulled to the forefront of her mind.

"Wait!" Bryn stepped up next to the man who rarely gave much of himself away, and she wondered how Caden even knew as much about Kessler to have told her what he did. He was quiet, communicated mostly in grunts, and glowered.

Kessler stopped, turning to her as he crossed his arms, and it reminded her of the defensive position she took when someone was intimidating her. She'd laugh out loud if that wouldn't shut the man down. He was built like a brick wall and just as difficult to knock over. No one messed with him.

"Could you make me a weapon of some kind, nothing fancy, but something that could help should someone take it too far sometime . . .?" She stopped her rambling and watched a happy glint shine in the normally dour man's eyes. He *had* wanted her to ask when all along when she felt like it would have been overstepping. Bryn never wanted to be the burden her aunt told her she was.

"Sure thing, Brynnie," he said with such affection she blushed. She knew he saw her as a little sister, much as she was sure Travis, Caden, and Justin did, but she could see the appeal in Kessler. The beauty of him when he smiled, something so very rare, that she felt blessed to be one of the few to see it. "I'll get on it right now."

She almost told him it was no rush, but he moved with a determined gait to the door, and she couldn't, no, she *wouldn't* take that from him.

Bryn moved to step out of his way, his arm brushing her hand as he reached out to grab the doorknob. A shock of static like the one both Sage and Declan had given her made her jump a little, the hair on her arms back up, but no vision.

Realizing she was standing frozen, still somewhat in his way since he was big enough to be a building himself, she gave a nervous laugh and moved to Sage's side.

With a raised eyebrow, Kessler shook his head before opening and closing the door quietly behind him.

Why was she getting shocked when she touched people? She only had visions when people were close to the realm of the dead, but usually if there was an accidental touch with no vision, there was just . . . nothing.

Perhaps this would happen with others, but she ran the risk of seeing someone's death if she started touching people, and that was emotionally and physically painful.

Was it worth the risk to investigate further?

She wasn't brave enough to find out.

Chapter 7

Sleep was not coming to Bryn anytime soon, so making her excuses, she escaped Sage's cottage, sticking to the shadows as she made her way back to the clinic. The church bells rang, and she wondered what state the church was in to still be having service.

Her mind was exhausted, but her body was somehow energized. An odd conundrum that she'd never experienced before.

Rubbing at her gritty eyes thanks to the sand, she moved between the buildings as she mentally ran through what her options were to keep her occupied until nightfall since sleep was obviously out.

Though her body was ready to start the day, she could feel pressure behind her eyes, warning her of one of her headaches coming on. She rarely had them these days, though her youth had been full of them due to the stress of moving and her father's death. She'd thought she'd grown out of them, so a second headache in one week seemed off.

What isn't off right now, though?

Growling, she closed her eyes, wishing something in her life could be simple for once.

Declan's warm voice carried over to her, and she peeked around the corner of one of the buildings. He worked with some of his men to assess the damage to the Cauldron, standing before the place with their hands in their pockets as they took in the old wooden building that had somehow withstood such a strong storm.

Hammers were already nailing wood across broken windows, and the loud pounding was worsening the aching throb in her head.

Declan was the one who, when there was an item they wanted but did not have the ability to make or grow, had a permit to leave the gate and trade with Tanwen. It never failed that he was able to secure supplies considered by others as unattainable. If something was needed, Declan could obtain it, and the Cauldron had it. It was part of the reason Niamh had alcohol in her establishment, something banned by the church.

The man could haggle anyone out of anything for nearly free.

Not to mention the seeds he brought back to the farmers that were toted as magical. There was a saying among them: "If Declan Rafferty didn't bring the seeds across the gate on his person, I want nothing to do with them."

Everyone had laughed until another one of Declan's authorized men had brought them through, and the seeds never even attempted to bloom. Another few tests and they all figured Declan was damn good at getting the best seed.

It all equaled up to him being the most valuable trader in the entire country, which was vast outside of the town, and Bryn wished she could explore it. Maybe go even further and explore the parts that King Bres hadn't yet brought to heel under his rule. To see what it was like when culture wasn't contained and controlled by a man far away in the farthest city to the west of Ifreann, Drystan.

It was all words to Bryn, never having seen even a picture of the king, yet she knew since the town paid a tithe and honored the king's favored religion they were left to their own devices. As long as they followed the rules, the wraiths would not be making a surprise visit.

Closing her eyes against a sudden wave of dizziness, she leaned back and was met by a hard chest.

"Look what the cat dragged in," a voice whispered into her ear, making her jump.

Jumping and spinning away, she saw Travis stop where he was walking to make sure she was all right before moving quickly down the road toward the meeting hall. Bryn breathed a sigh of relief at seeing him in one piece after working the guard tower during the storm. She knew it had to have been him who sounded the horns.

Turning back to Caden, he smiled at her, his white teeth in contrast to his dark olive skin and long black hair pulled back at the nape of his neck. Always ready for some good humor, the man lived to tease her.

"Don't scare me!" Bryn clutched at her shirt over where her heart was, taking a deep breath as she stared down the bartender she had seen only hours ago.

A loud guffaw from the man brought the attention of those on the street to her and Caden. That included Declan, one of the many people whom she had hoped to avoid.

She was so tempted to touch Caden's arm and see if she had a vision but stopped herself. The temptation to see if it was only Sage and Kessler she could touch without an issue was strong, but the thought of seeing a friend die was too much. Unless he was old and surrounded by loved ones, she couldn't handle it.

When Mr. Rafferty walked down Saints' Road at a clipped pace, everyone's eyes followed him. Declan's too, before he cut a look to her that promised a conversation later before he continued with his work.

Mr. Rafferty went into the sheriff's office just after Travis, the door slamming shut behind him. She figured it was a meeting about the storm, but why the sheriff's office and not the meeting hall?

"What's going on, Caden?" she asked, watching Declan making a motion with his hands to the men to continue on before jogging over to follow his father in. The man was graceful for being well over six feet tall and built like a mountain. Both him and Kessler were huge compared to the rest of the men in town.

Leaning too far forward, Bryn stumbled from the step of the porch, almost meeting the dirt road face-first before Caden grabbed her hand.

No vision, but no shock either.

"Whoa now!" Caden laughed, his face going from humorous to confused as Bryn rounded on him. She had no idea what her face looked like, but Caden took a small step back, putting his hands up before they went back to his sides. "Time for bed, Brynnie-bear."

"I've got her. Thanks, Caden." Jace's voice flowed over her, and she turned to her cousin as he moved his medical bag from his right side to his left side so she could take his arm. A static shock just as with Sage and Kessler moved between her and her cousin.

"Let me know if y'all need anything. Looks like it'll be a hot minute before this place is up to par." Caden gave a nod, concern marring his brow for a split second before he shook his head and sauntered off in the same direction Travis had gone. Bryn wanted to follow but thought better of it.

Giving Caden a nod, Jace pulled Bryn behind him, walking them to the clinic.

"Are there lots of injured?" Bryn asked as she pulled out of his grip, needing some space. Touching people could be overwhelming when one wasn't used to it, and she needed a moment to reset her thinking.

Her mind still spun with the visions and realizations she'd come to in the past hour, but thankfully the sensitivity to her environment calmed down as they walked. Almost as if just the nearness of her cousin helped to divert all the excess energy and soothe her frayed nerves.

"Yes . . . but there is more than that," he whispered, looking around, then moved them faster to the apartments above the clinic, Bryn trying to keep up with him. She hoped Mallory was with her beau so she wouldn't have to deal with the woman on top of everything else. One crisis at a time. She'd had more than enough to deal with today.

His shoulders were tense, his knuckles white, and anxiety was palpable as he gripped the doorknob to her apartment door.

She wondered if somehow he took her fear and nerves onto himself.

Ridiculous thought, she chastised herself.

Throwing open the door, Jace all but pushed her in before slamming it closed behind them, making Bryn wince. If Mallory was home, she was sure to investigate now.

Turning on her, she watched Jace attempt to calm himself and gave him a minute to gather his wits before she started in on the questions.

There was not a thing in their tiny little town that she could think of that would set him off like this.

Jace was always so calm, even in life-threatening situations, which made him a wonderful doctor.

"What is going on, Jace?"

She'd given him long enough since, unlike her stoic cousin, she had no such patience.

Putting his finger to his lips as she had done with Sage only half an hour ago, Jace pushed her into the center of the room before shutting the curtains of her tiny window. As if someone would care that Bryn was in her own apartment.

A thought struck her then.

"Did something happen, and you worry they will hold me accountable?" Her voice was quiet and embarrassingly meek. The shroud of fear she hated to wear with every ounce of her being took hold and started to suffocate her.

Why would he care if anyone outside could see in? Especially since she was on the second floor where it wasn't like someone could walk past and look inside. He was being paranoid, and that was the only logical explanation her mind could think of. Someone thought her guilty of something, and he was trying to protect her.

There were few people who would stand up on her behalf against the town if everything were to go sideways, and she did not want to know what the angry townspeople would do to those loyal to her.

She would be killed or exiled, she already knew that. The whole town probably already had plans in place to do just such a thing once they had enough evidence. Enough evidence that they felt they could go above the law, the law being Mr. Rafferty and Justin, to take things into their own hands.

Had something more substantial than a sandstorm happened in Ifreann? Did the townspeople think she was the cause of it? That Bryn had called on the beast of a storm with her unnatural witchy magic?

Bryn was about to find out.

"Out with it," she demanded, sitting on her bed and folding her shaking arms across her chest as Jace paced her room with his hands in his blond hair. She tried to ignore the flicker of the unnatural shadow in the corner of the room. Bryn was sure it had to be her imagination. If not . . . well, one crisis at a time.

"There was more than sand thrown past the gate when the storm rolled through." Jace moved to the trunk in her room where her few dresses and even fewer personal items from her past lay within. "There were two people standing at the gate."

"So? We've had more people than I can count sitting, standing, or lying outside our gate. Refugees from Tanwen, for example, looking for the good Baleros lifestyle. Perhaps they were lost in the sandstorm and trying to take cover?" she asked, wondering why this was so shocking.

How many times have people come seeking refuge in Ifreann? One would think by now people were catching on that no one was allowed past the gate. Just to keep walking if they see Ifreann because there was no quarter there for outsiders. The deadly desert would be more friendly and welcoming.

Ugh. If there were bodies, there would be no sleep for her. She'd hoped to clean the pyres out tomorrow, but if there were deceased that needed to be burned, she had to do it now.

"Not at the gate, Bryn," Jace broke into her thoughts, agitation and fear clear in his voice. She stopped her musings to look at him and saw real fear in his eyes. "They were already inside the gate. *Alive.*"

"Inside . . .," she parroted as Jace nodded. "Alive? How?"

Jumping up from the bed, Bryn was the one pacing now.

"Did the storm knock down the gates?" she asked as she watched Jace shake his head no.

"Then how? I watched them secure the gate after you came back in! There is no way anyone can get them open aside from the city guards!"

That anyone could make it past the gate without prior authorization, well, it was impossible. Guards were placed all along the walls and at the gate. Messengers were never allowed inside, only given what they needed for their travels back to wherever they came from, and if someone showed up without a permit authorized by the crown for trade, they'd be turned away . . . without supplies.

Not to mention that the walls around the town were far too high to climb, and even if they were easy to overcome, to do so during a sandstorm was beyond anything Bryn could comprehend.

"Maybe they were here before? Snuck in while the gate was open when you and Arioch left?" she asked, but she knew the truth. The gate was monitored all day and all night. City guards held posts at both sides of the gate on the rare occasions they opened it.

"There were two people. An old lady and a young male. Them being here is why I was walking home with my bag since I was needed to check them for signs of sickness. They claimed to have come in with the storm." Jace raised his brows at the words as he said them.

Well, that certainly changed things.

Chapter 8

"There was a prophecy . . ."

Bryn's eyes opened as the sun set outside her window, Sage's words carrying over into the waking world as her mind clawed its way back to consciousness.

Blinking the grit of sleep from her eyes, Bryn was happy it was sleep instead of sand. A quick scrub last night had managed to get her somewhat clean, but she still found sand in unfortunate places. Even fully clothed and no epic sandstorm, sand was still a daily nightmare for Ifreann.

Jace had asked her to keep a low profile today, not because she had done anything, but because when the town feared something, anything they already deemed a threat to them was in even more danger.

Best not to remind them she was here if word got out about the sandstorm stowaways.

Night was upon them now, so she could safely walk the streets. Pyres would have to be done at night, too, if bodies were to show up, and she hadn't thought of a way to pull that off yet.

People were bound to notice fire and smoke since she couldn't guarantee an entire town would stay asleep.

If only it were so easy for her to obey in other areas of life. If she went to church without questioning it and followed in her father's footsteps, she'd be welcome anytime in Ifreann. Day or night.

Shaking away useless thoughts, she was happy to be back on her schedule of sleeping during the day. Standing and stretching out the kinks of her body, her linen shift fell to her knees as her hands caught on her nest of hair from going to bed with it wet and uncombed.

Tangles galore.

That was going to be fun to deal with. Perhaps the crow she'd seen could enjoy a nice nest on her head.

A squawk sounded outside her window, and for a split second, she wondered if her thoughts had summoned it.

Wavering between ignoring the crow and opening the window, she bit her lip in thought. Was it worth inviting more trouble? She was sure a crow, a bird that hadn't been seen in this part of the world since before the Collapse, was not a sign of anything good to come.

The decision was made for her when the crow went about tapping its beak against the glass of the window a tad too loudly. Throwing her wild curls out of her face, she made for the window, hitting her knee on the edge of her wooden bed frame in the process. Cursing Justin for his sturdy woodwork, woodworking being his hobby when he wasn't in the role of the town's justice, she slammed her palm on the window ledge.

With another few curse words to color her dull and drab world, she threw open the curtains.

Narrowing her eyes at the bird, the crow stared back in challenge, almost daring her not to open the window.

What was it with this weird animal?

"I would have assumed this was a mental health crisis had my friend and cousin not seen you too," she muttered as she unlatched the ancient brass window and swung it open. With dust motes and sand fluttering through the air into her room, the bird sauntered in and looked around, its head swiveling to take in the entirety of Bryn's small room. If she hadn't thought she was losing it before, the look of unimpressed ambivalence on the crow's face would have done it.

Taking flight, the crow landed on her headboard before beginning to work over a feather at its side.

"Make yourself at home," she mumbled, shutting the window and latching it before turning to stare at the crow, crossing her arms as she studied the avian stalker. "Well, I have a crow, something that hasn't been seen in over two hundred years in Ifreann, sitting on my headboard. Not at all a reason to be concerned."

Sarcasm was usually not Bryn's choice of armor—no, that was normally disassociation—but it was the one she was apparently going to wear after everything that had happened the last day or so.

"My name is Cyerra." An irritated voice had Bryn freezing, her knees weakening at the sound of a voice in her head that was not her own.

Swallowing, Bryn looked around the room for any other potential reason for the voice aside from the crow. She knew logically there would be no one there, but desperation had her on the edge of acting unreasonable.

If only it hadn't sounded like it had been in her own head, then maybe she could rationalize it. Someone outside the door was talking, or . . .

A hesitant laugh left Bryn as she stepped closer to the wall, leaning against it as her weak knees lost the fight, and she slid along the wood paneling until her butt met the floor.

"You seem so much weaker than before." The crow tilted her head as the words rolled through Bryn's mind. She was going to have a very serious nervous breakdown if she wasn't already in the midst of one.

"Than . . . before? You are talking to me . . . in my head? A crow?"

Bryn was hardly impressed with her wit, and the crow even less so.

"Simpler, too, it appears." Its beady eyes somehow held a look of disappointment. Bryn wanted to laugh, and then cry. She was transferring her insane emotional state onto a bird.

"Simp . . . simpler?" Bryn released the unhinged laugh she'd been holding in. Of all the ridiculousness . . .

"Bryn?" Jace knocked as both her and the crow, Cyerra, turned to look at the door at the same time. "Are you all right? Can I come in?"

Looking back to Cyerra as if in question, Bryn shook her head, standing up and reaching to unlock the door as shadows rolled over the doorknob. Yanking her hand back, her heart pounding, she looked around the room for the cause.

Nothing made sense anymore. A shadow should be the absence of light, yet these moved through her room as if light did nothing to faze them.

"Fomori demon," Cyerra sneered, and Bryn knew instinctively that the crow was not referring to her. *"You dare show yourself to our queen?"*

Queen? Fomori demon?

The shadows undulated on top of each other before forming into a human shape between her and the door.

A battle cry came from the crow as she took flight before dive-bombing the shadowy person, making the shadows disperse.

The door flew open, almost hitting Bryn. Jace, having chosen to pick the lock for the first time since childhood, stepped into the room where a crow was flying overhead, cawing.

Everything went to absolute mayhem in a matter of seconds, and Bryn was having a hard time processing it all.

Bryn stood frozen as she stared at her cousin, his jaw dropping at the scene, waiting for his reaction to the chaos unfolding in front of him.

"This is real, right? There is a crazy-ass black bird, circling my head, preparing for war?" Jace's words were barely audible over the noise.

Bryn would have laughed at the look on Jace's face had she not been holding her own freak-out in check. There was no telling how far down that rabbit hole she would go once she allowed herself to think about what this all meant.

"Crow . . .," she whispered, keeping her eyes on her cousin, seeing the nervous tell of his shaking hand moving thoughtlessly through his hair.

Swallowing, Jace only nodded instead of saying anything.

Her eyes moved to the scarred wooden floor as shadows rolled over her toes.

"Are both of you thick? Poor, poor Danu . . .," the crow lamented as Bryn turned to stare at the bird. Jace's eyes followed her lead.

"She thinks we are thick," Bryn whispered, and Jace looked at her in disbelief.

"Who does?" he asked, his voice wavering as if he didn't truly want the answer.

Bryn pointed to the crow who had settled onto the headboard once again.

The shadowed form of a man a few inches taller than Jace appeared between them, Cyerra ruffling her feathers in irritation, her wings flapping as if to take off again and attack the trespasser.

As the man's form took on an ethereal quality, she watched the lines of his face grow more defined. Black hair and silver eyes watched her, his body transparent enough she could see through him to Jace standing behind him.

A ghost stood before her and watched her with intense, mercurial eyes as she stumbled back, falling onto her butt as a strangled scream left her throat.

Jace, moving around the shadow man and giving him a wide berth, made it to Bryn, grabbing her elbows to pull her up, only to shove her head back down as the crow dive-bombed the ghostly man made of shadows again.

Crawling from the room, Jace and Bryn slipped through the door, pulling it behind them with a loud bang, the noise of Cyerra on a warpath covering the noise of the door.

Padding down the hall on bare feet to Jace's room, they snuck in, both of them turning to look at one another with their eyes wide, faces frozen in shock.

Pointing to her room with a shaking finger, Jace shook his head and said nothing as he turned away from her and began to pace.

"There is a violent black bird in your room!" Jace grabbed his hair in frustration that Bryn felt all too keenly.

"A crow. It was a crow," she stated again, as if that was what mattered most right then.

Jace spun on her so fast she wondered if he'd fall over dizzy.

"Do you think that matters right now? I don't care what the hell's damned breed the bird is!"

Jace was one to love science. That everything could be explained in some form or fashion, which was why if he hadn't been the town doctor and a man, he would have been as hated as she was for believing more in science than religion.

None of this was logical, so therefore, Jace was done with all of it before it had even begun.

"There is a black bird, 'a crow.'" He made air quotes just to irritate her, but she let it slide. He was having a mental health crisis. She would know since she was in the middle of her own. "And a shadow . . . man . . . thing, in there with it. Those two are now fighting and tearing up your room."

Bryn looked back toward her room as if she could see through the doors before turning back to Jace.

"It seems so."

Placing his hands on his hips, he cocked an eyebrow.

"It seems so, she says." His lips twitched as he turned away from her, repeating the words again before the end of his tangent was cut off by a snort.

"Are you laughing right now?" she asked, moving around to face him as he pressed his lips together and shook his head. As if she'd believe for a second he wasn't.

Throwing his hands up, he let the loud laugh free to bounce off the paneled wooden walls of the small room.

"It's so insane that it's incredible! We all have desert madness from one little sandstorm!"

Bryn folded her arms, rolling her eyes as she let her cousin laugh until he fell back onto his small bed.

Turning away, she really had nothing to focus on in his room. Nothing to take her mind elsewhere for just a moment of time. A simple mental reprieve.

His entire apartment had minimal décor.

Where Bryn had pillows and furs to the point she had her own nest, candles everywhere, her small space decorated as much as she could manage with modest means, Jace's was utilitarian. There for basic functionality and nothing more.

Sitting on the floor, her back to his tiny mattress, she hit his jeans-covered knee with the back of her hand. He grunted before letting loose a borderline hysterical chuckle.

They both jumped when a knock sounded on the door, bringing them back to reality. Jace stood up far too quickly, his gait as he walked to the door showing he wasn't immune to a bout of dizziness after all.

Pushing his hair back, he gathered himself as she retreated into herself. Folding her arms like a shield across her chest, she kept her eyes to the floor, lest it be Aunt Mallory on the other side.

There was no way in hell the woman would lose an opportunity to torture Bryn, so if that was her, Bryn needed to be ready for it.

Bryn's only hope was that Mallory would continue her trend of not lashing out in front of others.

When Justin stepped in, Bryn let out a huge internal sigh of relief, but it was short-lived as she realized Justin may have heard the battle in her apartment.

How would she answer any questions related to that nightmare scenario without everyone thinking her crazy? What if only Jace could see the shadow man? Maybe not a logical thought, but these were not logical times.

"I need you both to come to the office. We have some questions," Justin informed them, his tone completely official, but she caught the hitch in his words. The worry in his stormy blue eyes and the clench of his jaw told her this was far more serious than she'd be prepared for.

Watching people, learning their tells, was what had kept Bryn alive all these years. To not know was to make one vulnerable, especially when allies were not there to stand at one's side.

So, she read Justin like a book and knew with certainty her gut reaction was right. Her life was about to get so much more complicated.

"Yeah, we will head over there in a few. No need for the escort." Jace motioned to where Bryn was in her sleep shift and barefoot, sitting against the bed. "She needs to get dressed first."

Bryn worried that Jace speaking of her getting dressed might cause Justin to inquire about why she was in Jace's room in sleepwear, but he only nodded and left, shutting the door with a soft click at his departure. No questions asked, which she was mightily thankful for. Had it been any other man's room but her cousin's, she doubted Justin would have been so quick to dismiss it all.

Jace walked her to her room, the quiet stillness behind her own door either a boon or a warning.

Opening the door, they were met with an indignant squawk from the tiny, feathered beast once again sitting on her headboard as if Bryn's battle-torn room, candles knocked over and clothes everywhere, were not at all her fault.

"We've had a long day, and it seems it'll be all that much longer." Jace ran a hand over his face, and Bryn caught the bags under his eyes as his hand moved to his mouth.

"Get dressed and I'll meet you in the hall . . . and maybe get the crow out of your room before it poops everywhere." Bryn appreciated her cousin's attempt at levity after both of them dealt with the extreme highs and lows of their dizzying emotions, but she wasn't in a state to give him any more than a small smile as she closed the door behind him.

Sighing, Bryn sat back on the bed and rubbed her temples, staving off another headache as her adrenaline waned.

All this commotion in one day could not be healthy.

The thought of a nice bath was out, having used up her water ration for the week already. If she wanted to get clean again, she would have to take a cold bath in one inch of rusty pipe water.

Not worth it.

The large gravel-filled tanks underneath the town only held so much water. The windmills outside were starting to run dry as they pumped the last of the season's rainfall into homes and businesses from the main water reserve.

The rustling of feathers had her turning to really look at the bird. Beautiful black feathers covered the small creature, and she noticed a small feather of silver on its chest, another unique marking compared to the birds in the illustrated books she'd skimmed through.

"The demon has been banished ... for now," the crow's voice whispered into her mind as she preened. Her job as Bryn's valiant knight defending her from the shadow man had been done and done well, obviously.

One imaginary creature taken down at a time.

"What do you mean 'demon'?" she asked, wishing her voice was less tinny and fearful.

"Bryndis Kenneally. So much different than your other selves and no knowledge of your past at all. I am saddened by this." The crow's beady eyes looked her over.

"Sorry to ruin your day with my ignorance," Bryn replied with a dry tone. The crow must have been eavesdropping for a while to know her full name.

"Apology accepted. We must remedy this of course. I cannot fight near as strong as I can when we are bonded."

"That might be too much information or too little. I can't decide."

Shaking her feathered head, Cyerra hopped closer.

"The demons are from below, and one was here. I never trusted him, and that he follows you here worries me. You must talk to Danu and figure it out. Soon. We don't have much longer."

Without further explanation, the crow took flight and disappeared through the window.

Bryn followed the crow with her eyes, trying to form words. The crow had just flown through a window . . . that was closed.

Jace knocked impatiently on the door, and Bryn closed her open mouth, shaking the shock from her overwhelmed mind.

"We've got to go, Bryn!" his muffled voice ordered.

Standing, she riffled through the swirling thoughts in her mind. Obviously there was something happening in their tiny town, especially if Justin and Jace were rattled. Not much ever bothered them.

Of all the things to dream up and create in her own mind, it was a man made of shadows.

Bryn mindlessly zipped up her boring and bland brown skirt as she wondered how they committed people in her day and age. In the past, people went to places called hospitals and were given medication and therapy to work through their psychosis. Now she assumed she'd be too much of a burden and would be exiled to the desert. Or worse.

A crow feather floated in the air in front of her, lazily making its way back down to Bryn.

Reaching for it, a jolt of static electricity jumped from the feather to her finger, giving her a start as she grabbed it out of the air. The same jolt she'd felt with Niamh and Kessler.

Twirling it in the last of the sun's light, she admired the darkness of it.

Well, there was no turning back midstream down shit's creek.

It was time for Bryn to figure out what in the hell was going on.

Chapter 9

Bryn stepped outside next to Jace into the dying sunlight, the heat still stifling enough to feel like she had stuck her face into the hearth.

If only they lived somewhere cold. The freezing season was her favorite time of the year, and while it was an extreme cold, it was tolerable for a few days to not have sweat make clothing and sand stick to skin, dripping into a person's eyes as they tried to work.

Ifreann was a miserable place most of the time, but once the freezing season set in, Bryn had more freedom, another reason she loved that time of year.

The days were shorter with people staying in more, hating the cold just as she hated the heat.

Just more proof she didn't belong here. She was supposed to be somewhere covered in snow and mountains, not plain, flat, and drab like Ifreann.

Ignoring the sting of the sand around her eyes, she pulled her scarf tighter around her face and turned her head away from where it was blowing in over the wall. It wasn't the nightmarish sandstorm from earlier, but it wasn't comfortable either. As if the desert were unsettled and continued to react.

Almost as if it worried it would be forgotten even after all the damage it had caused.

The horses were being moved to the stable for the night, their hooves clomping on the ground in agitation as their keepers worked to place gear meant to protect the horses' eyes and ears from the grit.

Most everyone else was indoors now, a few stragglers working their way to their homes as they ended their day.

Only two of the townspeople heading home sneered at her in passing as she walked down the street, but most of the others ignored her, lost in the exhaustion of the day. She wondered if she could actually consider that progress.

What a sad thought.

Jace was again a ball of nervous energy next to her, pulling her by the elbow away from people if they stepped a little too close. Losing himself to a growl when one of the few people that noticed her gave her a look. He had always been protective, but not this much, and that worried her about what he thought might happen at this meeting.

The Cauldron was across the road with two personal guards, or Declan's thugs as Justin jokingly referred to them, stationed on either side of the doors. The torches lit on either side of said doors fought to stay lit in the whipping wind, the soldiers like statues, hands on weapons, at the ready should they need to put someone down. Declan was going into overdrive if he had his guards posted outside, the men usually only working when readying to leave for trade beyond the walls of their town. He obviously felt he needed to make a statement.

A happy little thought.

Almost to the sheriff's office, Bryn heard the small caw in the alley to her right between the buildings. Stepping away from the road, she watched Cyerra settling on a metal pole sticking out from the wall with twine knotted at the end, whipping in the wind where it had torn free from the other building. The clothes that had hung there were long gone.

"Come on, Bryn. We need to move it," Jace grumbled, his hands in his pockets as he looked around the road, unable to stand still. His eyes constantly moved, assessing for a threat, so unlike the calm, even-keeled man he was only yesterday.

Holding a hand up for him to wait earned her a scoff as he crossed his arms and leaned against the side of the smooth redbrick building.

"Planning to follow me everywhere now?" she whispered to Cyerra, testing her limits as she put her hand out for the crow to perch herself on. Without hesitation, Cyerra flew to her hand as if this were something the two of them did regularly.

The calmness of the crow did not last long as a shadow fell over them, her feathers puffing up, and Cyerra let out a battle cry that shocked Bryn. It was far more intense than the one with the shadow man as it left the little beak.

"What have we here?" The voice moved over her like oil, suffocating her and stopping her breath in fear.

She watched Jace stiffen out of the corner of her eye, and he stepped back as if to put himself between Bryn and their new arrival.

"Bryndis, I've yet to see you back at services . . ." Scrios Arioch smiled as he prowled like a predator around Jace and toward her, stopping and narrowing his eyes at Cyerra before he pointed at the crow. "What is that? Is that a crow?"

Bryn felt Cyerra's tiny claws dig into her hand, drawing blood at the man's words.

"Go on, find somewhere to rest," she whispered to Cyerra, hoping the crow listened.

Naturally the crow refused, not budging from her post until Bryn moved her hand, curling her fingers into a fist, no longer giving Cyerra the option to stay. Even though she did leave Bryn's hand, she only went back to the metal rod, keeping her keen eyes on Arioch as if she could take on the man herself.

Perhaps she could. Cyerra hardly seemed normal compared to what Bryn had learned of birds from a time long ago. Nothing in the literature stated humans were able to communicate telepathically with their avian friends back then either.

The scrios clenched his jaw, his eyes moving from Cyerra back to Bryn as something flashed in them, but it was far too quick for Bryn to catch. Arioch looked back toward the Sanctuary where Niamh stood now, looking through the window at them, before turning back to Bryn. "Taken up a new line of work since medicine doesn't seem to be in your wheelhouse?"

She wished she could have slapped the creepy, self-indulgent smile right off his face, but she didn't think she would enjoy having to sleep with one eye open for the rest of her life when Mallory found out. No, her aunt worshipped the scrios almost as much as she did the god she proclaimed to serve.

At least his focus was off Cyerra.

"No, sir. You know my friend Niamh lives there, and I like to visit her." She pasted on the sweetest smile she could without rolling her eyes. She tried, oh how she did try, to not lose her temper with these people, but they pushed at her control. Had she not grown up terrified of her aunt's reaction behind closed doors, she would have liked to think she'd terrorize the people here as much as they did her.

As Cyerra readied for battle once again, the sound of ruffling beautiful black feathers resonated in Bryn's ears, but she didn't dare remove her eyes from Arioch.

The scrios stared back at Cyerra, a growl coming from nearby had Bryn hoping that meant Finian was close enough to jump in should Arioch try anything. The scrios wouldn't use his hands, but instead his words, and they could be deadly all their own should the right people hear them.

"Well, one would think you a witch with the familiar the way you two act." His smarmy smile had her freezing, as was his plan if the widening smile was any indication.

His graying hair was pulled back at his nape, his cold blue eyes frozen with maliciousness that could only be honed from years of hatred. She hadn't realized he'd backed her up to the wall until she felt the bricks at her back, his arms quickly caging her in.

Jace was at his left just as fast, vibrating with anger and clenching into his hands into fists, ready to throw them toward the scrios. That was until he finally turned her way and caught the look in Bryn's eyes.

The warning there was clear, she hoped. If he were to do anything, he'd only make it worse for her, and she prayed he picked up on that.

Overwhelming relief as Jace stepped back had her knees buckling a bit. Jace didn't leave, and he still vibrated with anger, but not with the look of unrestrained violence he had before. It was obvious that his body was ready to spring into action should Arioch do anything more than run his mouth, but he was giving her a chance to handle this, and that was all she could ask for.

"A young lady like you should stick close to the good men of this town. Marry and lay down some roots." His gnarled finger ran along her clavicle and over the shirt she wore, thankfully not touching her skin.

How this man could be called holy flabbergasted her. Something had always been off about him and Daran, Mallory's betrothed and Arioch's brother. She wished she knew what it was so she could point the finger back at him. "You out roaming about in the evening like a whore might let the men of this town think they can—"

"Get away from her," Jace growled, no longer heeding the warning in Bryn's eyes.

Damn it, Jace.

Arioch only looked over his shoulder, letting out a laugh of indulgence one would have toward an errant youth posturing for a battle he would only lose due to age and inexperience. Ignoring Jace, Arioch turned his eyes back to Bryn as his tongue ran over his yellowed teeth.

"Until today, I'd had my hopes up that you'd leave your wicked ways and all that behind." Arioch eyed her lips before they roved down to her chest and back up again.

Her fake smile dropped, and his eyes narrowed as she pulled the ends of her drab-beige shirt sleeves over her hands. Even though the sleeves of what she thought of as her daily uniform were sweltering in the heat, she couldn't chance someone, most especially Arioch, making contact with her skin. To be at his mercy during one of her fits was one of her worst nightmares.

"I'd rather not marry, thank you." She put her arms between their bodies and broke away from him using her forearms.

Grabbing her elbow once she was freed, while Jace grabbed the other, Arioch leaned in, his lips close to her ear, making her shiver in disgust.

"It'd be best for your safety if you did. I'd listen to those wiser than you, girlie."

"She listens to herself, and I think that makes her plenty wise." Jace growled, pulling her away from Arioch and spinning Bryn toward Saints'

Road, leaving Arioch behind without a glance. She could feel Cyerra watching her as she left and hoped the man left the crow alone. That he seemed unfazed at the crow's appearance made her wonder if he knew Cyerra had been here even before Bryn did.

Just more proof that Arioch had his own dangerous secrets. Ones she hoped in no way would affect her or her place here in Ifreann.

"You do not pretend to be weak as I thought. I had hoped it was all a ruse." Cyerra's presence left her mind as she walked, and Bryn tried not to feel like she had let down a crow of all things. One that knew some version of her from some imaginary past life when Bryn had no idea where the crow had come from.

Bryn's teeth ground down as she ran the crow's words through her mind. Had she ever tried to stand up and show her strength? Or had she always backed away with her tail between her legs?

An unsettled sensation moved through her at the thought.

The next time she could, she was going to ask question after question about what Cyerra knew now that Bryn's panicked state had decreased enough to have some semblance of rational thought.

"You survived a life surrounded by enemies," Jace started speaking, as if he could hear her thoughts. "You do what you need to in order to see another day. You continue to gather your strength, and one day, you'll hit back so hard they'll all regret the moment they set you in their sights as prey."

And wasn't she so very tired of being prey?

Chapter 10

"You give him too much of your energy," Niamh said as she followed Bryn into the sheriff's office. It had the same bare wooden walls as the rest of town. The chairs and desks that Justin had made were the only redeeming quality of the décor. Yet the entire room was still brown. Always brown, no matter inside or outside, in their depressing town.

Two cells with bars that were situated against the left side of the room were so rusted it looked like a slight breeze would reduce them to powder. She knew the jail had hardly seen any use aside from the town youth finding creative ways to get in trouble, and even that was rare.

A small closet-sized room, also entirely brown aside from the beige papers strewn across the desk, was for Justin to work in relative quiet without dealing with the rest of the bulls in the pen.

It took Bryn a moment to realize Niamh was assuming she was thinking of Declan when she'd walked in the room, fresh with the misery of Arioch's ambush on her face. Poor Declan had just been the first in sight when she'd entered the sheriff's office.

The man in question stood up at the look on her face but stepped back at the tension radiating from her cousin next to her.

Giving Niamh a half smile, she stepped past her friend into a separate room next to Justin's office with a long table that the deputies and sheriff met at every day for their tasks. A podium was at the front of the room, a chalkboard behind it with names and schedules written out, the once-black board now chalky white from being used so much.

Bryn felt like she was in a coffin with only one, tiny window in the room and moved toward the chair closest to it.

Caden was at the table already, speaking and laughing with Sage, which only amplified the stiffness in her cousin's body. Placing her hand on his shoulder, she wished she could somehow calm him down before the stress of dealing with Arioch made him tear into Caden in a fit of jealousy.

"I'm not the problem today," Declan said to Niamh, and Bryn did not look back to see the stare off that Niamh and Declan were no doubt caught up in as she moved to the chair she had scoped out.

There was some serious animosity between the two, so she knew somehow Niamh must have figured out what had happened between her and Declan.

Kessler scowled from the corner, obviously agitated he had been summoned from his forge for some mystery meeting, and Bryn couldn't say she blamed him.

Jace settled on one side of her as the chair next to her was pulled out by Declan only for Niamh to slip into the seat before he could himself, giving him a pat on the hand and a thank you.

Sage let out a small laugh as Declan gave Niamh a quick look of irritation before moving to stand next to Kessler along the wall. Everyone ignored the open seat at the head of the table near where Justin was currently sorting papers.

"I adore Declan as a friend, but anything more is exhausting," Bryn murmured to Niamh as the woman tapped her bloodred fingernails on the table, everyone around them talking among themselves as they waited to find out why they'd been called here.

Bryn watched Travis poke his head in to summon Justin, the room quieting as they watched the exchange before whispered conversations started again when Justin left the room.

"They all are, darling," Niamh said, looking back at Bryn with her dark, almost black eyes, and Niamh shrugged. "Best to not mess with them in the first place. Live a long life and acquire many animals."

A small laugh left Bryn as she shook her head.

"I don't exactly see your place full of animals. More of 'do as I say, not as I do'?" Bryn asked, relaxing as much as she could with the fear of what she may find out in the next few minutes hanging over her head.

"Oh, there are animals there, I just make sure they are kept in hand." Niamh winked as Justin walked back into the room looking unsettled.

Clearing his throat, everyone quieted as Justin looked over the room, Mr. Rafferty coming in behind him and closing the door softly. The sounds of people milling about outside had quieted down substantially as well.

Bryn looked at who all was gathered with her in the room aside from Justin. Jace and Niamh were next to her, Sage and Caden across the table. Declan and Kessler leaned against the wall, and Mr. Rafferty stood next to Justin at the front of the room.

The only thing they all had in common was their friendship with Bryn as far as she knew, and even then, not all close friendships. Her heart stuttered as she wondered if this was it. The moment when their alliance with Bryn put them in peril.

"I've asked everyone but us to leave the office," Justin stated.

At his words, everyone else in the room straightened but Mr. Rafferty, who obviously already knew what was happening.

Justin leaned forward, his hands on the table as he gathered himself before looking up at everyone through his blond hair. Shaking his head, he pushed away from the table, running his hand along the scruff of his jaw.

Stalling.

"This information stays in this room. I wouldn't even be telling you all, but our governor here thinks it's best." He motioned to Mr. Rafferty, who stood tall with his hands in his pockets. After he gave a nod for him to continue, Justin turned back to the room to finish what he had to say.

"Immediately after the sandstorm dissipated, two people not from here were found by the gate. Jace here"—waving to Jace and earning a nod in return— "checked them over and found no illness, hell, they didn't even look like they had been wandering the desert. No horses or other form of transportation was found around town."

Justin waited a beat for them all to take in what he had said. Bryn felt guilty that she was relieved it had nothing to do with her, but when a person lived in fear for so long, it was habit to assume the worst.

"Two people." Justin held up two fingers as if to clarify. "One a male in his mid-twenties and an elderly woman who could not have possibly survived desert conditions."

"Then how in the hell did they get here?" Declan asked. "Teleportation?"

A few of the group laughed, but Justin was not one of them.

"If I believed in that sort of nonsense, I'd say that was the only explanation."

"How were they dressed? Could they be from Tanwen?" Sage asked, and Bryn could see the hope in her eyes that maybe family or someone from her birthplace might have come for her.

"Like nothing I've ever seen. Weird cloaks with animal fur around them, and not from any animals I've seen in my lifetime. Their clothes are all stiff and look like it could cook a person in 'em if they stayed out in the sun for more than a minute. The old woman called it wool. Belts with purses on 'em . . ."

"Even the guy?" Kessler asked, earning a nod from Justin.

"Even the guy, but his belt was rope. Weirdest clothing I've seen, but when have I last roamed the country looking for the latest fashions?" Justin shrugged.

"Why are we here?" Declan turned to look at his father as he said this, but Justin was the one to answer.

"Here's the thing. The old woman seems to be looking for her kin."

Everyone raised their eyebrows at this. Sage, Kessler, Caden, Travis, and Justin were orphaned young, but they knew who their parents were. Was there someone in Ifreann that she was related to? If so, why would Mr. Rafferty have demanded this meeting with only this group in particular?

Was anything ever going to make sense in her life ever again?

"Okay, and she thinks we will find them for her?" Jace looked at Mr. Rafferty as well.

"No," Justin murmured, crossing his arms over his chest as he let out a weary sigh.

"She thinks it's us."

Chapter 11

Bryn sat frozen as the voices of her friends rose in varying degrees of disbelief and agitation around her, but her mind was able to cancel them all out as the words reverberated through her brain.

They were all kin?

A tapping at the small window broke Bryn's thoughts, and she looked to see Cyerra standing on the sill, a look of avian annoyance on her somehow expressive face. Bryn was quick to wave her away before anyone saw her. She did not need to answer any questions about the obsessive crow when emotions were already high.

Her eyes moved around the room to see if anyone noticed the crow. No one did, but it took a moment to realize the grimace on Declan's face meant he had caught on to what she had been thinking about before Cyerra interrupted. It was the same look of horror she was sure had just been on her own face.

Was she related to Declan? Her stomach twisted, and she tried not to wretch right there in front of everyone.

That was far too much. She'd take the talking crow and shadow man, but being related to her ex . . .

"Calm yourself." Niamh's hand moved next to Bryn's but did not make contact. A tap of Niamh's pinky next to her own had been a signal created between the two and used ever since her father had died. It meant that Niamh would handle whatever was needed and Bryn was safe. "There is no way everyone in this room is related. So don't worry, you didn't sleep with your cousin."

Bryn heard the mirth in Niamh's voice, and had she not been in the midst of her own spiraling thoughts, she would have thrown some sharp words the woman's way.

The chaotic and panicked voices of her friends went eerily silent all at once, and Bryn glanced toward the door to see Travis guiding an elderly woman and a young man with golden curls wearing a white cloak into the room. Bryn wasn't sure if it was the pure panic running through her or the room going quiet so abruptly that made her ears ring.

These were the two people who had made it in under the radar. Two completely unassuming individuals that looked for all the world like a grandmother and grandson. Yet somewhere in Bryn's brain, she sensed something dangerous about the pair that she couldn't quite put her finger on.

It was the same thing as when looking out at the horizon, a small cloud of dust actually being miles of dangerous sand and wind.

One didn't know they were in danger right away, and that was how it felt to be in the room as the two new people stood before her. Bryn's skin tingled in anticipation of what was to come as she watched the elderly woman look them over.

Travis trailed them in and closed the door, the sudden feeling of being a caged animal made sweat break out along Bryn's hairline, and it took everything in her not to start pacing and growling. The fact that Travis kept his hand on the pistol at his hip did nothing to calm her nerves.

Justin watched both of the newcomers like a sand serpent as the young man helped the woman to sit, her frail hand patting his youthful one in thanks.

Turning a grandmotherly smile on everyone in the room, she looked at them individually, taking her time as if memorizing their every detail.

"You are all so different than I remember . . ." The woman spoke with a thick accent. One that could have been a song in the lyrical way it rolled off her tongue. Her eyes moved over Kessler, and she gave him a warm, affectionate smile. "Looks wise at least."

A shadow moved behind the woman, resembling a man for a flicker of a second before it moved to the corner, blending in with the other shadows. Bryn looked around to see if anyone noticed, but their focus was only on the older woman.

"Well, I am sure I've surprised you all with my visit." Placing her folded hands on top of the table, she steadied herself, the young man who came with her keeping his place at her side.

His eyes were curious, but otherwise his expression was stoic. It was as Justin had said, the man wore a rope around his waist as if it were a belt, a velvet bag hanging from it. Velvet was something she had rarely seen in her lifetime and only the church could afford. She wondered if that meant he was a religious man.

He kept his hands folded behind his back as he waited for the woman to speak again.

"So different, wouldn't you say, Callum?" she asked the young man at her side.

Giving her a nod, he placed his hand on the velvet bag at his waist.

"Stop right there," Justin growled, his gun already in hand. "I warned y'all about this before we came in here."

The older woman put her hand out to stay the young man as she gave a nod of acquiescence to Justin. The young man released the velvet green bag on her order and refolded his hands behind his back.

Justin, Travis, and Caden had gone on high alert, and Bryn was sure the older woman did not miss it.

It was bizarre how calm the woman and young man were as the intensity in the room ignited. Bryn wondered how many of the others were holding their breath, concerned about what exactly the young man, Callum, had planned to do.

"You can relax. We mean you no harm." Her words did nothing to quell the tension. "My name is Danu."

Bryn felt like she'd fallen into a void and was spinning endlessly, unsure of which side was up. Cyerra had told her to speak to a woman named Danu, and what were the odds that a woman with the same such bizarre name would fall into her lap? Zero. Everything causing her world to crumble around her was this woman's doing.

"I have waited so very long to have you all back together again," Danu stated, her eyes watering, and her frail fingers attempted to wipe the escaping tears away. Ever the gentleman, Mr. Rafferty offered her his handkerchief. "Excuse me. I had hoped to stay more composed when I set eyes on you all again."

"No offense, but we have no idea who you both are," Declan intervened. "You show up literally out of nowhere in a town full of people who are ready to shoot anything that walks different. On top of all that, you say you are kin to all of us." He waved to the room around him. "That about sum it up?"

"There is always more to the story, young Declan." She smiled, and Declan shot a look at his father. Bryn guessed Declan had yet to meet her, and her knowing his name had sent up a red flag.

As if this whole scenario wasn't one giant red flag.

"Then please, educate me." Declan leaned back, folding his arms, his whiskey eyes narrowed as they took the older woman's measure.

A shadow moved again, and this time Sage turned her head toward it, furrowing her brows before looking back to the woman.

Nope, not crazy, Sage. We can see men made of shadows now and crows that talk.

Bryn wished she could put a voice to those words, share that not only could she see the end of people's lives on earth, but now she could apparently talk to animals on top of a new friend made of shadows that popped up in random places.

How many more secrets must she keep? How did everything that was happening even correlate?

She was so tired of carrying the burden of secrets from her friends. If only she could have someone to help her carry it, she would be forever grateful.

A flicker in the shadows moved again in her peripheral vision, but she ignored it.

"I am here because I am dying . . ." Danu let her words trail off before taking a deep breath.

Caden let out a whistle, shaking his head.

"I am real sorry to hear that, ma'am, and I mean nothing discourteous by this question, but what does that have to do with us? You're a stranger to us all," Caden asked as he leaned back against the wooden chair. Declan nodded in agreement as he worked his jaw, the words he wanted to say stuck to his tongue.

She could only imagine what those words would be. Declan was not one to hold back his thoughts on the best of days.

"Caden, was it?" she asked, earning a nod from the bartender. "I have yet to meet you and Travis, and while I've heard stories of you, you did not exist as the rest of your group has. Your paths were meant to cross with everyone here, of course, since you both will help them meet their destinies. And along the way you will find your own. Though the road will not be a smooth one. Heartbreak and pain await you both."

Travis looked at Caden, but Caden shook his head with a sardonic smirk. He wasn't buying any of this, and Bryn wished she could say the same. Had it not been for Cyerra using the woman's name, she might have been more skeptical.

Settling back in her chair, Danu sighed as she placed her hands in her lap.

"I had hoped you all retained some piece of yourselves. That certainly would have made this all so much easier, but it seemed the more cycles you went through, the more you lost of yourselves. It has been so difficult to find you all along the same timeline, and I fear this is my last chance. I cannot hold on for much longer."

Bryn was sure everyone's eyebrows went up at the same time as each person exchanged looks with one another. She could imagine everyone's heartbeats within the room grew in sync, amping up in their intensity.

"I am not hearing answers, only more questions," Declan whispered, and earned a chastising look from his father.

Danu gave Declan a warm smile, not at all offended.

"What do you all know about the Tuatha Dé Danann?"

Chapter 12

"The tootha-what?" Jace asked before anyone else in the room could.

"The Tuatha Dé Danann were warriors from long ago. They held god-like abilities and resided in the Otherworld, which of course has different names depending on the people and the region they resided in. That was unless they were needed upon this plane, which they crossed the veil to attend to the earth and the humans' needs. Some of them stayed for long periods of time upon this plane, others came and went, but all were my children."

Silence engulfed the room as Danu looked at each of them expectantly, her eyes growing sad as she realized nothing was triggering a memory for anyone.

"They have other names, of course, perhaps one of those would help you remember. The folk of Danu, tribe of the gods, sidhe—"

"Sidhe . . . like fairies?" Sage broke in, and instead of disbelief, she looked excited. Bryn could only smile at Sage's enthusiasm as the woman tried, and failed, to tamp it down. Bryn knew as soon as they left the room, Sage would be lost in her books for hours if not days.

Danu gave her a motherly smile.

"All myths come from some form of truth, child."

"What does this have to do with us?" Declan murmured as he stuck a toothpick in his mouth, the wood bobbing with his words. "You're a fairy?"

It was a joke, of course, so everyone laughed . . . except Danu, Callum, and Mr. Rafferty. The sudden quiet stole over the room again when they did not join in.

Looking at Declan, she watched as his eyes narrowed in on his father. Turning to Niamh to see how she was handling the news, Bryn realized the pale woman somehow managed to lose even more color.

Placing her hand on Niamh's covered shoulder, her friend jumped as if she'd been brought out of some incredibly intense thought. Niamh attempted to give Bryn a smile but failed terribly at it. The worry wouldn't wash away that easily. Bryn knew that as much as her own name.

"I suppose it depends on your definition of a fairy," the older woman replied.

Jace rubbed his hands over his face, the first sign of irritation for him. It was obvious the men were running out of patience, fast.

"So, who and what are you, and why do you think we are family?" Sage asked, and while Bryn saw the men's thankful looks that someone was cutting to the chase, Bryn knew it was Sage's thirst for information, not her desire to wrap this meeting up.

"You are all my children," she said, but Bryn wasn't sure if anyone heard her correctly.

"I have a mother, thank you," Jace broke in, and Bryn realized that he was the only one here who did.

Declan had his father, Jace had his mother, Bryn had her father before he passed . . . but none of the rest did. From what she knew, all of their parents had perished from the sickness that went through when Bryn was little. The outsiders brought it with them before the gate closed, but she hardly remembered the fine details of it all.

One day her school friends were laughing, living life, and readying themselves to find apprenticeships, all of them between the ages of ten and twelve, Bryn being the youngest at age eight. The next, they were just hoping for someone to find it in their heart to care for several children on the cusp of no longer being children.

An elderly woman, who had died years ago, took the orphans in and raised them: Sage, Justin, Travis, Kessler, and Caden.

No, the woman before them was not the same woman who had stepped in to help raise the orphaned youth of Ifreann.

Bryn knew their adopted mother was long gone since she was there when they ran the pyre and did the funeral rites. Her father always brought her along to the pyres when they were lit. A reminder of why he did what he did, he would tell her, and so she would accompany him and wonder where the souls of the bodies were going.

No. No matter what trick this woman did to get in past the closed gate, Bryn doubted she could survive fire.

"Not in the way of giving birth, but in creating you all."

Bryn was concerned the men were going to lose their minds soon as she watched their faces turn beet red. It was possible that in the next few minutes their heads would explode from anger at having no direct answers.

Soon enough, tempers were lost, and angry words were shot like bullets at the older woman with the vague responses.

"Stop!" the young man, Callum, ordered with his hands up. "She is Danu. Mother of creation, and you are the children, the warriors, she created to fight." His eyes stayed on Declan as he spoke. "You went across the veil when the Fomori destroyed our lands and were reborn into human vessels. We have kept you safe until you were of age to take back your powers and not a moment later since the earth is dying, and with it, Danu."

"This is absolutely ludicrous. I am done here. I have shit to do." Declan pushed away from the wall, walking toward the door before his father stepped in front of him.

"Sit down, Declan Rafferty," Mr. Rafferty ordered, his voice deeper and full of enough power that had it been aimed Bryn's direction, it would have bent her will.

"Everyone here"—Mr. Rafferty's eyes moved and caught each and every one of theirs to imply how important it was— "this is all something you need to hear."

"You actually believe the crap these two strangers, who breached our walls during a sandstorm, are selling?" Declan asked, aghast.

Bryn couldn't blame him. It was beyond anything she'd ever heard, even the crazy stories from Sage's contraband books. Not to mention, should any of the conversation leave this room, the entire town would come down on the two new people.

Nature and gods? That was prime sinful witchcraft. This town would raise a stake in a matter of hours.

While Bryn could understand Declan's frustration, she couldn't ignore Cyerra's demand she speak to the woman named Danu. Even if this was all a farce, just a small piece of her *wanted* to believe. To have evidence that she wasn't the outcast the town made her out to be. That her connection to death, her visions, really were some greater power.

Something more than this little town, and its simple ways, could understand.

It was all a dream, she knew, but one she would allow herself to stay in just a tad longer.

Her mind spun, thoughts of the meaning and consequences of what the woman had told them overwhelming her rational side, which was the only possible reason she could have said what she did next.

"Does this have anything to do with me being cursed?" Bryn blurted out, her mouth running without the go-ahead from her brain. Cringing, she realized she could have asked that question a bit more delicately. Perhaps it was not the best sentence to voice in a room full of people who didn't realize she was as abnormal as the people outside claimed her to be.

"You are not cursed!" Jace yelled, slamming his fist on the table, shocking everyone. Never had anyone here seen this behavior in him before, and his eyes widened as everyone gave him a surprised look. Settling back in his chair, his cheeks pink, he folded his arms. "I apologize. I haven't slept well."

"Why do you think you are cursed?" Danu asked, and Bryn looked at Jace before she said anything else. His eyes moved to hers, and she saw sadness there. Sending him an apologetic look, she turned back to Danu.

"I'm supposed to be a healer, but I cannot heal anyone. In fact, most people I try to help—" Her voice cut off. Should she really be airing her issues when the governor and law were here to listen? They had protected her to this point, but if they *knew* some of what was whispered about her was true, how long would they put themselves on the line to protect her?

"You see their deaths," Danu answered her, and Bryn actually felt her mouth drop. Her heart ran rampant as she looked around the room, fearing they would drag her outside to be put to death. Everyone looked at her in shock except Danu, Callum . . . and Mr. Rafferty.

His eyes held hers before he looked back to Danu. He knew?

He knew!

"You do?" Jace asked, but his voice was lost to her as she watched every small movement Mr. Rafferty made before she looked back to Danu.

"How did you know that?" Bryn asked, worries carrying through her brain like a parade. Could this woman have been the reason this happened? But how when she had only come to town in the past day and her visions had been ongoing for twenty years?

"I know all of your secrets." She looked to each of the people in the room, and Bryn wondered if anyone could feel the undercurrent of power surrounding the woman. "All of you."

Were witches actually real, and this woman was what they were like?

Bryn couldn't help the sadness that overcame her. The woman had walked into a town that would see her dead by sunrise.

On the opposite side of that thought, Bryn selfishly wanted answers before she never saw Danu again.

"That's not at all unsettling to hear," Travis muttered.

Danu smiled at Travis, her eyes lighting on the stoic man.

"While you and Caden are human, you have your roles in helping my children. That is why you are here. I am unsure of the future, but you are part of getting the Tuatha Dé Danann to where they need to be."

"So, you know all our secrets, huh? What's mine?" Declan challenged, bringing Danu's attention away from Travis. His eyes held a dare in them that most people backed away from when he gave them that particular look. Danu was completely unfazed and ready to respond.

"Ah yes, I am not surprised you are the first to ask. I think it's absolutely darling you named your general store and trading post the Cauldron, and with this post, you have the ability to keep this town thriving. Never will anyone here go hungry as long as you are near since the crops and livestock will thrive with your gift, but I am sure you've already noticed that trade goes much better when you're the one doing the exchange.

Always were able to sway the emotions of those around you." Turning to look at Callum, she let out a little laugh. "Dagda and his harp could sway any man."

"I play guitar," Declan muttered, but his voice held no heat in it as he stared off, seeing nothing but his own thoughts. Shaking his head clear, Declan pointed to his father.

"And what secrets does my old man have?" Declan sneered, and Bryn felt for him. She knew all too well what it felt like for one's world to begin unraveling at the seams.

A bang on the door interrupted any further discussion, but the look in Declan's eyes promised he'd have his answers. Bryn could understand that as well. She would be right behind him in demanding them.

Voices rose in the building outside their room as Justin and Mr. Rafferty headed to the door.

"I am most likely needed, so I will see what I can do to get them outside so you can stow away our surprise guests." With those words, Mr. Rafferty moved out of the room and into the rest of the building, his voice taking on that of a politician. A shepherd guiding his sheep outside with soothing words.

Justin nodded, cueing Travis to escort Danu and Callum to wherever they were holding them, but before anyone could leave the room, Justin held his hands up.

"This, as I said in the beginning, cannot be spoken of outside of this room. Is everyone in agreement?"

Bryn wondered what would happen if they disagreed, but no one did since everyone knew where Justin's concerns stemmed from. Mr. Rafferty knew the older woman, knew she would be considered a witch, and so she was to be protected.

Justin may have disagreed, had questions himself, but he'd follow the rules. Mr. Rafferty had laid them down in front of the lawman in black and white knowing Justin would follow them to the letter.

At everyone's acknowledgment that they would remain silent on this, Justin left without issue.

Danu stood, and everyone in the room watched with careful eyes as the woman made her way to the door with Callum's help. That they all remained watchful told Bryn they'd felt the same strange feeling emanating from Danu.

"When can we speak again?" Bryn asked, breaking the silence as she stood to walk around the table toward Danu, stopping when Callum moved between the two women as if Bryn might harm her.

"Callum," Danu chastised. "I may be dying, but I can still destroy anyone who dares threaten me."

The breath froze in Bryn's lungs right as someone's chair scraped across the wooden floor.

"You are a witch . . ." Caden's voice carried across the room, but Bryn kept her eyes on the woman.

Danu smiled benignly.

"Anyone who walks, talks, and fu . . . screws different is a witch in this place." Niamh laughed, and Bryn couldn't disagree. Danu looked at Bryn as she moved around Callum, reaching for her, but Bryn took a step back. If the woman was dying, she didn't want to see and feel her death.

Not at all offended, Danu gave her an understanding look.

"We have a very limited time, so believe me when I say it will be soon. I will wait for the sheriff and governor to handle this disturbance before we convene again," Danu stated as she looked over the people she had referred to as her children. "I know this is all a lot at once, but I cannot maintain against the evil that corrodes our world forever, and if I die . . ."

Looking back at Callum, he stepped forward, his hand taking hers, and she perked up a little, as if drawing strength from him. Turning back to them, her face held a graveness even with that boost of energy.

"If I die, so does our world."

Chapter 13

It hardly surprised Bryn that Declan, Kessler, and Caden took off. She doubted any of what Danu had said made much of a difference in how they felt when she knew they didn't believe a word of it.

Still, she wondered if it was actual disbelief or if they had their own weird happenings, like her visions, and Danu cut to the quick of it, scaring the men. Scared them enough that they were defensive and shutting it out of their minds until it was dropped in their lap again.

Bryn did not have that issue at all; in fact, she *needed* to know. It was for that reason alone that she followed Sage to her cottage.

If there were answers, it was most certainly in the books Sage had hoarded from the time before she moved to Ifreann. Sage's mother had been an avid reader and kept everything she could from her life in Tanwen. Before certain books were banned by the church, Sage's family library was a wealth of information that very few were privy to.

While most of Sage's collection had been burned after the death of her parents, Sage had found a way to copy many of them discreetly, though seeing the originals lost forever broke her teenage friend's heart the way a first love might.

It had been the closest Bryn had ever come to fighting back, and it was at the sight of tears in Sage's light-brown eyes.

Cyerra flew ahead of them from wherever she'd hid during the meeting, seeming to know where Bryn was going. She desperately hoped no one noticed the crow that seemed to have attached herself to Bryn.

Chances were slim Arioch would keep it to himself that Bryn was talking to a bird, and people would be paying more attention to her because of it. Midnight pyres were a beast all its own, but she couldn't slip in and out at sunrise or sunset now. She'd have to be even more vigilant.

Looking up at Cyerra, the bird landed on the railing of Sage's porch as Bryn waved Sage quickly inside.

Hands on hips, she leaned down to where she was eye level with the bird when she heard Sage's door shut behind her.

"I met Danu."

"Was she as annoyed with your thickness of the mind as I am?"

"Har har. Once I finish talking to my friend, I want some answers." Bryn pointed to the bird as she stood. Once she had enough information from Sage's texts, she could see what Cyerra could fill in for her.

"Looks like you're not the only one."

Taking flight, Bryn turned as Jace ran up, grabbing the fabric of her shirt and pulling her into Sage's cabin, before shutting and locking the door behind him.

Sage already had a book in hand but merely raised her eyebrows at the scene before her.

"How long, Bryn?" Jace demanded, his rage barely contained as he spoke. "How long have you been keeping this secret, and what other secrets have you kept from me?"

Sighing, she sat in one of Sage's kitchen chairs, the mismatched eclectic collection of muted purples and greens from Tanwen usually gave her a sense of calm. One of only two places she could find reprieve in the drab-brown town, the other being the Sanctuary.

Her calm was lost to her at the look of betrayal in her cousin's eyes.

"All my life, Jace. The seizures, those are when I have visions of people's deaths."

Unable to look at his face, to see the betrayal in his blue eyes, she picked at some of the threads of Sage's amethyst tablecloth.

To see him judge her as others did . . . it would break her.

"That's not fair," he broke into her thoughts as he kneeled before her. "You're my family, and you lumped me in with all those who judged you. I would love you no matter what, and I would have been here for you if you had given me a chance." His eyes shimmered, but she knew now it wasn't his own hurt he was emotional over, or not all of it anyway. "I hate that you lived every day in hell, and there was no one at your side to weather it with you."

His hands folded over hers, not caring if she pulled away. He needed that connection, and to be honest, so did she.

"What else?" he demanded, though it was a demand built on concern and kindness. "What else don't I know?"

Bryn opened her mouth, the urge to spill every grizzly detail of how his mother had harmed her, both physically and emotionally when he wasn't around. The excuses she made so he didn't know who his mother truly was beneath the surface.

That him being an apprentice to her father, having taken the role her father had promised she would fulfill when she was younger, had made it where he was hardly around in those days.

That in and of itself gave Mallory time for her abuse, which made it feel like it was a cosmic punishment for her own failure as a healer. All hinged on her guilt that he had to take that job so they could stay in Ifreann made it easier to justify keeping the secret from him. That somehow she deserved it because she had let her family down when they needed her.

That was her penance since she was the one who had failed her family because she was broken inside.

It was easy to lie when she thought it would save him from the horrible truth.

"Found it!" Sage yelled out, oblivious to the seriousness of the conversation happening at her dining room table.

Bryn withdrew her hands, giving Jace a small smile. His eyes warned her that this conversation wasn't close to being over.

But it was. She had been almost weak enough to tell him, to change his relationship with the only other family member he had, and with her. As much as she wanted to share her burden with him, she feared what would happen.

Bryn feared deep down how much it would change their own relationship. He was all she had left.

Standing and turning, she walked into the small living area where Sage already had several books open and was moving between them all.

"She always like this at home?" Jace asked, watching her with a small, infatuated smile. Oh, he was in so deep with her. Bryn almost smirked at the thought before Sage slammed a book shut, bringing their attention back to her.

"I found it!" She jumped, grabbing another book, and running around the couch to sit. Placing the open tome in her lap, she patted both sides of her on the couch in invitation for them to sit.

Taking the order, they sat next to her, seeing a large drawing of a tree taking up the two open pages.

"It's a tree," Jace stated, his voice indicating how very unimpressed he was at her revelation.

"The tree of life! So many mythologies have something similar, but this one is specific to Celtic mythology, which of course . . ." Turning the page as she trailed off, the next one held the words "Tuatha Dé Danann" and the pantheon of the Celtic gods.

There were not any photos, and not a ton of information for them to go on, but there were descriptions of powers next to the names.

Bryn's eyes caught on Dagda, and it was just as Danu had said. Declan seemed to have a propensity toward the ancient god's gifts.

"This is all too surreal. None of this makes sense to me, I am sorry. It's . . ." Jace stood to start his pacing that Bryn lovingly referred to as Jace's dance of anxiety.

"It is, but there are not a lot of alternatives to explain everything," Bryn replied as Sage moved her finger along the page.

"Visions of death . . .," Sage murmured, and Bryn wished it was all a ruse then. The truth she had sought out was in front of her, and *now* she was scared to grab hold of it. Not to mention how uncomfortable it was to speak about a secret she'd kept to herself for so very long. "The Morrigan!"

"Does she always randomly yell out bits and pieces of what she reads?" Jace asked as he settled into a chair across from them.

"Yes," Bryn answered as she took the book from Sage's hands, pulling it onto her own lap as she ignored Sage's agitated, "Hey!"

Bryn was used to the random spurts of frenzy and then complete silence as Sage moved onto a new topic before randomly yelling more words from the next thing that caught her eye. Something Bryn found charming when the topic wasn't about *her*.

Turning the book to the page labeled "The Morrigan," Bryn looked upon a woman draped in black sitting on a throne of skulls, a sword leaning against the side. Her umber eyes staring back at Bryn.

Running her fingers along the braided black hair and crown of silver, Bryn took in the woman that held the power she supposedly carried inside herself.

Bryn felt no kindred spirit or pull from the woman on the page, but she wished she had. Wished that the truth was easy enough to verify from a memory or some opening of light upon the house from the heavens.

The crow on the back of her throne could mean anything, as could the shadows moving at her feet.

Underneath, it simply stated, "The Morrigan," along with various other names before a small paragraph of text.

The Morrigan. The Phantom Queen. The Great Queen. Banshee.

"A deity of Celtic mythology with the ability to move across the veil using her shadows. Her dark nature allowed her to take worthy souls from the battlefield, but not before predicting their deaths. Could change the tides of war with her premonition and ability to shape-shift. Her animals are a crow and raven . . . How did they know all this in Tanwen?" Bryn asked, her eyes moving back up to the crow on the picture as she stopped reading, not at all like Cyerra who was the size of a domesticated cat with a silver feather on her breasts.

As she focused in on the crow, Sage stole the book back.

"Because we were all interested in history and where we came from. Now, let's see what you are capable of, Phantom Queen," Sage joked as she looked for where Bryn had left off in the paragraph. The woman was so excited to be reading up on this as if there were not actual people this was affecting.

"... tides of war ... yadda yadda ... crow ... Ah! Goddess of death, war, prophecy, shapeshifting, and witchcraft."

That last word had Bryn jumping up before her knees buckled. Jace moved quickly to catch her as she fell to the floor, his hands grabbing her arms to keep her from slamming her knees on the ground.

"It's true," she murmured as tears slipped down her face before she had even realized she was crying.

It was all true.

"I am a witch."

Chapter 14

Opening her swollen eyes, Bryn took in the room she had woken in. Not hers, but from the plants everywhere and the smell of lavender, she knew it was Sage's bed she'd slept in.

From one blink to the next, everything came crashing back on her. She was a witch after all, just like the town had been saying for years. Tears tracked down her face at the revelation, and she was surprised there were any left after curling up into a ball and falling apart. She must have exhausted herself and fallen asleep.

Never had Bryn felt so alone. Even when they found her father on the other side of the gate, a sacrifice of the desert with his clothes torn apart and bite marks deep into his flesh, she'd had Jace there. They'd grieved the loss together, holding each other tight as the body of her father was moved to the pyre, covered in cloth stained red from his blood.

He'd been attacked by a wild animal while out checking on a group of people at the gates asking for refuge. The scrios was the only one to return alive and covered in blood.

It was then, as the scrios walked past the gate covered in blood not his own, that Bryn felt deep inside that Arioch and the Church of Baleros was wrong in a way she couldn't explain. Something under her skin warned her to stay as far away as possible, and so she did.

Listening as Arioch had said the words to carry her father's soul to wherever people went when they died, she'd watched the man closely. There was not an ounce of true compassion in his soul. His eyes were dead, and she wondered how none of the adults had noticed that about him.

His brother Daran was the same, something about them screamed predator, and she kept a wide berth ever since.

Thankfully, Daran was usually at the church, Mallory as well most days, doing something there to "help" for daily services while Arioch roamed about tending to his flock.

A wolf in sheep's clothing, pretending to be one of the sheep he professed to love, woke every day to guide them down the holy road Balor had set before them.

The day of her father's funeral, his eyes had caught hers, and something in them changed. As if he read her mind, knew she was catching on to something even she was unaware of, he took the first step toward damning her.

He'd looked at her as he'd prayed for safety from witches.

Not one of the congregation members attending missed it either.

If not for Mr. Rafferty moving her to the pyres when her try at healing after her father's death had failed, which she now questioned since he seemed to know far more than he let on, she was sure she'd have been put to death when the sickness passed and her body count didn't go down.

From the day of her father's funeral going forward, she was the "witch," and she knew Arioch had everything to do with feeding that rumor as the town scrios.

Now, he didn't need to pretend. He was right. She was a witch, and the proof was all there now for him to haul her into a witch trial. The trial he'd been waiting and planning for the last ten years, she was sure.

A sob broke free as she squeezed her eyes closed.

"None of that," a familiar voice chastised from behind her, and Bryn turned away from the wall to see Niamh sitting beside the bed, knitting of all things. Bryn never would have imagined her seductress of a friend would knit.

Nothing was as it seemed anymore.

She wished she had energy to do anything but cry because she would have enjoyed ribbing Niamh about this particular secret.

"Quit crying or I'll knit you a diaper since you're being such a baby about all of this."

"Sage told you what she found?" Bryn asked as she sat up against the headboard, wiping her tears and snot with her shirt in the epitome of womanly behavior, she was sure, but thankfully Niamh ignored it.

"She did when I demanded an explanation. Sage was out of her mind with worry when she grabbed me and pulled me, sans explanation, across the street to care for our friend who was curled into a literal ball of emotion on the floor of her living room. I wasn't going to let that go without more information once I saw you. It was a breakdown to end all breakdowns."

Embarrassment colored Bryn's cheeks.

"None of that either," Niamh chastised again, turning her nose down and giving Bryn a stern look.

"They were all right about me, Niamh. I am a *witch*."

"Good," Niamh stated with finality as she moved her knitting needles fluidly like an old pro. "Witches are powerful. These people here are not, and so they *should* fear you."

That was not at all what Bryn expected her to say.

"They *burn* witches, Niamh!"

"No." Setting her needles and work in progress down, Niamh leaned toward Bryn. "They burn innocents that do things they are afraid of. Witches, most especially the Morrigan of all people and gods, have power and can protect themselves. From *everyone*."

The emphasis on the last part of her sentence told her Niamh wasn't just talking about the enemies in their town, but the tormentor two doors down from her own.

It confirmed that Niamh had known to some extent what was happening at home, and Bryn wasn't sure how she felt about that.

Then the rest of the words hit her. Sage had informed Niamh of who Bryn truly was. Who else had she told? She knew deep down that Sage wouldn't betray her, but a tiny part of her, the part that had severe trust issues, wondered if she did by accident in her haste and excitement. That outside the doors, right at that moment, there was a mob waiting for her to step outside.

"How much did you know about this, me"—Bryn waved to herself—"before Danu came? You seem to know more than you let on."

Niamh sighed as she worked on a stitch, redoing it, before putting it down and rubbing the bridge of her nose.

"How much do you know about geases?" Niamh asked, stumping Bryn on where she was going with the topic.

"Next to nothing."

"Before you came here, I was put under a geas and cannot tell you anything until I am released from it. Nothing about yourself or others of Danu's children." Niamh's jaw clenched on the last part, making Bryn suspicious of what she knew of the others, but she continued. "But I can tell you my story, and perhaps that will settle your nerves, and mine, if there is one less secret between us.

"Now it is not something I enjoy rehashing, naturally, but I've lived a long time, and it is almost like someone else's memory now."

Bryn waited while Niamh looked off into space, gathering her thoughts, and then shook her head before she started.

"It happened so long ago that I couldn't tell you dates or places with any sure accuracy, but I digress. I was a lord's daughter in a time when daughters were nothing more than political playthings." Bryn settled in, listening to Niamh, knowing now after speaking to Jace that it helped to speak of the pain, to share it with someone, even if they were not blood. Niamh was her family, and she needed to trust her family more.

"I fell in love, a taboo love, and hoped to stay unmarried." Niamh's jaw clenched, her eyes glittering with anger. Oh, Bryn had so many questions, but she chose to let Niamh tell her story instead of interrupting. Scooting to the edge of the bed to be closer to Niamh, she folded her hands in her lap as she listened.

"My father wanted me to marry higher, and I was betrothed to one of the wealthiest men in my city. I married him since I didn't have a choice really, but he was horrible. Always using his fists and then taking me every night, willing or not. I went to a village healer, I didn't know she was a witch of course, to prevent pregnancy, and she gave me the herbs to do so. I thought they were only that, to prevent a child. I wonder now if the bruises I tried to hide were why she gave me something more."

Niamh gave a small sardonic smile as she tapped her nails on the arm of her chair before her face went serious again.

"Every day was worse with him, until he finally snapped my neck in a fit of rage."

Now Bryn was the one to put her arm around Niamh, squeezing her closer, careful of her skin.

"They buried me. A pauper's grave since I had not produced an heir." She laughed, and it was a painful sound. "I didn't know that the witch had given me more than birth control. I rose from my grave with a blood lust, and I killed my husband while he was in bed with his mistress. Her too. Found my father soon after and I tore him apart." Niamh's hand went to the ruby-red diamond necklace at her throat, and Bryn realized she'd never seen her friend so distraught.

"The town hunted me, and one day they found me. I had been looking for my love only to find out she had been trying to find me. My husband . . . he did horrible things to her before he killed her. I lost it." Niamh looked up at her with tears of blood welling in her eyes. "I killed them all and became the focus of the church to dispatch. They would have, too, had you not stepped from the mist to offer me refuge among the shadows."

"I was there when this all happened?" Well, the Morrigan, obviously.

With a nod, Niamh swallowed.

"You saved me, and I never forgot that. When you went across the veil to close it behind you that final time, I promised you I would find you again. And I did, although it was accidental since I had just come to Ifreann a few years before you did, and I was unsure until people started dying while under your care."

Bryn dropped her hands to her lap, staring at them. Unsure herself if she was actually who Niamh, Danu, and Sage thought she was. There was so much information thrown at her in such a small time frame, and she hadn't had time to take it all in. Where did she even start?

"I can't tell you much else, but I can tell you this." Niamh placed a polished red nail under Bryn's chin, lifting her face until their eyes met. No vision and no spark. "You, my darling, have always been powerful. Morrigan or not, and that is why they fear you so tremendously. If you were allowed to spread your wings, you'd be unstoppable."

Bryn realized Niamh was waiting for something, so Bryn gave her a nod.

"Good." Niamh nodded in return as she picked her knitting back up like they hadn't just had such an intense discussion about Niamh's past.

"You were meant to fly, Bryn, but they clipped your wings," Niamh whispered, and Bryn felt the power of those words, and what they meant, infuse her.

"It's time to get back into the sky. Hard to burn a witch from up there."

Chapter 15

A meeting was to be held later with Danu. Bryn had wanted to catch Cyerra for some answers, but she was keeping her distance, staying to the sky so she could follow Bryn, but not allowing a conversation between them. On purpose? Probably. It was only a matter of time before she made the bird spill.

Bryn was thankful that Kessler had summoned her while she slept since it meant she had something to do while she was waiting for the meeting. Niamh had gone back to the Sanctuary and Sage to her books. Justin and Mr. Rafferty were working hard to keep the new arrivals under wraps, the citizens of Ifreann none the wiser.

Crossing Saints' Road, the townspeople were leaving the evening service, heading toward their homes to settle in.

Stepping back onto the porch, Bryn observed them as they passed by, thankful no one noticed her.

Watching the people after a service, she saw there was a noticeable difference from when they walked about working and conversing during the day. They were radiating hostility, something she would think at odds with just having attended a religious service.

As far as she'd read, the old religions had brought people peace and calm . . . at least to the majority of people of faith. Others took it to extremes, but they were a small percentage.

The Church of Baleros seemed to only rile some primal instinct in its followers. She wondered at who Balor was, this god they worshipped so studiously. There was not any history of who Balor was in the book on religions she'd found in her teens, only that he came to save the people who deserved a second life after the Collapse.

Perhaps she'd looked in all the wrong places for the answers. She needed to look through all the books in Sage's library since there had to be something on him somewhere.

A large portrait was all she could remember from going to church, having to sit on a bench while the scrios spoke of Balor coming to save them all seemingly from nowhere. The horned bull masks they wore were in honor of him, but his face was human. Black hair, black eyes, pale skin that was ghostly. A large scar crossed one eye, the tissue puckered. He wore black and silver, a sword sheathed at his hip with a scarred hand resting on the pommel.

Bryn wanted to ask questions as a youth: What did he do to save everyone? Where did he come from? Why did the king demand they worship a particular god instead of letting the individual choose who and what they wanted to believe in?

It took one question, a slap to the face from Mallory, and Bryn didn't bother anymore. Bryn could still smell the cloying burning leather smell of the incense in Mallory's room from that day, the smell forever held in her brain as something horrible. The sting from Mallory's palm across her cheek, one of the few times she'd hit Bryn somewhere that she couldn't hide with long sleeves.

One of the only times in her life that Bryn had *begged* for a vision was when she was in her aunt's presence. To know that when her aunt laid hands on her, she'd die soon, and Bryn could have peace.

Those visions never came, though, and it'd been years since she'd questioned the church. Perhaps all the talk of gods lately was bringing those memories to the forefront of her mind.

Ava's tinkling laugh caught Bryn's attention as the woman left the chapel doors arm in arm with her friends. That woman had set Bryn's teeth on edge long before she had found her curled up with Declan.

She tried not to compare them, but Ava was definitely the better choice for a man of Ifreann looking to hold his golden throne as the governor's son.

Ava was all tan skin, honey-brown eyes, long lush blond hair, and the best dresses. Ones far higher in quality than Bryn's. Ava's father spared no expense for his little girl, and her stepmother doted on her to the point that Ava was sure she was the world and everyone in town just revolved around her.

Bryn had red hair, curly and wild, with greenish-blue eyes, and pale, freckled skin that was not made for a person living in the desert. Her drab-brown and beige dresses were sown together over and over again, only one dress in her possession in any decent shape. She blended in, though, and that was a blessing when avoiding the townspeople, but she wished she could walk around during the day as Ava did, have her pick of men, and just . . . be free.

Bryn shook the thoughts away before she became depressed and ignored Kessler's summons to go cry in her bed.

Things that were not to be were not worth dwelling on.

As the crowd thinned to a trickle, Bryn cautiously made it to the open wooden double doors of Kessler's shop.

The heat of the forge hit her immediately as she stepped inside, moving out of the way of the door should there be any stragglers outside. How he could stand in this all day long and not pass out was beyond her.

"You grow used to it," he responded, and she realized she had said the words aloud. Slightly embarrassed, she fidgeted with a button on the sleeve of her shirt.

"But it feels damn good to be in here during the freezing season. People are always bothering me during that time. This"—he waved to the fires that blanketed the place in horrid heat— "keeps people from bothering me. I'll take this discomfort over mindless chatter."

"Perhaps I should take up working in here with you," she joked. Oh, to never be bothered by hateful people and have a normal sleep schedule.

"Welcome to it. You are one of the few who isn't blathering on about needless shit to keep the silence away." He gave her a small smile as he put something burning hot into water, the sizzle and pops making her aware of how humid it was in the room. Her curly hair was going to be an ongoing issue tonight.

"I can't handle the heat, so I'll stay out of the forge." Moving to a chair, Bryn took a seat, watching the man work. His muscles moved in a rhythmic dance under his shirt and leather apron. The sweat glistened on his skin, and she wondered why she'd never seen him as a potential partner. He would have been a lot easier to deal with than Declan, that was for sure.

The feeling just never came for her to act on. For either of them, she assumed since he never tried either. Perhaps she was an idiot, or perhaps she went with the one man whose protection guaranteed her safety. Letting him court her until she let her walls down and eventually opened her heart to him. He was quick to hug her, take her hand, almost like he was trying to prove she didn't need to worry about fits.

So she'd fallen into his bed instead of another man's. Worries of a vision lost to the bliss she felt in his bed.

A bed she bet Ava had visited as well.

At a lull in Kessler's hammering, she finally said something to keep from woolgathering further.

"You called for me?"

Kessler's head popped up from where he was working, almost as if he had forgotten she'd been there this whole time.

"Yes!" Turning, he moved to a wooden table where he did the negotiations and designs of items for his customers and pulled out something wrapped in cloth. Opening it, she gasped.

A dagger, beautiful in the seamless lines of the blade, the hilt black with bits of red catching the light.

It was exquisite. Reaching out to touch it, she stopped herself, putting her fingers to her lips instead.

"I cannot afford to pay for such . . ." Stepping back, she shook her head, unable to say more.

Overwhelmed was the best description she could come up with of how she felt.

"I didn't make it for coin, Bryn. I made it for *you*." Wrapping the dagger back in the cloth, he placed it in front of her on the counter. "Take it. Please."

Her eyes moved to his face, and she saw how much he needed her to take it in his eyes. There was so much more to this than she knew. Hesitantly, she placed her hand on the dagger but didn't wrap her hands around it.

Shaking his head, Kessler put his hands on the table in front of him, looking down at the floor. Was she dismissed?

Stepping back, she folded her arms, readying herself to leave, when his coarse voice caught her like a fly in a web.

"You remind me of my sister . . ."

Kessler had a sister? She'd never known or heard about her.

Bryn didn't dare ask where she was. His body language told her this was not a happy story.

Looking up at her through his dirty-blond hair, dirt and sweat marring his brow, he grabbed a rag from his apron and wiped his face. A movement meant to give them both time to decide whether they wanted to share this or walk away oblivious.

Bryn stepped forward and leaned on the table. Her choice was made, and Kessler nodded.

"She was three years younger than me. A newborn when we came to town. It was at my mother's request that we left our home, some place northeast of here that I cannot remember the name of now. Who even knows if it is still there. I never knew why we left, and there is no one to ask any longer."

Leaning back against the wall behind him, he crossed his arms and ankles.

"Mother fell sick, so naturally, Father fell to the drink. He was gone almost every night after she passed. He grew angrier by the day, yelled about how if your father had come earlier to town, she'd be alive."

Bryn's eyes grew wide at that.

"For a while, I blamed you both too. Until I realized there wasn't a damn thing to be done to save her. Even if you'd showed up before, she was too sick. Went too quick."

"Still, I am so sorry, Kess," she whispered, the man giving her a small nod of thanks in return.

"My sister, Ariana, started to take to looking like Mom more and more as she got older. Dad grew in his anger and drink, and soon he was coming home to throw some punches at anything with a heartbeat. I watched Ariana go from a fun-loving and curious girl to fearful of everyone's touch." His eyes focused on her now, and she sensed she knew where he was going by telling her this.

"I was older, so I stepped in to take most of it. Thought it was just me he went after. One night in his rage, he yelled how he should have killed me the moment he found out I wasn't his. I was angry he would say anything about my mother like that, that she'd cheat, so we went head-to-head, and I lost."

Bryn's mind went back to a time when Kessler wasn't at school for a month, her father had been going to see him a lot, so she figured he'd been sick.

"I was too beat up for him to really enjoy his time hurting me without killing me . . ."

Closing his eyes, he took a deep breath, steadying himself.

"I found her."

That was all he could say. Shaking his head, he turned away from Bryn.

"Oh, Kessler." Bryn's lips trembled, but she couldn't say anything more than that. There were no words one could say to undo such horrid ties to the past.

"I heard nothing. She never made a noise. The whole time. Her broken body . . ." Pinching his nose, Bryn took a chance and moved around the counter. She had not gone into a fit from touching him earlier; even so, he needed comfort. Wrapping her arms around the big man, she let him tuck her into him like she was a beloved teddy bear. A sob left him, and she hugged harder.

"He'd beat her so bad, Brynnie . . ."

Closing her eyes, tears slipped from them as she wished his father were still alive so *she* could kill him.

"I held her as she slipped away from me. Promised her I wouldn't let him ever hurt another. You remind me so much of her, and the thought of this town . . . I know your aunt is evil too. I see it in her when she looks at you."

Bryn froze, but Kessler tightened his grip.

"Promise you won't let it go further? If . . . I am here, all right?"

Her lungs were stripped of air. So many people knew her secrets, and yet she thought she'd been doing so well at hiding them.

How many others did? Embarrassment flooded her, and she spun out from underneath his arms, her heart beating too fast to be healthy.

"I am sorry, Bryn," he whispered, his voice broken.

Folding her arms across her chest, she turned to him, unable to meet his eyes.

"Your father?" she asked.

"Met an unfortunate accident."

That was all she needed to know. Nodding, she took a deep breath, trying to stretch her lungs so she could breathe easy again.

"Please take the dagger. You remind me so much of her, and I can't fail her twice."

The dagger was suddenly in front of her, his hands shaking as he held it out for her to take.

Placing her hands under his, she took it, finally meeting the eyes of a man living in his own hell.

A kindred soul.

"Thank you, Kess. For everything."

Chapter 16

Determination burned in Bryn's veins after speaking with Kessler. She wanted answers, and only Danu knew them.

The caw in the sky pushed at her resolve as she ran to Niamh's place, having been told before she left Sage's after her breakdown that Justin was keeping Danu and Callum there.

"I'll be getting answers from you later, little crow," Bryn seethed through her teeth at the bird as it flew past her, far too close, in what Bryn took as a taunt. Narrowing her eyes, she ignored the bird, promising revenge later.

Stepping onto the wooden steps of the Sanctuary, Bryn clenched her fists as she took a steadying breath.

Yes, the world thought she was a witch and had tormented her for years because of it. Yes, perhaps they had been right, but if she was going to wear that title, she needed the information on how to do so.

Justin met her in the entryway, Caden sitting near the door in the seat he used when Niamh needed him there as security instead of serving drinks.

It always amazed Bryn how Caden worked in the Sanctuary, and the townsfolk treated him like anyone else in the community, yet they shunned the women working at the very same place.

Fair? Not in the least, but that was the world they lived in.

Didn't mean she had to like it.

"I can tell by the look on your face you're determined, and lucky you, Niamh is promising us uninterrupted time to ask the questions we need answered." Justin gave Bryn a small shoulder squeeze with his words as she nodded and stepped past him into the drawing room.

"You sure you want those answers, Brynnie?" Justin asked from behind her, using the nickname Declan had come up with during their courtship.

Justin was concerned for her, but she was so tired of being seen as weak, and if she had a slight chance, even the smallest of chances, to be powerful enough to control her own destiny, she was taking it by the throat.

"That I do, Justin. That I do," she replied.

"Let's see if we can finish what we started, then," Justin said as he shut the door behind her, staying in the hallway to welcome any other guests, or keep the uninvited out, she assumed.

Walking to one of the old leather couches in Niamh's drawing room, Bryn watched the man made of shadows move between several chairs to the wall. It wasn't long until the shadows fell apart, but she had to wonder who he was and why he followed her everywhere.

"Have a seat." Sage patted the spot next to her on the couch that had once been gold, time and use wearing away at the color. Bryn moved to sit when she saw the look of utter annoyance on Niamh's face from the seat across from her.

"Are you all right?" she asked, Niamh not answering, her mind elsewhere.

"Arioch came by before we got here. No idea what he wanted since Niamh has been mentally planning his death ever since he left," Sage told her, curling into the corner of the couch with a pillow. The drawing room was one of Bryn's favorite places growing up.

Much like Sage's, colors were everywhere compared to outside the doors of the Sanctuary. Blue walls, golden colors strewn throughout the décor, large, framed paintings of places Bryn had never believed existed until Niamh told her otherwise.

Bryn imagined this was what a room in a castle might look like. Whereas most of Sage's colorful items were from Tanwen, Bryn had no idea where Niamh's things came from. Probably from all over the world now that she knew how long-lived Niamh was.

One could accumulate a lot as an immortal.

Settling onto the couch as they waited for the rest of their people, Bryn reached out to the table between the couches where a glass of water sat.

The moment her fingers touched the etched glass, her vision went sideways.

A sensation of her body being lighter than normal told her she was in a vision, yet she hadn't touched another person.

Also, the fact that she was no longer in the drawing room but standing in the middle of Saints' Road as the sun set was another pretty clear clue it was a vision, human touch or not.

Screams tore through the night behind her.

Bryn turned to look, hearing yelling, gunfire, but the people making all the noise were moving as if stuck in molasses. Never had a vision been like this before, and unless the person who died was near other people, or killed, she never saw more than one person.

And never from her own perspective instead of the victim's.

The flash of a gun firing several feet away from her lit up the air around the weapon for minutes instead of less than a second. Bullets moved through the air at a snail's pace, all the while Bryn's movements were not slowed or hindered in any way.

Walking through the center of the fighting, knowing this was a vision and she couldn't be harmed . . . or so she hoped, she watched as Arioch stepped into the middle of the road with a weapon trained on a hooded figure. The stature of the individual was not recognizable to Bryn, but the large black-as-night wolf that came out from nowhere caught her attention.

A wolf? When had there been wolves in Ifreann? Hell, Bryn thought, *when had there been crows for that matter?*

And when the same wolf went for Arioch's throat, tearing it out, Bryn screamed until her world went black.

Chapter 17

"So, who's death did you foretell?" Danu asked as Bryn took a sip of water from a new glass.

Knowing the glass she had touched had been Arioch's, she wasn't sad about his death as much as she now had visions from items people touched. Danu had said her powers would grow, but visions from inanimate objects was going to make her life even more hellish.

Wasn't that grand?

Everyone was in the room now, and all watched as she seized on the floor. Her day just continued to get better and better.

Hopefully, the vision didn't ruin the drawing room for her. It was one of the few places of refuge she had.

Sage was still on the couch next to her, Jace now on the other side of her. Niamh and Danu were across from them on the other couch, while Declan, Kessler, Mr. Rafferty, and Caden took chairs. Travis stood next to the door, hand on his pistol, as he watched Callum's and Danu's every move.

Jace bit the skin around his thumb. Pacing was one thing, the biting at his nails and skin was a whole other level of concern. She'd really worried him.

"Arioch," she whispered through her parched throat. Even with the water, her throat was raw. She must have done some serious screaming during her vision.

"How did he die in the vision?" Justin asked, leaning forward in the chair. She wondered if he actually believed her or wanted to know so when Arioch's body showed up, he knew who to blame.

Bryn stopped her thoughts there. That was unfair of her. If she didn't want people to always believe the worst of her, she didn't need to do the same to them.

"Wolf tore his throat out," she whispered, and Justin let out a little huff of laughter before responding.

"You sure these visions are real? People haven't seen a wolf in these parts since before the Collapse."

"Haven't seen a crow either," Bryn snapped before closing her eyes. Taking a deep breath, she opened them again to see that Justin held a pensive look on his face but said nothing more.

So, Bryn needed a little more work on the trust front. She could admit her flaws.

Apparently during her vision, Cyerra had suddenly appeared in the drawing room, flapping her wings, and making a nuisance of herself until Danu ordered her away.

The crow was out of the bag in Ifreann.

"Well, if we are all being dragged to the circus for another encore, let's get on with the dancing monkeys," Declan grumbled, folding his arms as he watched Danu with the obvious skepticism he was wearing like a shield these days bright in his whiskey-colored eyes.

"I've thought long and hard on how to handle this. I thought to tell you all about your past selves, but after seeing how Declan reacted to just small truths, I believe actions would be far more profound than words." Danu turned to look at Callum, putting her hand out for him to take.

Standing, her body trembled with the effort, and Callum took her elbow as they walked to the person nearest to them in the room, Justin.

"Hold out a hand," Danu ordered, and Justin gave an exasperated sigh but did as he was told. Callum, at Danu's nod, reached into the velvet green bag belted by the rope at his waist and withdrew an orange-and-yellow stone before gently placing it in Justin's hand.

From there, they moved to each person in the room, placing a stone in everyone's outstretched hand, all except Niamh, Travis, Mr. Rafferty, and Caden.

All of the men, aside from Mr. Rafferty and Callum, wore matching looks of irritation and disbelief.

They didn't believe a word Danu said, thinking her crazy. Bryn could see it in their eyes as they watched Callum dispense with the stones.

Sage was ready to bounce out of her seat at the prospect of something new happening that she most likely would go home and journal about after.

Bryn turned the black stone in her hand under the sconce, watching the veins of red catch the light.

"These are called soul stones, and no, there is not a soul in there. The soul is in each of you, but that stone holds your power. I am simply reuniting you with what is already yours. I'd ask if you have questions, but I know you do, so let's get you set to rights, and then we can discuss everything further."

Callum assisted Danu in taking her seat again after she finished speaking, and Bryn wondered at what she meant by the inanimate stones holding power.

Watching as Callum took Danu's hand in his, both of them began speaking in a language Bryn had never heard before. A lovely language that sounded all too much like song as they spoke, the notes lilting.

As they chanted, the stones in everyone's hands began to crack, an inner light shining through.

Bryn jolted as the black stone she held disintegrated and became a powder, swirling as if air currents were moving it, yet Bryn felt no wind.

Suddenly invisible arms were holding her to her chair, and her inner animal panicked, ready to claw and maim its way to freedom.

Before she could try to escape the invisible bonds, her lungs seized, and panic overtook her as she tried to breathe.

"Relax, my children," Danu soothed as Bryn tried to force her chest to open up and let air in.

The powder swirled closer, and before she could do anything, it forced itself into her mouth and nose.

Trying to breathe through the feel of sand moving into her lungs, the grittiness stuck to the sides of her throat, she choked. Her body tried to sneeze, but whatever hold Danu's power had was pushing her natural instincts aside to force the powder in.

Choking could be heard around her, but she didn't know if that was her or not. Caden was yelling at Danu to stop, but Bryn was fixated on the red vines eating into her vision. The room trembled around her as she finally was able to release a scream, joining in with the chorus of other screams in the room.

Her ears flooded with smoke that felt like liquid, as if she'd dipped her head beneath water, yet she was on dry ground. The red in her eyes closed over completely, her vision gone, her body slowly going numb as she lost the fight.

Through the darkness of her vision, lights flashed, and she wondered if her brain was dying.

Visions started moving through her mind, ones she'd seen before and ones yet to come, she was sure.

All the deaths of people that she'd seen die and the ones yet to happen. Both those she knew and those she didn't, all swirled into a soup of images that melted together to make up the same drab-brown color she saw every day when she opened her eyes.

Swirls of shadow moved over her vision before the shadow man was standing before her in her own mind. Fear struck her as she could no longer feel her body.

The human shadow, the man, with silver orbs for eyes, was in her line of sight. A crooked smile on his face.

"Stop fighting it," a deep baritone voice soothed in her mind. *"It should be over soon."*

She wanted to scream, beg him, whoever he was, to return her to her own body. To tell her why he was there and to plead for his help.

"Let the power have you. Give yourself over to it. Soon you will be my equal, and we shall finish what we started."

His shadowed hand moved in front of her, and she wished she could bite at it, the fury inside her bubbling over at the lack of control.

"Push through the pain, Phantom Queen. I am curious to see how much of you is left in that pathetic mortal shell. I want an equal in the battle ahead that leads to your final death."

The strange man smiled, and nothing hurt near as bad as the fire that tore through her at the snap of his fingers. The shadows swirled around her as black encroached on the edges of her vision.

The fire engulfed her until she lost consciousness.

Chapter 18

Groaning, Bryn rolled onto her back, her arm going over her eyes.

The realization was slow to come, but she was outside lying in a field. When had she ever fallen asleep outside?

The sun beat down on her, and she lifted her arm to shield her face, but she wasn't sweating. In fact, she was pleasantly cool, which was never something one felt in Ifreann.

Putting her elbows onto the soft ground, she pushed herself up to sit before she realized it was not sand she was on but grass. Looking out over the land around her in astonishment, she wondered at the beauty of a side of nature she'd never seen. At least not in the real world. She'd only ever seen lush green grass like this in the children's books she'd read as a child.

The vibrancy of the world around her held her frozen in awe.

Even Niamh's and Sage's places couldn't compete.

Trees, actual healthy trees! An entire forest of them surrounded her full of vibrant life. The colors of the world were so much more than the dull tans and browns she'd grown up with in Ifreann. Brighter and just absolutely beautiful. She wondered if she even knew the names of all the colors around her.

Standing, Bryn walked toward an open path in the trees, an instinct telling her to move down it, and she heeded the call. Nothing here felt dangerous like it did in her small world.

Stepping past the first line of trees, crows flew in and out of the branches overhead as she watched and took in the fluid avian dance. As they played, swooping above her, the sun gave way to the moon in mere minutes instead of hours, and the path beckoned her farther along.

As she walked, the moon tripled in the sky, before becoming one again. Curious, she still didn't feel fear as she thought maybe she should. Instead, it felt familiar.

If anything, she felt right at home here. This was all a dream, it had to be, but oh how she wished it were real. To have a vision of the future, knowing she'd be in such a place was more than she could conceive.

Howls called to the moon, and Bryn could see the shadows of wolves running through the trees on both sides of her. Between the wolves and crows keeping her attention, she stumbled as she walked into something, catching herself on a stone. No, not just a stone.

A headstone.

Strong wind gusts pushed her forward, and she stepped farther into the cemetery, something she'd never seen before since their dead were burned on the pyres. She hated that the Church of Baleros would never allow bodies to be buried or anything put in the ground to remind them of lost loved ones.

Death begets death.

Lies.

It just seemed so wrong to just forget their loved ones because the people of their town feared death so much.

Bryn was never allowed to speak of her father again to Mallory. Only in the dark of night when she had a nightmare, and Jace slept on her floor, did she speak of her father to another person.

Sensing something heading her way, almost like a beacon of power in the back of her mind, she tracked it until a horse, black as night, broke through the trees, making its way toward her.

A kinship with the animal pulsed through her before the large war-horse halted its canter at the gate of the cemetery. Snorting, it walked steadily over the hallowed ground, tossing its mane, and watching her with eyes of the purest black. No light reflected in the equine eyes.

Senan.

The name whispered to her, and she knew instinctively that this was her horse and that was its name. At least some former version of herself anyway.

"You return to us finally, my queen?"

Putting her hand to Senan's neck as the horse approached her, she noticed blue tattoos all over her arms and hands.

Taking her hand back from Senan's neck, earning a nip of agitation from the horse, Bryn turned her hands over, the blue markings running up and down both of her arms. The curves and twists were all symbols, but she had no idea what they meant. Intertwined rings and triangles . . . they had to mean something.

"Will you take back the mantle you were born for?" An echo of voices wove in the air around Bryn as a howl tore through the night, met by another.

A silver wolf broke through the tree line as it ran toward where she stood next to Senan. While not hostile in its demeanor at all, she held her breath.

Bryn held still while the silver wolf sniffed her before licking her hand playfully, its dark-brown eyes almost black looking up at her with an affection that caught her breath before it could leave her lungs. Her hands ran over its fur, and the wolf leaned against her in appreciation.

An affection was there with the wolf she wished she could take back to the waking world. He seemed to care for her even more than Finian.

Two ghostly figures in black cloaks, one short and one close to her height, approached her from the woods, and the silver wolf growled, putting itself between her and the figures. She pushed her fingers into the ruff at the back of its neck, trying to calm it, but the wolf stayed on high alert.

"Hello, Bryndis Kenneally," one woman said, her voice much older.

"No need for your guardian. We mean you no harm," the other one, a youthful voice, stated as the women pushed back their hoods. Before her stood an older version of herself and herself as a child of barely ten. Both of them looked at her with an intensity that made her palms sweat.

When she didn't answer their greeting in return, too awestruck to respond, they moved as one to her with outstretched hands. Their blue markings matched the ones on her own arms, line for line.

The silver wolf whined, and she gave it a scratch behind the ears before stepping forward and taking their extended hands in her own. To her shock, they pressed their thumbs into her flesh, breaking the skin, and blood beaded the surface.

The pain ignited as cold flooded her veins, her body freezing inside out. She tried to hold back the scream, more and more of her breath being stolen with each passing second of time as the puffs of visible air leaving her lungs grew smaller and smaller.

The silver wolf growled, snapping at them before Senan nipped at the wolf, making the wolf turn its annoyance on the horse.

Releasing her hands, the women stepped away from her, and she was able to catch her breath again.

Looking up at the two women, ready to curse them into oblivion, she froze as there was no longer two versions of herself lost in time, but where the crone had been a crow. Where the young version of her had stood was a wolf. It was the same wolf she had seen in her vision.

The one that killed Arioch.

Both animals were black as night and watching her with expectation, yet before she could make a move, the two animals became smoke and shadows, swirling around her as her eyes caught on Senan. The horse reared back giving an equine war cry that made Bryn's eardrums bleed. Her silver wolf friend turned to shadow as well before it wrapped itself around her body.

The shadows moved faster until they closed in on her completely, and all she could see and breathe was smoke.

The darkness took her back into the opaque oblivion she had awoken from only moments ago.

Chapter 19

As Bryn attempted to open her swollen eyes, she could see candlelight flickering on the wall of a room that was very much not her own.

Turning her head, Niamh sat in a chair next to the bed, déjà vu from only hours before.

"What . . . happened?" she asked, her throat feeling like someone had run sandpaper up and down it. *Again.*

"You keep passing out, and I will have sweaters for all of Ifreann knitted," Niamh responded.

"Well, that would be useless in the desert."

"Yes, so you are wasting my time with this nonsense. You took power from the stone by snorting it all up. Everyone else is out too aside from Travis and Caden, who were fit to be tied when you all hit the floor. Now Danu is proclaiming she did not intend for anyone to lose consciousness and went on about being separated for too long . . . Anyway, are you well enough to walk, darling?"

"That . . . was a lot," Bryn replied, blinking slowly at Niamh.

"Yes, this is all tedious. We spend years in boredom, and you notch it up to ten in a week. Let's get you to your feet so the old woman can settle her old bones."

Niamh stepped forward to take her hands, but before Bryn's sluggish mind could stop her, Niamh was pulling her to stand, only to release her just as quickly. Bryn fell back onto the bed, catching herself before she rolled off.

"Niamh!" she yelled, but Niamh was staring at her own hands before looking up at Bryn in shock. "What is wrong with you?"

"Nothing." Niamh shoved her hands into her skirt pockets and turned to the door. "I'll see you downstairs."

Without another word, Bryn watched her friend all but run from the room, closing the door behind her with a slam.

Laughter cut into Bryn's focus, and she turned.

The shadow man stood, leaning against the wall, his shadowy arms folded, but he was more of a man than he had been.

Scrambling to stand, wanting to be on an even playing field, she watched the man of shadows. He was still somewhat ghostly in his appearance, but she could see some of what he might have looked like if he'd ever been alive.

Tall, lean muscles, black hair that fell into his face. His eyes were light, but she couldn't tell if it was a light blue or the silver she'd seen in his shadow form from where they stood. His black shirt sleeves were rolled up, showing similar blue tattoos on his arms that she'd seen on her own in her dream. There were more across the top of his chest and some on his neck as well.

Raising one black eyebrow at her, he smirked.

"What the hell are you?" she growled, not liking the predatory way he looked at her.

"*Who. It's offensive to refer to me as a what.*" His voice was deep, smooth, and oh so very arrogant.

"*Who* the hell are you then?" she demanded.

"*Depends on who* you *decide to be to me, Phantom Queen. Should you choose to be my ally or my enemy.*"

"As much as you're endearing yourself to me in this moment, I am not thinking fond thoughts."

Was it possible to slap a shadow? The temptation was unreal.

The man tilted his head, and the black strands of hair fell across his forehead and into his eyes as a smirk crossed his lush lips. She was honest enough with herself to admit that the arrogant shadow man was a looker.

Pushing away from the wall to walk toward her, as if he had an actual physical body, his shadowy presence moved closer until he was right in front of her.

She looked up into his mercurial eyes and could see swirls of silver that moved with the light.

So, silver it was. Not blue.

Moving her eyes across his face to take in the whole of his features, her jaw dropped when she saw his ears. They were pointed, unlike her rounded ones.

"*While my memories are not whole, I do know a few things . . .*"

Reaching out to touch a strand of her curly auburn hair, he smirked. He wasn't able to actually touch her, but she could imagine him tugging on a curl and watching it bounce back into place.

"*. . . I've just woken up, so I am not from this time. My name is Kian, and . . .*" He smiled, his eyeteeth sharper than the rest.

"*. . . I know that you were the one who killed me.*"

A soft knock at the door had Bryn turning her head, but not her back, on the shadow man who had just dropped yet another bomb in her lap.

"Time to head back downstairs. Niamh said you were awake," Travis's deep voice rumbled through the door.

Panicked, she looked back to where the man named Kian had been, only he was no longer there.

Composing herself, she walked to the door, opening it to see Travis leaning against the frame, his rifle at his side.

"Sorry if I startled you," he said.

She must not have composed herself enough. Shaking her head, she smiled.

"Wasn't you, Travis. Sorry. It's been a rough couple of days." She whispered the last words of the sentence.

Catching her off guard, Travis pushed into the room, shutting the door behind him. Motioning Bryn to take a seat, he pulled a flask from his pocket, offering it to her.

"Take a minute to gather your wits about you. I'm sure the mother of all drama downstairs has more surprises loaded in the barrel."

Bryn took the flask with an appreciative smile, sipping it and coughing as fire lit up her mouth and throat. Handing it back to him, she struggled through the burning, the air pushing through her esophagus only reigniting the flames.

"What the hell do you drink, Travis?" She coughed, her face turning red as her eyes watered.

Placing it back inside his vest pocket, he smirked.

"Special make using some of the good stuff Declan sneaks in."

Wiping her tears, she laughed, though it hurt.

"You could strip paint with that."

"You actually can. Justin has used it a few times for some of his projects."

She laughed, but Travis hadn't been joking. If she woke up tomorrow coughing blood, she would haunt him after she died from blood loss.

Leaning back in his chair, rifle settled across his lap, he sighed.

"Shit will pile up for a good while, but you'll get a reprieve. The quiet times are never long enough, but it's enough to where you think you can manage to hang on just a little longer."

Bryn watched the man as he moved his jaw side to side. The urge to ask him what he meant, what caused the shadows in his eyes, was strong, but she wouldn't do that to him.

"I suppose it's why I keep to myself. I can't much handle people too close to me, knowing what I've had to do. The things I've been told were best for this town, only to find out it was the agenda of one and not the good of all."

Travis looked at her, his eyes cold, but she felt no threat coming from the man.

"This town will break a person. They're good at it here. Don't let them take that last spark I see in you. Watching you night after night, walking with your head up when this town wants you under its boot heel, well, it helped me to push through more than you could know on the really bad days."

"I never knew . . .," she whispered, but Travis just shook his head.

"Most don't, but I've seen the skeletons in your closet the past few days, so I decided to show you you're not alone. We may not be close, but I consider you a friend."

Emotion clogged her ravaged throat.

"You're a good friend, Travis," she whispered, another cough reigniting the flames in her chest.

"My apologies, Ms. Kenneally. I've yet to grasp the role of nursemaid." Giving her the cup of water from the bedside table nearest him, she took it, grateful as the water was cool enough to help her abused throat. His words finally penetrated her thoughts.

"Thank you. Is everyone else all right after . . . whatever that was down-stairs?"

"Well, they're recovering, but to be honest, they were far worse off than you. You're the first to wake up."

"Knock, knock." Caden opened the door before Bryn or Travis could answer, earning a scathing look from Travis.

"Look, I'd wait and be a gentleman, but I knew you were in here, so no one was naked. Since Justin is down, you're up. Gotta problem for ya."

At Caden's words, Travis stood, looking down on Bryn.

"I've got it," she said in answer to the silent question. Giving her a nod, Travis and Caden stepped out into the hallway, closing the door behind them.

Curiosity bloomed inside Bryn, so much like a young child, she leaned against the door to eavesdrop.

". . . yeah, which is inconvenient when we had a group of rovers turn up at the gate while Justin was horizontal dancing across the floor."

"More rovers? We've never had this many before. Are they still alive? Jace is down, so I am not sure how we can check for sickness when he is the only doc . . . and I ain't killing innocent people at the gate, Caden. Never again. Arioch fooled me when I was younger, but I've learned."

Bryn's hand went to her mouth at his words. That was what haunt-ed him. Arioch had him kill people at the gate. Instead of letting them through, he made Travis end their lives.

"I wouldn't let him ask that of you ever again, but no, not this time. Travis . . . it . . . the new guy, Callum, said it looked like a sacrifice. It is not pretty. Fancy dress, too, which makes us wonder who exactly is hanging out near town. No heartbeats, so no one to ask."

"Sacrifice?" Travis asked as confused as Bryn was. She understood the meaning of the word, but her brain could not correlate it to what he was saying.

"Dead. Eyes gone. Throats slit. Jewelry and goods were left on their person, dressed up like they were living in the king's palace. Same across each body. They had to have had their clothes changed after they were killed too . . . since . . ."

"No blood."

A shocked numbness crept over her as she settled back against the door, her heart stuttering. Squeezing her eyes shut, she tried to loosen the stunned thoughts stuck in her mind.

Yells from downstairs broke out, and the heavy footfalls of Travis and Caden told her they were already halfway down the stairs.

Rubbing at her tired eyes, she wondered if she should head down as well, though what she could do to help during a brawl was beyond her.

Irritation had her clenching her jaw. Irritation that she and her friends were in a position where everything was unknown, sacrifices were left on their doorstep, and a ghost told her that she was the one who had killed him. What this all meant, she'd been trying to figure out, stumbling along the way and still knew very little.

It was time for *all* the answers about her past to be brought to light, and she was going to get them.

One way or another.

Chapter 20

J ace was an ace at medicine. A man with a natural gift for healing that
surpassed even her father. His patients had always recovered, and the
townspeople had long ago started to refer to him as a miracle worker.

So it came as very little surprise when Bryn heard a conversation between
Danu and Jace as she stepped onto the last stair that his power was that of
healing.

"Dian Cecht was the name of your past self. He was a gifted healer to the
Tuatha Dé Danann," Danu explained. The clinking of a teacup hitting a
saucer followed her words.

"I am still . . . me, though, right?" he asked, his voice breaking Bryn's
heart. It reminded her so much of the little boy Jace had been after his own
father had died.

A lost little boy who tried to find himself, having no father of his own to
guide him, and trying as he did, her father wasn't *Jace's* father. A beloved
uncle, yes, very much so, but Jace needed his dad. Especially because his
mother was not the nurturing type, and while she treated Jace better than
Bryn, she wasn't exactly the type of mother to kiss his skinned knees.

"You are," Danu comforted him as Bryn peeked around the corner into the drawing room where they were talking. She watched Danu place a comforting hand on his shoulder in such a grandmotherly way it tightened her sore throat. "You carry the soul of Dian Cecht, you are him and he is you, only now you are called Jace instead."

If that was the case, Bryn was someone who embodied death while Jace embodied life.

Jace was a miracle worker bringing people back from the brink of death, while Bryn seemed to push them over. It fit, she could give the universe that much.

Placing her hand on the railing, she thought of the first time a vision had come after seeing her uncle's death. It was after they had moved to Ifreann. She had seen blood pouring from the person's mouth, and her younger self had woken from the fit screaming, thinking it was real.

It wasn't then, but days later, when she was with her father on his many errands during his day off, it had happened just as the vision had shown. A man murdered another man, right on the street, the old sheriff not as keen on keeping his streets lawful back then.

Bryn had only been six at the time and had been in the process of getting a hard candy from the shopkeeper. It took months for her to be able to even walk past the store again.

That was when the first whispers of her being weird had started. Not yet a witch, but perhaps cursed. They were laying the foundation for Arioch's accusations later.

Children at school heard from their parents about the "fit" the doctor's daughter had gone into. The things she'd said when the vision was over as her father worked to calm her.

It mostly was young children and their whispers, adults playing it off as children being cruel.

That was until Bryn took to working as a healer during the second round of sickness brought in from someone passing through the gate. Until she lost more patients than she could explain, the "fits" coming so often that her cousin worried about the health of her brain.

Word carried, as well as the stigma, into the homes of those families who lost someone until just like the disease, it spread through the whole community until she was ostracized for being different any time she was in public.

But it was Arioch that threw the last match on the pyre of her reputation.

Words carried to her before the footfalls on the wooden stairs.

"These bodies need to be put in the pyre sooner than later. Not any of ours, but they were left on the edge of our territory. Had been there long enough to draw the attention of scavengers. Last thing we need is those monsters moving in."

Bryn squeezed into an alcove next to the drawing room to avoid being noticed as Travis's voice carried from the entrance of the Sanctuary. He made his way toward the front door, Caden following him and holding the door open for his friend.

"Not a priority right now I would think with half our people down with whatever the hell the old lady did to them."

"Need to make it so. We have to figure out why they were left there. People have been screaming and hollering all day, and I am sick of it."

"A warning?"

"Who knows, but lucky for you, I saved you the paperwork." Bryn heard the hearty slap on someone's shoulder and decided to make her entrance into Jace and Danu's conversation in case the men came back instead of leaving and caught her eavesdropping.

She wasn't ready to work the pyre. Not when she wanted answers first.

"Hello, Bryndis. Tea?" Danu held up a cup, not even looking to see if it was in fact Bryn entering the drawing room.

Moving to sit in one of the lush chairs next to the couch Jace and Danu were seated on, she caught Niamh poking her head into the room, seeing who was all there before disappearing once again.

Oh, she would be asking her questions later as well.

"Now we have powers, correct? What do we do with them? You said we needed to fix everything before you died, right?" Bryn demanded as she faced the woman who had brought far too much trouble to her doorstep.

"One thing at a time, dear. Perhaps we should wait for the rest before we speak again?" Danu asked, taking a sip of her own tea.

Curling her fingers into fists on the arms of the chair, she growled at the older woman.

"I am tired of interruptions. I want answers."

Jace looked at Bryn before narrowing his eyes on Danu. While he was in the process of discussing his new persona, there was still what they needed to do with the newfound powers they had been forcefully bestowed.

Not to mention the shadow becoming a ghostly man with a vengeance. She would have to sleep with one eye open and hope he didn't become real enough to stick a knife in her.

"Fine. We have very little time, so I will cut to the heart of it. Everything that has happened here this day all comes down to how you can defeat the king and his Fomori brethren who roam this earth doing the king's bidding. The wraiths are some of them, and not even the worst. The Fomori rule now as you all once did, and until we put them back underneath from where they came, this world and I are doomed."

Both Jace and Bryn stayed silent as Danu talked about regicide like she was simply planning a dinner party. Before Bryn could ask if the woman was out of her mind, she caught on another word Danu had said.

"Fomori? How many new enemies will we continue to gain as we become the Tuatha Dé Danann? Should I start making a list?" Bryn asked, trying, and failing, to keep the snark from her tone.

Sighing, Danu put her cup on the saucer.

"The Fomori are from another realm. They are demons with chaotic magic. Their magic, while based in nature much like the Tuatha Dé Danann, can cause destruction. Therefore, the earth being abused by humans was a perfect opportunity for them to expand on that. Earthquakes, fires, horrid natural disasters that were not the fault of human's abuse alone."

Jace leaned back on the couch, his hands fisted in his lap, his eyes staring off into space as Danu continued on.

Bryn was unsure about Jace, but little shards of memories flashed at the edge of her consciousness as Danu spoke. Quick, but there, and Bryn knew it was the Morrigan's memories, not her own.

Before Bryn could ask for confirmation, Callum stepped into the room, taking his place at Danu's side as he placed a hand on her shoulder, giving her a bolt of power that perked the older woman up a bit.

"I am the goddess of earth, and while I have worked to maintain it enough to keep humanity alive, they are not able to undo the damage alone. Until the earth is healed, I grow weaker and will soon die a final death. I need my children to fight, to push the Fomori back into the realm they came from and bring us back to what we once were."

"Which was what exactly?" Declan asked as he walked into the drawing room with Kessler and Sage following him.

"Free to roam anywhere you pleased as the earth was suitable all over. Trees, plants, and life everywhere." The sadness as Danu spoke was catching, and Bryn felt herself fall into her own melancholy at what could have been. Of what *had* been.

"And these Fomori created this new world?" Sage asked, sitting in the chair next to where Jace sat on the couch. He immediately straightened up at her proximity.

Bryn wondered at the new tension in Jace, but if their nerves were as raw as hers were after inhaling magical stones, she was sure *every* sensation was amplified.

Danu nodded at Sage's question.

"So how do we use our magic stone powers to fix what they broke?" Declan asked, his eyebrow raised and the sardonic smile there in his beard.

"Slowly, your powers will return to what they were. Memories may as well, but I am unsure of how much you will remember from your original selves. Never have you all made it to adulthood at once, so I have never done this before and do not have all the answers you seek. For that, I am sorry. I am unable to guide you further in that regard."

"So, we will what? Just remember how to sword fight?" Declan laughed.

Everyone else might be fooled, but Bryn could read Declan more than most, and she knew he was faking. Something happened after the soul stones broke apart and gave them the powers that made him a believer. Perhaps a vision like she'd had.

"Yes."

Danu said nothing more than that as she let her eyes move over the people in the room before settling on Bryn's face.

"The lines you've all descended from are of my people, even without the powers of the Tuatha Dé Danann. You are descendants of the people of the isles from long ago."

Waiting, she held Bryn's eyes.

"You've forgotten your heritage. To know what you're capable of before the church told you what you are not."

Callum stepped forward, breaking the stare down between her and Danu before lowering his head with a small bow.

"I will be working with you all to try and push your memories to the surface as much as I can in the amount of time we have left," he stated.

"Time we have left? You mean before . . ." Bryn broke off, nodding to Danu hoping they picked up on what she was saying so she didn't need to be crass about it.

"Before the old lady kicks the bucket?" Declan tilted his head.

Well, so much for that. Sighing, she looked at Danu who wasn't the least bit offended, thankfully.

"Once you have remembered your powers, you must decide where you can make a stand against the king and the Fomori. While this place would be ideal as a location, no large water sources around, you must consider the people here and if you're willing to let them die as fodder in the war."

"No one dies unless they decide to put themselves in harm's way," Justin said as he walked in with Travis and Caden flanking him.

"Does everyone just listen right outside the door until they can make a grand entrance?" Jace muttered under his breath. Bryn and Sage looked at each other over him, a smile on their faces since that was exactly what they had both done.

"Bryn, we need you. The dead are not getting deader, but they are getting smellier, and it's attracting undesirables." Justin turned before she could nod, pointing to Travis. "You head out with her to help. There are too many, and it'll take too long to handle it herself."

"I will assist her in this endeavor," Callum offered, and Justin turned narrowed eyes on the man.

"Will you now, new guy? I am not sure how much I trust you running around my town when I still have no grasp on how you got in." Justin was not going to budge on this, Bryn knew it, but she wanted Callum to go.

He, like Danu, had answers. This would give her enough time to pick his brain without interruption.

"Oh, Justin, so much of Lugh and his need for justice has prevailed in you." Danu smiled, but Justin just cut her a look before settling his eyes back on Callum.

"She is the goddess of war. I do believe she can handle one man," Callum said with a calm expression, while Bryn wasn't sure she would have kept a straight face saying those words.

Everyone but Jace and Sage, who already knew, looked at her.

"War?" Declan said with disbelief, as if it made more sense for someone, anyone else, to be the goddess of such a thing.

Bryn couldn't argue with that. She was not the most violent, nor did she crave it. Confrontation? Nope, she broke into a cold sweat at the thought. Blood? Pass right on out, thank you.

She had about as much ability, mentally or physically, for war as an apple. *At least an apple could be used as a weapon*, she mused.

Justin shook his head as if trying to dislodge the thought.

"She is scared of blood," Declan blurted out, everyone in the room looking at him at his outburst.

"Perhaps"—Danu tilted her head as she looked at Declan— "she is not scared of blood but of herself. Some say those who were built for war, but never tasted it, knew once the blood flowed, their thirst would never be quenched."

Bryn hardly thought that was her problem as her stomach bottomed out at the thought of being near blood, much less bloodthirsty.

Something about Declan's resolve in this told her that he was nearing a point of no return in offending Danu, and she would not let that be the reason she lost her temper with Declan today.

"Callum can come with me. I am sure he will behave," Bryn offered, but Justin and Declan were unmoved.

"How do we know he won't do something to her out of our sight? I mean, hell, he damn near killed us with you here watching!" Declan yelled, his arm waving toward Callum as he stared at Justin.

Justin's eyes moved to Bryn's face as if taking her measure.

"I think Bryn can handle it with Callum helping. Everyone else is needed elsewhere. If there is an issue"—Justin looked at Declan before returning his eyes to her own— "you call, and I will have someone stationed nearby to help. I can't have them watching you, we lost too much in the storm and have to focus on saving what we can, but they will be close enough to help."

The last word was pointed at Travis, who nodded in affirmation that he would be the one to stand nearby as guard.

Declan was having none of it and moved to stand in her way of the door, the stubborn glint in his eye all too familiar to her.

"Bryn, I'll go with you." While it sounded like a demand, she knew him enough to hear the plea there. He was more concerned than anyone in the room about her being with Callum alone.

While some might think it sweet he cared so much, she found herself angry that he thought so little of her.

Goddess of war? He would never see it nor believe it if she gave in. *She* would never believe it if she constantly stepped aside for other people's wishes.

"Push past the fear. He may be a mountain of a man, but I've known you to move mountains if you so will it," she heard Danu say into her mind. Not looking at the older woman, she kept her focus on Declan as she lifted her chin.

"Move, Declan. I am a grown woman, and I can take care of myself."

Narrowing his eyes, she wasn't sure he would move. That he would make a scene, more of one anyway, but before she had to do more, he stepped aside, his jaw clenched.

Nodding, she stepped out into the hall, not looking back to see if Callum followed.

It felt like more than walking out to handle pyres.

It felt like the first step to owning her power.

Chapter 21

Pulling her gloves on, Bryn looked out over the bodies lined up in the sand near the pyres as Callum came to stand beside her.

"How do they know for certain they are sacrifices? How can one know that this wasn't a murder or threat?"

Yes, it was certainly a weird way to die, horrible if Bryn was being honest, but at least there wasn't any blood. She didn't need to say that was the only part of this she was thankful for. Blood was what would most likely topple her house of cards, and that house of cards was already far too unsteady.

"They are sacrifices." Callum pointed to the one closest to them, the coin over one eye. "They did not just fall over dead, bloodless and their bodies positioned in such a way as they were at the gate."

Turning her head, she looked at the man.

"What are you not telling me?" she demanded, gloved hands going to her hips as she stared at him.

"Long ago, the Fomori sacrificed humans like this to bring back the ancient ones of their religion."

Bryn turned to look at the bodies, the waxy pale pallor of their skin making the slice at their throats all the more obvious.

"So they were brought here to give the king a power up?" she asked, now knowing the Fomori and king were all related and working to keep hold of the powerful reign they had overseen for the last two hundred years.

Danu being here . . . the sudden sacrifices . . . it was all connected. The first domino had fallen.

"Who are they, Callum?" With those words, she realized no one had even bothered to find out who *he* was. His blue eyes glittered as if he could read the words on her mind. Pulling the hood down and allowing the sun to shine on his blond almost white hair, he looked so young.

Closing his eyes, he took in a deep breath as if he could smell anything but death around them.

"They are from Arthmael." His brows furrowed. She was going to ignore his need to scent them to figure out where they came from. Sometimes weird was too weird.

"Where?" Bryn asked. It wasn't like anyone traveled this new world to know where other cities and places were positioned. A person knew what was closest to them, and they stuck to their little spot in the dangerous new world.

"It is far north, near Cethin. Those are the two countries who continue to resist the king's reign. They are always at war with him."

Cethin. The name was familiar.

"They sound like intelligent people," she muttered, walking toward the first body as she wondered if that was near where she had come from. Sadly, she did not know the name of her own people.

"The king knows, doesn't he?" she asked, standing over the poor souls who had lost their lives for evil to continue to reign.

Callum stepped up next to her, and he knew exactly what she was asking.

"The moment the stones broke, you regained access to your powers. Those powers would have been that of a beacon, telling the king that you were all back."

Callum closed his eyes, taking another deep inhalation before he opened them again and continued.

"It is best you find a way to pull those memories on how to defend yourselves to the front of your mind quickly because the first tide of war is heading this way. The sacrifices will continue as well, the king hoping to bring his father back. His father is the one that sent you, the Tuatha Dé Danann, across the veil long ago."

There was so much to process, but still work had to be done. For the first time, Bryn was glad of it. She needed to decompress as much as the rest of them. After she'd had time to work through it, compartmentalize it all, she'd get with the others, and they could discuss their next steps.

It was quite obvious they couldn't continue on as they were, not with this much at stake. It was hard to argue that Danu was crazy and senile when the moving pieces of the puzzle of her life were forming a picture that lined up with everything the woman was telling them.

Walking to the first body, she stood over it, unsure of what prayer was to be said. Did she pray to herself? A stressed-out laugh bubbled up at the thought.

They had to have died near town since the bodies were not in a horrible state of decomposition. Were they traders nearby, and the Fomori found them?

A shadow fell over her, and she tilted her head to see Callum looking down at her.

"Allow me?" he asked.

She stood and offered him a pair of gloves, which he took with a puzzled look on his face.

Yeah, he was ten kinds of weird, but she wasn't going to be the one throwing stones. Nope, that was for the citizens of the city to do, sadly. She wondered if she could protect him from the people. If there was a way to keep him and Danu safe without hiding them away in the Sanctuary.

Moving to take the shoulders of the body, she froze as Callum carefully placed the gloves back on the ground next to Bryn, standing back and looking at the body.

"You have a tight hold on your powers, and they cannot fully return until you release them. There is a block, yet you will not open yourself to it. Why is that, Bryndis Kenneally?"

She'd had the powers for five whole minutes. How was she supposed to know how to "open" herself up to them?

"Not sure about a block. I don't know how to access these wonderful, brand-new shiny powers because I've had them for less than a day. Besides, how would you know?"

Callum lifted a hand toward the body at her feet, and Bryn gasped, stepping back as it started vibrating until it began to levitate.

Bryn turned again to see if anyone was nearby in a panic.

"Stop that! They will burn you alive for this!" she growled, almost tempted to throw herself over the body to hold it down. Callum ignored her, moving the body to the pyre before snapping his fingers and igniting the kindling.

Staring at the flames, she tried to school her expression as she turned back to Callum. There was a brewing terror under her skin from what she had just seen, and if anyone else might have seen it.

Wiping her sweaty palms on her drab-brown skirt, the movement doing nothing since she forgot she wore gloves, she could only stare at Callum as she waited for an explanation.

"I am a Druid, Bryn. I can sense magic, I can hold it in my hands, and I can control it with the elements around me. I also know our history, who we are. Who *you* are. When you are ready to push through the human block you have on both your powers and mind, I would be honored to assist you with the knowledge I have obtained from generations of our people."

They stared at each other, Callum calmly folding his hands in front of him as Bryn looked him over.

"Seen a lot of shit, huh, Druid?" Her voice wavered on the words, tripping over the curse. Her hands felt numb as she shook out her limbs in a nervous gesture.

Bryn moved to the next body before looking back at Callum, unsure of what to say.

A small smile pulled at his lips.

"Yes, I have been around a long time and, as you say, have seen a lot of . . . *shit.*"

"Hurt to say that didn't it?" She gave a nervous laugh but was beyond relief when Callum assisted her in a more human way, bringing the body to the fire with his hands instead of his magic.

As nice as it would have been for him to just wiggle his fingers and move them with his mind, it was far too dangerous. The pyres were right behind the church, and anyone could walk around and see them at any moment.

Working side by side with the Druid was actually relaxing. He was incredibly quiet, not saying much unless she asked a question, but the silence was a comfortable one. Aside from the words he had said earlier, she did not feel like he was expecting more of her. That he would allow her to come to him in her own time.

It was nice to not be pushed into something or have expectations she was sure she couldn't meet hanging over her for once.

Placing the second to last body on its own pyre board, Bryn folded their hands over their heart. Her mind going into the prayer she could say without thought, it was so instinctual.

The words . . . she evaluated them in her own mind while they pushed the board gently into the fire.

May you walk among the kin who've crossed before you, sadness at your back and light guiding your path. No pain. No fear. Only the never-ending feast of our ancestors."

How much of that prayer was something from lifetimes before? Something passed down from the very ancestors Callum spoke of.

"Callum, where do people go when they die?" she asked as she watched the flame take the shell of who the person was, hoping it released their essence in return.

"Across the veil, to the Otherworld, where the guardian of the dead, Arawn, awaits them."

Arawn. The name tickled her memory, almost like a word on the tip of someone's tongue . . . just out of reach, but there all the same.

"Then, they join in the warriors' feast with all those who passed on before them if they are worthy to participate in the celebration of life with the Tuatha Dé Danann."

That answered her earlier question. The prayer was from lifetimes ago, something her soul held on to, and that gave her some small bit of hope. Hope that she would recognize her power if she called on it.

She visualized the Morrigan saying the prayer over the people she found worthy before she moved across the veil, delivered to the guardian of the dead who would watch over them.

Bryn had a lot to learn, but knowing where the prayer came from, she felt her first sense of rightness since Danu had quite literally landed in their lives.

Turning back to the last body, she moved to take their legs, Callum deciding halfway through to take the heftier part of them as Jace usually did. Putting his hands under their arms, she placed her hands around the man's ankles. Though she touched his skin, she knew since he was dead and she wore gloves, it was safe to do so.

The deceased man's eyes opened, milky white, and his body jolted up to a sitting position. Turning his dead eyes to look at Bryn, she fell backward as she stared at the man in horror. This was nothing like the visions she'd had of the living on the brink of death. Nothing at all.

It was all very real and had happened while she'd been wearing her gloves. Those same gloves having been her only protection from visions until now.

"Glaoigh ar a mbás! Déan mar a gheall tú dár muintir!" the dead man yelled, his voice piercing her ears as she covered them, but it was to no avail since he was speaking into her mind. The man repeated the words until Bryn was in the fetal position, screaming for him to stop, squeezing her eyes shut to block out the noise and pain.

Hands pulled her back up to sitting, her vision wavering as Callum moved into her line of sight, his presence calming her.

He kept quiet as she kept her focus on him, and she imagined galaxies of stars in his eyes before he blinked, his eyes returning to the blue she recognized.

"You . . . Did you see that? That . . ." Bryn pointed to the very unmoving dead man that lay in the same position he had been before he came back to life.

"While it was a vision for you, I did feel your pain. I heard the soul's painful screams as well, though I could not see him as you did."

Flexing her fingers in the leather gloves, she calmed her breathing, Callum still touching her shoulder.

"Your powers will grow stronger. It is best to embrace them as they come and not fight against them."

Shaking her head, she pulled away from him.

"He was speaking, but I'd never heard that language . . . did you happen to hear what he said? Between all my screaming?" she asked, her cheeks flushed with embarrassment.

Callum nodded, helping her to stand.

"What did he say?" she asked, and Bryn already felt the chill in her bones before Callum said a word.

"'Call for their deaths. Do what you promised for our people.'"

Chapter 22

A hard hit to the door woke Bryn from where she had dozed off half dressed in bed, having come straight home after working the pyres, exhausted mentally and physically.

Groaning, she rolled over, but the knocking was relentless. A feather fell onto the pillow next to her head, and she sighed. Cyerra was molting so much Bryn was sure she was about to see what a naked crow looked like.

Yet the crow was never around when it was just the two of them anymore. As if she were avoiding answering the questions that she knew Bryn had.

Rubbing at her face, Bryn stood, her legs wobbly from just having woken up, which was why she would chastise herself later for opening the door without checking first.

The moment Bryn undid the lock, her aunt barreled in like a bull full of rage.

Before she could steel herself, her aunt was pinching her in the soft flesh under her arm, and Bryn wished she'd had a vision right then that told her that her aunt would not be her problem for much longer.

A gasp left her not just from the pain of the pinch, but as Mallory twisted the skin between her bony fingers.

"Explain to me—" her aunt seethed as she twisted the pinched flesh even harder, breaking skin, and Bryn felt blood dripping down her arm.

Bryn finally found the mental fortitude to pull herself from the shock of her aunt's abrupt appearance and ripped her arm away. Running her hand over the sore area, her fingers came away with quite a bit of blood. *Oh boy*, she thought as the nausea rose.

"—why is Arioch saying you are speaking to crows? Why are you *still* hanging around that sinful brothel during the day with that demon woman after I forbade it? Explain why my son was seen there as well!" Mallory yelled, her face mottled in rage as she moved in far too close to Bryn's face.

Mallory's clawed hand reached out to grab her arm again, her nails digging in. If Bryn tore her arm away this time, she'd have bloody claw marks, which would be more difficult to hide.

"You know better than to embarrass me with the company you keep. I am to be the wife of one of the most powerful men here, and choosing to make me an enemy is not in your best interest." Mallory's hot breath against her cheek did nothing to quell the chills running over Bryn's skin.

A seed of rebellion pulsed through her before it was lost again to the anxiety and fear Bryn felt when in the woman's presence. Even though she was an adult woman herself now, the memories of her childhood were far too close to the surface when her aunt was around to be able to push them back down so easily.

Mallory shook her as Bryn tried to form coherent enough thoughts to answer the raging woman.

Trying to pull her arm back without losing more skin, Bryn was stuck in a time when she was a younger version of herself, grieving her father and finding her tears were met with slaps to the face for crying.

She could never be adult Bryn in these situations, always reverting back to the time when she was helpless, and she was sure she would, just like before, cover the bruises and play it off when her friends asked.

"I was helping him with someone—"

"Don't lie to me!" Mallory yelled, her face so close that spittle hit Bryn's cheek. Shoving Bryn hard enough that she hit her back against the door, Bryn slid down it, thinking about rolling away.

As Mallory stood over her, memories of being kicked in the ribs and stomach overtook Bryn. Curling up into a ball, she covered her head and felt every ounce of bravery drain from her.

"I've allowed you to stay under this roof for the sake of my husband's brother. Now, your father is dead, and I owe him *nothing*."

Placing her hands on the ground to push up, Bryn bit her lip when Mallory stepped on her fingers, pushing down with her heels. A crack sounded, but Bryn wasn't dumb enough to cry out.

Mallory loved it when Bryn cried out, and it always made the torture last that much longer.

"Witches can be burned, dear Bryn. Remember that," Mallory warned before twisting her foot on Bryn's fingers.

Whipping open the door to hit Bryn in the shoulder, Mallory gave her one last kick before she walked out and slammed the door shut behind her.

Sitting up when all she wanted to do was collapse, Bryn sat back against the door, the tears in her eyes from both the physical pain and relief that it was over. Pulling her hand to her chest, she closed her eyes and worked to steady her rapid breathing.

"Why do you allow her to touch you in such a way?"

A laugh bubbled up in her throat as the tears trailed down her face.

Of course, Kian was watching that all happen. Probably enjoyed his killer getting her comeuppance.

"I've spent years trying to *not* let her touch me that way."

Judgmental prick of a shadow.

"With your powers back, your hand should be healed now," he whispered, and she wanted to lash out at him with her own brand of fury, angry that he had seen her at her lowest.

Looking at her fingers, flexing them, she realized they were in fact fine. Then, running her hand along her arm where the flesh had torn, she noted that the skin was smooth and unblemished.

Only her emotional wounds were still festering.

Laying her head back against the door, she attempted to ignore the shadow.

Bryn needed time to come back to herself after Mallory did things like that. While it wasn't the worst she'd done to Bryn, it never got easier to bounce back from.

Focus on breathing, Bryn.

In . . . out . . . in . . . out . . .

"Hard to believe someone like you killed someone like me."

Opening her eyes again, she was startled to see him sitting on the floor next to her with his knee up, his elbow on it, and his hand hanging down as he watched her with a mix of curiosity and some sadness.

It was the sadness that pissed her off.

"Sorry to disappoint. Seems if I am that pathetic, how much more so were *you* to be killed by someone like me? Not sure who should be offended here."

A laugh startled her. His eyes held mirth, and she had to hold her breath. He was heartbreakingly gorgeous . . . *for an asshole*, she reminded herself.

"Touché."

"How did you die?" she asked, watching him.

"You mean how did you kill me? That I cannot remember."

"You hardly seem upset about it."

His eyes flickered over her as he stayed quiet, his face pensive as if he were thinking about how to answer.

"Perhaps I feel like that was not the end of my story, and soon I will have my vengeance."

Okay, it was subject-change time. Bryn did not feel like discussing what exactly he had in mind for his vengeance. She looked at his blue tattoos and remembered her own from the vision she'd had.

"Those tattoos . . .," she whispered, moving to touch his skin, her fingers hovering above his arm.

His eyebrows went up as he put his arm out for her to see.

Bryn touched the cold air where his arm would have been had he been a man made of flesh and blood.

"You've seen them before?" he asked, no inflection in his words to give her an idea as to what he was thinking.

"In a vision . . . I had them too. They were all over my arms."

"What else did you see, Bryn?"

Settling on her knees, she tried to recall all she could remember.

"There was a horse called Senan . . ." She stopped as her brain caught up with her mouth.

She shouldn't be telling him this. Perhaps she had killed him because he was in fact a Fomori, like Cyerra had said.

That would make him her enemy, and if they were enemies, she needed to rethink what she said to him. Bryn also needed to figure out how to know when he was skulking around so that he didn't learn any valuable secrets about her or her friends.

Kian made a carry-on gesture, but she bit her lip. Raising an eyebrow, he smirked.

"She learns."

"You said we could be enemies or allies, but I am not sure where you fall. Who were you that I would have killed you?" she asked, wanting him to say the words. To verify her suspicions.

Looking away from her, he closed his eyes but said nothing.

"Was it that bad?" she asked, feeling an apology on the tip of her tongue and then the ridiculousness of such a thought. It would hardly make him any less dead.

"Like I said, I can't remember. I just know you killed me, and now I am tied to my killer in death. Whether it was against my will or not, I do not know."

Fantastic.

"Have you gained any new memories since you woke up?"

His silver eyes grew unfocused as he recalled his past.

"I was raised not by my parents, yet I know somehow they were alive. The same as I knew I hated my father. Those emotions I can feel deeply, but alas, they hold no specific memories for me." Shaking his head, he looked at her.

"I was also a master archer and had many interested women should I have chosen them for my bed." He smirked.

"So sorry I took such a stud from the world." She stood, rolling her eyes.

"As you should be. I am sure many of the women wasted away in grief."

She snorted, then in embarrassment, turned away, pushing her hair behind her ear as she focused on where Cyerra usually nested down. Where was the crow when she could use a distraction?

"Your ears . . . they are human . . ." Kian stared at her just as she had when she first saw his pointed ears.

"Yeah, I am human." Crossing her arms, she stared at Kian, feeling vulnerability at admitting that but not knowing why.

Kian straightened, his face stoic once more as he swallowed, his Adam's apple bobbing.

"Stop letting the human woman hurt you. Figure out who you are so I can know if I should return the favor of your death."

And on those encouraging words, he swirled into shadows, disappearing.

Bryn knew it was a threat, but something bothered him at seeing his killer tormented. Perhaps he wanted the honor all to himself.

But something deep, deep down inside her said he wouldn't actually hurt her.

No matter who she turned out to be.

Chapter 23

The sound of footsteps coming up the clinic stairs broke Bryn from the book she was trying, and failing, to lose herself in. An attempt to calm down after Mallory's visit, knowing it had been long enough that Mallory had moved onto something else and was not coming back for an encore.

Focusing on the cadence of the steps, she knew whoever this was, it was not someone she was familiar with. She had learned the sound of her aunt's footsteps long ago in a sense of self-preservation.

Snapping the book closed as she jumped off her bed, her pulse thrumming, she walked quietly to her door.

Carefully turning the knob to where it made no noise, she made sure to only pull it open a crack so she could see who it was before she announced herself.

"I am so glad you could come, Scrios. Daran and I . . ." The words trailed off as Arioch walked into Mallory's apartment, closing the door behind him.

Panic held Bryn tightly by the throat. She knew instinctively they were talking about her, and the possibility of the three of them deciding to do something extreme, that they were colluding, did not bode well for her future in Ifreann. Especially after Mallory's intrusion and subsequent freak-out earlier.

Stepping into the hallway, careful to stick to the wood she knew wouldn't creak, something she learned as a fearful youth trying to avoid Mallory's wrath, she closed in on her aunt's door to listen.

"Bryn!" Jace yelled from the other stairwell coming up from inside the clinic, and the thought of throttling him hit the forefront of her mind, right after the jolt of panic. Spinning, she placed her finger to her lips as she quickly moved over the stable pieces of wood back toward her door.

"Mr. Rafferty called a meeting. Let's go." He ignored her obvious determination to remain quiet, and without waiting on her, he turned and ran back down the stairs.

Bryn quickly followed, hearing Mallory's door open as they left and breathing a sigh of relief she hadn't been caught. Far too close of a call. Another second and she would have been fending off another enraged session of torment courtesy of her aunt.

Scrambling behind Jace, they ran to the Sanctuary, making their way back to the very drawing room that was quickly becoming less of a refuge for Bryn and more of a reminder that her life was vastly different from only days ago.

Danu sat with everyone as before, but Bryn could feel the difference under her skin as she stepped past the threshold. There was a pulse of energy in the room, and it was coming from different sources.

Coming up behind her, Mr. Rafferty placed a hand on her shoulder, ignoring her squeak of surprise as he leaned down to whisper into her ear.

"Once we are done here, no matter how this goes, we still need to work on what the dead man said."

With a squeeze of his hand at the words, she looked to Callum, who gave a nod. So, they had discussed the vision out in front of the pyres without her. Agitation thrummed under her skin at being excluded from the conversation, but she let it go . . . for now.

Moving to a vacant seat, she watched Declan's eyes, full of rage, as they followed his father across the room.

Ignoring the impulse to go to him, ask what was wrong and offer her support, she was happy when Danu took the lead and pulled everyone's focus to her.

"Now, we can get down to business. I hate that I have to give you such a narrow timeline on all of this, but the Fomori have never bothered to work with us on anything." Danu took Callum's hand as he moved to stand beside her. "As Bryn now knows, Callum is a Druid, and it's his power that sustains me as I try to continue feeding the earth. Without him, I would have died long ago."

"So the Tuatha Dé Danann have powers based in nature?" Sage asked, her fingers tapping out a rhythm on the arm of the couch.

"Without the Tuatha Dé Danann, nature and life itself cannot thrive. The fall of the Tuatha Dé Danann over two hundred years ago is why the earth is as it is now. Each of you held a power that worked in tandem to keep the balance. A balance that the Fomori threw into chaos and now the earth has no strength to continue."

A collective breath was released. They were going to get answers so they could move forward and slip into their new roles. She looked to Niamh, but the woman wouldn't look back at her, instead cleaning under her nails. Her focus completely engulfed in the task.

"We each have a role you said, so I am Dian Cecht, the healer of this group," Jace started, placing his hand to his chest before pointing to Declan. "You claim he is Dagda . . . who is . . . ?"

"Oh, his outburst confirmed he is in fact Dagda." Danu smiled at Declan, his face continuing to remain a scowl. Ignoring his attitude, she continued. "A very Dagda way to handle it. I am glad to see some personality still shined through without your powers in play, but to answer your question, he is the leader of the Tuatha Dé Danann and has power over the natural order of life. He is most likely what kept this town from dying from starvation," Danu replied, adding on to what she had started explaining before.

Bryn thought of the seeds the farmers swore were magic and his ability to trade. It all made sense now.

"Then there is Arawn, the opposite to Dagda, who watches over the dead. The Otherworld is his domain. In some stories, he is call Donn, others he is called Manannán," Danu stated.

"Then the man claiming to be my father swoops in and takes the dead to his home away from home?" Declan sneered at Mr. Rafferty.

Bryn's head snapped up to look toward where Mr. Rafferty stood with his arms folded near the door, his eyes narrowed on his son. He didn't deny it.

Arawn was Mr. Rafferty. Here this whole time, and yet he said nothing to them about who he really was.

"As you all now know, our dearest Bryn calls for death as the Morrigan and walks the battlefield for worthy souls before she brings them to Arawn to care for," Danu continued, ignoring Declan's outburst, but he wasn't one to be ignored when in a temper.

"He knew who he was this whole time and never said a word!" Declan slammed his fist into the wall, creating a hole in the plaster and ignoring the ire in Niamh's glare.

"Declan—"

"Nope! No more lies. How could you pretend to be one of us?" Declan was hurt by more than the omission, and Bryn realized that not only had Declan learned he was someone else, but he also realized his father was too.

Her heart skipped a pained beat for the man she had spent so many years loving.

Standing, she moved to take his hand in her own and gave him a reassuring squeeze. The look he gave her shimmered with tears before he blinked them away and refocused on the man in question.

"I am your father, Declan. Maybe not by blood, but I've cared for you all the same." Mr. Rafferty's gaze held Declan's, a change in the normal self-assured politician as his eyes begged for forgiveness.

Letting go of her hand, Declan spun away from them and left the room, slamming the front door to the Sanctuary.

"Give him time. He has always been a bit hotheaded." Danu waved away where he had left.

"Who am I? I looked through all my books . . .," Sage asked with a curiosity that was beating at the walls of her words. Bryn gave her friend a look of thanks for taking the heat off Declan.

"You, Sage, are wisdom. You hold so much of it inside yourself and desire more. You can heal with herbs in a way others cannot, correct?" Sage nodded at the words, her fingers rubbing together in a nervous gesture. "You protect mothers, you bring life into the world. You are Brigid."

Bryn could already see Sage making a mental note to look into Brigid the moment they left.

Turning from Sage, Danu took in the large, quiet man in the corner.

"Kessler, my dear Goibiu, you are a miracle at bringing to life the inanimate. Your smithing skills are something I've long thought a true blessing."

Kessler simply grunted as Danu faced Justin. Bryn could tell Kessler was still skeptical of everything, but Bryn could understand that. He didn't have a crow and shadow man speaking into his mind or leaving feathers all over his room.

"You are my golden one. My Lugh, bringing us justice."

"Guess I picked the right line of work then, ma'am."

Danu's face lit up, and Bryn swore she could see the woman's skin illuminate, a shimmer of who she once was lighting her up from within.

"So, two hundred years later, we finally made it across the veil again to fight the Fomori?" Jace asked.

"Oh"—Danu shook her head— "several versions of yourselves have been born. Each time, I hid you all the best I could so that Bres would not find you. Getting you to the age that you could take back your powers has been difficult since every one of you needs to be in the fight for the natural balance to be sustained, but every time in the past, one or more of you has never made it to adulthood. Bres would hunt you all and kill you the moment he laid eyes on you.

"This is the first time he hasn't, but now that you have your powers, he knows you've awakened. Finally, you are all here, alive and well, which I am extremely thankful for because this is our last chance. I will not survive another lifetime waiting for you all."

"We live, get our powers, and are ready to fight? Why couldn't we fight them before instead of getting exiled from the world?" Justin asked.

"That, my dear children, is a question I have yet to figure out. They are darkness where you are light, but that was not enough in the past, when you had greater strength due to earth breathing life into your powers. Now, we must figure out how to fight demons in a hell of their own making."

Chapter 24

Bryn ran after Sage, the woman taking off at a tear.

The moment Danu had told them about the demons they were up against, Sage was on the move. It was going to surely be an underdog story for the ages . . . if they lived.

If there was a way to have knowledge at their fingertips like their ancestors, Bryn would find a way to get that for Sage just to keep the hummingbird of a woman in one place for more than a minute.

"Sage, wait!" she yelled, following her through the alleyways of the buildings as her friend didn't bother to slow down.

Making her way to the cottage, Sage disappeared inside but left the door open behind her for Bryn.

Footsteps thudded behind them, and Bryn knew they'd have company soon, she just hoped it was company that wouldn't bring pitchforks and torches.

As Bryn broke through the doorway, Sage's focus was already completely on the shelves of books in her home.

Turning back to the footsteps following them, Bryn stood guard and relief ran through her as Jace and Justin ran into the cottage. Kessler sauntered in at his own pace, tipping an imaginary hat to Bryn as he moved past her. Closing the door behind them, the room not large enough to hold three large men, she was barely able to maneuver her way through to Sage.

Unfortunately, there was a lot of skin contact, but she was relieved when no visions came. Her friends were not going to die anytime soon, and that was the only balm for her confused state of mind.

No shocks either, which she found curious but decided to focus on what was at hand.

"Here!" Sage put the book on the table. "The Fomorians, or Fomori. Celtic mythology. They were demons who rose from the sea to fight the Tuatha Dé Danann and lost. They were then forced back underground."

"It doesn't seem like we won at all," Jace whispered as he looked around the room. "Obviously they came back with a vengeance."

"They had the opportunity to since our ancestors destroyed the world for their descendants," Kessler murmured from his place along the wall.

"The king is Fomori himself, which means we have to kill him to end it all . . ." Jace worked out, as if saying the words aloud would make more sense than they did in his head.

"Sure, that sounds easy." Justin laughed, crossing his arms as he shook his head. "This is all a joke. We have an old lady running our minds in circles and trying to get us to commit regicide."

Killing the king did sound like a terrible idea, and like her friends, Bryn was rethinking this whole thing now that they were no longer face-to-face with Danu.

What evidence did they actually have that Danu was who she said she was? There was nothing to prove who the bad guys were. They would hardly wear nametags proclaiming them the enemy.

Perhaps all the happenings that Bryn took as proof of Danu's theory was just Bryn going deeper into madness. It certainly made a lot more sense.

Sage stopped pacing, holding a book. She turned a page, then turned back again with a hitch in her breath. Her fingers went to her lips, her mouth forming a soft *O* at whatever she had just read.

"I . . ." No more words came forward as her body went so still Bryn wondered if she still breathed. Sage was a living statue as Jace moved toward her.

"What is it, Sage?" he asked, taking the book gently from her hands, her head moving up and her eyes meeting Jace's. Something in Sage's eyes said she was terrified, as if pleading for him to read it, to tell her that what she had just read was wrong.

Giving her a pat of reassurance on the shoulder, Jace looked down at the book, his eyebrows furrowing as his eyes moved over the page, then to the top as he bit his lip, his breath quickening. Turning the page, his face went slack.

"No . . . no . . .," he whispered as he turned the page back and forth just as Sage had. The book fell from his fingers, and he made no attempt to grab it again. It was a testament to how shocked Sage was that she didn't bristle at the mishandling of her precious tome.

Justin grabbed the book, looking for the passage that had Jace and Sage wound up. His fingers skimming through, turning page after page, while Bryn worked to calm Sage, who was now breathing far too quickly, as Jace started to pace.

"Oh, holy shit fire," Justin muttered, another curse leaving his lips as Jace flew into a panic as if Justin's words were a starting pistol, before grabbing the book and running outside.

Bryn immediately ran after him, hearing Justin order Kessler and Sage to stay put.

Jace was moving toward the chapel, which was thankfully empty as he fell against the doors, all but falling into the building.

Finally slowing his steps, he made his way to the altar and stopped in the middle of the aisle as he looked up at the painting of Balor. Bryn took a look around, having not stepped into the place since she was a teenager. Nothing had changed, which made this all so much worse somehow.

Moving to stand next to Jace, she grabbed his shirt to keep him from running off again before she stepped around to face him. Her heart broke to see tears streaming down his cheeks.

On a sob, he dropped to his knees as if begging forgiveness, but not to the Church of Baleros. No, he was kneeling in front of her.

"What is wrong?" she asked, kneeling next to him as Justin ran into the church, turning to secure the doors only to find Sage and Kessler following him in, and Declan too. He must have seen the chaos of them chasing Jace and came to investigate.

Each of them made sure the door was shut, keeping an eye out through the windows. Keeping them safe while the world fell apart around them. She was never more thankful for her friends than right then.

Without a word, Jace turned the book to her, his finger on a passage.

The drawing of the leader of the Fomori, the one who had led the campaign against the Tuatha Dé Danann long ago, looked back at her with a smile that sent a cold chill down her spine.

Shoving to stand up, taking the book from Jace, she turned to the altar where the scrios stood twice a day to save his town from the sin that was people like Bryn. Her eyes moved between the picture in the book and the painting in disbelief.

The man with the dark hair and pale skin . . . the scar across one eye.

The greatest enemy to the Tuatha Dé Danann was Evil Eye, his true name . . .

Balor. Baleros.

Their greatest enemy was the god the people of Ifreann worshipped.

It all made sense in such a sick and twisted way, she wished she could laugh. Instead, she held back a scream, her body vibrating.

"How is it possible?" Declan asked as he looked over her shoulder at the book. At the damning photo.

"This whole fucking time!" Jace yelled, standing, pulling at the seat cushions, and throwing them at the altar. Grabbing sacraments to the town's god and throwing them down, breaking them.

Justin ran up, grabbing Jace by the arms, telling him to calm down, but Jace was wild with anger. Absolutely feral in his movements as he swung at the lawman. Justin managed to get his arms around Jace, being larger than her cousin working in his favor.

"Get something to knock him out with!" Declan yelled, Sage taking that as an order directed at her as she slipped out the chapel doors.

"Jace . . .," Bryn whispered, reaching out as her heart tore in two at the sight of her calm and easygoing cousin losing his mind.

"I guess we know now where we stand, Phantom Queen."

Not taking her eyes off Jace, she could see Kian moving into the corner of the room from her peripheral vision, looking up at the picture of the god on the wall above the altar.

Sage ran back in with a needle, jabbing it into Jace's neck, making Bryn flinch.

"Take him to the Sanctuary," Declan ordered as Justin faltered at the sudden stillness of Jace as he went unconscious. Kessler moved to help him. "Make sure no one sees him."

Turning, they followed Justin out with Jace, except for Bryn, who stepped forward to see what Kian meant when he claimed he knew where they stood.

"Who is he to you, Kian?" she asked, her hands shaking at her sides.

"The man who sent me to kill you before you killed me yourself."

Her eyes met his silver ones in the low light of the church.

"I'll ask again. Who is he to you?" she demanded.

Giving her a small smirk, he crossed his own arms, and she felt some part of her lose the small hope she'd had. The hope that perhaps they could be more than enemies, that maybe he was safe in a way she couldn't understand. That maybe she hadn't been the one to kill him since he couldn't remember.

"He is my king."

And with that, any lingering hope she held was crushed at his words.

Kian was in fact Fomori as Cyerra had said.

Bryn stared at the man who was nothing more than an enemy to her now.

"If you manage to come back somehow, I will end you again," she vowed.

"I can hardly wait for you to try." He smiled, disappearing into the shadows once again.

Chapter 25

B ryn settled in a chair beside Jace's bed. Pushing a strand of hair out of his face, she knew he was out for the count since he didn't flinch. He was also drooling quite a bit, and Bryn was never more irritated at the lack of photographic equipment in their lives. This would have been a wonderful form of blackmail for later.

"He will be out for a while . . .," Niamh whispered as she looked in the door, checking on Jace and still not making eye contact with Bryn.

"What did I do wrong, Niamh?" Bryn asked, looking at her cousin since she found herself unable to look at Niamh either.

Niamh, who had been a friend and confidante for so much of Bryn's life, found out who she was and now couldn't even look at Bryn.

"What do you mean?" Niamh asked, stepping into the room, the anxiety in the air unmistakable

"You fear me now," Bryn stated what had been obvious all along, and yet she'd ignored it, refusing to believe anything could hurt their friendship after all they'd been through. The two women the town hated and feared had once stood together to face the world, and now they couldn't be further apart.

"I . . . do."

Bryn closed her eyes at the admission, trying to hold the tears back.

"But not because of anything you did. When I touched your skin . . . it triggered my geas as if I had said the damning words myself," Niamh admitted. "It hurt, and I panicked, unsure what to say to you since I couldn't explain without further triggering it . . . and"—Niamh took a slow, deep breath— "because I worry that when it all comes out, when the geas is gone and I can finally tell you everything, you'll hate me."

Bryn opened her eyes and turned to look at her friend. A woman stood before her, but it was not the Niamh she had known. Not the lively fire starter who did not care a wink what anyone else in this town thought.

No, this was a woman terrified that what Bryn was becoming would mean the end. That when her own secrets spilled, it would be enough to push Bryn away.

"I will love you always, Niamh. You've been the truest friend I've had." It was a promise Bryn would keep. There was nothing in this world that would change her love for Niamh.

"I do hope you'll always feel that way." Niamh opened the door the rest of the way.

Her thoughts went to the Founder's Day Festival, and Bryn started to put two and two together.

"It has to do with Declan, doesn't it?" Bryn asked, wondering what could have happened to make Niamh give him such a murderous look.

Niamh closed her eyes, her knuckles going white as she squeezed them tightly.

Bryn wet her lips, her body tense as she prepared to ask a question she really didn't want to know the answer to but felt compelled to ask anyway.

"Niamh, did you ...?" Bryn couldn't finish the words. They hurt far too much.

Niamh's eyes popped open in horrified shock.

"Gods no! I have done nothing with him. I may have crossed some lines, but that is not one I ever will. Plus ... my tastes do not go that general direction ..." Niamh let that statement hang in the air, as if awaiting judgment.

Ah. Right. Bryn remembered her true love had been a woman from when Niamh had told her of her past. How had she never known Niamh liked women?

"Get that look off your face," Bryn chastised. "I hope that's not the secret you think will make me hate you because I didn't think you'd ever think so low of me."

"No." Niamh sighed, and Bryn watched a weight lift from her shoulders. "That's my own secret. No, what worries me about you hating me is a secret that's not my own, but I cannot tell thanks to the geas. Which means I cannot tell you until the truth comes to light on its own. If I could, you can guarantee I'd spill everything in a heartbeat."

Bryn did know that, could tell it was true, so she nodded to her friend.

Niamh smiled, reaching for Bryn, but stopping since she knew Bryn hated to be touched.

Without a second thought, Bryn stood up and walked to Niamh, pulling her into a hug.

Unused to reaching for another person, to give affection, she pushed aside her own fear. Her friend needed comfort, and so Bryn would give it.

The two people she thought of as her siblings, who meant so much to her, were in this room. The two people she would fight any demons, including her own, to protect.

Stepping back, Niamh moved the hair that had escaped Bryn's ponytail back over her ear. "You should get some rest, darling. He will be out until the sun rises."

Niamh left quietly after her words, letting the door click shut and leaving Bryn to the quiet of the room and her own thoughts.

Yes, Bryn needed rest, her world was spinning out of control, and she was having a hard time hanging on to herself.

Instead, Bryn moved to look out the window onto the street below. People were hesitant to leave their homes since the storm, but some still worked on the small community farm. She watched as they made their way down Saints' Road, the last of what was left of the crops in tow.

While most of their food was brought in from outside, the import and export of needed items controlled by the king, Ifreann never had to go without like she'd heard Tanwen had.

As if the very reason for their abundance was summoned, a flash of auburn hair caught her eye, and she watched Declan walking into the Cauldron with his massive shoulders bowed. Declan had been dealt even more upheaval than anyone else in town. Finding out his father was not who he thought he was, Bryn could feel for the man even after he'd hurt her.

Checking on Jace one more time, she made her way to the Cauldron. An odd feeling after she'd worked so hard to avoid it since their last conversation, or fight, where they had broken up.

Stepping into the large trading post, several of the men Declan had hired as personal security watched her with narrowed eyes. The suspicion had always been evident even when she had been dating Declan. Thankfully, they did not stop her as she made her way upstairs to Declan's apartment above his office.

She never visualized she'd be back in the Cauldron after the day she had walked out of his life.

Tapping lightly on his door, she questioned her judgment in coming here. The conversation was bound to lead to the end of their relationship, but perhaps it was better to stop ignoring it so they could have closure and move on.

They had enough to deal with, especially without adding old drama to it.

"Not in the mood, Mikey," Declan growled from the other side of the door, and Bryn remembered Mikey was one of the traders from downstairs. She had liked Mikey. Maybe he hadn't been outright nice to her, but he hadn't spat at her feet either.

"It's not Mikey, Dec," she replied, and heard quick footsteps before the door swung open, Declan looking down at her in shock and disbelief. She had promised not to return and had managed to do so until today.

Waiting for him to move out of the way and let her in, she wondered if she was even welcome. She'd said so many harsh words due to the pain of finding him cuddled up to another woman downstairs in his office.

"I just wanted to check on you," she stated, stepping back after the beat of silence had gone from awkward to weird. Why had she thought this was a good idea again?

"Wait!" He stepped forward, holding his hand out for her. "Please come in. I just, I am shocked to see you here, but I am happy as well."

Biting her lip, she placed her hand in his and followed him in.

Nothing had changed. The dresser she'd used when she'd been slowly moving in with him was still there, her belongings in the same spot as before. It was as if he were sure they'd take back up where they left off or scared they wouldn't and couldn't remove the items as the last piece of her in his space.

For a whole year, they'd had a life together here where Bryn had felt truly safe for the first time. The room represented a year of shelter from her aunt.

Then she had been betrayed and left, moving back into her apartment even though that meant dealing with her aunt since there were no open rooms at the Sanctuary, and Bryn refused to displace one of the girls.

Thankfully, Mallory had started her courtship with Daran and was not home much anymore as they prepared for the wedding and worked at the church. It kept her aunt busy enough to where Bryn could slip in and out without running into the woman.

Feeling worthless and rejected, she'd thought she deserved him cheating. Just as she thought she deserved the abuse. She always thought being happy in her mind meant another shoe would drop. That there would be punishment for every smile.

"Stop it, Bryn. None of that . . ." He ran his hand down his face and over the scruff of his jaw. "I let my guard down, and she snuck in. Nothing would have happened, and had you come in seconds later, I would have broken off the kiss."

She'd heard the words before, refused to believe it then, and had a hard time even now believing them.

Bryn never let him get past those words. Never let him explain that day, unsure if it would change her stance, if she'd be a fool and fall back into his bed so it could happen all over again.

Her trust was such a fragile thing, and he had broken it that day.

"I am sorry everything went so wrong," she responded, sitting on his bed. Taking a seat next to her, he took her smaller hand in his much larger one.

"Me too. Everything is even worse now, but even if we are not romantically together, I still care for you, Brynnie."

Closing her eyes, she laid her head on his shoulder, breathing him in. Even his recent cigar didn't hinder all that was Declan. The hint of tobacco only added to his rich male scent.

It was comforting, and right now, she really needed that, even if there were consequences later, which with Declan was very possible.

Looking up at Declan, his whiskey-colored eyes met her own. His holding so much love for her, her throat felt tight, but not with love in return, fear.

Fear that he would say *the* words, that it was all a mistake and what they had was real. She didn't dare chance opening her heart up to him again.

"Bryn, I still lo—"

Panic flooded her, and she cut him off with a kiss. A simple press of her lips to his to stop the exact words she did not want to hear. Letting herself have a moment to remember the feel of his lips, chapped from the sun and sand, against hers since she knew it would be the last time.

Gathering her strength, she pulled away only to find herself staring into his wide eyes, which were shocked at her behavior.

She'd come to comfort him but threw herself at him instead. A complete turnaround to when they were together before, and he was always the one making the first move. Her fear of touch kept her from doing so.

The way his jaw tightened, his open hand moving along her lower back until it curled around her hip, pulling her closer, she thought perhaps words were not in fact what was needed. Perhaps, just this once, she could use her body as a comfort, both of them familiar with each other in that way.

Bryn was never great with words anyway.

Declan framed her face with his hands as he brought her mouth back to his, pushing the kiss farther, his tongue running along the seam of her lips until she opened for him.

Like a man starved, he took her mouth, his tongue emulating what she grew hungry for him to do to her body with his own.

Something in her broke, and all the pain and anger she had reverted to in order to protect herself, the armor she'd created, was gone.

Some version of her that was older than the town, some ancient feminine feral part of her took over, pushing Bryn backward in her own mind.

As she moved herself around to where she sat on his lap, a small grunt of surprise left his lips as she tugged at his hair and deepened the kiss further. His large hands engulfed her waist, and she couldn't help herself any longer as she bit his lip, the coppery taste of blood barely registering in her mind.

Something in Bryn knew the blood should bother her, yet she rubbed her center against him as he groaned into her mouth before pulling his lips from hers, his panting breaths sending the smell of tobacco into the air around her.

"You sure you want this, Brynnie?" he asked, his voice thick with lust as he moved to lay gentle kisses along her neck, a growl leaving her at how delicate he was being with her, treating her like glass that could break.

Without a word, she pulled away, her fingers moving to the top button of her shirt, his eyes watching her hands intently as she undid the buttons one by one. Something primal in her loved the fact that nothing could take his focus from her unveiling inch after inch of skin. The absolute power she felt flooded her system.

His hands covered hers as he began kissing her neck, down her now-exposed chest, and continued lower with each undone button. Her head fell back, reveling in the feeling of his lips on her skin again.

"Say it, love," he murmured between kisses as he slowly moved farther down her neck and chest, pulling her shirt down her arms and throwing it to the floor. His hands moved quickly to unhook her bra as he moved to take her lips once more.

"I want you, Declan," she breathed as she took him in hand through his jeans, a sigh leaving him as he kissed her, his hands working her skirt.

Moving her hands up from where he was hard against her, she grabbed his shirt, tugging it off to expose his wide chest, and ran her nails over his work-hewn muscles.

A mountain indeed, she thought.

Grabbing the back of his neck to bring him closer again, she ground her hips against his, feeling the friction of how much he wanted her. A throaty moan left her as her core tightened in anticipation.

Pushing him away from her, her eyes laid a challenge out without saying a word.

Declan unbuttoned his jeans, pushing them to the floor and leaving himself completely exposed.

Bryn found herself falling to her knees, taking him in hand, and with a squeeze, she placed her lips around him. His groan rolling through her as she took more of him into her mouth.

"When did you learn this—" He cut himself off by grabbing her under the shoulders, pulling her back up.

"Forget it. I don't want to know," he whispered against her lips as he took her breasts in his large hands, his thumb and forefinger rolling her nipples between them before he leaned down and flicked one of them with his wet tongue.

"I forgot how good it feels to have you in my arms," he whispered against where he had just licked, his breath against the wet flesh making her purr.

"Obviously, I did too," she admitted, but something chafed at her holding back.

Before she made another move, a smile crossed his lips as they took hers, his beard tickling her nose, but she focused on the feel of his hands and lips on her.

With a gentle shove, she was on her back as he moved his face to between her thighs, his beard rubbing the sensitive skin there as well while he made her moan out his name for the first time in so very long.

He was a man starved as he lapped at her, her hands finding his hair and pulling as her thighs closed around his head.

How had she lived without this?

Kissing his way back up her stomach, that feral part of her took over.

She *needed* the hunt. She didn't want to be a docile lamb as the wolf took what he wanted.

Putting her hand to his chest, she pushed him back, rolling out from underneath him. His eyes widened in confusion as her own desire ignited into something far more out of control than before.

Turning, she took off to the larger room that he used as an entertainment space. She had almost made it to the couch before Declan had her by the hips, spinning her to him.

"What are you playing at, Bryn?" he grumbled, his eyes narrowed, but she ignored it. She wanted to play and let the woman that had been trapped for so long inside herself out. No longer pushing her down to fit some preconceived notion of what human males wanted.

Blinking at the thought, Bryn didn't have time to calm her wild side before she felt Declan's arousal against her thigh. The erotic nature of it had her reigniting. She wanted the desire of the man she cared for to ignite like a raging inferno in his eyes.

Moving her hand along his jaw, she snapped at him with her teeth when his hand did the same, and Declan's eyebrows shot up. Something in her was trying to pull the beast beneath his skin to the surface.

It was what she both wanted and needed.

Moving her face to his neck, she bit down, not enough to draw blood, but enough to get something stirring inside him, and the growl that came from her made him jump.

Spinning her around, he pushed her down over the arm of the couch, but she escaped as she twisted out from his hands and pushed him down onto the couch instead.

His eyes widened before they closed as she climbed on top of him and pushed onto him, sheathing him inside of herself with an aggressiveness she'd never shown nor felt before.

Her fingers dug into the coarse fabric of the couch as she rode him, his hands in her hair as she moaned, trying to pull her down for a kiss, but she didn't want that. Not then.

No. She wanted to keep this feeling of power that so many women before her were denied. A sense of being in control of their own body, and no one could tell them to hide themselves.

This was how a woman should live. Her own rules for her own body, including finding her pleasure with a willing mate.

Pulling away, she growled again at him, not wanting to kiss, but he managed to get a better hold on the back of her neck and found her lips anyway.

She allowed it as their sweaty chests pressed together. His slick body rubbed along hers, the sensitive flesh igniting her nerves with the friction of their movement.

Bryn could feel her release building as she twirled her hips, hitting the right spot that sadly was never found when she was on the bottom. Throwing her head back, she screamed his name, sure she interrupted their demon service down the road at the very chapel where they worshipped her enemy.

Declan pulled her face down to look at him again as his eyes locked on hers, something making her show her teeth as he growled and threw his own head back, his thrusts erratic as he spilled himself inside her.

Closing her eyes, she let herself feel the power of the strong male before her losing himself inside her body, and for the first time, Bryn felt closer to who she truly was on the inside.

She felt *powerful.*

Chapter 26

"You drugged me!" Jace yelled as soon as Bryn's foot hit the landing of the stairs to their apartment hallway.

"I did," she agreed as she turned from him and walked into her apartment. She was too tired to fight, and her bed was calling to her.

Declan, as per usual after sex, had passed out. That gave her the opportunity to leave without chatting about what this all meant.

So much for closure and starting new, she chastised herself.

As she had walked home, Cyerra had followed her, as usual, but said nothing to her.

Honestly, had Finian not come galloping around her for some slobbery dog kisses, she worried she might have punched someone.

There were enough townspeople around staring at her to light her last nerve on fire.

She'd slept with Declan, and yes, she'd finished during the act, but it wasn't *her.*

Bryn had not really been in that room with whoever those two people were, and that felt all kinds of wrong.

Sitting on her bed, she focused on getting her boots off and not the ache between her thighs or the angry man in her doorway.

Could she just let her and Declan pretend they were together? Would it be so bad to have that relationship rekindled when they both needed someone on their side in all this?

She was the broken one, and it seemed that Declan had accepted that part of her. Why would she turn away that affection? People married for less than love around Ifreann all the time.

"You know how I feel about that, Bryn," he growled, and she had to remind herself that Jace was talking about her drugging him and not marriage to Declan as she looked up to face him, throwing her boot on the floor and flexing her liberated foot. Standing, she walked back to the door, Jace stepping back out into the hallway with an angry scowl.

"You just had a whole cart full of shit land on you. We knew you wouldn't rest unless you had help. So, we helped. You're welcome." Slamming the door in her cousin's face, she felt a little bad about that, but the subsequent kick and curse before his boots thudded back to his room cured her of any ill feelings about drugging him.

It was the only way a man like him would take a break.

The fact that he should have been out for far longer told her that in the future, Sage would have to up the dosage. Apparently with his newfound powers, he pushed drugs out of his system faster.

Sitting back on the bed, she took her remaining boot off as she wished for a bath, thinking hard on if it was worth it. As she unzipped her skirt, Cyerra tapped on the glass.

"I've waited for you to show up for a while now, but I have my answers, so you'll excuse me if I don't jump up to greet you."

The tapping grew in agitation.

"Why bother pretending you can't get in? Figure it out," she mumbled, stripping naked before pulling on her nightgown, ready to bed down for the day.

When had she gotten so mean?

Lying in bed, she rolled onto her back. Usually, she'd have bent over backward to tell Declan all the sweet and nice things lovers were supposed to say, not slip off after the man's first snore.

Her reaction to Jace was especially surprising. Never in a million years would the old Bryn have slammed a door in his face.

Pushing her body deeper into her nest of pillows, she stared at the ceiling as she considered walking down the hall to apologize to her cousin. However, if she did it right away, he'd probably return the door slam.

A lot had happened, and he had just woken up in a fury. He needed to work through it, and them flinging accusations and hurtful words would do nothing to help him or her.

A knock sounded at her door, and she groaned. Jace coming back to argue more was very unlike him, but they were all changing these days.

Opening the door, her jaw dropped to see not Jace, but Declan. The consequences of her actions were now here, standing on her doorstep.

Waving him in, he bowed his head and stepped through the doorway as Bryn stepped back, the discomfort between the two of them palpable. Not to mention, Declan rarely came to her apartment while they dated. He'd asked, of course, but it was so much safer at the Cauldron where Mallory couldn't invade her personal space at any moment.

She could only imagine her aunt finding her having premarital sex.

Turning to shut the door, she noticed Kian's shadow flicker in the corner, and she wanted to groan. This was not a conversation she wanted to have in front of him.

"Look, Declan—"

"I'm sorry, Bryn—"

They started at the same time, and she was glad Kian didn't make a sound. If only she could throttle the shadow and murder him again as he played peeping tom to what was going to be one of her most embarrassing moments, she was sure.

"I, uh . . ." Declan ran his hand through his hair. "It's not at all that I didn't enjoy our time together, Brynnie, please don't think that . . ."

Oh gods. This was about to get really weird, and the light cough from the corner covering the laugh of a certain Fomori demon was thankfully missed by Declan.

"You were just . . . it was a bit much, Brynnie," he whispered as if using his nickname for her might soften the blow.

A snort from Kian had her closing her eyes, visions of killing a shadow dancing through her head.

She was glad Declan couldn't hear the idiot.

"The sex, Declan?" she asked, crossing her arms, and his eyes widened at her bluntness. She'd never been so outright with him, the word far too aggressive for her to use in his opinion, she was sure.

"Yes, you were so . . . not like you usually are. It was a bit too much for me. I think we were both looking for comfort in what we knew, with everything changing, and that . . ." Declan rubbed the back of his neck before dropping his hand to his side. "That was very much not how it used to be."

"So I wasn't docile and submissive like before is what you are saying?" she asked, walking around Declan and backing her body into the laughing shadow in the corner that she wished she could smother.

"I am not saying it like that, but you were so . . . just so . . . wild."

Wild. She was *wild*.

Never, ever, had she been accused of that. She almost . . . *liked* it.

"I was too wild for you?"

"Yes!" Declan said before he dropped his relieved smile, realizing he had just stepped onto a minefield.

She smiled back, a cold tingle from Kian being directly behind her pushed her forward toward the door. Kian knew to disappear before he was seen by Declan, but what did she care now?

"That is fine, Declan. It was a one-time deal anyway. We both needed comfort, and that's what I received. Sorry if I was too much for you and you did not get what you needed during our time together."

"Brynnie—"

"No, I think we are done conversing on the subject. Thanks for making me aware and have a great day, Declan." She all but shoved the man out of her apartment, putting her head to the wood as the shadow laughed out loud from behind her.

"Why is that so damn funny to you? That for once I wasn't a wildflower holding up the wall?" she growled into the wood before turning to look at him.

Pretending to wipe tears away, he calmed himself, a slight hitch to his words as his laughter was not totally under control.

"No, it is that you were never anything but *wild. Humanity tamed you as much as it could, but your roots are deep, Phantom Queen."*

Chapter 27

*T*omorrow.

Tomorrow she would address all the pending issues. She would deal with all the loose ends of her poor choices made in the last day.

Settling into a book to calm her mind, Kian leaving to go laugh in the dark abyss of wherever he went when not following her like a lost puppy, one with big teeth, she was finally losing herself to sleep.

Bryn could finally rest. Leave the worries behind as she slept in her *own* bed like she should have instead of heading to Declan's and adding another bad decision to her growing list of terrible choices.

While her attitude had grown, her ability to make intelligent decisions seemed to be thinning.

Closing her eyes, Bryn felt Cyerra settle onto the pillow next to her head. Not quietly either. Cyerra let her tail feathers tickle Bryn's ears and nose more than was necessary. She knew it was the crow's way of showing irritation for having to use her own magic as opposed to Bryn going out of her way to open the window for her.

"Cyerra!" Bryn yelled, opening her eyes and swinging her arm out, the crow squawking in annoyance as she flew to the headboard. "I'm beyond irritated with you."

"I am aware, but I have no answers to give you. Everything you are and everything you need are inside of yourself or for Danu to provide. I am not privy to as much as you think."

Bryn narrowed her eyes.

"I bet you'd have answers about Kian and who he is."

"Ask him yourself. I had nothing to do with that demon when he was whole, and I'll have nothing to do with him in his spirit form."

She knew he was Fomori but hearing it again made it even more real.

"I was there at every battle that demon was. We did not chat in between the bloodshed. I did not have you telling me your secrets either, and you were powerful enough should I have pushed, I'd be nothing but ash and feathers."

Fair enough. She let some of her ire at the crow go.

"They worship Balor here," she confided to the crow, the beady eyes staring at her.

"Disgusting."

Yeah, Bryn couldn't disagree with that.

"It makes me wonder about some of the customs here. Surely you knew of Balor if we battled side by side in the past?"

"As much as Danu—"

"Quit foisting me off on her! You were in battle with *me*! You can help me find the memories of the Morrigan so we can defeat him, and you know it."

Cyerra moved back to settle on the pillow near Bryn, picking at a feather before looking back up at her.

"Balor feared you all and knew his power was weakened when you were near. Now, I cannot imagine how difficult it will be to beat him with the natural world so very ill."

"So, there is no hope." Bryn felt her newfound fight dwindle at those words.

"No, it means we must find another way to do so, and that requires all the Tuatha Dé Danann together. Including Danu. If she dies, it will push all of you, and humanity, across the veil. The Fomori will roam the earth in your absence."

Cyerra's head turned to the window as the church bells rang out for one of the daily services.

"I will go explore this religion of Balor. Perhaps I might glean something for our cause that is helpful."

Without a word from Bryn, Cyerra was gone, leaving another feather after her disappearing act.

"At least it's not poop," Bryn muttered as she grabbed the feather and tossed it away, turning and letting out a scream at seeing Kian there.

Kian was back and sat on the chair next to the bed, half shadow, half-ghostly figure as he stared at Bryn.

Shoving to sit up against the headboard, she noticed the dangerous look in his eyes, and her muscles tensed as she reached for the dagger under her pillow that Kessler had made for her.

"I should kill you."

Bryn waited for him to say something, anything, else. He remained silent as he stared hard at her.

"If you even could in your state of being, well for lack of a better word . . . dead, would you? After speaking to me every day, knowing me, would you still choose to do it?" she asked, pulling the blanket up like a shield with her free hand.

"When I saw the painting of Balor in your chapel of worship—"

"Not mine," she corrected, but he ignored her.

"There was something that told me we were in fact enemies, but that I do not have the whole story. That you are not the enemy I think you are. The enemy that I know you were."

"Your conscience?" she asked, and he raised an eyebrow, his smile sardonic.

"Very deadly of you to assume I have one of those."

She gave him the same sardonic smile in return, and he laughed, shaking his head.

"Answer my question," she asked of him, already knowing the answer. It was easy enough to ask him that since there was nothing he could truly do to her in his state. Should that change, she'd need to be prepared.

"I would have killed you already. I knew my assignment. I failed, but had I another chance, I would complete it and return home . . . wherever that may be now."

"To all the women who would fall for your amazing archery skills?"

"Droves of them, I assure you."

A true laugh left Bryn's lips for the first time in days, and it was at the hands of the man sworn to kill her.

Looking up, Kian was smiling at her, a small one, but true in its sincerity.

"I'd be sad to kill you, Bryn," he said with an honesty that made her shiver. The fact that he would still kill her lingered in the air, yet she didn't feel fear like she knew she should.

"Bold of you to assume I wouldn't kill you first . . . again." Her eyes were growing heavy as the man sat there, his fingers tapping out a soundless rhythm that lulled her in its dance as she drifted.

Ghost, shadow, or man.

"Rest now, Bryn. Tomorrow's worries can wait," he whispered as her eyes closed, her mind drifting, her body growing vulnerable when an enemy sat only inches away. Yet she felt safe, and there was no understanding why except that he couldn't hurt her physically.

But as she fell deeper into sleep, she could have sworn Kian somehow squeezed her hand.

Chapter 28

B ryn stood in the middle of Saints' Road, her breath visible in the frozen air surrounding her.

Was this a vision? A dream?

There was no way the freezing season had already begun with the stifling temperatures that Bryn had been dealing with. The temperature was known to drop dramatically sometimes, but never this much, this fast.

Yet the frozen air said the freezing season had begun, moving in overnight, quick as can be. Never had that happened in her lifetime, but then again, when had they ever had a sandstorm such as the one that had passed through?

The church bells tolled, and she blinked, the darkness outside not a great indicator of the time of day during the freezing season, so she always had to be extra vigilant roaming the road this time of year.

Pulling the fur coat tighter around her, she stopped, thinking on how when she had fallen asleep, she'd only had a sheet because of the heat. She'd also been in her nightgown made of linen, not fully dressed for the day.

Screams pierced her thoughts, the sound of pounding feet on sand had her turning to see several of the men in her community running past the clinic, pushing women and children into buildings. Yelling for them to barricade themselves inside.

Hounds bayed in the distance, and she heard the horns follow in the wake of the howls.

There would not be a sandstorm during the freezing season, she knew that, so something else had them terrified.

A pull in her chest demanded she be in the center of the chaos.

Protect the city at all costs.

Where the words came from, she didn't know, but when she moved to run upstairs, to grab the dagger Kessler had made for her, something stopped her.

Reaching into her coat, she pulled the dagger out and realized that this was the battle she'd been fearful of if she was already prepared to fight.

Fear pulsed through her veins as she ran to check on Jace, making it up the apartment stairs faster than she ever had. The hallway outside her room was empty, and that worried her. Running to Jace's door, she banged on it, pleading with any deity listening that he was safe. Giving up on the courtesy of knocking, she kicked the door open.

His room was empty; in fact, his clothing and gear were gone.

What the hell?

Bryn ran down the backstairs to outside, falling to her knees once she hit the bottom, holding her head as a stabbing sensation, like a knife being driven into her brain, had her begging for death.

Visions flashed through her mind: *A gorgeous woman made of light. Mist. Mountains. Screams. Death. Chaos. Shadows. Wolves. Crows.*

A scream tore through her chest before escaping her throat as her body fell to the frost-covered ground.

Rolling to her hands and knees, she dry heaved as the visions lessened and disappeared from her mind entirely.

Fear and adrenaline pushed her to her feet, her equilibrium off as she stumbled around the building to Saints' Road.

Bracing herself on the brick wall next to her, Justin ran past her line of sight, dressed in his warm sheriff's clothing as if he'd already been awake for a while, yet it had to be night by the fact that no farmers or merchants were moving about the streets. The sconces flickered, running out of oil, verifying her guess.

"Shut down the city!" Justin yelled from the street, his orders heeded by city guards who moved into action as he ran to the gate. "No one in or out without my say-so!"

Time sped up, and creatures she had never seen before tore through her town. They moved like predators, tearing down anyone who stood in their way with swords, the bullets shot from the law enforcement surrounding the city doing nothing to the horrible things.

They continued to smile with their split mouths, hooded cloaks keeping it so she was unable to see their eyes as they killed innocent people—a visual that would haunt her dreams.

"Wraiths. They are not human, so you need to be careful. Make sure to separate their heads from their bodies." Kian was suddenly next to her, looking around at the carnage. The caw of a crow was a balm to her soul in all the chaos and pain as Cyerra landed on her shoulder. Her feathers ruffled in agitation, and Bryn had a feeling Cyerra was waiting on her to make a move.

"Wraiths? I had thought those were the king's very *human* assassins for so long . . . but these are the stuff of nightmares," she whispered as she worked to steady herself and make a game plan.

"Not human, pure demon, and they are very hungry," he whispered, his eyes staring off as if he could see through the wall that Bryn was currently hiding behind. *"I cannot remember much about them . . . but I've fought them before. They have something on their forehead that you have to hit, or it will not be easy to take their heads."*

"What the hell does that mean?"

Turning to shadow and reappearing between her and the onslaught happening just around the corner, he looked at her. His eyes raged, and she wondered if the anger was for her alone.

"Perhaps it's best if you stay here. I can get Danu and Callum—"

"Like hell, shadow boy. Move." Bryn was walking into the street as cries rang out into the night. A plea for a god not listening. A god who created these monsters that razed this town whose only crime was worshipping him.

Turning to take in the scene as she pulled the knife free from her coat pocket, the wraiths ignoring her, she halted as her eyes caught on Travis as he fell to the dirt, Caden falling to his knees next to him, his hands coming away with blood.

"Travis!" she yelled, already in motion, running to her friend. Hoping Jace would make it to him first, though she had yet to see her cousin. A fact that was worrying her to the core.

With her dagger in her hand, she stabbed out at the wraith closest to her as she kept on toward Travis, all the while hearing the screams of the people she had known since she was little.

"You cannot save him without sacrificing yourself!" Kian yelled as he took form in front of her again, sagging in relief as she halted her footsteps. The crow was going wild in the air, diving around her as if to get her attention.

As a wraith came near her, she swung out at them.

Since her dagger did nothing to the wraith she'd attacked, she knew then this was a vision since nothing was happening to her. The wraiths moved as if she did not exist. Not until one ran through her did it confirm her thoughts.

"Perhaps *you* should stay here," she replied with a voice full of anger that was dissipating as she grew numb, watching the carnage around her before her mind began to disassociate.

Bryn moved to step around Kian, though she could have walked right through him, but that seemed rude, she supposed. Why that had popped into her head now, she wasn't sure.

While most of the townspeople meeting their deaths wouldn't bother with her should she be the one in peril, she wasn't cold enough to ignore their cries and screams.

A hand landed on her shoulder, stopping her, and she turned to fight whoever had dared to stop her from reaching her friend.

Once she turned, she saw the cemetery from her vision laid out before her instead of Saints' Road.

The silver wolf was there, along with Senan and the crow. This time the black wolf that killed Arioch in her other vision joined the fold as it walked toward her, the silver wolf sniffing the air before turning to her and lying down on its belly. A soft whine leaving its maw.

"I don't understand . . .," she whispered, unsure of how she was having a vision in the middle of a vision.

"You've managed to call on your powers during a vision and have crossed the veil as you would when moving a soul. Welcome to the Otherworld, Bryn." Mr. Rafferty's voice spilled into the night as the man himself stepped out of the darkness.

The silver wolf growled as it stood back up and moved to stand between Bryn and Mr. Rafferty.

The governor she'd grown up with was the same aside from small differences as he walked from the darkness toward her.

His hair was pure silver and his eyes black with no whites. He wore a cloak that looked like living shadows made up the black garment. She hoped the shadows kept up the work covering the man's body.

Some things could not be unseen.

The blue markings she had on her arms were all across the exposed areas of his skin up to his neck, and surprise, surprise, his ears were pointed too. Like the books she'd read about fae.

Mr. Rafferty was fae.

Kian was fae.

"Mr. Rafferty," she greeted, swallowing her panic. She could *feel* his power as it wrapped around her, invisible, but then the steady thrum of it was soothing her soul like a mother's heartbeat would a child.

"Arawn will do just fine now that we are aware of one another's souls once again."

Nope. Too weird. He would always be Mr. Rafferty.

The silver wolf pushed into her side as several hounds left the trees, coming in behind Arawn but not moving into the cemetery. They were huge beasts, with bloodred eyes, black coats, and yet they made no move to attack.

The pitch-black wolf turned and sat on its haunches next to her.

"Was there ever a Mr. Rafferty?" she asked.

Arawn walked to a headstone, wiping off some dirt from the top before leaning against it. The silver wolf next to her curled its lips but did nothing else. The crow, not Cyerra, landed on a cross nearby but remained silent as well.

"There was. He left town as a young man and died out in the desert sands. I took over his identity, the face I wear is his, but I can change as needed. Taking on his face and identity, I returned to Ifreann after gathering all of you up, having been tasked by Danu with overseeing your care."

"You rounded us up? I came with my father—"

"At the suggestion of his good friend, Aaron Rafferty, who promised that his daughter would be seen to and cared for in Ifreann."

He had played quite a long game, she'd give him that.

"Declan?" she asked, her voice wavering a bit. She might have made things incredibly awkward between them, but she still cared for him.

"He was orphaned during one of the plagues in Osgar. I took him and called him my own as I led your families in. He is my son, Bryn, in all but blood. I do care for him."

"Even if you've lied to him all this time?" she asked. Arawn shook his head as his hounds growled and started moving back and forth along the fence.

"The lie was to protect you all, and so I am not sorry for it."

"Yet you knew this whole city worshipped our greatest enemy?" The wolves at her side growled louder at her statement.

Arawn, Mr. Rafferty, whomever he was, tilted his head.

"Every time he found you after you'd been reborn, he killed you and always made sure to burn your bodies so we couldn't bring you back. Then his son created a city to follow his religion, the one he created in honor of his father. A place where to worship nature was witchcraft and where he burned all the bodies of those who died as a sacrifice. We knew the best place to hide you all was right under his nose." Arawn shrugged, such a human gesture. "And it worked."

That explained much more about why the church did what it did.

"The king is Balor's son . . .," she started, and Arawn nodded. "And he is planning to bring Balor back, but to do so, he needed to keep his father's power tethered here through worship, which he did, and sacrifices to Balor."

Sacrifices. Like the ones at the gate.

Arawn nodded again at her words.

"You never said a word. Just let this all fall in our lap and watch us fumble around in shock."

"I can speak of it in the veil but not in the real world. For us to acknowledge the sacrifices, every death you've been through, gives him more power since we are more than human. Until the stones gave you the power to protect yourselves, it was too dangerous." His black eyes focused on her. "Ifreann has ears, dear Bryn. I've yet to ferret out all the spies, but I am keeping my eyes on a particular few and seeing what I can find out about them."

"Daran and Arioch?" she asked, almost hopeful. "Mallory?"

Tilting his head, his hounds growled, a chilling sound.

"With time, you will know. Until then, I must see to this myself."

Stonewalled. She could take a hint. She'd been with her powers for only so long while he had been at this for years.

"Why were you not reborn as well?" She folded her arms, her tattoos almost glowing in the moonlight as she did so.

"I do not belong to earth and cannot receive power from it like the rest of you do. I derive my power from the Otherworld, so I am able to move across the veil as I please. I was not weakened by the dying earth as you all were."

"Why am I here?" Perhaps that was the most important question. She'd been on the street, surrounded by fighting, and yet . . .

"Your memories and powers are coming back, but not as fast as the others. Declan, Sage, Kessler, and even Justin are farther along in their journey back to themselves. You are allowing your past to hinder your future by repressing who you are."

Bryn snorted, earning a raised eyebrow from Mr. Rafferty before he continued.

"Your subconscious mind, where the version of you that is the Morrigan resides and is communing with the return of your power, saw the vision as real and brought you here so that you could guide your warriors across. This is where you bring them, to me, and I take them home to care for them."

Arawn waved to an island off in the distance.

"Paradise," she whispered, and Arawn nodded.

"And the ones who don't deserve to live in such a place? The evil of the world?"

"The souls who do not deserve such a place, well, we *hunt*." His face lit into a devilish smile as the hounds bayed into the night.

Her wolf included.

Chapter 29

J olting awake, Bryn fell out of her bed in her desperation to check outside.

It was almost night, the sun setting, the heat of the window letting her know it was in fact all a dream.

A creepy as hell dream, but a dream. If it were a vision, though . . . and she hadn't imagined the Otherworld and Arawn . . . she needed to make sure she was ready.

Bryn needed the memories of the Morrigan to keep her friends safe.

Perhaps, she should find Mr. Rafferty and have him work with her on crossing the veil at will and whatever else the Morrigan was supposed to do.

Probably wouldn't hurt to learn how to actually fight, something that still hadn't come to her with the power, which was incredibly embarrassing to admit since she was supposed to be a war goddess after all.

Better to die from embarrassment than a knife to the gut.

Jace first, she thought as she dressed herself and went over the words of apology in her mind as she walked to his room.

The door swung open before she even had a chance to knock, and then she was pulled into a hug that both her and Jace desperately needed.

Her cousin understood her, and the pain of never giving him the chance to get past the walls she'd built to keep everyone else out struck her with a ferocity that brought tears to her eyes.

No more, she promised herself. She had people who cared about her, she was just too blind to see it through her own pain.

He may not need the words, but she would give them.

"I am so sorry, Jace. For drugging you . . . for everything," she whispered as her cousin pulled her into a tighter hug.

"I am so sorry I was angry at you for drugging me. You are my family, Bryn," he whispered into her hair. "The last of who I can trust in this world, and I overreacted because I feel like I am losing someone. Someone I have thought of as a sister . . . and the drugging just pushed me over the edge. Please, *please*"—he stepped back to look at her, his eyes teary— "let me in. We're all that's left."

Those words hung in the air between them as she took his hands with a nod.

His mother was so entrenched in the lie of who Balor was, they could not know if her love for Jace would be enough to walk away from the religion and life she'd made for herself.

Some people come to rely on the lies they've told themselves, even if its foundation was built on quicksand.

They'd happily sink beneath thinking it was an honor and a sacrifice, though it meant nothing to the world around them.

Clasping his hands in hers, she told him about her dream, holding to the promise she made to let him in. Bryn was going to keep to her vow of no longer keeping any secrets from him.

"Okay, so we talk to Danu and figure this out before the cold snap." He nodded, and the light in his eyes, the pure appreciation that she had let him in, sent a fresh wave of guilt. A feeling she tamped down since it was not a necessary emotion at the time, and she found herself in wonder that she could do that. That she could calculate and disregard an emotion that she deemed unnecessary.

A very un-Bryn-like behavior. Perhaps there was more of the Morrigan coming to the surface than she thought.

"They are staying at Niamh's as far as I know. Pretty sure Justin figured that was the safest place for Danu and Callum a while ago," Jace told her what she already knew before giving her hands a squeeze and releasing her to grab his bag. Why did he need his bag to go to the Sanctuary?

Looking out the window, the sun was now up, and it suddenly made sense. He'd play off their being about the town and going to Niamh's as being called to a bedside.

She was an absolute idiot to have kept anything from this man. Her life would have been so much easier with his quick-thinking and problem-solving abilities.

Also, she was off schedule. Again. Her days and nights were so mixed up along with everything else happening in Ifreann.

On a nod, they headed to the Sanctuary, the curtains closed in the windows of the building and the door shut tightly.

Giving a knock Bryn had never heard before, Jace waited until the door opened, nodding to a man she'd never seen before, but who obviously worked here.

"Nigel, this is my cousin Bryn. She is also a friend to Niamh." Jace walked into the room, the introductions following, but not Bryn since the large man named Nigel was staring down at her with an expression that could make the strongest in nerves tuck tail and run.

"Bryn . . ." He chewed on her name before nodding and letting her through.

"What the hell is that about?" she asked, having never come to the Sanctuary during daylight, usually only at night when the doors were open, and the music was carrying into the street.

"He keeps the Sanctuary safe while the women and Caden sleep in after having been up all night. You don't see him because he is only here during the day and never leaves," Jace explained as they headed upstairs, him knowing the way better than she did since she didn't feel like exploring while there at night. The moans and grunts of men who were at their crescendo for the evening being enough to make her feel like she needed a shower.

"If I am correct, the suite she'd use for our particular guests is this way." Jace led the way to where she hoped Danu was with Callum so they were not running from room to room, seeing men who should be cuddled up to their wives wrapped around another woman.

A door opened, Jace freezing as Bryn ran into his back. Jace's hand flung out to keep her from moving around him, but she pushed it away as she looked past his shoulder at what had made him halt so abruptly.

The sight of the man who was stepping out and closing the door of one of the rooms froze her heart.

"Declan?" she whispered, and his head snapped up to look at her, his eyes full of panic before turning to remorse.

Something physically cracked in her chest. While she hadn't been in love with Declan like she once thought, they had been intimate and perhaps on the verge of establishing a new relationship that suited them both. One that worked with where they were in their lives now.

She'd been willing to try at least.

"Brynnie . . ." He reached out a hand, but not before a fist slammed into his jaw, knocking his head back.

At first she'd thought Jace had done it until she felt the throb of her knuckles.

Shock hit her like a horse's rear kick. She'd never hit anyone before. Ever.

Holding his jaw, he didn't curse her as she'd have liked, giving her a reason to see if she had a decent left-handed punch as well.

"Don't ever call me that again," she seethed, and Jace moved between her and Declan when the large man with a bruised jaw tried to step toward her again.

"I think it's best if you walk away, Declan. The damage is done." Jace held himself firmly in place.

"I don't even get to explain. Damned before I've had a chance to prove my innocence?" Declan asked, some blood on his teeth making her woozy.

"If you'd kept your hands to yourself in the past, Declan Rafferty, she would most likely be more inclined to hear you out. Now, if you would please leave my establishment, I am sure Bryn has a valid reason to be here, and it seems your visit has met its conclusion."

Bryn froze, hearing Niamh's voice behind her, the coldness in it telling everyone that Declan had crossed a line that not only could Bryn not forgive, but Niamh wouldn't either.

"You—" Declan started, but Niamh stepped around Bryn and Jace, clasping her hands in front of her as she stood regally in front of him.

"You didn't know your power then, when you tricked me into the geas, but now that Bryn knows about your extracurricular activities here, I am no longer bound by it."

That was the geas Niamh had told her about.

Declan stared at Bryn for a moment longer, before sighing and shaking his head, leaving as quietly as possible. The temptation to go into the room he'd just left was strong. She wanted to see for herself the state of the woman in there, have the proof burned into her mind the next time she felt weak around the man.

But something in her heart didn't need it. She'd been with Declan for the last time, and she was only now catching up to the truth of it. Trying to force a relationship because of previous history was a recipe for disaster, and even if he hadn't been caught leaving a brothel after having spent the night with a woman, she couldn't be his.

Even during the sex, she wasn't his. It was mere satisfaction of body meeting body, but there wasn't anything deeper than that. That was why that part of her didn't want him to kiss her during the act.

Everything made so much more sense now.

"You all right, Bryn?" Jace asked as he turned to face her. His eyes full of concern.

"Yeah, I am. Surprisingly." Turning to Niamh, she waited for her friend to meet her eyes, and when Niamh finally did, they were glassy as she worried her lip.

"I would have told you a million times over if I could that he frequented this establishment during your courtship, but due to the geas, I was unable to form the words or give any clues to guide you to this knowledge."

"How could you have told me?" Stepping up to Niamh, Bryn hugged her, and Niamh released the breath she'd been holding. "I don't blame you for Declan's actions, Niamh. He is a grown man who made the choice all his own."

A wet, tear-filled chuckle left Niamh's lips before she spoke.

"I love who you were and who you will become, Bryndis," Niamh whispered into her hair. "I've never truly had family until you came along, and I will treasure our bond."

Bryn stepped back, realizing there was something Niamh wasn't telling her.

"I can only hope when you see the true me for the first time, you feel the same."

Niamh turned and walked down the hallway to where Danu had to be, leaving Bryn stunned at her parting words.

Chapter 30

Bryn worked to steady herself after Niamh's mysterious statement, telling herself it was not the most important item on her ever-growing agenda right then.

Sitting across from Danu and the others in the drawing room of the Sanctuary, her mind went to how thankful she was that she didn't have to face Declan, and her throat burned from the thought of all he'd done behind her back for so long.

Steadying her breath, she repeated the words said to her in the vision from the dead man at the pyre to Danu.

Callum had to repeat the actual language, which helped her settle her mind enough to speak of the dream from the night before. Danu's face blanched at her words.

"I thought we would have more time," Danu whispered, her frail fingers going to her paper-thin lips.

"Then he is sending his wraiths. Just like in my vision." Bryn leaned forward, her elbows on her knees and hands clasped tightly in front of her to keep her from shaking answers out of the older woman.

"Before they were aware you were all here . . . Arawn is right, I did make sure to hide you among the enemy, as you are well aware of now that you've seen the church in a whole new light." Danu spoke the words aloud, but Bryn felt like she wasn't speaking to anyone in the room.

"You've been watching us? How? We never see you around town, and from what Justin has said, you were supposed to be on lockdown!" Jace was losing the patience he was known for yet again, but who could blame him these days?

"Young Sage has been stuck in her books and coming to me almost hourly. I've always loved her thirst for knowledge but forgot how tiring it can be." Danu took a sip of her tea, but she did not look like a woman put out by Sage's antics. If anything, she looked pleased.

"Yes, Sage loves to read. We know." Bryn was not letting Danu go down a rabbit hole. "Now, we know that the king is wanting to bring his father back through the sacrifices at the gate, which still rattles my brain. How do we prepare?" Bryn was reaching out for her patience and finding no purchase.

"Balor was taken down by you when you, the Morrigan, were closing the veil. He is on the other side now doing who knows what in a prison of the Tuatha Dé Danann's making. Now, his son as the king has spent so much time looking for you all, knowing that he has to defeat you again and to make sure the veil closes with Balor on this side and the Tuatha Dé Danann on the other. Permanently." Danu's jaw clenched before she spoke again.

"Killing you in the past did not bring his father back, so I am guessing he has finally worked out that he can only bring him back fully by killing you all after you've been bound to your powers once again. Should that happened, what is left of this world . . . Well, there wouldn't be anything left. They are demons of chaos magic, creating horrible natural events. It would quite literally be hell on earth."

"So, the sacrifices at the gate we are dealing with right now? You said something about the deaths being because our powers were a beacon, and if what Arawn said—" Bryn didn't finish before Danu spoke.

"Those sacrifices are to feed his power enough to tether his father to this world through the veil until the time is right. When the veil is wide enough, Balor can step back through onto mortal ground."

"The small deaths keep the veil open just enough, and yes, yours would rip it wide open until you got to the other side to close it again. That's when he can trap you," Callum responded, having been quietly listening at the window the whole time.

"We were so much stronger than we are now," Jace said more to himself than anyone in the room. "Seems almost as if we are walking into a suicide mission if we go against him. We lost when we were stronger . . . No." Jace shook his head, Bryn unsure what he was saying no to, but she had a clue.

Mr. Rafferty was right. She was behind the others in grasping her memories.

"It would have been so much worse had you and the rest of the Tuatha Dé Danann not stepped in. If sacrifices hadn't been made." Danu looked sadly at Bryn as she said this.

Bryn gave her a look of confusion in return.

"Are you speaking of us losing our power?" Bryn asked, and Danu waved Callum over.

Callum with his cumulative knowledge of all their history. A walking encyclopedia of who Bryn was long ago.

"When the veil was threatened, the Tuatha Dé Danann fought and took their last stand against the Fomori, not the first of their battles. Yet, this time, they were about to breach the levels of the veil with their wraiths, the very ones the king uses even now."

Settling onto the edge of the couch near Danu, he folded his hands on his lap, his eyes focused on somewhere far away from where they were as he continued as if reading it all from a book in his mind.

"The Morrigan and her Clan of Shadows held the line until the rest of the tribe could make it to where the veil meets our world. She"—he finally looked at Bryn— "you knew the veil needed to be sealed to keep the Fomori from taking over the Otherworld, or as it was called at the time, Faerie. So, with Danu's assistance, you all gave over your powers to the soul stones and went across the veil so that you would all be reincarnated and born mortal. If you crossed with your powers then, you would have been stuck there, and the earth would not have its warriors."

Breathe, Bryn. She was unsure if she had any more space in her brain for new information.

"As the last to go through, you refused to leave your clan vulnerable against the soldiers of Balor. So you split their souls, making them immortal as one part of them lives on each side of the veil and therefore cannot be killed."

Callum nodded as he finished and stood back up to return to the window.

"Clan of Shadows?" Jace asked before Bryn could.

"They were your mortal warriors who fought under your banner as the Morrigan. Fought beside you in every war you took the lead in and helped you to keep the balance in the wars between the mortals," Callum responded.

Jace looked at her wide-eyed.

"You had an army, Bryn."

Yes, one split in two so that she would have to figure out how to unite the two sides of themselves should she need to call upon them to fight Balor.

Another priority to add to the ever-growing list.

"The moment those stones released your power back to you, a beacon would have gone out. Not just for Bres, but for others who remember, which is why the man you were handling the rites for called out to you for the deaths of Bres and his people," Danu finished for Callum.

The man had been one with the knowledge of who she was, knew what to expect when she came back. His people must still speak of the Morrigan long after she left the earth.

It was not only the king who would search for her and the others to destroy them.

How would she know friend from foe?

What she did know was the wraiths were coming for the first time to a city who had no idea, and to warn them would only condemn herself.

Never had Ifreann been at the mercy of the wraiths, being that King Bres most likely thought his devout followers would never allow his enemy in the gate. Now that he knew they had, they were doomed to a visit from his assassins.

Unable to sit any longer, Bryn stood up and looked down at Danu.

"Then we should leave here before they come in order to keep everyone safe from the wraiths."

"You think the people who have ostracized you for most of your life deserve your loyalty?" Danu asked, voice calm yet raspy. "That you should sacrifice the home you've made here as well alongside them whether they liked it or not?"

Danu shook her head, looking out the dirty window covered in the never-ending sand of said home.

"It's time to face your own fate. Now everything is in motion once again, and roads will need to be traveled. Paths cut for those to follow. I suggest you look into who in this town truly deserves your loyalty."

Bryn thought back to the times she'd simply walked down the street and been hit, knocked over, spit at, pinched, or just simply called a witch in a threatening tone.

Of all the times in the past that Bryn had been vulnerable and only her friends were there to stand beside her.

It was obvious that Bryn was in need of comfort when her father died, and yet the townspeople chose to close their doors and ignore her.

Perhaps it *was* time to take a good look at who was truly on her side.

"It doesn't matter, though. You cannot leave just yet. The prophecy has an order to it, and the first stand must be made on the ground of your reawakening." Danu looked away to Callum as she spoke.

"The prophecy? So now there is some kind of prophecy?" Bryn snorted, earning a look of censure from Danu.

"Yes, the prophecy of gods and crows was what it was referred to after you'd closed the veil." Danu sighed, her eyes closing. "So much of you is still in there, but you keep pushing the real you down. Fear of the unknown was never an issue with you before you stood in this mortal skin. The unknown is where you *thrived*. With gods and crows, or so the prophecy goes."

"Cute," Bryn muttered.

"Hush," Danu growled, her tone stunning Bryn into silence. "The Fomori, with their chaotic powers, were able to take over, and the earth being weak from human neglect for centuries made it all the more easy. Those wraith-like creatures, they are part of the Fomori and entered this world after pushing out the earth's protectors. Those demons, which is exactly what they are, currently reside with your king in his castle fortress."

"Some job we did as protectors," Bryn grumbled as she folded her arms.

"Yes, you sacrificed yourselves to close the veil so the demons could not make it to the Otherworld. You sacrificed pieces of yourself to protect those who followed you." Danu's eyes narrowed in on Bryn. "The prophecy was created because King Bres will be looking for the gods who would come back from the veil to return the earth to her former glory."

"Yes, we know. The gods being the Tuatha Dé Danann . . . us." Maybe if Bryn said it enough, she'd believe it one day.

"The prophecy all begins with a god and a crow . . ." Danu looked at Bryn, a smirk crossing the older woman's face that agitated Bryn. "The first of the gods to arise, ready to slay those who dare threaten the good of the world, and the last one to enter the veil."

Bryn knew all too well who Danu was referring to since Bryn was the first to wake up after their powers were released back to them.

"That . . . sounds like the ravings of a mad person. I am sorry, this is . . ." Bryn stopped, unable to continue, her mind spinning. "Whoever said that is wrong." They had to be. Who in their right mind would think Bryn could save the world, even with a team behind her?

"Oh, darling Bryndis, it was you. You and your prophecies. Your sight. You predicted all of this before you left us, and so we shall follow your lead."

Oh hell.

Chapter 31

B *lood. Battle. Swords. Travis dead on the sand, blood everywhere.*

"Wake up," a voice finally penetrated the fog of her dream, and Bryn shot up out of bed, the sun setting on the horizon outside her window.

Kian stood next to her bed, his eyes narrowed on her as his shadows moved around him, Cyerra watching him from the foot of her bed.

She guessed Cyerra had given up on murdering him since there wasn't a ruckus with his entrance, and her room was as it had been before she fell asleep.

"You are quite a violent sleeper. A lover would have died tonight had someone been brave enough to slip into bed with the Morrigan. Aside from that idiot that watches you with stars in his eyes," Kian joked, and Bryn spun on him.

"Did you watch me having sex with Declan?" she screamed, not bothering to keep her voice down in case Mallory came barreling in with a vengeance. His eyes widened in shock at her declaration before he started to laugh. Shaking his head, he pushed his hair out of his face.

"No, I was unaware the two of you took back up. You used to be married to him, when you were both the Morrigan and Dagda, and quite angry about it since he couldn't seem to be bothered keeping his pants buckled around other women."

The laugh that left her lips was as sharp as a knife's edge.

"Danu must have been right, then. We retained more of ourselves than we thought."

Turning, she took in Kian, who said nothing in response to her words. Perhaps he was thinking about her being more like his old enemy when he was only just beginning to see her as Bryn. His face was pensive, and she wanted to know where his thoughts were right then. Would have paid good coin to know, but he shook his head.

Bryn pulled her sticky nightgown away from her skin, the sweat cooling her now and giving her a chill. Cyerra stretched out her wings before disappearing, and Bryn wondered if the crow watched over her while she slept. She knew the crow was in the sky while Bryn moved about, seeing her move through the lamplight at night and taking up a perch to be near her, but never overtly in her way.

Sitting back against the headboard, she rubbed her eyes, exhaustion lingering like a heavy blanket over her weary body.

"What did you dream of?" Kian asked, and she wondered if there would be any harm in telling him. None if her vision, and his part in it, happened the way she had seen it.

"The wraiths will come soon," she told him, closing her eyes and leaning her head back against the headboard. After a long silence, she finally gave in and looked up to see his face in profile as he looked out the window toward where the town was winding down for the night.

"Then the king knows you are here. I wondered how you were able to stay out of his all-seeing eye for so long. Balor is not one to let things go unmissed."

"It's Bres," Bryn whispered, watching Kian as he turned a shocked look to her.

"What happened to Balor?"

"Do you not report to anyone now that you are back in our world?" she asked, wishing she'd thought of this earlier and blamed it on him being a shadow. That he was unable to physically harm her made it so that her questions about him were not at the forefront of her mind with everything else happening, yet if he could talk to another as he did her . . .

"I am only able to communicate with you. When I am not here with you, I am in a dark place where there is no light or sound. I come and go as I can, trying to avoid that place until my reserves are too low to be here."

Bryn knew he haunted his killer. That his death at her hands tethered him to her. While she also knew she'd haunt anyone who killed her, that was for sure, the thought of being in a place where all of your senses were blinded . . . that was a horrible punishment. Who knew how long he'd had to endure that. It wouldn't be but mere hours of it before Bryn went mad.

"What happened to him?" Kian asked as he settled into a chair near the window.

"I don't know. All I know is the Tuatha Dé Danann gave up their, *our*, powers to cross the veil and be reborn, sealing off the gateway, so Balor's army was unable to get through. He apparently slipped by and is imprisoned there." Standing from her bed, she took the chance of being near him. He was her enemy, but he had lost the entire world he had been used to along with his life.

Bryn settled on the edge of the bed closest to where he sat.

"I wish I could remember something more." He put his hands into his hair, his elbows digging into his knees as he leaned forward.

"Same here," she joked, but he didn't respond. She waited in silence for him to process the changes to his reality while she looked out the window.

"He was so determined to rule Faerie, or the Otherworld as I've heard Danu call it, as he was to rule this world. His greed must have finally won but at great risk to himself," Kian finally whispered before looking up at her, his hair in his eyes making him all that more attractive, yet so very broken, and she felt pained at the sight.

"The worst part, Phantom Queen?"

She nodded for him to continue.

"Is that you're my enemy, yet I am glad he is dead, and I do not know why."

Bryn couldn't find the words to reply.

Chapter 32

B ryn heard the church bells ringing while she pulled her long curly hair up into a ponytail, waiting for Callum to meet her by the pyres. There were no bodies tonight, thankfully, but she wanted to learn everything she could about the magic she held underneath her skin.

The nip in the air was making her nervous, but it would be a few days or so before the cold winds brought the freezing season in.

Before her vision came true.

We still have time, she tried to remind herself before the worry took over, *just not as much as I hoped.*

Her eyes moved to the north of Ifreann, her thoughts going to her father and why he would move them here. Obviously, Arawn had a lot to do with that, but if her father had made a life elsewhere before coming here, why did he choose to come to Ifreann just because some strange man promised safety for Bryn? Was it so bad to be there after her mother had died in childbirth? Why would her father have trusted him in the first place?

She had a hard time believing her father had thought religion could cure her no matter what he said to the contrary.

The townspeople there could not have been any worse than they were in Ifreann.

Dangerous thoughts, she knew, but she wondered what her life would have been like had her father not taken her from her birthplace.

No one had ever said a word about where she was from except that it was one of the last few strongholds to defy the king. That in and of itself was blasphemy to her aunt, so anything outside of Drystan Territory did not exist for her.

She smiled at thinking of what her father must have looked like when he stepped foot into Ifreann for the first time. The shock that must have taken the entire town into a stranglehold. She liked to visualize her father showing up in his underclothes having been unused to the heat, with a young, bedraggled daughter in tow, and seeking refuge.

Her father would talk about their home before Ifreann on very rare occasions. Mostly it was about how he didn't miss the cold as much as he thought, but he did miss the mountains. Other than that, he never spoke of her mother or her homeland.

"It's beautiful there," Callum said from behind her, and she wondered again if he could read her mind. "If you're looking to the north in thought, I'd assume it would be for the land of your birth."

She nodded.

"I was. I know nothing of it." Turning to Callum, his eyes were not the blue of every day, but the swirling flecks of gold and silver, a galaxy within him.

"It is beautiful, and I can only hope the king never manages to squash the rebellion there. They are amazing people who are fierce. You remind me so much of them."

Looking away, she swiped the rogue tear that escaped from hearing his words. Taking a deep breath, finding her inner strength, she turned back to Callum. There was no point in speaking on a place that was no longer hers to call home.

"How do I use my powers?" she asked, and he shook his head.

"It is not on and off as such. These are ingrained in you, but I will work with you to recall as much as you can. Most of the rest is instinctual, and you can call upon them when you're ready."

Cyerra landed on a dead tree branch near them.

"And if you can't figure it out, everyone dies. No pressure, Phantom Queen."

"I think the crow is being snarky with me."

Callum laughed a genuine belly laugh.

"Yes, I imagine she is quite frustrated you did not wake up with all the memories you left with. She never had patience, even when you were the Morrigan."

Bryn tried not to let the words bother her even if she knew the others were far ahead of her in their memories, or at least in control of their powers, returning. They may not remember who they were as a god, but they were working with their powers and finding new ways to make their lives easier.

Which was why it was difficult to be around them. She could admit she was jealous.

She still did not have a grasp on the visions she'd dealt with *before* Danu had given her that damn stone.

"We are going to Faerie?" the crow asked as she tilted her avian head, and Bryn looked back at the crow. Those words were the most excited she'd ever heard from Cyerra, her voice usually bordering between exasperated and sarcastic.

"Correct, and we will need your help crossing for the first time, Cyerra."

Bryn snapped her head to look at Callum.

"You can hear her?" she asked, feeling a little less special that her familiar could speak to other people.

Mature? No. Not at all.

"Only when she pushes her words into other's minds can they hear her," he explained as he sat, crossing his legs, and gesturing for Bryn to do the same.

"Since this is her first time, you can act as a tether for her while I make sure nothing happens to her physical form," he said out loud to Cyerra, the crow flying over and landing on Bryn's shoulder.

"Can I say how weird this is?" she thought aloud as Cyerra hit her in the face with her tail feathers.

"Bryn, release yourself from your mortal form and walk to the other plane," Callum ordered, folding his hands in front of him as he waited. "Once you've grown in your power, you will be able to take your physical body, but until then, let's focus on your mind."

"Uh . . ." She looked from Callum to Cyerra. "How?"

Bryn could feel the disappointment radiating from the crow. She was glad the little bird said nothing this close to Bryn. She had surprised herself when she hit Declan, and so she wasn't sure she was above strangling the crow. It wasn't like Cyerra could die after all.

Callum tilted his head as if baffled this was not something she already knew.

The long, pained sigh in her mind came from Cyerra, before the crow spoke to her.

"*Close your eyes, Bryn,*" Cyerra's voice rang in her head. "*Feel that darkness in your mind, that part of you that you hide in the shadows?*"

Trying to take this seriously, she visualized a door, shadows spilling out from beneath it.

"*You need to go through that door.*"

Walk through the creepy door of her psyche? How could this possibly go wrong?

Stepping forward in her mind, she put her hand out. The same hand as was in the real world without tattoos.

Pulling open the door, a vast blackness spread out from it, reminding her of the place Kian had told her about.

Hesitant, Bryn waited, but the shadows had other ideas as they wrapped around her arm and tugged at her, pulling her toward the threshold.

Trying to pull her hand back was no use as the shadows only strengthened the more she struggled.

Panic had her trying to open her eyes only to realize they were already open in the very darkness she'd proclaimed not long ago would make her go mad. Closing her eyes, she pretended that was the reason for the darkness. It felt easier to accept somehow when she felt in control, even if it was false.

"It's safe. Relax and walk through. I will be waiting on the other side," Cyerra assured her, and Bryn took a deep breath before following Cyerra's advice.

Hands out in front of her, she felt the wood of another door and moved her hand until she felt the cold metal of a doorknob before twisting it open.

Stepping through the pitch-black door, she emerged on the other side.

Opening her eyes, the shadows remained around her before finally letting go and dissipating.

Everything around her was the more colorful version of her world, just as it had been in her visions, but it felt different this time since she had come through on her own. She could feel the breeze more than she had before, and a pulse timed with the rhythm of her own heart seemed to shudder through the land.

It was as if the Otherworld, Faerie, had its own heartbeat.

She was still next to the pyre, but Callum wasn't. The dead tree that Cyerra had just been on was lush and full of life. Greens of varying colors wove through the tree, the sun shining above sending flares of sunlight through the leaves and onto her, colors glittering along her skin. Holding her arms out, the tattoos were once again inked where they had been every time before.

A chuff caught her attention, and she turned to the silver wolf who was watching her from where Callum had stood moments before. Getting to her knees, she ran her fingers through its fur, its eyes closing as it leaned into her touch.

Cyerra was flying, meeting other crows in the branches of the trees that surrounded town.

"Are you Callum?" she asked the wolf, its head shaking dramatically in a very obvious no, and she wondered who the beast was that had become a protector for her in this realm. Could it be another familiar?

"If only you were this real outside of here," she whispered, and the wolf opened sad eyes before giving a nod and a bark.

Laughing, she gave the gorgeous beast a kiss on the forehead, earning a slobbery kiss on the side of her face in return that reminded her of Finian.

Standing, the wolf whined at the lack of pets but followed her as she roamed.

It was as if the veil laid directly upon her world. She could see all the buildings, Niamh's, and the Cauldron clearly. The gorgeous grass that grew between her and the brick buildings and trees that stood outside the walls built to keep people in. No sand to be seen anywhere.

It was as if they'd saved the world already, the Fomori gone, and it returned to the beauty it had once been so long ago.

A piece of her soul longed for what she now imagined the world could have been. Unsure if it was possible to ever get it back to the way it once was.

Overwhelmed by the loss of that place she couldn't remember but grieved for, she fell to her knees in the middle of Saints' Road along the plush foliage and plants that thrived and screamed.

Vines moved along the ground, wrapping around her wrists, but she felt no malice from them. Where she'd landed, the grass had thickened, making a soft carpet for her knees.

All the anger and loss that both the Morrigan and Bryn had felt left her lips. The dangers that they would face, it all left her body in the violence of her voice. The howl of the wolf next to her brought more howls from the woods beyond the Faerie version of Ifreann. The birds rose in their own song, and Senan took her place at Bryn's side.

It was a battle cry.

As the scream left her breathless, she stood, turning to see the crows along the tops of the buildings, Cyerra nearest her. But what left her even more breathless was the black wolf that stood before her, and the many wolves behind it, all looking to her as if for guidance.

The beauty of the pack struck a loose chord in Bryn's soul, one that tightened, and a physical golden string moved along the wolves until it hit the black wolf, who turned and walked to Bryn before taking its place on the other side of her. With the wolf on one side, Senan on the other, Cyerra moved to Bryn's shoulder.

The silver wolf moved to the front of the pack where the black wolf had just stood and took position in front of them. It was as if the silver wolf was the beta of the pack to the black wolf's alpha.

A howl broke free of the silver wolf, and all the pack returned the call.

"Now, my queen, you have an army. Call when you are ready for them to fight at your side once again."

The voice did not seem to belong to anyone in particular, the echo of it androgynous.

"You are always welcome here, child of Danu."

Something deep in Bryn knew then that it was the Otherworld, Faerie, that had spoken to her.

Faerie was sentient.

Chapter 33

Moments after Bryn had returned from the veil, stunned by the knowledge of all that happened in Faerie as she now referred to it, Sage had run to her, grabbing her arm, and pulling her to her small cottage.

"Okay, I can explain . . . maybe." Sage held her hands up as Bryn walked into her cottage, her eyes wide as she shut the door behind her.

"What the fresh hell . . .?" Bryn reached out to touch one of the vines that had wrapped itself around a sconce, the smell of far too many herbs in a small room was overpowering and made Bryn's eyes water. It was so much like her vision in Faerie, Bryn almost thought she'd left the veil open long enough for something to slip through, and her blood froze.

"It's a damn forest, Sage!"

"I know!" Sage responded, pressing a knuckle against her lips, her eyes panicked. "I was trying to see if I had magic with the herbs like Danu said, so I started trying different things . . . and well . . . I do . . . have magic that is."

It was Sage's magic. Faerie hadn't slipped through, and Balor hadn't slipped out.

That was all Bryn's battered emotions could take before she started laughing so hard that tears were coming from her eyes. Bending over, she put her hand out to grab a vine-covered chair as Sage stomped.

It was from the hilarity of the room around her and the relief she hadn't left the door wide open for Balor with a "Welcome back!" sign awaiting him.

"It's not funny, Bryn!"

That only made Bryn laugh harder.

A knock at the door had Bryn attempting to calm herself, Sage walking past her to check who it was before giving Bryn the evil eye and opening it.

Bryn responded by wiping away the tears and flicking them at her friend.

"Good gravy, Sage, you weren't kidding." Kessler walked in, his eyes wide as Bryn was sure hers had been upon seeing the newly forested cottage.

Bryn snorted, covering her face as it turned red from embarrassment.

"I am sorry, Sage. I don't mean to be cruel. I honestly wish my power was less deadly . . ." Bryn stopped herself from continuing.

This wasn't a competition. She needed to remind herself of that.

Running his hand through his hair, Kessler whistled as he looked around.

"Well, the rest of us have been trying to figure out what our powers are, and it's going about as well, so perhaps this is not such a shame after all, though you'll need to redecorate," he stated as he lifted a bundle of herbs that had overtaken the table.

"I did find out I can sense where there is water." Sage beamed at that revelation. "Not too shabby for people who live in the desert, huh?"

Bryn couldn't help but smile at her friend's thirst for knowledge and achievements. If anyone was able to figure this whole mess out, it was Sage.

"Oh my . . ." Danu was suddenly in the center of the room with them, and Bryn had to grab her chest to keep her heart within the confines of her ribs. A yell that was a bit more high-pitched than Bryn would have expected came from Kessler and had her turning wide eyes on the man.

"Where in the blazes did you come from?" Kessler growled, his own hand clenching his shirt near his heart.

"I felt a surge of power from this area and came to investigate. I've been curious how you are all fairing, most especially since you are not updating me hourly as my dear Sage is." She gave a look to Kessler.

"With all due respect, ma'am, every time I see you, you turn my world upside down."

"Yes, well, our timeline was moved up with all the bodies showing up." Danu didn't bother expanding on her revelation.

"Bodies?" Sage asked, beating Bryn to it.

Not again. Not. Again.

"Yes, at the gate. Perhaps you should try speaking to me once in a while if you want to know what is happening outside of this little town you all hide in."

Well, that wasn't fair at all, but Bryn let it slide as she slipped out of Sage's home and made her way to the sheriff's office where Justin would be ending his day. At least he should have been anyway.

Justin was easy enough to find as he was holding off a crowd from the gate, but it wasn't the crowd of people from Ifreann that halted her in her tracks, it was the crowd she could *sense* outside the gate.

"Looks like I have my work on both planes cut out for me, as do you." Mr. Rafferty moved to stand next to her, looking like the human she had grown up with, his ears no longer pointed and the gray only threaded through his hair instead of taking up the entirety of it.

Danu appeared next to her, this time Bryn was focused enough that her sudden arrival was not the equivalent of the old children's toy called a jack-in-the-box from long ago.

"As you each learn your powers, you will grow stronger. It looks like you are about to be thrown into the deep end, my dear." Danu patted her shoulder as she spoke before turning and walking away with too much pep in her step, whistling a tune that grated on Bryn's nerves.

Callum walked to stand on the other side of her in Danu's absence.

"I can be of assistance working with her once again to cross the veil as we did earlier today," Callum offered, and Mr. Rafferty nodded.

The fact that Callum and Danu were out and about, and no one in the whole town noticing, did not bode well. Could they not be seen?

Wishing she had the ability to turn invisible, Bryn turned to Mr. Rafferty, but he cut off any words she was about to speak.

"That would help. I cannot go back and forth across to move souls when I need to make sure they are settled."

With those words, he turned on his heels and walked away, leaving Bryn and Callum without her getting a word in.

They were all pushing her buttons today.

"We should move this to your domicile since I am unsure of what to do with your physical body once you cross over. It is one thing to do so at the pyre when the town is in a state of calm, but there are too many agitated people, and agitated people do not know how to stay still."

"I understand," she replied, torn between listening to Callum and watching Justin try to calm the people gathered, but her eyes found Arioch and Daran leading the group before she walked away. Figured they'd be those *townspeople*.

They obviously forgot their torches and pitchforks at home. What a shame.

"Come, let us begin so the souls do not have a chance to turn." Callum touched her elbow, her body walking before her mind could catch up with what he had said.

Turn?

As if privy to her innermost thoughts, Callum answered as they walked side by side to her apartment.

"Many things can happen to a soul left on the earthly plane. Myths have been created from the souls walking the earth, looking for hosts. But that is for another day."

Ending the conversation by heading to her apartment stairs, she followed him, Cyerra hopping along with them on the railing.

Getting settled into her bed once they reached her apartment, she let her mind cross over.

The moment she crossed into Faerie, thinking of it as such since Otherworld seemed a terrible name for a sentient entity, she could feel the pull and tug of the souls.

With a thought, she was outside the gates of town, leaving her apartment in a blink.

"Don't panic. That's probably normal . . . I hope," she whispered to herself.

The souls were speaking in a hushed panic, trying to figure out where to go and what to do as Bryn stepped forward. Every one of the souls turned to her as if magnetized.

"I really wish you could tell me what to do, help me figure out how to do this," she said to Faerie, and then the silver wolf was there, giving her a bark in greeting, before moving behind her to push her forward with its nose.

"Okay, okay . . ." She walked toward the souls, each one frozen as they looked at her, watching carefully.

Whispers not from the spirits but nearby caught her attention. She turned to look, and just like before, Faerie overlaid her own world.

Though the sound was muted, the colors vibrant, if she focused, she could see through the gate to where the townspeople surrounded Justin just as they had been before she crossed the veil.

The silver wolf pushed against her, bringing her attention back to the souls. Cyerra fluttered to the gate above them, not speaking to her here, and she wondered if the crow even could.

"I am straddling the line and not fully in Faerie, am I?" she asked, and both the wolf and crow gave her a nod.

Walking up to the first soul, an older man, he took her hand in his. She felt the urge to pull back but let her hand settle there. He was dead, so she wouldn't see, or feel, how he died . . . she hoped.

She was wrong.

Bryn watched each battle of his life, both on the field and in his own mind. His life's highs and lows, regrets and triumphs. It made her dizzy, but she held on until she looked upon the man once again.

"You may pass," something ancient in her said, her voice stronger than when she was herself in the world outside of the veil.

"Thank you, Phantom Queen," he said before he broke apart into a ball of pure white light and moved away from the group toward where Arawn stood on the horizon. She'd not seen him there, but it made sense. He would be guarding the ones he took the paradise.

Bryn continued moving through the people until she came upon a man in his late thirties. Touching him made her skin tingle, and the visions she got from him disgusted her. Trying not to lose the contents of her stomach, she pulled her hand back, thinking only burning her flesh would rid it of the wickedness that spread through the man like a cancer.

"You're evil," she seethed. "You are not worthy."

The man narrowed his eyes and grabbed for her hand again, earning a fierce growl from the silver wolf.

"Let me through," he demanded, stepping into her space, the silver wolf snapping its teeth at the man.

"Call your general off and let me through!" he yelled in her face, but she held steady.

"No," she returned, bracing herself in case the man took it further, which he did. Shoving at her, he tried to run around her, toward Arawn.

A deep well of power filled her. Like being struck by lightning, all of her hair stood on end.

"Stop." Her voice was but a whisper, but the man froze as she walked up to him, her hand out. Getting right into his face, she looked into the eyes of evil. The monster who wore the mask of a human. Of someone who mistreated and used the life around him. Both humans and creatures. "*You may* not *pass.*"

Placing her palm on his forehead, the man shattered into millions of pieces before turning to dust and floating away.

Falling to the ground, her body exhausted, the wolf nudged her to continue.

So, she did, her energy depleted with each soul she moved from the mortal world.

"Do I need to be near my body to go back?" she asked, thankful when all the souls were through, it was over, and she could rest.

The wolf only whined, pushing at her with its nose.

"General, huh?" She pushed her fingers into its fur, the wolfish smile making her wish again that she could pull the wolf across the veil with her.

Letting go of the wolf, she pushed to stand up and stumbled back to her apartment. The pulling sensation was gone now that the souls were handled, but she did not feel lighter. If she could curl up into a ball and sleep for days, she would do it.

The stairs proved difficult, but the constant little nips kept her going and earned the wolf some colorful words.

As she entered her room, her eyes caught on the mirror.

"What in the hell . . .?" Touching her ears, which were pointed, her skin still pale, but without the freckles she always saw in the mirror. Her hair was darker, but the most striking change was that her irises were black, the whites of her eyes red.

It was still her . . . but not. It was more.

Jumping up on his hind legs, the wolf shoved her with its paws until she landed on the bed.

The moment she hit her furs, she blinked her eyes, and she snapped back into her own world with a gasp.

Callum stood over her before giving her a nod and saying good night. The door clicked softly behind him as he left before she could even catch her breath. Her mind was still stunned by the abrupt change in worlds.

Kian was over her the next moment, looking at her as if concerned she might not be whole.

"Worried?" she said with a weak voice.

"That someone killed you before I could? Yes. I still have a job to do."

"In time. You'll get your chance, but I'll put up a good fight."

"Promise?" he asked, yet his words did not have the levity he usually had when speaking of their final battle. Opening her eyes as much as her exhaustion allowed her, she nodded.

"I promise to give you the fight of your immortal life, Kian." Her eyes closed after those words, her body losing its heaviness as she fell asleep.

"Rest now. Cyerra will be here all night as she always is to watch over you."

"It's a shame you cannot kill me in my sleep, huh?" she mumbled as she rolled over to shove her face into one of her pillows.

"Such a shame indeed."

Chapter 34

The large gathering outside the church the next day did not bode well for her, nor any of her friends now that they all could be considered witches according to the Church of Baleros.

People were riled and scared, and Bryn did not have to read as many history books as she did to know that was not a good thing.

What also did not bode well for their future health was the cold snap that had come in overnight, everyone now in their freezing-season clothing. Bryn had put her furs on that morning with trepidation.

"Do you have any idea what is going on?" Jace asked Bryn as he walked up next to where she stood looking out the clinic window.

"Probably a little peeved their chapel of sin was destroyed."

Jace gave her an irritated look.

"I heard enough about that from my mother the other night, thanks."

She was sure he had. Mallory probably lost it completely when she walked in and the altar was torn apart. Never in a million years would she think it was Jace who did it and instead probably just added it to the list of charges against Bryn.

"Then what have you heard, dear cousin?" she asked, looking back out to the chapel.

"Nothing more than that. My mother is tight-lipped. No one has come into the clinic or called for me in a few days, and I know for a fact the Halsey twins have a cold in need of herbs. They refuse to let anyone in the home, so I left something to help with the fever on their doorstep with instructions."

Looking at Jace, she knew how much that had to bother him. He thrived on helping people, and now they knew why. That being a healer was more than a vocation. It was a huge part of who he was as a person.

"The bottle is still there, isn't it?" she asked, and the clench of his jaw told her well before the nod.

"People are scared. A large group of bodies left at the gates not once, not twice, but three times? While the desert and illness are logical answers, this is a religious town. Their minds will go to witches and demons."

His worried eyes looked to hers, and she knew that worry was more for her than anyone else. She was the witch of Ifreann after all.

Bryn turned to the gathering of people entering the church. Oh, to be a fly on the wall . . .

She wished she could skip over to Faerie and straddle the veil, but without a way to tether herself, she worried she may be lost there if she tried on her own to cross. Callum had promised to help her practice more that night, but she was worried leaving and looking for him now would cause issues. The sun was almost down, but the people were still out and about.

"Cyerra," Bryn gasped as Jace turned to give her a look of confusion.

"Who?" Jace asked, but Bryn ignored him as she reached out to see if she could speak to Cyerra and initiate a conversation. She hadn't tried it yet as the crow usually spoke to her first. Perhaps opening a line of communication was something else she would need to practice.

Bryn felt like an idiot for never trying before.

"I am already listening in on this madness, you have no need to take over my mind. Get to a spot where no one can see you, and I'll share my eyes with you."

Stepping away from Jace, Bryn had no idea what Cyerra meant, but she trusted the crow.

"What are you doing?" Jace whispered, following her.

"I am going to see what is happening in that church without going in there myself."

Turning, she ran up the stairs to her bedroom. She didn't need to ask Jace if he was following since she heard the stomp of his boots on her heels. She was sure he had officially concluded she had lost her mind. Powers or not, there was still the possibility she was mad. She smiled a little at the same thought that used to terrify her.

"Let me know what you see. I'll watch your back," Jace whispered, as he moved to stand guard. He had to be the best cousin, trusting her as he did after she withheld so much. She couldn't help but relax knowing even if he thought her crazy, he believed in her.

Lying back on her bed, she closed her eyes, letting Cyerra do whatever it was she needed to do.

"Relax your mind, Phantom Queen," Cyerra ordered, and Bryn was suddenly happy she couldn't hear Cyerra in Faerie now. It was a nice break from the angsty crow with far too big an attitude for her little body.

Closing off the rest of the world, Bryn let Cyerra tug at her consciousness. She'd have to see if there was a way to do this without being vulnerable to the world around her like Callum said she'd be capable of someday.

That day needed to be sooner than later.

An out-of-focus picture played across her eyelids, and she waited as Cyerra pushed the picture further into her mind, putting it into focus for her.

Bryn could see the inside of the chapel from high up in the rafter overlooking the entire sanctuary. Arioch was at the front as he always was as the scrios. His brother, Daran, sat with Mallory in the front pews facing Arioch.

The giant painting of Balor at the head of the chapel had her sneering, and she could feel Cyerra's agitation at seeing her former foe being honored.

She went to the services growing up. She'd heard of Balor and his greatness. Smiting people with his poisonous eye that he kept hidden under a patch to protect his followers.

The same god that created their very town and kept them trapped there through fear.

Bryn had wondered about the old religions, like Christianity and Judaism, that she had read about in Sage's secret book stash. It was obvious they were not kept from leaving their towns. Bryn had always wondered why Balor required its disciples to stay holed up in the pit of the desert. Required them to never leave their little spot on the earth.

Now she knew.

Cyerra hopped to another plank, one of the townspeople looking up, and Bryn realized Cyerra must have made a noise.

"Be careful, Cyerra," she warned into the crow's mind. A sensation that made Bryn dizzy came over her, and she wondered if the crow was trying to purposely make her throw up by moving around so much.

"Not the first time I've scouted. Pay attention and quit blathering."

Scolded, Bryn focused on where Arioch, in his golden scrios outfit that Bryn thought was a dress as a child, stood at the front of the chapel.

"Calm yourselves in the name of Balor, our great god!" Arioch lifted his hands above him, and all the people whispered the name of Balor the Great.

"Now, I know the last few days have been trying on our town. The sin of the nonbelievers is bringing death and doom on our people now."

Yelling started, several men standing up and calling for the death of the heathens.

"Now, now, calm yourselves. Balor did not leave us to weather the storms on our own. He has spoken of those who would come to our lands and take it for their own."

Had they? Bryn wished she'd paid more attention when Mallory had dragged her to the chapel as a youth. It never sat well with her, the things she did hear, so she was more than happy to make the choice not to conform, even if it meant walking the night and staying indoors during the day.

"They are coming! This is the sign! Bodies at the gate."

Bryn felt a cool breeze come over her mortal body and hoped Jace was still watching her.

"I know, my people. It has been written that the enemies of Balor would return from another realm. That the bodies would come, people hoping to assist those who would harm us would be killed and left at our gate as a show that Balor is watching. That he knows the enemy has risen and the witches grow in power."

"What do we do, Scrios?" a woman holding a baby asked, a small child with bright-blond hair clutching its small fists in her skirts.

"We know the only way for these demons to get to us is through those who sin in our presence. Now, I know we've had this come up before, and the governor had stood firm in trials of justice. Unless we have indisputable proof they are a witch, we can do nothing. That whore at the brothel cannot be burned for spreading her legs. Mallory's witch of a niece has been coy in keeping her craft out of sight, giving us enough to know her evil, but not enough to hang her with."

A loud crash sounded from someone breaking a chair in the back of the chapel in anger.

"But justice is no longer being upheld in our town if we allow witches to walk our streets!" Arioch yelled as if in response to the violence.

The crowd roared in approval. A mob being created to hunt the monsters of their own imagination.

Bryn's blood turned to ice as Mallory made her way to the front. Keeping her hands clasped, she looked like the demure and devout person she pretended to be.

"I have been living my life in fear. Fear while in my own home knowing a witch is two doors down from me. I worry for my son, that he would fall prey to her wickedness and join her. I have tried to bring her around, to know Balor, but she refuses."

The booing was loud enough that Cyerra hopped in agitation, ruffling her feathers as Bryn shushed her in her mind, hoping the crow did not bring attention to herself.

Arioch stepped next to Mallory, readying himself to preach to his people.

"I have offered my hand to Bryndis Kenneally, hoping to make her a good wife, but she refused my suit and chose the darkness instead. Even now, she wakes up to walk the night, spending her time at the devil woman's brothel, and speaks to black birds in alleyways. Now, we have to take this into our own hands before these witches bring the demons down upon us," Arioch finished, standing next to Mallory in solidarity.

"Burn the witches!" the crowd chanted over and over again, and all the while, Mallory smiled.

Chapter 35

Coming back into her body, Bryn reeled as she tried to sit up. She felt sluggish as if she had fallen into a deep sleep.

The words she'd heard reverberated through her mind until fear flooded her brain, zapping her nervous system back into gear and waking her body up with adrenaline.

"They are going to burn me at the stake!" she cried out, grabbing Jace's arms as she pulled herself up.

"No, they wouldn't . . ." But as he said the words, he realized they very much would.

"Niamh . . . I have to warn her!" Pushing away from Jace, she ran at a hobble as her legs were the last of her body to wake up. Jace came up beside her to grab her arm and hold her steady.

The people were still in the chapel, so it had to be now. There was not any time to wait.

"Get the others, please. We have to make a plan and figure out what to do next!"

Not waiting for Jace to respond, Bryn ran before slamming into the doors of the Sanctuary, the music in the main room going as one of Niamh's girls played the piano. The party had already started for the evening, unknowing of the mob taking up arms just down the road.

"I need Niamh and Danu!" Bryn yelled, knowing someone in the house would find them.

"What in the world is wrong?" Niamh was quick to come from her office, her dress and makeup perfect.

"The church is planning to burn us at the stake!" Bryn yelled, her voice and body shaking. She knew she should be quiet, even if there were only a few patrons in the Sanctuary, but her panic was superseding her logic.

"Do they now?" Niamh looked toward the door with a contemplative look on her face. One that showed very little fear.

Declan, Justin, Caden, and Travis ran inside, and without question, Niamh went to the drawing room, ordering tea for her guests as if they were having a party and not discussing the town's plan to kill them.

Soon enough, Kessler and Sage were there as well. Jace and Mr. Rafferty were the last two to come.

Yet there was no sign of Danu or Callum.

Telling them what she saw, everyone in the room flew into a frenzy at her words. Declan moved closer to her as if to protect her, and though she wanted to be as far away from him as possible after his betrayal, their drama was not important right now.

"Hold on, let's think," Declan yelled over them.

Bryn sat down, Sage taking her hand and squeezing as she sat on the arm of the couch next to her.

"Dad, what can you do?" Declan asked, knowing that Mr. Rafferty had been the one to stop such atrocities in the past.

Sighing, he shook his head in response.

"Nothing. They called for my resignation this morning after the mob lit into Justin. At this point, I will not be in power much longer."

"On what grounds?" Declan demanded, clenching his fist.

"Take your pick. That I let heathens run free and put their town in danger. That I am partial to some and not putting the needs of the town above my own. There was a list I believe." Mr. Rafferty rubbed his eyes under his glasses.

"Failure to put the needs of the office before his own personal affairs is what was on the very unofficial-looking paperwork I was given," Justin grumbled. "Not much I can do, though, if the whole town is calling for it."

Shock stole Bryn's breath. If anyone else moved into the governor position, there would be no stopping Daran and Arioch. Mallory would be queen, reigning over Ifreann, and it would finally earn its old moniker of Hell's Gate.

"We have to leave, then. There is no choice!" Jace yelled, pacing as he fidgeted with a bracelet on his wrist. His hands were shaking.

"There will be a trial first," Mr. Rafferty assured. "Maybe not a fair one, but it gives us a little time to plan."

"Then let's start right this second. How will we travel? Horses will only get us so far in the desert. We'd be at the mercy of the sand and the sun. Gods or not, we still have human bodies," Sage stated, her logic grating at Bryn's nerves as she lost herself to working on and formulating a plan with limited options.

"Where is he?" Mallory's voice could be heard through the wooden doors well before she barreled her way in, two men following her that were in the chapel moments ago. Bryn couldn't remember their names, but the look in their eyes chilled her blood. "My son does not sleep with whores!"

Niamh rolled her eyes as she stood up from her chair, but Bryn hesitated, wondering if she should get up and help Niamh, but she remembered people of the town feared Niamh for a reason. Bryn stayed seated, hoping to see firsthand as to why.

Curiosity was a strong mistress.

"You!" Mallory pointed to Niamh. "You have brought nothing but trouble to this town, you demon! Now my son hangs out with whores." Her eyes snapped to Jace. "Get back to your apartment, now!"

"Ms. Mallory—" Declan started, her face whipping to look at him, taking the whole of him in. A gleam glittered in her eyes, followed by a crude smile.

"Ah yes. The man my own niece whores herself out to. Now you've your hooks in my son? She wasn't enough to corrupt?"

"I'd watch your tone, Ms. Kenneally. I'm allowing you this moment to collect yourself since we've had many a tragedy happen within these walls, but I won't tolerate your behavior for longer than a minute if you keep it up. I still run this town." Mr. Rafferty stood taller, Mallory only then noticing he was there as well.

"Not for long. We all know you're not fit to lead, not any longer. Soon enough, you'll be gone, and you'll take that waste of oxygen I've been forced to call a niece with you. Whether it's to outside of these walls or to the death where Balor help you should he be merciful enough to forgive your sins."

Bryn wondered if Mallory knew Bryn was in the room and was blatantly ignoring her. It seemed the more her world changed, the meaner and more ignorant the woman became. The fear making her dig her heels into her beliefs even more.

"Balor will smite you all. Remember that when you do your demon worshipping here in the house of sin!" Mallory spat on the floor.

"Been waiting on your god to do some smiting for a while now. Guess he is busier than you thought watching this little town, and it's less than a hundred population. Busy man." Caden smirked, and Mallory straightened for another tear when Danu appeared behind her.

"You believe that your god would forsake you on the beliefs of another?" Danu asked, moving between Mallory and the rest of the room. Bryn had forgotten in all the chaos of the past few minutes that Mallory, and most likely the rest of the town, was unaware that an outsider was being kept within their walls.

Mallory's face somehow became scarier, and Bryn started toward Danu, only to be pulled back by Declan.

With a finger pointing toward Danu, Mallory growled.

"Every one of you hid a witch in our presence, and you bring more into our town. Our safe place has been breached." Turning to the men with her, she pointed to the door. "Go! Tell the scrios what you've seen here!"

The men ran out of the building, leaving Mallory with the "witches." Had Bryn actually been dangerous, Mallory was an idiot to have left herself vulnerable.

Looking at Danu, Mallory roared a scream that was almost hilarious had the atmosphere not been heavy with dread.

"Stay away from me and my son with your witchcraft and pagan beliefs!"

Danu only smiled, not the least bit cowed by Mallory's obnoxious and unhinged behavior.

"You would do well to remember you are in my house now, Ms. Mallory." Niamh floated closer to her aunt.

The smile fixed on her face as she stood between them, and Mallory made something primal in Bryn's brain warn her that right now Niamh was dangerous, and Bryn needed to tread carefully.

Moving to slap her friend, Mallory's hand was caught in Niamh's without anyone seeing her move.

Mallory's eyes widened as she stumbled back, trying to pull her hand away from Niamh but to no avail. Niamh only gripped her tighter.

"Now," Niamh's voice was feminine yet deep, "are we going to behave, or will we be having a *chat*?"

"I . . . I won't . . . I'll go." Mallory was vibrating with fear.

Niamh released her, and Mallory stumbled, barely catching herself before she fell. Without another one of the venomous looks she was so fond of, she was out the door as if a demon itself was hot on her heels.

Straightening her dress, Niamh took a minute to touch her face, checking her makeup before she nodded and turned back to the group.

"Now, where were we?"

Chapter 36

No one said anything after Mallory's outburst and subsequent fleeing in terror.

The fear in the room was palpable in her absence, and from the look on everyone's faces, no one really knew why. Their entire lives were in danger here, and they needed to leave as soon as was possible, yet they were staring, frozen, at Niamh.

"Oh, please." Niamh laughed. "Every one of you is infinitely more powerful than Mallory and her little army of ignorance," Niamh said as she waved her hand to the door where Mallory had just fled.

"Then why was she so scared of you and not us?" Sage asked as she tilted her head, her inquisitive mind piqued by Mallory's abrupt departure.

No one moved or said a word. Bryn wondered if anyone was even breathing.

Niamh looked at each one of them before her eyes landed on Bryn's.

"If you'll excuse me. You all have much to discuss." Niamh nodded, turning to leave, but Danu moved between Niamh and the door.

"I release you from your geas, Lady Niamh Gwyer of Waterford, the original Dearg Due," Danu whispered, and power flooded the room.

"What the hell is a Dearg Due?" Justin demanded.

"Like I said, every damn time I am near her, something new pops out and turns everyone's lives upside down again. Just when we find right side up," Kessler grumbled.

Bryn moved toward Niamh until her friend held her hands up to keep Bryn back.

"It's safer if you stay away," Niamh whispered, her voice normal now, but sadness threaded heavily through it.

Ignoring the warning, Bryn moved to take Niamh's hand and faced her in front of everyone in the room.

She had no idea what a Dearg Due was, but she would stand beside her friend through something she could tell would be difficult to speak on.

"You're still Niamh," Bryn whispered, and Niamh took a stuttered breath. "You're still my friend. I promised you that before I knew you could scare the pants off my aunt. Now we are best friends."

Shock was there first before Niamh gave her a sad smile, moving her other hand over their joined ones.

"I understand secrets, Niamh. I have plenty." Bryn had wondered what was so huge that her friend kept her real self locked away.

"Yours are out in the open now. You have allies even though they know the real you. That would not be the case if they knew the real me," Niamh whispered, the room around them growing in agitation at the lack of information, but no one demanded they speak just yet.

"Not all . . .," Bryn stated, staring at the divot in the wood floor, most likely from one of Niamh's high heels.

"You don't have to tell me anything—" Niamh started, but Bryn cut her off with a wave of her hand.

They were all in this together now. There was nothing left to lose, so her secrets no longer held the same weight they once did.

"Mallory is perfect to everyone here," Bryn started, drawing on the courage to speak, keeping her eyes to the floor.

"I know that woman is evil. I am sure you have plenty of religious lectures growing up that were the epitome of hypocritical." Niamh laughed, but Bryn didn't.

She didn't look up at Niamh's face as her friend grew silent. If Bryn was going to tell them all, she needed to not look at anyone.

"She didn't bother after a while," Bryn started, and she could see the tips of Jace's shoes as he stepped forward. He didn't touch her, but he was still lending his strength to her. "I was too broken. When she fell in with the church, my father was alive, so she would do small things no one would notice. Pinches and hits that he wouldn't see since she did it during my bath time.

"Saying that I brought death and that death took my uncle because of me. Soon, she would tell me I killed my mother, should have died with her . . . and then after my father . . . that I killed him." Bryn had to stop and take a moment to calm her breathing.

A hand went to her shoulder, but Bryn feared touching it right then and making her shaking hands obvious. A curse passed someone's lips, and Jace pulled her face into his shoulder, Niamh still holding her hand, but Bryn pulled away from them both.

She appreciated their strength, but she just felt like she needed to not be touched while saying the words of her tormented past.

"After my father passed, she was so angry that she'd lock me in her closet. I'd get so hungry and so scared of the shadows . . . that it would be her coming back. Then the closet meant I didn't have to endure her words that came with the physical hits . . ."

Wiping a tear away from her eye, Niamh pulled Bryn in closer, Jace and Niamh holding her up now that her legs were buckling, and she had no other option but to let them.

"When my fits happened while working with Jace after dad died, she tried to get the demon out by beating me. Once I recovered, she'd do it again, which is why I was in my room so much in my teen years." A sob escaped, and she rallied to control herself so she could finish.

"I am going to kill her with my bare hands . . ." Declan's voice was terrifying as he said the words Bryn had wished to hear on those nights when she prayed for a savior.

"That's for me. I've earned my vengeance," Bryn whispered as she wiped her eyes and finally looked at the room around her.

Justin had his jaw clenched, eyes on fire, and he looked ready to snap. Most of the men did. Sage looked so sad on her behalf that Bryn had to look away again.

The silence was too thick for Bryn to handle, and the urge to flee the looks of both pity and promised retribution were strong, but she had relived that time for a purpose.

"Now everyone knows all my secrets. We should all feel safe in each other's presence because like it or not, we are a family all our own now, and we need each other to survive."

Turning to Niamh, she wiped the tears away and tried to smile.

"You don't have to tell us, but know it is a safe place, here with us"—Bryn waved around the room—"for when you are ready to share."

Niamh nodded, almost frantically, and then her bloodred lips spoke.

"A Dearg Due is . . ." Niamh took a deep breath, settling herself as she tightened her hand around the one Bryn offered again. "I am what you call a vampire."

That was not at all what Bryn expected.

"Like, you drink blood vampire?" Kessler asked, everyone's eyes in the room huge at her revelation.

Niamh nodded before swallowing. Looking at the ceiling, she composed herself again and turned to the room.

"Only people who are willing. I have control of it, so no need to fear me."

"I thought I'd be a lot more scared to meet a vampire," Justin stated, scratching his head.

"She is the same as she was twenty minutes ago," Caden said with a defensive tone of voice.

"You knew?" Travis accused.

"Yeah, I knew!" Caden replied. "I am one of the willing!"

Travis's jaw dropped at that, his hands going lax at his sides in shock.

"The girls?" Sage asked, pointing to the door where the women who worked at the Sanctuary were going about their nightly activities.

"They are like me. All women found to be in need, scared and broken, that come to me under the cover of night for refuge. I am known throughout the world for giving others like me a place to stay, and no, they don't have to serve the men here. They drink the blood of the patrons and that's enough to help these men find their pleasure without sex, though if the women decide to lay with the man for coin, that's their business."

Bryn didn't look at Declan as Niamh spoke.

"Who would think a group of vampires would live among the most righteous of King Bres's subjects? This is why my girls question nothing, including helping to carry you lot upstairs after you passed out from the stones."

The tension in the room was even higher than when Bryn had told her story.

"Enough. Niamh is not a threat to any of you. She is not the same as you all, but she is immortal and never had to be reborn because of a king hunting her. She is an ally, and you will all treat her like one," Danu ordered.

No one said anything, and Bryn wondered what she could do to break the silence before Declan did that for her.

"So, you were saying we have to leave our little slice of paradise?" Declan asked, settling into the chair he'd been leaning forward in to watch the drama unfold around him.

"Yes. The wraiths will come here, and then eventually, Bres will send his army to finish off anyone who managed to survive the wraiths," Danu replied, holding her hand out for Bryn. Giving the woman a small squeeze, Bryn felt a bolt of power run through her nerves and into her head before it settled, Danu moving back to the spot next to Sage on the couch as if she hadn't just lightly fried Bryn's nervous system.

It hadn't hurt, but it was a more intense shock than when she'd touched her friends after the sandstorm.

Narrowing her eyes, Danu gave her an innocent smile, taking her teacup and putting it to her lips.

"I thought the prophecy said we needed to be here to fight the wraiths?" Bryn asked as she settled down into the chair she had vacated to follow Niamh.

"Your visions did not say that you would be fighting more than the wraiths, and that is what concerns me." Danu touched her cheeks as she spoke.

Sage stared at a dent in the wood-grain coffee table. Pushing her nail into the wood, she tore a piece off as she was deep in thought.

"Are we all outsiders? I thought Declan was from the original founder until . . .," Kessler asked before stopping himself.

Oops.

Bryn forgot the rest of the group wasn't up to date on the newest revelations of Declan's parentage and Arawn's role in it.

"He was born in Osgar." Mr. Rafferty sighed, knowing it was time to tell them what he had confessed to Bryn in Faerie. "His parents were killed, and I took him with me to find the rest of you and push your families to move to Ifreann. It was the best way to keep you all safe, to hide you in plain sight."

Declan only sighed as everyone looked at him for a response. It was obvious he had already found this out about himself and may have even come to terms somewhat with the fact that the man who had raised him was not his biological father.

Though the scathing looks were still shot toward the man a few times in the meeting. It was odd to look at Mr. Rafferty, to know what he looked like in Faerie compared to the man who had adopted and protected them here in Ifreann as a man.

"Odd that they would let us in at all with all the panic and fear going on when we came here. Were any of us born here?" Jace asked.

Mr. Rafferty, Arawn, shook his head.

"I took on the persona of their founder's grandchild and brought you in under my wing. No one resisted it too much since I was of the blood of their people . . . or so they thought."

"So we have no living parents aside from Jace?" Sage asked, her voice small.

"And Bryn of course," Danu stated as if she hadn't just set a bomb off inside the room around her.

Danu looked at Bryn now, oblivious, or maybe not, of what she'd just said. Bryn stared hard at Danu, her eyes demanding Danu choose the next words very carefully.

"Your mother still lives in Cethin."

Chapter 37

Bryn shoved back from the table so abruptly that the chair fell backward, making a loud racket in the quiet space. Everyone in the drawing room stared with their mouths open and eyes wide.

"Liar!" Bryn yelled, her mind going feral at the implication that she had a mother out there. One that had not died during childbirth but lived and never looked for her daughter.

A daughter living in pain and ostracized.

"Bryn, we can go and find her." Jace stood, holding his hands out in a placating gesture, but Bryn only growled.

"Cut the crap, Jace!" She stepped toward the drawing-room door, scared she might lose her mind if she was kept in the slowly shrinking room full of people.

"Your mother might think you are dead just like you thought she was." Sage tried to intervene, reaching out for Bryn, but her nerves were too raw for the touch.

Bryn needed to tear into something or strike out at someone. She knew she was far too dangerous to be around her friends for much longer.

"Does she know I am alive?" Bryn growled, her voice gruff, as she turned back to look at Danu.

"I am unsure, but as of when you left, yes. She knew."

Declan ran a hand over his face.

"For the sake of self-preservation, Danu, the answer was no," Declan grumbled.

Danu shook her head before looking back at Bryn.

"She knew whose soul resided inside of you, Bryn, and knew who you would eventually become. That she would have to let you go."

Bryn didn't care why. All that mattered was how she'd suffered without any parent to look out for her all the while her mother lived freely away from the hellish place she'd resigned her daughter to.

"So she didn't care that I was alive, her daughter. Didn't care that I was taken to some rotting city in the desert. All she knows for sure is that I am some goddess wearing her daughter's face. Well, that makes me feel *so much better!*"

Bryn barreled her way out of Niamh's, ignoring the voices calling out to her from the drawing room as she ran out onto the road heading toward her apartment.

The anger was burrowing deeper into her marrow as she got closer to the apartments she shared with her tormentor. Knowing Mallory was nearby, her skull thrummed with the beat of her heart. A vicious part of her demanded she take every ounce of anger out on Mallory like the woman had done to her for *years,* but logically she knew she should avoid her aunt.

It was no good for her, or the rest of the Tuatha Dé Danann, to look for more trouble.

Focusing on the whiskey she'd hid in the trunk full of dresses in her room, she planned to lock herself in and get drunk enough to pass out.

Ignoring the growing chill in the air, she let her anger warm her. Her focus was on her rage and her destination that she stumbled, almost falling, when Kian appeared in front of her.

"Don't borrow trouble, Bryn. It is a volatile state this town is in right now."

Her laughter carried down the street, a few of the merchants closing up shop shooting her looks.

Not the fearful looks of a crazy lady laughing in the street, but one that told her they saw her as the enemy. That they were counting down the moments until her blood was spilled in the sand.

Walking around Kian, she ignored him, thankful that he was too ghostly for the people to actually see in the waning light. Hell, she could barely see him.

The fact that he was warning her like someone who actually cared for her well-being made her angrier. He wanted to kill her himself as he thought he was due vengeance, not because he gave a shit about her as a person.

Tearing through the clinic, Bryn stomped up the stairs to her apartment, standing at the top, looking between her place and Mallory's.

Biting back the urge to barrel into Mallory's apartment, Bryn started toward her own when Mallory's door opened behind her. Bryn slowly turned to face her aunt.

If I am supposed to be the Morrigan, then why do I fear this mortal woman so much?

That Mallory could have her burned at the stake should no longer matter. She was powerful and was letting Mallory, a human, keep her from everything she could be.

Come to me then, something inside of Bryn whispered, and she knew deep down this was the part of her that was the Morrigan.

The tingling along her skin, the headaches that pushed at her since the sandstorm, all the sensations that she fought, she gave in to.

To take out all the rage on Mallory as her aunt had done to her so many times when Bryn was young. When she was so small and unable to defend herself.

While her mother lived up north, blissfully unaware of the pain Bryn lived through every day.

"Bryndis." Her aunt seethed as Bryn watched Mallory move closer.

The woman narrowed her eyes, trying to figure out why Bryn wasn't cowering back yet, but there was a promise there that Mallory would find a way to make it happen eventually.

Bryn started laughing as she looked at Mallory posturing and the subsequent confusion when it didn't work as it once had.

"Think about what you are doing, Bryn. You can't take every decision back," Kian growled in her ear from where he had formed next to her. She spun, pointing a finger at his chest.

"Says the Fomori assassin," she growled.

"What in the name of all that is holy do you think you're doing?" Mallory found her voice finally as Bryn stood there, her fist clenched, her eyes moving from Kian to lock on the woman who had spent Bryn's childhood lying to her about her mother.

"My mother is alive, and you never told me!" Bryn yelled, slamming her fist into the wall, breaking through the plaster as white rained down from the spot she'd hit.

With wide eyes, Mallory turned and ran back to her room, but Bryn was quick to grab the edge of the door, pushing it open as Mallory tried, and failed again, to close it.

"Get out!"

"No," Bryn growled, pushing her way into Mallory's apartment. The entire place smoky from the incense she lit during prayers. The walls covered in propaganda to her false god. Balor was everywhere in this apartment, and some place deep inside of Bryn seethed at a level she didn't know existed inside of herself.

For once, Bryn did not feel judged or intimidated being here. She did not feel powerless.

Bryn turned to Mallory and waved the burning sage into her own face as Mallory watched.

"Guess it does nothing to repel the demons like you thought, huh?" Bryn laughed, sure that she sounded deranged.

Bryn was sure she *was* deranged at this point.

Mallory was a human who worshipped a deity that had ruined their world. That would see Bryn dead if she didn't take hold of the power she had been given.

Bryn's vision reddened, and Mallory's eyes widened. As if Bryn was physically different now, her anger changing her.

"Witch!" Mallory stumbled back, her eyes wide. "I always knew you were made of the dark magic!"

Bryn smiled until she thought her face might split. Oh, how close Mallory was to the actual dark magic and yet she had no clue.

A primal part of Bryn loved that Mallory flinched when she took a step toward her aunt.

"Bryn, keep it together and remember she is human," Kian's voice cut in, but Bryn was done trying to fit into a world that had chosen long before she had ever stepped foot in this callous town that they would not accept her.

Finally, Bryn chose to no longer accept *them*.

"My mother is alive!" Bryn's voice boomed, the echo of it filled with a power that Bryn was sure made the tiny hairs on the nape of her prey stand up.

Mallory shook her head, her fingers going into her ears as if trying to get something out, unable to hear.

"As far as any of us were concerned, she was dead! She was full of sin, and we had hoped you would overcome your sinful heritage," Mallory replied in a voice far too loud.

"My sinful heritage? And who is 'we,' because as far as I knew, my father loved me as I was."

A sickly-sweet smile crossed Mallory's face, one that told Bryn that Mallory had been waiting a long time to say these words. And she said them, though her voice shook.

"Your father was smart enough to take the child born to him by that useless feral bitch. She wanted to raise you in their sinful clans, and he refused. Why he even bothered touching a demon—"

Bryn's hand was wrapped around Mallory's throat before she could finish the thought.

Shoving Mallory against the wall, it took every ounce of willpower she had not to snap her neck. Bryn was desperately fighting herself, the Morrigan, and while fear ran along the surface of her mind that the Morrigan might take this too far, the fear in Mallory's eyes fed the monster inside.

The monster that begged Bryn to kill the weak woman. To protect the damaged girl that she had been by destroying the one who had hurt her and made her feel she was less.

"You dare speak of the woman who gave me life in that way? The woman from whom you stole her child?" Bryn asked, the echo in her voice sounding as if two women spoke at once.

Mallory struggled for breath, her eyes bulging, and Bryn lessened her hold slightly for the woman to speak, though she doubted she would get any insightful information. She had to end this now because Bryn could feel herself receding, the other part growing stronger as she could actually *smell* Mallory's fear.

"Where is my mother now? Is she still in Cethin?" growled Bryn, no longer seeing Mallory as a bitter aunt with whom she had to deal with the daily antagonism. No, now she was Bryn's enemy as much as the king and his demon wraiths.

Perhaps Mallory didn't maim her victims with a sword but instead used her words and neglect.

And sometimes that could be just as deadly.

"Mountains . . . outside . . . of Cethin."

Kill her. End all your troubles now. So easy to just snap her fragile human neck . . .

Fighting herself, the part that was the Morrigan yet familiar enough that Bryn knew that it had always been there in the deepest recesses of her mind. Bryn tightened her hand before she came back to herself and released her aunt.

Holding herself back from grabbing Mallory again, she watched the woman fall to the floor in a heap of shaking mess, the predator deep inside her screaming for her to finish off her prey.

Bryn stepped away, though she stayed ready to grab Mallory by the throat again should she move or speak in a way Bryn, the Morrigan, didn't like.

"The Dearil Mountains. My mother lives in the death mountains?"

Rubbing at her throat, Mallory looked up at Bryn with eyes full of unleashed anger.

"Does it really surprise you that you were born of death?"

Bryn couldn't say it did anymore. Not when she was learning more about herself, and her deadly abilities, every day.

Chapter 38

Grabbing her old, beaten leather bag she had used long ago when providing lackluster medical care, Bryn stuffed her meager belongings into it.

"You cannot go out to find your mother alone. The wraiths will surely destroy you too." Kian appeared near her as she shoved a bra into the bag, his eyes laser focused on the item for a second longer than she thought a guy without a body might.

Looking up at her raised eyebrows, he gave a panty-melting smile. *"Still have the mind of a man who was once very much alive, Phantom Queen."*

Bryn snorted, wishing she could bask in the playfulness he was falling more and more into each day, but instead, she moved to the trunk that held her extra items for cold and her dresses.

The whiskey was already packed.

The Dearil Mountains were known to be some of the coldest areas left in their world. Nothing she owned would prepare her for the drop in temperatures, but she hoped even if she didn't find her mother, she would find goodwill among her mother's people.

But did it actually matter where she went? She knew she couldn't stay here. Mr. Rafferty wouldn't be running Ifreann for much longer, and with her having attacked Mallory, one of their most fervent believers, that only guaranteed her death here.

Stopping her erratic packing, Bryn put her hands on the bed, taking in huge gulps of air as she realized she was not as settled with the idea as she thought.

"I would hate . . . to begrudge . . . you my . . . death at your hands," she whispered between pained breaths.

"Exactly. It would be a great disservice to me."

Steadying her shaking body, she took a huge breath in and centered herself before moving to grab her candles when the door swung open, hitting the wall, and leaving a dent in it.

"You attacked my mother?" Jace asked from the doorway, his eyes shining as his world fell apart just as much as her own.

Staring at him, she really looked at him. He almost seemed taller since taking his power back, his eyes alight in gold, and she wondered if that was what Mallory saw when she called her a "demon" earlier.

"My mother is alive, Jace, and she kept that from me!" Her face was wet. When had she started crying? Maybe she had been crying the whole time.

"My mother!" Bryn's voice broke, and she wiped the tears that dared to leave her eyes. "She has been alive this whole time, and your mother helped my father leave with me. They took me from someone who could have loved me after my father's death." She ended on a sob.

Bryn would need to unpack all she felt toward her father on that matter, but that would have to wait. She had too much happening now, and she wasn't sure she had anything left in her tank.

"Still, antagonizing her puts a larger target on your back!"

"Exactly, Jace!" She stepped to her cousin, face-to-face, and noticed the true differences between her and her father. Between her and her cousin. Where they had blond hair, hers was a deep red. Their bright-blue eyes to her mixed green and blue. Tan skin to pale.

She must resemble her mother.

"Exactly. It doesn't matter anymore. They planned to kill me before I even showed any potential power, and you know it. This was all the catalyst to put their plans into action."

"Even so, Danu said we have to fight here. On Ifreann's soil. It's all a part of the prophecy. If you leave, then we are doomed to fail."

Without looking at Jace, Bryn left the room and moved to the pantry of the kitchen they shared.

She needed to find enough food to make it to the closest town, but who knew what state Tanwen was in or how she would even get there.

Anxiety built in her chest as she put her head against the pantry shelf and slammed her fist into the wall. Tears of frustration leaking too fast for her to bother with wiping them away.

Bryn let herself have a moment to fall apart before she wiped her face with her sleeve.

She was so *damn* tired.

Steadying herself again, she grabbed a few more jars of preserves and turned only to run into Jace.

His eyes were red, his jaw clenched, and she feared he had come for a fight that would end with her leaving her cousin here on bad terms.

When he reached forward, she flinched, but he pulled her into his arms, wrapping her in a tight hug.

"I am so sorry for all the pain she has caused you, Bryn. So, so sorry."

Tears leaked from her eyes as she hugged Jace back with everything she had left in her.

"If you are determined to leave against my advice, then I am going with you to find your mom. I owe it to you to help you find yours after what my own did."

"Jace, no." She stepped out of his hold, but his hands gripped her shoulders, tightening his fingers into her shirt.

"I am not letting you go out into the wild desert without me at your back. What will you do if you get injured?"

Bryn kept her eyes focused on his, moving between them as if she could pull his thoughts to the surface and see if this was all simply guilt or his own desire to leave town.

"Probably help to have backup and someone who can find food," Declan's voice interrupted them, and Jace turned them to face Declan. "Seems the town has no need of me or my father any longer. Arioch is the interim governor."

"Worse yet"—Justin followed Declan in— "Daran is the new town sheriff."

Bile rose in Bryn's throat.

Sage ran into the clinic, standing at the top of the stairs, her eyes wild. She ignored the men as she stared at Bryn.

"They are gathering wood. They made a pyre in the middle of Saints' Road."

"What about a trial?" Bryn demanded, turning to Justin. "Mr. Rafferty said there would be a trial first!"

"There should have been. It's in the bylaws," Justin replied, pinching the bridge of his nose. "But I am guessing Arioch and Daran aren't too worried about following the letter of the law."

"Can they do that after removing Mr. Rafferty for what they deemed the very same issue?" Jace asked, bewildered.

"They have enough of a mob to where they can do anything," Declan remarked, his hand moving to point at the wall, as if they could see through it to the townspeople out there planning and preparing for Bryn's death. "Those people are not rational right now. They are being fed a steady stream of poison in the form of anger and hatred, and we have no antidote."

Everyone was silent at Declan's words before Sage spoke up.

"Then it looks like we are leaving together. Screw the prophecy."

Chapter 39

Waiting for Jace to grab his medical gear, Bryn watched as Travis and Caden came out of the back door to the Cauldron, bags packed and rifles slung over their shoulders. Caden gave Bryn a wink and a smile when he walked up to her.

"We are going to need each other, and this town is no longer the place to make our stand against the king."

"And where would that stand be made?" she asked, watching him as he strode by with a cocky look on his face. She knew where she planned to go but was unsure if everyone else was on board.

Bryn hoped not to have to split off from them on their travels, but she would find her mother and answers.

"Wherever the goddess of war decides it is." Caden snickered as he walked into the small barn behind the Cauldron.

Of course it was.

Declan and Kessler were the next to stride around the corner of the Cauldron, moving to the back barn that Declan had kept for himself and where Caden and Travis had just gone to.

How long had they been planning this? This was a little coordinated for a spur-of-the-moment decision.

But she knew that Mr. Rafferty most likely knew the tides could change at any moment, and he created several backup plans.

The power structure in the town was far too fragile not to have an escape plan years in the making, and one was now being enacted.

Breaking away from where she'd been leaning against the building, she caught up to Declan and Kessler, both of them larger than her by far. She was almost childlike in height next to them, and that was saying something since she was not a short woman.

"What are y'all up to?" she asked as Justin walked up with his own bag, Finian loping to Bryn and smothering her in his canine affection.

Rubbing Finian's head, she looked to Declan as he took her elbow and pointed to where Kessler moved to something huge under a tarp in the barn.

"Backup plan." Declan winked, confirming her thoughts as Kessler tore the tarp off, jumping into the back of a monster made of metal.

She knew what it was, but they had long since been rendered useless due to the war on resources after the Collapse. Food, gas, anything that could keep a person at the top and alive was coveted until the king came in and started controlling the import and export trade.

People still fought for food and land, but things like gas and fuel were long gone.

So, without the fuel to power it, why this was some amazing thing struck her as odd.

"A truck," she stated, trying to keep an optimistic tone but failing horribly.

"A truck," Kessler said with a pride she'd never heard from the man of few syllables. "Been working on her for a while, but with that magic rock igniting something in my blood, now she works!"

He smacked the metal side as if it were a prized horse.

"You can magic the metal to drive it?" Sage's voice joined them, holding the awe she was sure the men had hoped to hear.

"Sure can." Declan looked at Kessler as the man admired his work.

"Beautiful, isn't she?" Kessler jumped down next to them and stared at the metal contraption. Various colors adorned her from where he had somehow managed to find random metal to weld together, most likely during the rare times he went with Declan to trade outside the walls of Ifreann.

"Yeah, Kessler, it really is," she replied as she walked around the truck, taking it all in, never having seen one before in person. How he had come to own one and kept it secret for so long baffled her.

"I need to pack and make sure I have all my books and herbs," Sage started, ending the sentence by continuing her mental list silently as she ticked them off on her fingers. Without saying another word to them, she turned and began walking back to her cottage.

"Can we leave soon?" Niamh asked as she walked up to the group, looking between Declan and Kessler.

"The moment everyone in this town is sound asleep in bed, we are gone," Justin replied, leaning against the truck, and earning narrowed eyes from Kessler that he ignored.

"We will have to push the truck out to be safe. I've had to cause a lot of ruckus to cover the noise of testing to make sure it starts." Kessler popped the hood of the truck, messing with something Bryn couldn't identify if she tried.

A cool breeze moved around them, giving Bryn a chill that felt like a warning.

It was as if Mother Nature herself was telling them to get a move on.

As Justin had said, they would need to slip out once everyone was tucked away and the guard shifts had changed. That gave them the night to move the truck and . . .

"The gate?" Bryn turned to Justin. "How will we get past the gate if you are no longer sheriff?"

Justin smiled and looked at Travis.

"Lucky for me, a good friend is on shift and can get them opened up."

"And you can get down in time to join us?" she asked, not willing to leave any member of their group behind. Travis nodded but said nothing else.

Did this mean if they left soon, she could save him from the death she saw in the vision? What was even the point of seeing such things if there was nothing she could do to stop it? Being the Morrigan must give her some power to take control of the future.

They knew from speaking to Danu that the wraiths were after them since the king had felt their awakening.

If they left tonight, maybe Travis wouldn't have to die, and neither would the people of the town. At least that was what Bryn was hoping for. Not everyone who walked these roads was guilty. She couldn't bear the thought of innocent children caught up in this.

Bryn wished she could show up and leave without a trace like Danu. To just pop in and out of places without a soul being aware. That would have been a handy power to have in their escape.

Kessler shut the hood, taking the bags already brought in and throwing them into the back of the truck, organizing them as everyone remained silent.

"It'll be tight, but we can make do. We can bring the tarp to make a cover for the back, but let's make sure we have what we need."

Declan walked over, taking Bryn's small leather bag, not saying a word about the fact that she had so much less baggage than the others.

Sage walked back toward them as Niamh placed her bags on the floor. Sage's luggage, much like Bryn's, was worn with age.

Niamh's looked like a princess going on a royal tour. Bryn shot a smirk at Niamh who replied back with one of her saucy looks.

"I've waited years to leave this gods forsaken spot in the sand." Niamh smiled.

"Could've left whenever," Travis responded as he tucked his own gear into the truck, keeping his pistol on hand and rifle slung across his back.

"No, I couldn't . . ." Niamh gave a tender look at Bryn. Mush. That was the feeling deep within her at that look.

Niamh was what her mother should have been to her. A protector and nurturer. Something that Bryn doubted came naturally to the woman, but she somehow managed to do it with Bryn, and she could never repay her.

"Where are we headed?" Travis asked, checking over his bag.

"Ultimate goal? North and as far away from Drystan and the king as possible. Maybe the wraiths will stay focused on the area nearest the coast, giving us time to get Bryn to Cethin and see what we can find out about her mother. Hit Tanwen along the way for supplies and plan our next step from there," Declan said with authority.

Bryn watched as Kessler threw the tarp over the back of the truck with their gear tucked away, leaving a few open spots for them to sit in the back since the cab only held three people. Justin, Travis, and Caden were already offering to sit in the back of the truck to take care of any "issues" before they became problems while traveling.

"That's about it. Finish packing what you need and get your asses back here as soon as possible. We will set out as soon as Travis is on shift to get the gate open for us." Justin nodded to each of them as he moved to help Kessler grab the bricks next to the tires that had kept the truck from rolling.

"Leaving right now would be a hell of a lot better," Declan muttered, earning a look from Justin.

"We need the cover of night, and you know I have no control over the guard shifts anymore, Declan."

Everyone went quiet at the reminder except Finian who made a small whine as if he could understand what the men were saying.

Shaking his head, Declan walked off without another word. The rest of them followed, all except Kessler and Bryn, to get the last of their things before they stepped outside the gate for the first time since they could remember.

Straight into the wilds that was the rest of the world.

Chapter 40

B ryn felt a tickle along her neck as she sat on the tailgate of the pickup
truck, waiting for her friends to return so they could leave. Running
her hand over the top of Finian's head as he lounged beside her, she pushed
away the fear plaguing her as she mentally willed her friends to hurry up.

They were supposed to have all met back up within thirty minutes, yet
here they were . . . Bryn looked at her watch. Okay, so it had only been
fifteen minutes.

She was a little antsy, she could admit it.

Kessler was moving around the truck, checking tires and saying words
that made no sense to her.

Caden had come back fairly quickly and kept an eye out for anyone
sniffing around that shouldn't be.

Travis had gone to work his shift at the gate.

Her body tingled with nervous energy at what was to come, the excitement and fear pulsing through her in equal measures. Her legs were
swinging constantly in nervous anticipation, which had irritated Kessler as

he worked on the truck, but he was good enough to stop his angry grunting at her after the first few times.

She knew him working on the truck, double-checking everything, was his own version of restless waiting.

The only person they didn't need to wait on was Mr. Rafferty. He could just cross the veil to wherever they needed to be, so Declan had planned for him to wait on the other side of the gate and cause a distraction if need be.

Cyerra landed next to her, her feathers ruffled, as a sudden wave of freezing air stole over the town, and Bryn sat up. Kessler stopped and walked to her as they looked together at the walls of the city. Finian jumped down from the tailgate to investigate what had everyone wound up.

"That is in no way normal," he whispered.

"Neither was that sandstorm," Bryn responded, and looked to Cyerra who was on high alert as well.

"Am I in another vision?" she asked the crow as Kian took form near the driver's side door of the truck.

"What in the blazes?" Kessler murmured as he caught sight of Kian, seeing him for the first time, and Bryn wondered what Kessler thought to do with the wrench he was holding like a weapon against a man made of shadows.

"Kessler, this is Kian. He is a shadow man who I killed as the Morrigan and is waiting to become human and take his revenge. Kian, this is Kessler. He is an alive man who is a very good friend so attempt to mind your manners."

Bryn pushed off the tailgate of the truck as Kessler murmured something more to Kian, but she wasn't listening to them any longer.

"*Not a vision,*" Cyerra answered as she flew to Bryn's shoulder. "*It is time to leave before the wraiths come for you.*"

A huge gust blew through, and Bryn watched the fire in the city lamps struggle to stay lit in the onslaught of wind.

It was time to leave Ifreann, and she was happy to do so. She just hoped the wraiths were not so close that they were able to stall their escape attempt.

"We need to go," she yelled as she spun around, running to the front of the truck. "Where is everyone?"

Kessler looked at Kian one last time before moving around the man of shadows to the driver's side of the truck.

"No idea, but we gotta move this closer to the gate before we do anything. Declan has a spot picked out so they can all meet us there."

Nodding, Bryn moved to the back of the truck, closing the tailgate as she readied to help him push it.

"Darling, you are not moving that hunk of metal." Kessler gave a small tilt of his head for her to move out of the way as Caden ran up from where he had been playing lookout.

Raising her hands, she stepped back and watched as the wheels began to turn on their own, Kessler concentrating on the truck but not touching it.

"Holy hell, Kess," she whispered, watching him move the giant metal beast that had to weigh several tons all with his mind. "That is a cooler power than I have."

Kessler grunted, not with effort from moving the truck, but just with typical Kessler speak.

Grabbing the lantern they had set up nearby as Kessler had double-checked everything, she followed the truck and both men to the area near the gate.

"You think moving a metal object is better than warfare and guiding the dead?" Kian asked, his voice full of disappointment.

"Sure is." She smiled at Kian, feeling some relief that they were making small steps toward leaving. "Do you see Kessler having to deal with you?"

At those words, she walked faster to where Kessler was slowing the truck, a bead of sweat dripping down his forehead. A concerning sight with the freezing air surrounding them.

"Are you going to be able to get us to Tanwen?" she asked, reaching out to touch his arm, her fingers hesitating for a second before she remembered that she could touch him without a vision.

As she laid her hand on his arm, he nodded.

"I am getting better. There had been some trial and error, but the concentration is more from trying to move this thing while not making a noise between buildings in the dark. Open road? No problem."

That made sense.

Looking at her watch, it was time for the others to be here. Justin broke through the darkness first with a mini personal armory and his bag. Finian nipped at Justin's heels before jumping into the cab of the truck the moment Kessler opened the door and took a seat. Bryn tried not to laugh as Kessler whisper shouted for Finian to get out of there.

Sage followed soon after with more books and herbs, a sad look on her face as she gave her possessions to Kessler to load. Bryn gave Sage a side hug knowing it was hard for her friend to have to give up so many books since there was only so much room.

Declan moved on silent feet, something that had always astonished her for a man of his size, as he handed off a crate of provisions from the Cauldron to Kessler.

"How will we make everything fit? This is too large, and with all the people, bags . . ." Kessler furrowed his brows as he looked back to the truck.

Declan slung a pack off his back, opening it up to show that it was empty.

"Turns out one of my powers is quite a boon when escaping hell." He smiled, his teeth white in contrast to the dark night. Taking Sage's books and herbs, he packed them into the backpack.

"What about your items?" Sage asked, watching him with curiosity as Niamh came around the corner after having done what she needed to do in handing the reins of the Sanctuary over.

"Already in there." Declan smiled and grabbed Bryn's bag from the bed of the truck, putting it in the backpack that should have been overly full by now. "It's like another pocket of reality, or whatever shit Callum went on about when I was barely listening. Anyway, I have all the space in the world once I open up a pocket, and here we are." He showed the stuff he had just put in was gone, the backpack still looking empty.

"I will kill you Declan Rafferty if anything happened to those books!" Sage growled, only earning a wink from the man in response.

Jace was the last one in, pulling a duffle over his shoulder full of his personal items while holding his medical bag in his other hand. He stopped when he realized everyone was already gathered and cautiously handed his belongings to Declan, who made them disappear.

"What in the—" Jace started but was cut off.

"You think to leave? Before you've fulfilled your own prophecy?" Danu interrupted, and everyone turned to the little old lady standing in front of the truck looking quite a bit more formidable than she ever had before with her eyes narrowed and hands clenched at her sides. The power she was radiating toward them was mind-numbing.

They thought her frail and that they could easily get past her when the time came, but Bryn knew they were wrong. The old lady facade was all an act, and Bryn remembered how Arawn stated he could change his appearance as needed.

Bryn could just bet that Danu could as well.

The tingly sensation that had run over her sensitive skin ever since right before the sandstorm was now threading through her muscles, attaching itself to bone and making her nervous system hum.

Cold chills ran down her spine as her hands and feet began to feel far colder than the rest of her. Her fight-or-flight instinct started to pump adrenaline into her blood as she turned to the gate, ignoring everyone else as her attention went to where Travis was on lookout.

Finian moved up beside her with a low growl, his hackles rising along his back.

"Bryn?" Declan's voice cut through her thoughts, and she shook herself free of the sensation that tried to hold her in its thrall.

"Something is coming," she responded. "We need to move right *now*."

Chapter 41

E veryone looked from her to each other.

"Then that is exactly what we should do. Let's head out, y'all." At Justin's words, Caden stood, strapping his borrowed pistol to his side and securing his rifle along his back just as Travis would have done, and she wondered for a split second if that was something he had taught Caden to do.

"You must stand your ground here!" Danu yelled, and Bryn worried that everyone in Ifreann heard the woman. "If you leave, everything I have done to this point is for naught!"

Grabbing gas lamps, Justin and Caden moved to the front to light the way for Kessler as he moved the truck closer to the gate since the sun had yet to make its debut for the new day.

The adrenaline pumped through her, her heartbeat pushing it through at a rapid pace as it flooded her body.

Only a few more yards and they were free!

That was all it took, the unfettered optimism for something horrible to strike and ruin all their plans.

Such as the men who stepped into the light of Justin's and Caden's gas lamps, the truck halting when Kessler noticed the new arrivals standing between them and the gate.

Bryn almost wanted to yell at them to just start the truck and mow them down, but she bit her lip instead. The torches the men held lit them in a way that made them look demonic as they wore the masks of Balor on their faces. All but Arioch and Daran, who stood at the front of the group.

Daran in his normal wear was nothing next to the sight of Arioch in his full religious regalia. The black-cloaked man with what she now knew as the Evil Eye Balor had been known for embroidered on the chest.

"And where would you be heading to?" Daran asked with a wicked smile on his face from where he stood next to Arioch, several townspeople flanking him.

The torches cast devilish shadows on the brick in mockery of the situation Bryn found herself in. As if she were in actual hell, demons surrounding her as they readied to torment and torture her for eternity.

All of them armed aside from Daran and Arioch, several with their own rifles pointed right at Bryn. As if out of all the people standing before them, she was the greatest threat.

She could see it all in Daran and Arioch's eyes; they had planned to send her to her death this night. The torches they held would be what ignited the wood at her feet.

Niamh moved around her, but Bryn held up a hand. She refused to stand behind anyone ever again.

Sage jumped down from the bed of the pickup where she had been organizing gear and moved to flank Bryn and Niamh.

"Figured you'd be pleased we were leaving," Declan responded as he came around to the front of the truck, keeping his voice calm, but Bryn caught the hand signal to Justin. What it meant, she wasn't entirely sure, but she was hoping for an amazing backup plan.

"Heard from Mallory while she was hollering about you attacking her"—a few of the townsmen let loose a string of muffled threats or curses as Daran spoke— "that you have some new gifts we can surely use, Bryndis."

Daran smiled, the men next to him aiming their weapons at Declan, while the ones in back grew restless with their torches. They were ready to burn some witches it seemed, and Daran's little standoff was cutting into their evening plans.

If only they had left earlier . . .

"Oh, so we are demons until we have something you want, then you have a use for us!" Sage burst out, her normally small voice booming with justified anger. Well, justified at least as far as Bryn was concerned.

"I am not sure what you are talking about, Daran," Declan stated, putting his hands in his pants pockets. "When has there ever been anything special about any of us?"

Someone snorted in the back, but no one else made a sound as Arioch stepped forward, except Finian whose low growl and full display of teeth made her worry someone might shoot him.

"Would you like to admit your crimes and come willingly, Bryndis Kenneally and Niamh Gwyer? Perhaps we can find a use for you instead of taking you to your deaths."

The men behind Daran turned to each other, glancing around and nervously shifting, their body language screaming confusion. They had come for blood, and Daran was offering the witches a way out.

"What are you talking to them about it for?" one of the men asked. "I thought we was here for burning the witches, not sitting down for tea and having a lovely conversation."

Daran looked back at the man with narrowed eyes before turning to face Bryn again.

"Balor taught us that sometimes we don't always see what we need right away, but we have to take it when we find it." Daran smiled with a piece of straw between his yellowed teeth. Something predatory flashed in Daran's eyes as Arioch strode up to stand before Bryn.

Bryn didn't miss Daran tilting his head to the side and showing his neck as Arioch walked past him.

She also didn't miss the majority of the mob as their movements grew in agitation, their bloodlust and adrenaline starting to wear off. She was unsure how Arioch wanted to play this since they were losing their momentum. A mindless mob growing in mindfulness was not what she figured his ultimate goal was.

"Balor?" Danu appeared from behind Declan, moving to the front of their group to face off with the men as if they wouldn't chew her up and spit her out, old lady or not. "You truly have no idea who the god you worship is, do you?"

The men in the back of the mob squirmed. The high and mighty holy justice they were going to dispense was petering out quickly now, and Arioch only had his backup for so much longer.

Maybe, just maybe, Bryn could wait them out long enough to work her way through. To negotiate with the rational part of the group to release her and her friends.

It was a nice thought for all of the five seconds she'd had it before she realized that Daran and Arioch were in charge now and no longer needed the people's vote. They could have what they wanted without needing the townsfolk to approve.

"Balor, the true god," Mallory piped in from where she had been hiding in the back. Nice to know her aunt was finally taking an interest in her, even if it was just to watch Bryn die.

"Mother? You're part of this?" Jace asked, and Bryn could hear his heart breaking. For that alone she wanted to walk over and break Mallory's jaw. Too bad she'd have to get through all the men armed to the teeth to do so.

"You planned to leave me!" Mallory whined, and something in Bryn relished at the smell of her distress and fear as it carried to her on the breeze. Strong and potent and familiar; at the scent of it, she was back in the apartment having it out with her aunt.

That memory sent the demon inside Bryn raging, shoving at the walls of Bryn's brain to get out.

Her control began to flounder as she watched Mallory walk around the group to where she was in view of Jace, but not close enough for Bryn to get to her without being shot first.

Still, she watched the woman closely as a wolf would a wounded rabbit.

"I was planning to go back to the apartment to talk some sense into you! To try and have a rational conversation and possibly work on you coming with us! Shot that all to hell now, haven't you?" he yelled, backing away from the townspeople he had known and treated as their doctor. From his mother, who was his own flesh and blood, gone turncoat.

Danu's laugh caught them all off guard.

"You worship the true demon himself! The one who brought this wrath and plague upon you and this world! The demon king's own father! Evil Eye himself!" Before Danu could go on, someone pulled the trigger of their rifle and shot her, sending everyone into a panic until a growl reverberated through the crowd that shot everyone's prey drive into frozen-deer mode.

Finian bit into Bryn's skirt, attempting to pull her away from the chaos, but Bryn only moved to cover Danu as Jace ran toward the older woman.

The look on Mallory's face told her she knew nothing of who they actually worshipped, and Bryn watched her aunt's eyebrows furrow as she puzzled out what Danu meant . . . but it was the grins on Arioch's and Daran's faces that said they were all too aware of who their master was.

They'd known all along.

Chapter 42

"Get back, Bryn," Declan ordered, and Bryn had the urge to punch him in a different head this time as he tried to take her place at the front of the mob.

"The hell I will! Quit trying to take my power, Declan," she growled, holding tight to her position as Cyerra flew in and landed on her shoulder.

Mallory's eyes narrowed at the crow, and it seemed that sparked the murderous mob back to life.

Oops.

Danu started to speak softly in the language Bryn had heard before from the dead man, her voice growing louder as the mob inched closer to them with weapons and torches raised. Someone had a rope ready to tie Bryn and Niamh down like a runaway calf.

The old woman was speaking prayerfully and *loudly* behind her, and all the while Bryn was trying hard to focus on the threat in front of her. The words started to pierce through Bryn's mind as she took a defensive position, her knees slightly bent, her hand moving to her blade.

"May the great queen of the Tuatha Dé Danann guide your blade in battle and see you safely to the other side of the battlefield, whole and alive. Should you cross the veil, know the Tuatha Dé Danann are honored among those in the Fae realm and will find their rest there," Danu said softly.

Bryn somehow suddenly understood the words in another language, and her skin became even more sensitive. Like a snake, it had grown far too small for her, and she needed to shed it.

The words Danu had said triggered something in Arioch and Daran too.

Her grip tightened on her knife as she watched the two men's bodies begin to violently shake.

Bryn stepped back and watched in horrified awe as Daran and Arioch sprouted hair, and muzzles extended from their faces. Their forms a grotesque mix of man and beast with yellowed fangs that dripped saliva onto the sand.

"Werewolves?" Declan asked Bryn as if she had any idea what they were or what was going on any more than he did.

Callum came up beside Bryn as the townspeople were shocked out of their stupor and ran into the night from the nightmares that Arioch and Daran had become. Horrified screams pierced Bryn's sensitive eardrums as she watched torches being dropped into the sand, rolling toward buildings as the townspeople ran from the very men they had worshipped almost as much as they did Balor himself.

"Oh no. Werewolves are decent people. These are the Wolfmen of Ossuary. Sinners who took the form of a half man and half wolf for their crimes when they were human," Callum stated as if in a schoolroom, teaching children math equations and not facing down the ugliest beasts Bryn had ever seen. "Watch their bite. It is poisonous. They have bitten several people in town in the past from the information I gathered, and those people died. I believe they blamed it on a sickness of some type."

Bryn stared at Callum for a blink before her brain put the puzzle together of what he had said in her mind.

Arioch and Daran were the cause of the sickness.

The beastly men gained footing as they moved in their direction, but before Bryn could move, Finian was in front of her and Declan, pushing them back.

"Finian! No!" Bryn cried as the large dog launched himself toward Daran, the beast taking a swipe at Finian but missed as the dog spun around and bit into the left haunch of the beast.

Justin came up next to them with a rifle, aiming at Daran before taking a shot that clipped the monster in the shoulder.

"Don't touch my dog, jackass," Justin yelled, aiming another shot at Daran as Caden aimed at Arioch.

Daran managed to dislodge Finian and clawed him to the side, Bryn screaming as Justin aimed and hit Daran's throat. She watched in horror as the beast that was Daran healed right before her eyes.

Finian had hit the wall of the town, but he was back up again, his canine eyes full of anger.

Most of the townspeople had fled in fear, as surprised and terrified as she was sure she would have been if she still thought she was human, and yet a few particularly less intelligent individuals still stood next to Daran and Arioch, not scared at all. In fact, they had removed their masks and looked positively gleeful. Their eyes shining with anticipation.

As if unlike the terrified humans, they'd already known who Arioch and Daran were.

"Just left us in the pan and looked to see who had the balls to hop out, huh, Danu?" Declan growled as he loaded a pistol and handed it to Jace.

Jace had never touched a gun before, and the look on his face made it very obvious.

Bryn maneuvered to the side, looking for Mallory. She knew she was the type to come in from the flank when everyone was distracted, and she was right. There Mallory stood in the shadows, but she had yet to make a move; instead, she was frozen.

Frozen in fear at seeing her fiancé turn into a beast? Bryn wasn't sure, and she sure as hell didn't care to ask.

If only Bryn had the ability to release the torrent of fire within her, her aunt would have been charred and unrecognizable.

"You can tear them up like you did Bryn's daddy. Full circle, Ari," one of the men next to the beasts muttered, rubbing his hands together.

Everything inside of Bryn stopped at those words, her eyes moved to Mallory's, but the shock on her aunt's face told the same story. She'd had no idea.

Shaking, Cyerra dug her clawed feet into Bryn's shoulder, trying to push a sense of calm and permeate the barrier of anger and fear that had engulfed Bryn.

"You'll do no one here any good if you lose control," Cyerra chided into Bryn's mind. *"Strategic battles over emotional ones, Phantom Queen."*

"There is no need to escalate to violence. Let us leave and we will take our so-called sinful behavior from this town." Declan walked forward, his hands up in a placating gesture. From the corner of her eye, she watched as Kessler readied the truck to start on Declan's command.

Bryn felt fire running through her veins as she held preternaturally still, watching Declan's back as he faced off with the beasts. As she stared at each face behind Daran and Arioch, the ones who had called her a witch, who had wanted to burn her alive, she found them lacking.

Jace came around to Bryn's side.

"Danu is fine," he said from the side of his mouth. Bryn said nothing as she continued to watch the townsmen come back with rifles, shaking like leaves, but the idiots still stood next to the monstrous versions of Daran and Arioch.

"Just kill 'em!" Daran growled, his elongated mouth and sharp teeth making it hard to understand him, but the men next to him moved forward, some even ready to enjoy their kills from the looks of unfettered glee.

Mallory stood back with her arms folded, doing nothing to stop them as Bryn watched Jace give her a pleading look.

Her aunt's only response was to turn her back. Maybe if it were just Bryn in the line of fire, but it shocked her that she'd turn away and let her own son be killed.

She knew she really shouldn't have been. A woman who believed the religious droll she was served to the point she beat and harmed her own niece, well of course she could turn her back on her own child should that child not fall to his knees at her belief system.

If there had been any compassion left inside of Bryn for Mallory, it was dead and buried now.

"Grab the witches, kill the rest," one of the men ordered since it was obviously far too difficult for the wolfmen to speak to the whole of the crowd and be heard in their state.

Rifles aimed their direction right as the horns blared.

Bryn knew what that meant before anyone else did.

Everyone in the group in front of her stopped listening to Daran as he yelled to shoot her. Instead, they focused on what the horns meant, turning like mindless creatures sharing a brain cell as they looked to where the gate stood just behind them.

"Here comes the minions of your god," Danu yelled over the deafening sound of the horns. "Now you reap what you've sown!"

The wraiths were here.

Chapter 43

The sky was darkening, the small amounts of light the sun was putting off as the rays broke over the horizon were lost to the cloud of darkness rolling in.

It was not another sandstorm, though. Instead, it was the very evil that Daran had just accused her of being. The people of Ifreann were about to learn the truth of their savior's lies in the worst way.

"Wraiths?" Jace whispered from behind her, and she nodded.

Daran and Arioch had finally stopped biting and clawing their way to Bryn, only to end up pushed back by a bullet or three. Turning away from her with the promise they'd finish Bryn and her friends off once they dealt with the reason for the horns, they too looked toward the black cloud of death coming toward the town.

Bryn was quick to move to Saints' Road, her boots throwing up sand as she skittered to a halt, the gate several buildings down from her, the black cloud behind it ominous.

She watched as the sentries along the wall aimed their guns, firing down on the wraiths. The bullets did nothing to penetrate the cloud of black-cloaked bodies moving in far too quickly. Bryn could barely make them out, the veil of darkness keeping them covered until they struck out, only to disappear back into the darkness again.

All too soon the firing of the guns turned to the screams of the men as they died at the hands of the wraiths.

Bryn watched, gripping her knife as the black cloud overtook the metal and wood structure that was their gate.

Please, Travis. Please have gotten out of there in time.

Kian appeared next to her, his silver eyes on the incoming darkness, before turning quickly to Bryn as the wraiths took the form of humans cloaked all in black. An army of darkness on her doorstep.

"They are not natural, so they cannot be killed naturally. Remember what I am telling you. They are soulless and can kill without striking a mortal wound by taking a person's soul if you look into their eyes. They are called Sluaghs, and the only way to kill them is to behead the mortal body they've stolen. The only way to get them immobilized enough to take their head is to strike the king's brand on their forehead, but you have to be quick."

"I will," she responded, Kian's eyes staying on her as if trying to recall something. "I'll stay alive. I promise if I am to die, it will be at your hand, not theirs."

The smile that crossed Kian's face gave her the boost she needed to stand before enemies that would tear her apart.

A hand softly touched her shoulder, and Bryn turned to look into the glowing gold eyes of Danu. There was something ancient in them as she whispered words to Bryn that made no sense until some part of her mind translated them.

"Call for their deaths, child." And with that, Danu was gone. Disappearing into the wind as if she had never stood before Bryn at all.

Justin was running through the streets, just as he had in her vision, yelling for people to get inside before making his way back to where the truck was.

The itch Bryn knew meant a vision was coming started in the back of her mind again, but so much worse than before. The predator inside her danced beneath her skin, singing the song of war, ready to be released on the threat in front of them.

"Bryn!" Declan grabbed her arm, swinging her around to face him. "Get to the truck!"

Screams were at a deafening decibel as the men that only moments ago had held a gun pointed at her, were running toward the assassins, and literally being torn apart.

The only ones actually faring well in the fight, if that was possible, were Arioch and Daran in their beastly forms. They tore apart wraith after wraith, clouds of dust falling where the wraith had been.

Bile rose in her throat. The predator from before being lost to Bryn's human revulsion at the macabre scene before her.

"They are here for us! We can't let them kill everyone who stands between us and them!" Jace yelled from where he stood near the alleyway Bryn had just run through.

"He's right." Bryn looked up at Declan as she said this.

"There are too many." Declan grabbed at her again, but her hands pushed his away.

She should be here, but deep down, she knew only coming into her powers so recently did not mean she was ready for battle and war.

Cyerra was nearby after having took flight once the wraiths breached the gate. Bryn could feel her in her mind, and the persistent push of her crow friend told Bryn that she should make a move. Give an order. Anything but stand there with her mouth gaping open.

A head of dark-auburn hair moved between her and the wraiths.

"No, we leave. When have they ever done anything for you?" Declan reached for her again, but she danced out of his way.

"Nothing. They've been horrible, but I am not them to where I can look the other way when someone needs help, and I know deep down you don't want to be either," Bryn yelled, but she could tell Declan was losing his patience and about to grab her and throw her over his shoulder. She knew it from the way his hands moved closer to her as his fingers flexed.

"Declan," she warned as she looked to him, but a wraith swiped at her from the side, and that was all Declan needed to grab Bryn and throw her over his shoulder. He took off at a run toward the gate where the truck was, ignoring her screaming at him. She beat against his back, her dagger in hand flipped so she didn't stab him, but oh how very tempted she was to do so.

"No! Put me down, Declan Rafferty!" Bryn yelled, her head going up right as the wraiths moved through another group of people trying to hold them off. There were kids in those buildings, and Bryn needed to stop the monsters who would see this town dead.

The baker was in his store, and she watched the vision come to life before her eyes. She knew his wife was in there with their newborn, most likely Ava as well since she was his daughter, and the man whose eyes she watched it all happen through.

A scream tore from her for him to stay inside, to not open the door. He couldn't hear her, and for that, he lost his head. Just as he had in her vision.

There was no one to protect the child if the mother fell next.

No matter what the parents chose to believe, Bryn would not have children lost to their parents' failures. To her own failures.

While she did not care for these people, all the hurt inside of her could not allow it; watching them be slaughtered was heart-wrenching. There was no one who deserved such a fate.

It was all too much. She could feel something far deeper than the first time, as if everyone's souls were screaming in her ears, begging her for help.

A headache pulsed in her temples as the world flashed bright colors as if she were straddling the veil.

That small amount of power, power she hadn't even meant to use, not at all meaning to cross the veil, had every wraith turning to look at her.

They were here for her and her friends, hunting and killing the innocents while Declan tried to save her.

But she wasn't meant to be saved from this.

"It's too late, Bryn! Stop fighting me," Declan growled, somehow getting the words out while sprinting full speed toward the truck at the gate.

Bryn was thrown into the passenger seat of the truck, but she wouldn't stay there. The wraiths were coming fast toward her now, and she had to do something. Turning to see what she was looking at, Declan froze as he watched the wraiths form the opaque cloud as they moved toward where they were.

Anger blasted through her.

The pressure in her head from the predator pushing against her skin was producing black spots in her vision as she tried to keep hold of herself. Tried to keep her own beast at bay, but it didn't take a seer or a prophecy to know the truth she felt in the pit of her stomach.

Bryn was going to have to let the Morrigan out to fight at the possibility of losing herself.

Chapter 44

Bryn pushed her way out of the truck, her dagger in hand as her friends gathered around her, seeing the cloud moving toward them.

Their buildings were burning if the smoke was any indication. People were screaming as they died, as their crops and buildings burned . . . soon everything would be gone. Anyone left alive would either be dead by morning or soon enough from lack of water or food.

The children . . .

A sob left her lips again, and Declan pulled her against his chest, whispering into her hair.

"Where the hell is Kessler?" Travis yelled from the bed of the pickup. "We kind of need him to run this beast!"

Travis had made it!

"I'm working on it!" Kessler yelled from somewhere nearby. "Someone tampered with it."

They all knew the scrios had been watching them long enough to know when they were leaving. It wasn't a stretch to think it would be him who would do such a thing.

She couldn't feel sad about his death if the wraiths managed to tear him apart.

Danu appeared in front of the truck, and the world around them froze with Danu's power. Bryn watched the older woman struggling, her face pinched, her body tense, as she worked to give them enough time to gather their faculties and ready for the fight ahead.

"You must face this trial." Her voice was ethereal and spread out through their minds as much as it did their ears. "You cannot run from it now. Not when the blood of the innocent spills into the streets."

Danu's eyes met Bryn's, and she knew Danu saw her will to stay, to not leave and let the wraiths finish what they had started as they searched for her and her friends.

"The innocents lost will roam the earth if the queen chooses not to release their souls to paradise," Danu finished on a whisper.

Bryn pushed away from Declan and moved to stand in front of the older woman.

"You know you must fight. I know you feel it deep inside of you," Danu whispered as her gnarled finger moved along Bryn's cheek.

Everyone stepped away from the vehicle, following to stand next to Bryn as she stood face-to-face with Danu. Bryn knew what she meant, as she'd heard the screams of the souls lost on Saints' Road all around her.

Niamh placed a hand on Bryn's shoulder.

The caw of the crow moved overhead, its battle cry all too familiar to the spirit within Bryn. Even if it were only in her head, there was a warrior soul in her that would see them through this.

Whether their end was here or on the other side of the veil.

"We need you to come back, Phantom Queen," Cyerra said into her mind.

Turning back to her friends, her skin on fire, she took a deep breath as Declan gave her a pleading look and motioned toward the truck. Her eyes moved from his as she took in the rest of their group, all of them waiting for her to take charge.

Even Kian hovered in the background unbeknownst to her friends.

It was time to dig in deep, to reach for her true self. The part of her that she was too afraid to let fully out. That thing inside her that she always thought a monster might just be what kept people alive in the end.

To do so, Bryn could no longer hide from her true nature.

Closing her eyes, she accepted there was no time to think this over. It was done. The Morrigan would be her best bet to guide her and, since she had zero fighting skills, her best bet to live another day.

Time to think logically and field a battle plan.

With a nod, she opened her eyes and looked at her friends who stood around her. She needed to plan quick as sweat beaded Danu's brow.

"Justin, Travis, Caden, and Declan, I need y'all to get up high with your rifles. Take point in the buildings and try to keep the enemy, both enemies"—Bryn looked to each of them, hoping they took her meaning—"at bay. Sage, please head around the back of the buildings, and I will see if I can guide people to you. Get them to a safe place, and Jace, you provide care to the wounded," Bryn ordered, the itch under her skin flaring back up again.

"Niamh—"

"I am with you, Bryn," Niamh stated, brokering no argument as her eyes glittered.

Nodding, she took a deep breath, readying herself for what was to come.

"You're kidding me right now!" Declan bellowed.

Bryn stood firm, staring him down.

"I am going to do this, Declan, so either strap yourself in and do as you're told or get the hell out of my way."

Turning away from him, Bryn rolled back her shoulders.

She worried that if she gave too much of herself over at once, she'd lose herself completely, so she would let the Morrigan have small bits of power. Danu may have said they were one and the same person, but it did not feel like it.

If Bryn didn't need to protect her people, she wouldn't bother with even the small possibility of losing herself completely to the predator. She knew that would only lead to the deaths of those around her if she lost control.

Would the Morrigan part of her soul even care if the people of the town lived? Bryn barely did and only because of the innocents like the children, so she couldn't imagine this goddess fighting for people who worshipped her enemy. No, it was best to keep that part of her soul contained as long as possible if Bryn wanted anyone but her and her friends to live.

Jace stepped forward and pulled her into a tight hug, then released her, his hands on her shoulders.

"Take care of the injured, Jace. Keep yourself safe," she whispered, pulling him into another hug as the other men grabbed weapons.

Declan took her from Jace's hold, his hands upon her cheeks as he pulled her face to look up at him.

"I don't like this. I know they say you're a war goddess, but I want you somewhere safe and sound," he growled, holding her face close to his own.

"I'd say I am sorry, but I am not. I was born for this, so let me fly, Declan," she whispered back to him, watching his jaw clench. She thought he would demand her to stay near him, but he shocked her instead with an apology.

"I am sorry for everything I've done to hurt you, Bryn. Regardless of our romantic history, I care for you as a close friend and hope to earn back the trust I lost."

Placing her hand over his, she gave him as much of a smile as she could muster with everything that was happening around them.

"Live through this and we will work on our issues. Promise."

With his own painful smile and a nod, Declan hugged her again before releasing her.

"Live, Bryn. Promise."

Declan did not wait for her response as he took a pistol from Justin. The men gave her one last look, Jace's eyes watery, before each of her friends moved off the street and back into the buildings.

Bryn was surprised Declan had done as she asked, but maybe he was growing and allowing her to grow as well.

"I feel like I should warn you away, but I am pretty sure nothing will or can touch you." She gave the same small false smile to Kian that she had just given Declan as she turned to face him.

"*Let that part of yourself rise, Bryn. You have more control over yourself than you think,*" Kian whispered into her mind.

"How do I know she won't take over?" Her fear was obvious in her words.

If Niamh thought it at all weird that Bryn was talking to a shadow, she kept it to herself.

"*Because you have her knowledge, but she is not separate from you. You are one and the same. The same soul, same person. Just with human memories this time.*"

Closing her eyes, she nodded, not quite believing him.

"Are you ready?" Niamh asked, her hand giving her shoulder a reassuring squeeze.

Bryn gripped her dagger tighter as she nodded.

"Thank you, Kian." She opened her eyes and stared into those violent swirls of silver as he stepped back into the shadows.

"*This will be good practice for our own epic battle should you live,*" he promised, his words carrying more meaning than she had time to unpack.

Turning away from the emotional onslaught her group, her tribe, and her family caused, she readied herself to take on a cloud of killer wraiths.

"I am going to die," Bryn whispered, earning a cackle from Niamh.

"Not on my watch, darling." Niamh winked as she stepped up beside Bryn sans weapon.

"You should go with Sage and help her find a safe place," Bryn ordered, but Niamh only gave her a smile.

"Darling, I am *very* difficult to kill."

"I'm holding you to that. Now, let's save the day and get the hell out of Dodge," Bryn replied as she started toward the cloud.

Danu was losing her hold on freezing time, the wraiths slowly starting to move again, so Bryn nodded for her to let go.

She tried to keep her mind calm as it was quite obvious that she was walking into a battle with little to no training.

Danu was so sure they would take to their powers like a fish to water, which she hoped the others had. Feeling selfish at the thought of not checking in on her friends during all this, she tried to be thankful she'd at least had the chance to know Faerie.

The entire world came back to life as Bryn stumbled. The utter chaos and torment happening only feet away from her dried up all the saliva in her mouth.

Her gorge rose as she watched a man who had for years tended to the church garden lose his head just for having been in the way of the deadly assassins. As the head rolled, it stopped at the toes of her boots, and she tried very hard not to lose her composure.

Or pass out from the blood.

Her eyes were so focused on the macabre sight that a wraith was able to make it to her, almost taking her head off had Niamh not been there to rip his own off instead.

Bryn felt her mouth start to water as bile rose in her throat.

"Focus!" Niamh yelled, using clawed fingers to gut another wraith.

Her adrenaline finally kicked into gear after another wraith stabbed at her, and she sliced at the creature wrapped in all black and shadows.

Managing to cut into its arm, Bryn faltered when she pulled her knife back to see that instead of blood, there was black ichor.

"What the hell?" she groused, immediately earning a punch to the side of the head from the creature.

Stumbling, her bell sufficiently rung, the creature moved to stand in front of her as it pulled its hood back. Her curiosity to see what kind of being bled black was abruptly halted by Kian yelling right into her poor brain still ringing from the hit.

"*Do not look right into his eyes!*"

A scream tore through her at the sight before her.

She stared at the mouth missing lips, its skin pulled tight and blue as if it were a walking dead person. As far as she could tell, the eye sockets were empty, though with Kian's words, she decided not to bother double-checking.

"*Dagger!*"

Shaking away the thoughts, she took the dagger she held and aimed at the top of the head, trying to miss the eyes. The moment the brand was cut, it froze, and the preternatural stillness was somehow even more disturbing.

Her panic took over, and she slammed her knife down into its eye socket, which was in fact empty, but she didn't look into them directly as the creature exploded into dust and ash.

"*That,*" Kian said, as he moved to her side, obvious irritation that he no longer had the energy to manipulate the world around him, "*was a sluagh weaponized.*"

"What?" Bryn's voice was borderline hysterical as she dodged another blade, about to yell at Kian to quit distracting her.

"*Soul eater. Reanimated in corpses, they move in packs to steal and eat souls. The symbol on his head weaponized him for the king.*"

As Bryn shook and Niamh tore into another wraith gunning for her, the man made of shadows looked completely calm and assured as he stared at the new soot smear on the brick building they killed the wraith in front of.

Another's scream unfroze her, and Bryn tightened her grip on her dagger, running in the direction of the yell. She could sense Kian following her and wondered when she'd become so in tune with him. He was nothing like the wraiths, yet he claimed to be Fomori . . . and he helped her kill one of them.

Nothing about their situation made sense. However, Kian was an enigma she'd have to figure out another day.

She saw Declan take aim with his pistol at the wraiths as he walked down the street; he managed to get several headshots, though most of the bullets went wide. Black dust was blowing in the air around them from the dead wraiths . . . or sluaghs.

Bryn promised to kill him herself once the battle was over for not staying in the buildings, but when she saw the child on the ground running back to its mother, the wraith now focused on Declan, she couldn't begrudge his decision.

Declan had figured it out, taking out the mark and rendering them to dust in one hit. The other men copied him as they came out of the buildings, following him, so obviously this had been a group decision.

Tripping, Bryn looked down to see a storekeeper grasping her ankle as he looked up at her with his remaining eye. He was one of the very few that hadn't followed the crowd and called her a witch. He had taken a huge risk in sneaking food to her as a young child when their crops were not faring well, knowing what that could cost him and his reputation.

To be sympathetic to the witch was as good as being one yourself in this town.

"Please . . .," he whispered, bleeding profusely from a gut wound. His entire body glowed yellow, his eye shining in a way she'd never seen before, as if it were a lit candle.

Bryn couldn't save this man, but still she knelt in the middle of the battlefield and took his hand in hers.

Taking a risk as he had done for her so many times.

A gunshot moving over her shoulder told her that the men were watching her back as much as Niamh was.

The world lost its intensity, the noise of battle a low thrum, the world going monochrome before flickering with vibrant colors. As if everything around her had moved to the background, time slower than before, Bryn ran her hand over the man's pinched features, his brow smoothing at her touch.

An onslaught of feelings and memories of his life hit her, and she bit down on her lower lip as it tore through her psyche, but she kept her hand on the man, giving him as much comfort as she could with her whispered promises.

As his soul split from his dying body, she saw herself kneeling over him from his eyes, hers shining gold as she looked down at him.

"Free him," the voice inside her head calmly ordered. A reverence there that had never been before.

The world had stopped around her. Time was still, and the world was now brighter as she crossed the veil into Faerie.

"You shall pass," she whispered, and at her words, his eyes lost the life within them as the yellow orb that was his spirit fully left his body.

Bryn held his soul in her hands as she stood, cradling it to her as she would something far too delicate to withstand the harshness of the world.

She whispered her prayer, feeling relief at knowing there was in fact a place for these souls after death, before lifting her hands above her body. She released the orb as it exploded into millions of tiny lights that swarmed her before rising up and swirling into the form of the shopkeeper, a specter of himself.

"Thank you," he whispered, before fading from sight, and the colors were once again the dull and drab browns of her own world. The one she knew all too well.

A man of shadow had stood over her as she released the soul.

Standing over her as she returned from Faerie and back to the world of pain and death.

Slowly, time started moving again until the battle once more raged around her.

Chapter 45

Cyerra dove over Saints' Road as the wraiths swirled in and out of the shadows, having already torn through one-fourth of their town before Bryn had even stepped out onto the street with Niamh at her side.

All because the king felt their powers awaken.

Bryn knew there would be no rest now until the king was dead.

One of the very men who had held a gun on her minutes before the horns had sounded stared at the sky, his eyes blank as death took hold.

The soul leaving his body was not the bright yellow of the others but stained and more of a sickly brown with black bordering. As the spirit stood up, looking around, his gaze settled on Bryn.

Turning away as Justin's shot hit the wraith that was about to attack her, she ignored the soul that was starting to walk toward her.

As she slammed her knife into another wraith's forehead, the wraith managing a cut to her side before she landed the hit, the soul hovered near where she was fighting.

The words he yelled at her, pleading with her to save him, were on the back burner since Faerie did not call for his soul yet, and Bryn honestly doubted Faerie would.

It was most likely he'd be hunted by Arawn's pack after the battle, and she did not want to know what happened to those souls.

His pleading turned to rage as he yelled at her to put his soul back in his body.

Funny how now he accepted who she was and was okay with it, when not so very long ago he stood ready to tie her to a stake. One she had been trying to ignore the whole time they had been on Saint's Road.

The stake stood as a morbid reminder in the background of the battle she was engulfed in, reminding her of another battle she had spent most of her life fighting. One physical to one mental.

Cyerra swooped down before landing on Bryn's shoulder, the soul backing off at the sight of the crow.

Interesting.

"How shall I serve you, Phantom Queen?"

Bryn looked at the crow on her shoulder, surprised at the lack of usual snark, but the crow was battle ready and focused.

Snark was for days off from battle. Got it.

"The name is Bryn, and your job here is to distract the wraiths as much as you can so I can manage to behead a few."

"And so it shall be. Don't die . . . again. It's annoying." Cyerra took off and dove in and out of the black mass, separating from the wraiths before any of them could physically harm her.

Once the whole of the black cloud was in the inner gate, Bryn watched them separate into well over a hundred more sluaghs.

Daran and Arioch were covered in the black ichor, fighting the newest wraiths in the middle of Saints' Road.

It would be a massacre, and she had to wonder if they could survive this even if she were at full power. These beings were far too difficult to kill, and at most, they had only dispatched twenty so far.

Her friends looked as bad as she did, each of them tired and weary as the battle raged on.

How much longer could they hold out?

"Be safe," she whispered as the crow swooped down toward a wraith fighting one of the town merchants before the man went down in a spray of blood.

"The people will be safer indoors! The wraiths are here for us!" she yelled out to her friends, and watched as Justin nodded, backing away but still aiming his rifle. She knew he would take care of it.

Declan was reloading each of the rifles now when the men ran out of bullets, and she realized they would never want for anything with him around.

"Get inside!" she yelled at a line of townsmen along the sides of Saints' Road, their weapons aimed and firing at the wraiths, but it changed nothing. The bullets hit them, but it was as if the wraiths themselves felt no pain.

"Shut it, witch! You brought them here!" one of the men yelled back.

Touché.

"Let them fall on their own swords, Bryn. You are doing your best," Niamh whispered, and somehow Bryn heard her clearly over the loud clashes of metal on metal and the booming discharge of the guns.

A tingling sensation made her turn as a sword barely missed her. One of the wraiths had been midswing to take her head off, but Niamh was already on it, dispatching the wraith as efficiently as she had the others.

Focus!

It was a ghastly soundtrack of bullets flying, the wraiths killing, the flames of buildings on fire from broken sconces, and children yelling for their parents as they were taken to safety. Justin was covering people as they made it into the buildings on the side of the road that were not on fire.

Travis, Caden, and Kessler were aiming at the heads of the wraiths in unison from between the buildings.

Callum was with Danu, holding her and giving her the power she needed to sustain her in whatever it was she was doing.

It was then that Bryn realized there was a push of power coming from Danu to her.

The woman was going to kill herself helping Bryn, and all because Bryn couldn't access her powers.

Trauma, Callum had said. Her trauma was making her push her true self deep down.

Turning to face off against the ones focused on her, more of the wraiths spilled over the gate, multiplying.

It was never ending.

They couldn't last.

"Get everyone to the truck! I will meet you all outside of the gate!" Bryn yelled, as she swung her knife like the amateur she was. She barely cut anyone or anything, only managing a few lucky strikes. She had no training to be some master at killing assassins, and it was all too obvious.

The cut of a blade into her side told her she was getting too close to death.

"Bryn!" Declan yelled, and his voice was closer than it should have been.

Damn it, Declan!

"Stay back!" she yelled at the men, yet every one of them ignored her, coming in closer to the center of the road where the heaviest fighting was taking place.

Declan, Caden, and Travis were backing each other up as they aimed at wraiths surrounding her with far more precise hits than she had been landing. Many of the wraiths moved to the men, the opposite of what she wanted to happen.

A wraith swung low at her with its leg, and Bryn was flat out on her rear, the sand between her fingers wet with blood. The wraith moved in to finish her off, but Niamh was suddenly in front of her, grabbing the wraith by the shoulders and biting into its neck, ripping its throat out.

"Hit the center of their heads!" Bryn reminded the men as their shots went into shoulders and chests, their panic taking over and their focus wavering.

Niamh grabbed Bryn's hands and pulled her up.

Bryn looked into her friend's eyes, and they were bloodred, her teeth serrated, and the canines elongated.

Right. Vampire.

Niamh rolled her shoulders back, sticking her chin out, waiting for judgment.

"Glad you're on our team" was all Bryn said as she moved around Niamh to strike out at a wraith coming at her friend.

"That's it?" Niamh asked, as she broke the arm of one of the wraiths, the arm coming off the body and Niamh throwing it to the side in disgust.

"That's it." Bryn looked at her, and Niamh gave her a nod in return.

Declan, Kessler, and Jace were next to her, aiming bullets at the heads of the wraiths, very few hitting the mark as the men grew far too fatigued and worn.

Jace was supposed to be helping Sage, but she didn't have time to yell at him. She'd have to save that for when they finished the battle.

Their bodies having taken enough hits to where they were covered in blood (she hoped not their own) and black ichor, which only made the dust of the dispatched wraiths stick to them.

They were a sad army of fighters. If they lived, they would have to train. The only ones making much difference on a consistent basis were Travis and Justin, who were quick to hit the literal mark on the heads and take them out. If the mark was only scratched, the wraiths went feral if they didn't damage the brain or behead them quick enough, leaving them with more problems.

Declan had the wraiths too close to him to fire his weapon, and he began to brandish the rifle like a club. Kessler following Declan's lead as he clipped the wraith with his own rifle, slowing it down enough that Bryn could stab into its head.

She didn't always hit the mark and turned more feral than she meant to.

Jace still managed a few hits with the last of his bullets from beside her, standing at her back and not in the safety of the building where he could tend to the injured.

A wraith moved on Bryn before exploding in front of her, Bryn barely getting her arm up to cover her face.

Black ichor and things she didn't want to think too hard on were covering her. This one had not bothered turning to dust at all. Its head hit the ground, still alive, and Bryn stabbed it with her knife, the head making dust.

Looking up, she saw Callum with his hands out.

"I am here to assist, Phantom Queen." Looking around, he did not wait for her thanks as he blew up another wraith. It was *gross,* but it was appreciated.

Turning away from Callum, Bryn readied her knife for another wraith. One was ready for her too. It walked toward her, its sword bloody, and she readied herself to fight. It had been luck so far, the hits she'd made. She knew it, and she bet her enemy did too.

Niamh was in front of her in an instant, killing it, but Bryn's eyes roamed the battlefield as she tallied where they were at and saw a wraith was moving in on Travis from behind.

She knew what was about to happen, and she ran, screaming at him to turn and look. Hope in her heart that she could stop this. That someone would turn and shoot the wraith, ending it before it made it to Travis.

A shot rang out, the echo of it ringing in her mind as the wraith blew to a cloud of dust.

Relief surged through her until Travis's knees hit the sand, and she took in the sword protruding from his chest.

"No!" she yelled, running faster as if she could stop it all, Caden making it to Travis first and catching him before he hit the ground.

Falling to her knees beside her friend, she reached out to touch Travis's cheek, but his eyelids were lowering, his throat unable to form words through the blood spilling from his mouth.

Closing her eyes, she slammed her fists into the bloody sand.

All the visions she'd had, and yet she was too weak to stop the deaths. To save her friend. If only she had warned him—

"I would have walked right out here shooting anyway. Besides, look at that. You are *a goddess, Brynnie."*

Chapter 46

T ravis smiled as he stood over her, a rare sight for the always serious man.

"Travis!" she cried, reaching for him, and going right through him. His hand moved to touch her shoulder but stopped before his fingers curled into a fist.

Time started to freeze as she pulled them across the veil subconsciously, or Faerie did it for her, she had no idea, but the moment they were in Faerie, she grabbed him in a hug. One he returned just as tightly.

"Best friends any guy could have." His soul looked to where Caden was frozen in yelling at him to wake up, and to where Declan and Justin stood having picked up his rifle and pistol, covering his body so no one could make it to them.

A tear fell down Bryn's cheek as Jace tried to save him even knowing it was too late. It was all there, frozen in time for them to watch play out. She was thankful he was given this, that Travis knew how much they loved him in the end.

Travis looked to her, the pain in his eyes that he'd held inside of himself in life was gone, and she wished she knew how to bring him back the way he was now.

"You can't, darlin'. It's my time." He smiled down at her. Pushing a lock of hair behind her ear, he laughed. "You *are* a damn fairy."

Bryn let out a sob as she moved her face into his hand, his thumb wiping away her rogue tears.

"Tell them that they need to keep going. No matter what. And Bryn?" His eyes were lit with an eerie blue, his body with yellow, his soul pure. "Listen to Danu, you can end this. Did some reading of my own and you've got some banshee in you. So, call for their deaths, darlin'. I know you got it in ya."

Touching his shoulder, she smiled up at her friend, his form blurring from the tears in her eyes.

"You shall pass," she whispered. As much as she wanted to hold Travis to her, to find a way to take him back, Travis had earned his rest. Earned the honor of living among the warriors that had come before him.

"Don't let them get you down, girlie," he whispered as his aura grew brighter. "Declan better be on his best behavior because I'll be watching." He winked, finding a peace in death he never had in life. Stepping back, he turned to where Arawn awaited him.

"I'll be damned." Travis winced at his words before chuckling. "Mr. Rafferty really is king of the dead, huh?"

"You get to go to paradise, Travis." She smiled, and Travis returned it, looking back over his shoulder at her.

Bryn watched as he walked to Arawn, giving him a slap on the back as they turned to walk off together, talking. Travis let out a boisterous laugh at something Arawn had said, and Bryn closed her eyes as the tears fell.

She needed to grieve, but that would come later because the world came back to life around her, the dulls of the desert angering her as she left Faerie and its comfort.

Shoving to her feet, she swung around toward the wraiths, jabbing her knife blindly with tears in her eyes. She would die, she knew this. There was no way to survive this but losing her friend . . . she would die taking all the wraiths with her. She would save the friends still breathing.

When the lack of gunfire registered, panic rose inside her.

The bullets had stopped.

Fear had her frozen, but something moved her, turned her body to see her worst nightmares come to life.

As if she were a mere observer.

Arioch and Daran were still in their wolfman forms, fighting wraiths, but she knew they'd turn on her and her friends the minute they could.

Declan scrambling back from a wraith that had him on the ground, the sword lifting into the air to strike him down.

Caden, right as a wraith sliced through his arm, severing his hand.

Justin shoving a knife into a wraith's head, not seeing the one behind him closing in.

Bryn's body shook as time sped up, her human body unable to move fast enough to do anything. Unable to save anyone.

The wraith slammed the sword into Declan's chest just as it had done Travis.

Caden went into shock, Jace grabbing him and pulling him back as Niamh moved in on the wraith.

Justin got a knife through the throat, gurgling as the wraith pulled it out, before exploding as Callum blasted Justin's killer apart.

Sage screamed as Jace yelled to Kessler who was surrounded by wraiths himself, trying to break through.

Bryn hadn't realized she was still half in the veil, her body sluggish. Something was tethering her, holding her back, and she was fighting through it, but her efforts were as good as struggling against quicksand.

Falling to her knees, Bryn hunched over, something in her tearing at her skin. The itch now a searing pain shooting lightning through her head.

Her fingers dug into the sand as she moved back fully into her world.

Jace ran past with Kessler on his tail, Sage having taken over caring for Caden and moving him toward where the truck was next to the gate. Caden, who was holding the bloody stump where his hand should have been, not aware of what was happening around him, was just going where he was told. His olive skin was pale with shock.

Her world was tearing at the seams.

Looking up, Kian was faint, but there.

"I can't save them." Her voice broke with the words.

"I thought you were stronger than this," he whispered into her mind.

Her hands fisted in the sand, her tears falling faster, running through the blood on her face.

A slice to her shoulder, a stabbing in her back, the wraiths were trying to finish her as Niamh held them off.

"You win," she whispered to herself, letting that latent part of her mind that fought against the cage she tried to put it in. The door she had closed long ago, the predator that moved closer and closer to the surface by the day . . . she had shackled it. Now, she opened the door wide, releasing the chains, and let the beast out.

Pushing herself up to stand, she fisted her hands and released a bone-chilling scream that was completely inhuman. Releasing her power in a call to the universe.

And death answered.

Chapter 47

Pushing open the veil, Bryn brought her army into her world from Faerie.

Arms opened wide as Senan, the crows, and the silver and black wolves followed by the pack escaped into her realm running past her down Saints' Road toward the wraiths before pulling back. They moved to her side as she closed the veil.

Nothing would get into Faerie while she stood between the enemy and their only place of respite.

Lowering her arms, her dagger still in hand, her empty hand went out to the silver wolf who stood at her side near the black wolf, the pack at their backs.

The silver wolf tried to push into her hand so she could run her fingers through his fur, but her hand went through him just as it did Kian.

The wolf wasn't solid in her world, and just like Kian, it was a shadow of itself on the mortal plane. Turning to look at her army, she took stock of each animal.

Senan was real enough, the black wolf from Faerie was, too, but the wolf pack and crows were the same as the silver wolf.

Shadows.

How could they fight the wraiths?

The silver wolf looked up to her with sadness in its eyes as it attempted to nudge her hand once more before turning away from her. It felt so much like a goodbye that she didn't understand.

"Wait . . .," she whispered as it moved forward toward the chaos.

"Just wait!" she yelled as the silver wolf took off toward Kian, who stood, bracing himself with furrowed eyebrows of confusion as the wolf aimed its body at him like a missile.

Her silver wolf had been her protector in Faerie, so it made sense that she would sense Kian as a threat.

"No!" she yelled to the wolf, not wanting it to kill Kian, if it even could. She had no idea, but it probably had a better chance than anything here in the real world.

The wolf took a running leap directly at Kian, but instead of hitting him, he was absorbed into him, the two entities becoming one in a flash of blindingly bright silver light.

As the light seared her eyes, her mind pulsed with memories.

Of Kian standing over her with a sword before she disarmed him. Keeping him as a prisoner in a forested area where other people lived with her, the Clan of Shadows. Him earning her trust, riding into battle with her. Becoming her general and leading her army.

The Fomori coming, him fighting alongside her, knowing it would mean his death. A death she refused to allow, and so she split his soul and took his other half to Faerie to keep him safe.

Kian was a shifter. He was Fomori. And he had been her most trusted friend.

Kian looked at his hands as the shadows moved to his feet, his body slowly losing its transparency, becoming tangible and real.

Not shadow. Flesh and bone.

Bryn took a hesitant step toward Kian and wondered if he remembered everything as well. If the same memories flashed through his mind.

He glanced up, and their eyes met, but it wasn't a smile of vengeance to be served on his lips.

As he looked at her, his expression held something in it that she couldn't have anticipated from the man made of shadows. Something she never would have thought to see in those mercurial eyes.

A look she wished long ago Declan had given her when he looked her way.

Where Declan's looks had been possessive, Kian looked at her in a way that made her feel powerful.

As she moved toward him, wanting to say something, anything, she was stabbed in the side from behind.

Turning, she stabbed the wraith in the head, dispatching him, and the wraith turned to black dust, the wind scattering it.

When she turned back to Kian, his jaw was clenched, his eyes on the wound the wraith had made in her side. A look of resolve took over his features before he looked to her, catching her eyes.

Just like the silver wolf had moments before, she was sure he was saying goodbye.

He mouthed the words, but she refused to accept them.

See you on the other side.

Turning away from her, his bones began to pop out of place, and his skin rippled as the muscles tore before restructuring and healing into a new form. Now the silver wolf stood, whole, flesh and blood.

Kian was the silver wolf.

His howl rent the air, a battle cry, and the rest of the wolves matched his call as they took up formation behind him.

All the wraiths were still, frozen before being released again, the feel of power being Danu who once again was using the last of her magic to help. Slowly, the monsters began to move, their focus on the newest threat before them. Recalibrating was a word that came to mind as they watched the wolf and the pack.

The silver wolf, Kian, stepped forward, his hackles raised before he broke into a run aimed directly at the wraiths who were moving faster now. The wolves of the pack followed, all but the black wolf that remained dutifully at her side.

Panic was a vice around her heart as she watched him throw himself onto death's blade and her being unable to stop him.

If he was whole, he could be killed.

Her voice was full of screams as her heart tore apart watching Kian sacrifice himself for her.

Senan ran past her, her back hooves hitting several wraiths as she bucked and stomped at them.

The crows flying in and through the crowds and the battles caused disorientation for all of Bryn's enemies who would see her dead.

Arioch roared as a crow swooped past him, before he swiped his large claws at a wraith.

Finian howled as he bit at the human who aimed his gun at Bryn, tearing into the bone and sinew.

The world was chaos and blood. Sand and death as it surrounded her and invaded her senses, but all she could see was Kian as he disappeared into the cloud of wraiths.

All she could hear were his howls of pain that followed.

All she could feel was anger and rage as they tore into someone she had leaned on in the past, who attached himself to her and, even thinking himself an enemy, kept watch over her.

All she could taste was her thirst for the blood of those who harmed her people. Her friends. Her allies.

Her family.

Bryn's vision turned red as she roared.

Her battle cry rang through the town, the stake standing behind her as a tangible threat of her past, while the threat to her future turned as one and faced her.

This would end here.

Finally, Bryn fully embraced the Morrigan.

Chapter 48

Turning toward the wraiths that were completely focused on her now, anger saturated her mind. As the red battle haze overtook her vision, Bryn's own mind went dormant, her conscience going to the deep recesses of her psyche that had once housed the powerful creature she had just released.

Now her body moved to prepare for battle, and Bryn was nothing more than a mere observer.

Opening her arms wide, her black wolf took up its place at her side, its fur on end, lips back, and silent as it readied for battle.

The crows from Faerie dove toward her and swirled around her in a tornadic fashion before fanning out and moving over the city.

The tattoos she'd seen in Faerie lit up along her arms, the blue a beacon to the wraiths. Darkness bent to her will as the shadows whirled around her, a fog encompassing her as she let her darker nature take over.

She looked from where she had thrown her head back to where her enemies stood, and she faced the wraiths with a smile.

The shadows moved along her feet as she stepped toward them, now a hunter.

A wraith moved on her from behind, stabbing her in the shoulder with his dagger. Turning, she stared the wraith down as she ripped the dagger out and stabbed the wraith in the neck with it, before pulling it out and stabbing it in the head.

Every one of these monsters sent by her enemy were doomed. She'd find a way to let the king know his message had been received and that his own death was imminent.

As she reached out to take a sword from the ground, abandoned by the wraith whose dust she wore on her blood-covered body, the tattoos on her arms glowed an even brighter blue with her kill.

The wraiths hadn't moved on her, and she didn't need a mirror to tell her that she was the Bryn she'd seen in Faerie.

As the monstrous creatures slowly stepped back, something jolted their bodies, as if someone else was pulling the strings.

Kian had said they were weaponized.

The wraiths now readied themselves to attack all at once, and she welcomed it.

Humans still alive now saw her as much of a threat as the wraiths, aiming their weapons at her.

Bryn called to her crows, guiding them from her own mind on where to go. In unison, they rose high in the sky before coming back down like a black feathered blanket. Once they broke the top of the buildings, they dispersed and flew around the humans, confusing them enough to where most shots went wide. The bullets that did make it to Bryn, she couldn't feel.

Her entire body was numb, except for the power that lit through her, moving her in the battle dance her soul had known for ages.

Growls from behind told her she was surrounded by enemies from both sides of the veil.

Arioch and Daran, those pitiful beasts that her human side had to deal with, had been focused on the wraiths until now.

So be it.

The thought that she would die didn't even stick in her mind.

No, she was *death*.

And death could not die.

Stepping toward the wraiths, she held the dagger as she tested the weight of the dead wraith's sword in her other hand. Muscle memory she'd earned from lifetimes ago finally taking over.

As she lifted her sword, the other more dangerous part of herself was happy to be allowed out to play, as her sword slashed through the wraiths, ichor spraying, as her mind let instinct take over.

Her dance of death led each of the king's wraiths to their end at the tip of her sword.

Cyerra flew over the battlefield as if laying the burial shroud for the annihilation of those who threatened her clan.

Brandishing her sword and dagger, she lost herself to the rhythm in her own mind. Humans that moved in on her met the same fate as the cut of the steel that was her weapon met any who dared to come upon death and think they could win.

Stabbing the wraiths in the head, she slashed and removed each head from their grotesque body as if she'd done this every moment, of every day, of her life.

Bryn had been *born* for this.

Arioch, having been nowhere near her mere moments ago, stared at her in his beastly form with seething hatred.

Bryn knew the Morrigan remembered him well since she had been the one to relegate him to the form. She had found it fitting at the time that he look on the outside what he was on the inside. A monster.

She'd always been a fan of things like that matching.

The Morrigan hated pretty monsters.

His beastly form took a running leap at her, only to be caught in the jaws of the black wolf from Faerie that Bryn had released.

Swinging, he attempted to dislodge her beautiful wolf, but she tore his neck wide open.

Bryn swirled around, her sword an extension of herself, and removed Arioch's head. His body turned fully human as he fell, his blood watering the earth beneath him.

Arioch's black soul lifted from his body, and he looked to where she had closed the veil, able to see the rift now that he was dead. She watched in amusement as Arioch made a run for it, hoping to push through to Faerie. He had lived a life of predatory habits toward young children, and so he had not earned peace, but he thought to take it.

Bryn laughed as the soul tried to escape his fate.

"Hunter!" she called out on instinct, as most of what she was doing was all rooted in some deep-seated knowledge.

Arawn stepped out of the veil, his beastly hounds at his side, and Arioch's black soul stumbled to a halt. The hellish-looking hounds bit at the air, their bodies dancing as they waited to hear the words that gave them permission to take Arioch to where he belonged.

"You may hunt!" she yelled, her laughter following as Arawn's hounds ran straight at Arioch, and the fear in his eyes ignited the prey drive in her own predator.

Arioch didn't make it far, though he did try, she could give him that. He ran, the hounds nipping at his heels in fun before they each took a part of the man's soul in their large maws and disappeared into the ether with him. Who knew where Arioch ended up, but good riddance.

Turning, she saw the humans quivering in fear before her, the dust floating through the air of all the wraiths she had destroyed right before their eyes.

Only glass stood between her and their petrified eyes, their trembling bodies, as they watched her walk forward, still holding the dagger and sword dripping with blood from their points to the sand at her feet.

They wouldn't have seen the veil and subsequent spirits moving through the gate to Faerie not being dead yet themselves, but they had seen her kill Arioch. It seemed that was enough for them to watch her like a deer would a hungry wolf.

Let them fear her. They did not think her worthy when she was nothing more human than they were.

"The wild hunt will conclude soon, and lest you be deemed unworthy, I will take you to your paradise," she whispered to the souls of those who'd died during battle, awaiting judgment with the slight yellow glow, ones that she would need to take soon enough once the threat was deemed no longer an issue.

Bryn stepped forward, stabbing several wraiths moving in on her in her distraction, leaving them as nothing more than dust motes. Bryn walked to another gathering of humans not hiding behind glass. Mallory was among them.

Standing before them, her eyes moved through the crowd until they met Mallory's. She trembled in fear, and the Morrigan aspect of herself let Bryn taste Mallory's terror as it saturated the air around them.

"Your god is dead. I am real. You chose poorly." Bryn looked right at Mallory as she said this.

Bryn turned back to where the battle was almost at its conclusion. There were very few wraiths left to fight as their maimed bodies reconstructed themselves enough to hold a sword once again. Bryn yelled out her battle cry as the last of the wraiths focused on her as if she were a beacon of light to their unholy darkness.

Senan was running through, stomping and hitting them, the crows dive-bombing them, and her shadow wolves were actually able to bite the wraiths since they were not of this world either. She watched her beloved pack tearing at the flesh of the monsters.

Her silver wolf was not among them, but the wraiths were not letting Bryn focus on that.

"In honor of the Tuatha Dé Danann," she growled as she raised her sword once more and ran through the last of the wraiths, beheading them as she went.

No matter what it took, she would finish what King Bres had started.

Chapter 49

The air stilled as if the world was aware that Bryn was coming back to herself and worried one wrong move might set her back on the warpath.

Standing in the middle of the bloody chaos, she raised her arms to the sky, holding her bloody weapons as if an offering to the heavens.

The crows dove down and aimed their bodies at her.

Instead of impact, they became one with her, the crows being made of her own power. A piece of the puzzle that was all her, the soul of the Morrigan, firmly in place.

The black wolf limped toward her, and Bryn wondered how a creature of her power could be injured as well, but as the wolf merged into her as the crows had, she noticed the bloody injury of her own leg.

Bryn was as much the wolf as the wolf was her.

"Queen of Shifters as well. You have a lot of names," Cyerra said from somewhere, and Bryn felt relief that the sarcastic crow had survived to annoy Bryn another day.

Her eyes moved over the bodies lying strewn throughout the street. Her other self, as she saw it, would need to move the souls over to Faerie or watch as Arawn's hounds took them to wherever the damned souls went.

The stake had withstood the battle, and the irony that those who would have burned her at the stake were the ones to die this day was not lost on her.

The girl who was scared of blood was covered in it.

"Come back, Bryn," Danu whispered from behind her, but Bryn could only focus on the viscous fluid running down her weapons and her body.

The blue tattoos were still on her arms, but they no longer glowed.

Looking at the people cowering in fear, huddled together in front of her, she thought she would enjoy this. The feeling of having power over the people that hurt her, but she didn't. She only felt . . .

Numb.

She wished she could explain that it wasn't her, but it had been. She had allowed it, letting her mind go dormant for the Morrigan to rise up from within her and take her pound of flesh.

Bryn's eyes made it to one woman in the crowd in particular. Ava. The woman who until this day had been a nuisance in pretty dresses. Always put together and out stealing boyfriends she thought more worthy of her than the women the men were already with.

This was not the Ava of yesterday. She was covered in dirt, bloody mud caked to her boots and the bottom of her dress. Her eyes were wild and her hair in disarray, and Bryn wondered then how she could have let this woman make her feel less than.

When it all hit the fan, Bryn was the one standing between the town and certain death, while Ava cowered.

If a man like Declan wanted a woman like her, he was well and truly not for Bryn.

Funny, Bryn thought, *how my mind wanders to such ridiculous things while I am absolutely sure I am about to have an actual nervous breakdown.*

A hand landed on her shoulder, making Bryn jump from her musings.

"You did nothing wrong, Bryn. You saved these people, and they are idiots if they do not understand it," Danu whispered, and Bryn cursed the woman mentally for bringing her back to the world around her.

Turning back to look at the children crying into their parents' shoulders, she knew they would think of her as the boogeyman under the bed for the rest of their days.

"I became a monster . . .," she whispered, dropping the sword and dagger into the bloody sand, and turning to face Danu.

"You became what was needed to defeat the *actual* monsters, love."

Niamh walked up to them, her clothes torn and bloody, but she had no obvious wounds.

"You're alive," Bryn whispered, breathing hard as her friend moved to pull her into a fierce hug.

"I am thanks to you." Niamh stood back, keeping her hands on Bryn's shoulders. "You were amazing, my darling. Absolutely magical."

Bryn swallowed the lump in her throat at Niamh's words. She had been anything but magical. She had been dangerous and felt such . . . joy in the bloodshed that it scared Bryn.

Callum moved to Bryn's side as Danu turned to face the humans.

"Get yourselves to rights so you can fix this town. We will be leaving soon, and the danger should be going with us." Danu looked to Mallory. "Do not do anything that could cost you your life after the danger has passed."

Mallory gave a pensive look to Danu before turning away, ignoring Bryn entirely.

That was fine by her.

Moving past Niamh and Callum, she looked out over Saints' Road.

She walked without thought to the body of one of her friends nearest her.

Justin.

Moving to him, Finian was at his side, trying to move Justin's hand with his nose. Whining when Justin failed to move, to rub his head, to do anything.

Her heart broke seeing them both like this.

Kneeling on the other side of Justin from Finian, she placed her hand on his chest and prayed. His soul was not one of the ones who had been waiting to cross over. Still, as she held her hand over him and waited for his soul to come up as a beautiful glowing yellow orb, nothing happened, and she wondered if Arawn had already taken them across the veil.

Perhaps Arawn had thought of it as a boon to Bryn, but she had wanted to say goodbye to her friends as she had Travis.

Rubbing at Finian's head, she made a note to come back to grab him before they left. She would take care of him now that Justin couldn't. A sob broke through at that thought, but she kept moving. To stop and think would mean she'd be stuck in her own thoughts, and they had to leave.

There was no longer a choice.

Walking to Declan, she checked his pulse and felt nothing there, telling her he was well and truly gone. Even though it was obvious he could not have lived, his blood running out into the street, she'd held out hope.

"I am sorry, Bryn." Niamh stepped up next to her, her hand going to her shoulder in comfort as Bryn prayed over Declan.

Standing, Bryn could only nod as she looked to where Jace stood, his eyes staring through her.

"We should head to the truck," Niamh whispered as she took hold of Bryn's hand, helping her to stand.

"We need to leave, and Kessler, though pretty banged up, claims he can still run the truck. Sage and Jace are ready to assist with injuries while on the road."

Bryn pulled away, looking back at her friends' bodies. It felt wrong to leave them like this. Would the people left in Ifreann honor them? She'd been friends with them and watched as Justin and Declan had killed several of their own in self-defense, but did that even matter to these people?

They always had their own skewed perception of the world, but Bryn supposed everyone had their own perspective.

"I need to be the one to put them to rest," she whispered, refusing to leave their bodies in the street, to neglect her friends in such a way. "I can run the pyres one last time."

"I will handle them," Callum offered. "You need to get going before the humans come out of their shocked stupor. I am sure it would pain you to have to kill innocents."

Callum's face was sincere, but it felt so wrong to leave them. To not say goodbye.

Mentally thanking Callum for not accusing her of already having killed innocents, she nodded.

A hand took her elbow, and she turned to face Jace, who had finally come out of his own stunned state.

"We need to go. I did the best I could for Caden, slowing the bleeding from the loss of his hand, but we can't wait. If another battle comes, he is not in any state, mentally or physically, to fight." Jace was hardly standing on his own himself. She wasn't sure if his holding on to her was for her comfort or just so he didn't eat dirt.

Bryn nodded but looked back.

"Let me say goodbye and I'll be right behind you."

Jace looked to Callum, who tilted his head in acquiescence.

Niamh and Jace walked away, leaving Bryn with Callum as they moved to say goodbye. She knew to make it quick, as Callum was keeping a close eye on the people who were starting to stand up and walk toward her. Not getting close, but they were not moving away in fear anymore either.

Bending, she walked to each friend, closing their eyes and praying, though it was obvious their souls were gone already.

"Bryn." Callum's hand landed on her shoulder, and it took everything in her not to shove him off her. "It is not the end. In a few hours—"

His words cut off when she heard a soft whine, and Bryn shot to her feet when she saw a silver wolf on its side, its breathing labored.

Kian.

"Kian . . ." She teared up as she crawled toward him through the bloody sand.

Her hands hovered over him as she tried to find a place to touch him that didn't look like it would be painful. There was so much blood and nowhere she could find to embrace him.

The whine that left him broke her heart.

He moved his muzzle deeper into her hand as she cradled his face, and even though the wounds on him there were extensive, she knew he wanted her to comfort him in his final moments.

"Why can't he speak to me anymore?" she asked Callum, running her fingers through his sticky and matted fur. The silver was now stained with his blood and the black ichor from the demon wraiths.

"The tether that kept him connected to you broke when the two parts of his soul merged. The only thing that kept him here, in this battle with you, was his loyalty."

Closing her eyes against the onslaught of new tears, she promised herself to find out later why Callum kept this all secret until now. It could have changed her dynamic with Kian.

"I wish I had known who you were before. I . . ." The words stuck in her throat, but the wolf looked her in the eyes with acceptance.

"Can he change back?" she asked Callum, unable to look away from Kian.

"Not in the state he is in, Bryn. I wish I knew the extent of your magic to know what it did to him . . . but I do not hold that knowledge. I am sorry."

"Please don't die," she whispered to Kian, choking on her tears. "I need you to stay."

She laid her other hand on his head, his tongue licking her wrist.

Before she could think better of it, she stuck her face into his neck, her tears running off into his fur. Her fingers continued to move through the fur on his head, his breathing growing more and more labored.

"I will give you time before we leave. Danu could use my assistance since some of the humans are causing a scene." She heard Callum walking away but kept her face in Kian's fur.

His breathing was slowing even more, and she held him tighter, crying more when the pressure of her hold no longer made his breath hitch. He could no longer feel the pain. It may have been a blessing for him, but she knew he was leaving her.

Swallowing down her sobs, she held him tighter as his breathing stopped completely, and he went limp in her arms.

"Kian, please come back," she begged, her voice hoarse. "Don't leave me."

"Bryn . . .," Mallory whispered from behind her. Bryn's ragged breath stung in the chilled air, but she could not let the monster that was her aunt near Kian. Alive or dead, she would protect him.

Pushing to stand, her own wounds starting to bother her now, she straightened her spine as she turned to face her aunt, keeping herself between Kian and the demon of her childhood.

Just another enemy. A wolf in sheep's clothing.

"Put the knife down, Bryndis," her aunt hissed as she stepped forward. Bryn hadn't noticed she'd grabbed a dagger dropped to the ground by a dead wraith as she stood. That part of her, death incarnate, was pushing back up into the driver's seat of her mind, and she doubted she would ever get it back in the cage.

And honestly, she didn't want to if it could protect her and those she loved from Mallory.

"Stay back or I will end you as I did the rest." Bryn's voice was more than just hers. The monster rose to meet the challenge that Mallory's appearance held as she stood before her.

"I am sorry, Bryn," her aunt apologized, and she stared into Mallory's eyes looking for the truth. Her mind confused, she stepped toward Mallory.

"Wh—"

Before Bryn could formulate the words, a searing pain roared through her belly. Her hands going to where the fire emanated from, she felt the blade sticking out from her. A gut wound. Bryn knew enough about those from some of the ranchers' injuries that such a wound would not be a quick death.

Mallory stepped back after having stabbed her, leaving the blade in Bryn.

"You never should have been brought to us. I warned your father over and over again you were a changeling and would be nothing but a curse." Her aunt spat at her feet, the knife she'd stabbed Bryn with was holding her blood loss at bay while she finished her tirade. "But he wouldn't listen, thinking you were his daughter from the gods. Blasphemy. I am glad everyone you love is dead."

Looking Mallory straight in the eyes, she stepped toward her aunt.

"May the wild hunt take your black soul." Bryn ripped the blade from her side, knowing she would die faster now, but she didn't care. With it, she stabbed Mallory right in her black heart, before ripping the blade back out and dropping it to the ground.

Unable to focus, Bryn hit her knees, falling onto her side in the sand, her blood mixing with the others' lost in the battle of Ifreann. Her vision turned red as the monster rose from within with the word "kill" on its tongue.

But the monster was in a mortal body, and as she lost her lifeblood, it grew weaker.

Fire pulsed through her weakening veins, her mind lost to the shock that her father might have known who she was all along.

A clawed hand went around her neck, picking her up from where she had fallen into the sand. Daran stared down at her, making his appearance after abandoning Arioch in the battle, leaving his leader to his death at her hands. Probably to save his own hide.

She attempted to pull from him, but he smiled with long, yellow teeth. Not at all worried she had just ended his betrothed. It seemed in the end the only one who cared most about Mallory had been Mallory.

And Jace. Oh, Jace! He had lost both family members this day. The sudden will to live pushed through her as she clawed at Daran's beastly hand around her neck.

Bryn could hear screams, some her name, some her aunt's, as the smell of panic grew stronger than the coppery smell of blood.

Words stuck in her throat as Daran leaned into her face.

"I knew you'd bring death, but I had no idea you'd try to kill us all. I am going to enjoy the taste of your blood, witch," Daran spoke into her mind right before his mouth was at her throat, his teeth digging in.

It felt like a lifetime, but it had been mere seconds from the point of him biting her until he ripped her throat out, dropping her to the ground like a used doll no longer cared for.

The pain in her throat seared through her as the blood gurgled from her torn flesh. Her body seized on the ground before the numbness took over, and then she knew, deep down, she was on the verge of her soul leaving its mortal form.

She would see them all again, and she knew that Justin, Declan, Travis, and Kian were waiting on her to cross over.

With that thought in her heart, Bryn let death take her.

Death.

Home.

Chapter 50

Faerie was as bright as she remembered it, yet the only one of her friends there to greet her was Travis.

"You sure can dole out a hell of a fight when provoked." Travis laughed, the light in his eyes catching the brightness of the world around them.

She tried to smile but couldn't.

Bryn thought when she passed on, she'd feel peace, but what she felt was nothing close to it. She'd failed even after giving herself over to the Morrigan.

"Where are Declan, Justin, and . . .?"

Would Kian be here if he was Fomori?

"That's a wonderful question. I am not privy to the universe's bullshit, so I have no idea. I assumed y'all just end up wherever around here. Kind of a big place."

Bryn realized she wasn't near the veil like she thought. She was in actual Faerie.

"You can move about as you please?" she asked Travis.

"Well, not many things you can do wrong here, so I figured I'd push until someone told me no."

His smile lit a dark place in her heart for a second of time before the caw of a crow called to her.

"Seems your bird friend wants to have a little chat," Travis stated, putting his elbow out for her to take as if they were going on a romantic stroll.

Travis walked next to her, not saying anything as day turned to night, and they entered the hallowed ground of Faerie. The cemetery she'd seen in her visions was before them with the lush forest surrounding it.

It was peaceful in a way Bryn had never felt.

"None of these tombstones have names," Travis noticed, and Bryn looked to see he was right.

Weird.

Senan, the black wolf, and the crows were near the fence. Bryn's heart broke again at not seeing the silver wolf there with them.

"I know now that death isn't the end," Travis whispered, his thoughts catching on to hers.

Turning, she held her hand out, and Travis grabbed it in response, before giving it a squeeze.

"And it shouldn't be. If you could go back, Travis, would you?" she asked, wishing she could send them both back.

"It sure is calm here, but I need the adrenaline rush of firing a rifle. Of standing between an enemy and my friends. I reckon I'll get pretty bored here." He laughed.

"I suppose we both will. Poor Danu." She kept Travis's hand in hers, the feel of him a reassurance and a balm to her nerves. "We were her last chance."

"Some of the Tuatha Dé Danann still live. There is hope. It just might not be how she had planned. Maybe they don't need all of you together . . ."

Bryn nodded, but she knew the truth. Only as a unit would they be powerful enough to kill King Bres.

A tightening in her chest caused her to rub at it with her free hand as Senan let out an agitated neigh.

The animals that had stood staring at them from the cemetery gates turned and left, running and flying back into the woods.

"You all right, Bryn?" Travis asked as her lungs started to burn, her vision blurring.

"I just feel really weird . . ."

Falling to her knees, she wondered if Faerie was punishing her for not upholding her duties.

"Bryn?" Travis helped her lie down on her back, keeping hold of her hand. She refused to let him go even if he tried.

". . . hurts . . .," she gritted out through her clenched teeth, closing her eyes as she arched in pain, her body tearing apart at the seams.

Bryn's eyes burned as she opened them back up, but the pain lessened. She was certain she had died twice, and yet here she was—in horrible pain. That was not the blissful death given to those who fought honorably, and she knew it. Death was blissful and less bumpy, she was sure. It had to be.

Blinking her eyes open, all she could see was blue. Blue plastic? The sun filtered through ragged holes as her body was bumped and jostled, reigniting her pain over and over again.

"You've awakened!" Danu moved into her line of sight, smiling down at her, as Bryn blinked her sensitive eyes.

"I—" Fire shot through her throat from trying to speak.

"Now, now, none of that. Your throat only just knitted itself back together, and Jace only has so much healing water until we find a natural source."

Finian's large mug filled her vision before Danu pushed him back, earning a bark from the behemoth of a dog.

The sound of metal moving had Bryn trying to turn her head, but her throat felt like it was tearing open all over again. Stuck in the prone position, she could only stare up at the blue plastic tarp as Danu placed her hands on either side of Bryn's head to hold her still as the truck swerved.

"She is alive, damn it! Focus on your driving!" she heard Justin's voice bark out the order.

Justin. Justin was dead! Wasn't he?

Her eyes widened, and Danu laughed as she looked down at her.

"It is not easy to send gods to where they do not plan to go, and none of your fellow Tuatha Dé Danann cared to cross over just yet."

They were alive . . . except Travis . . . and Kian.

A tear fell down her cheek, but a rough tongue licked it away before it could fall from her face.

Her eyes opened wide at the sensation. A whine left the creature that had just licked her as it brushed against her and settled in, warming her with its bristled fur. Finian was relentless.

The animal moved again, and a sob left Bryn's mouth as she caught the color of the fur from the corner of her eye.

Silver. It was silver!

Danu smiled again as she looked down at Bryn, her eyes full of laughter.

"Welcome back, Phantom Queen."

Thank you for reading!

Please consider leaving a review of my book! Reviews feed the dark demon of my soul long enough to where it has the energy to write more books... Okay, not really, but reviews help authors out a lot and are very much appreciated!

Also, sign up for my newsletter to stay up to date on any new releases and giveaways by scanning the QR code below or clicking on the image.

Or stay in touch via social media!

Website: www. authorcdbritt.com

Instagram: @authorcdbritt

Facebook page: Facebook.com/authorcdbritt

Join my street team on Facebook for exclusive content!

Also By C.D. Britt

Reign of Goddesses Series

Shadows and Vines

Sirens and Leviathans

Storms and Embers

Clan of Shadows Series

Prophecy of Gods and Crows
Omen of Blood and Wolves (2024)

Blood of Saviors Series

Thanatos's story (coming 2023)

Medusa's story (coming 2024)

Acknowledgments

I thank God every day I get to write and put my soul on paper for the world to read. This is my dream come true and I thank every single one of you for taking a chance on my books.

As I said before, Prophecy of Gods and Crows is nothing at all like the original outline. This book has put me through the ringer, but I found a piece of myself in these pages. Through my research, I connected with an ancestry my grandmother tried so hard to teach me, but as a young child I was much more interested in all the other mythologies out there.

If only I could show her what I have learned about her culture and thank her for teaching me about the strong women that we are the descendants of.

One of those women, my mother, made so much of this book possible by teaching me what it meant to stand strong and always take the risk. Thank you, Mom.

Thank you to Chrissy Wolfe from EFC services, LLC for taking a chance on this book and working with me on this constantly changing manuscript. I'm sure it was exhausting and with such strict deadlines, almost impossible, but you went above and beyond. I cannot wait to work with you again!

Thank you so much to my Alpha and Beta team! Your feedback always helps me to make it so much better than I could have ever imagined!

To my ARC/Street team, thank you a million times over for reading this far and for everything you do to get the word out! I feel truly blessed to have such an amazing group of readers to support me on this rollercoaster that is publishing!

Bari, Katie, and Jennifer, thanks for the wine and never letting me quit, even when I was ready to throw my computer out the window. I value our friendship and love y'all. I am so ready to move to the forest and raise Shetland cows together.

To my husband and children, the loves of my life, thank you for standing by me through this. For loving me even when I was at my lowest, unsure if I would ever finish this thing. You pushed me and loved me enough to persevere, and I did it! I love you more than you could ever know.

To my darling daughter, always use your voice. My fierce little girl, never let the world dull your sharp edges. They are perfect in my eyes, as are you.

About the Author

C.D. Britt began her writing journey when her husband told her she needed to use her excessive imagination to write stories as opposed to creating a daily narrative for him. Ever since she penned her first words, life has been a lot more peaceful for him.

She currently resides in Texas where she has yet to adapt to the heat. Her husband thrives in it, so unfortunately, they will not be relocating to colder climates anytime soon.

Their two young children would honestly complain either way.

When she is not in her writing cave (hiding from the sun), she enjoys ignoring the world as much as her children will allow with a good book, music, and vast amounts of coffee (until it's time for wine).

C.D. Britt is the author of the Reign of Goddesses series, Clan of Shadows series, and the upcoming Blood of Saviors series.